PASSION'S DESTINY

"Do you find it so difficult to believe that a man could fall in love with you?" Daken asked. "Or is it only that you have heard those words too many times before?"

"No," Jocelyn protested. "I've just never been sure how you felt about me."

"And you are also not sure how *you* feel about *me*," he stated.

Then, before she could begin to formulate a reply to that, he stood up and drew her to her feet as well.

"Come. We should go back now—back where it is safer for both of us."

When he released her hand, she let it rest against his chest and tilted her head to stare up at him. She wanted only to hold onto this moment, to feel forever what she felt now. And then, as they stared at each other, she knew she wanted him to kiss her. Her lips parted slightly, although she had no words to say to him.

Futuristic Romance

Love in another time, another place

Other Books by Saranne Dawson:
THE ENCHANTED LAND
FROM THE MIST
GREENFIRE

Heart of The Wolf

Saranne Dawson

LOVE SPELL **NEW YORK CITY**

LOVE SPELL®

August 1993

Published by

Dorchester Publishing Co., Inc.
276 Fifth Avenue
New York, NY 10001

Printed in the United States of America.

Heart of The Wolf

Prologue

The ancient cellars were cold and damp. She wrinkled her nose in distaste, but the smell wasn't bad enough to drive her away—it was just the moldy, musty smell of great age.

She wasn't supposed to be down here, which was why she was. And now, having embarked upon this rebellion, she really had no choice but to see it through. What fun was there in deciding *not* to do something you'd been told you shouldn't do? At least, so it seemed to her nine-year-old mind.

But she was being careful, and she was proud of that. She'd stolen a huge ball of yarn from one of the ladies, and as soon as she felt herself in danger of losing her way, she began to leave a trail of bright red behind her. When it ran out, she would go back; until then, she was safe enough.

Most of the storerooms here were empty; she'd

already passed through the ones that held the vast supplies of food and other goods needed to maintain the huge palace.

Now she hurried past the big, barred gate to the old dungeon. When her father pretended to be angry with her—and it was always just pretense—he would proclaim that he was going to send her to the dungeon. He always spoke the word in a very deep tone. Although she knew he didn't really mean it, the tone itself conveyed a message: this was the worst possible place in the whole palace.

Her brother, who was four years older, claimed to have seen the dungeon once. He'd told her that there was old, dried blood on the walls and floors and horrible machinery that had once done unspeakable things to people. When he'd launched into a gruesome description of one of them, she'd told him that he had to be making it up. Their family had ruled this land for centuries—and none of them would ever have done such things.

His tale *did* make her curious about the place, but since she couldn't get into the dungeon she ignored it as she walked along, unraveling the yarn and listening to her footsteps echoing loudly in the great silence. Fear was her companion, but it was the sort of companion that only added to the excitement.

There were twists and turns and many small sets of stairs. It seemed that no two rooms were on exactly the same level. She stopped occasionally when one of the rooms contained something to explore: old rusted armor, crates that held tattered bits of cloth that must once have been clothing, broken bits of crockery. Her concept of time was rather inexact, but she knew they must have been here for many years. This part of the palace was very old; in fact, no one seemed to know exactly how old.

She was nearing the end of the ball of yarn and the limits of her curiosity as well when she descended yet another set of stairs—a long and twisted one this time—and came to a halt before a door.

The door was interesting. Except for the dungeon, none of the other rooms had doors. And this one was very impressive. It was huge and carved in ornate fashion like the doors upstairs—perhaps even more elaborate. Even the wood itself looked different. The brass handle was so badly tarnished that it was nearly indistinguishable from the wood.

Why, she wondered, would there be such a door down here? It seemed out of place in this bare stone cellar. She glanced at the small amount of yarn remaining on her ball. She couldn't go much farther, but she could at least try to see what lay beyond this door.

With a slight shiver of anticipation, she grasped the handle and pulled at the door. She gave it a very hard tug, expecting that it would be difficult to open, but to her surprise, it opened smoothly, nearly toppling her in the process and causing her to drop her torch. She bent to retrieve the torch and at the same time peered into the room beyond.

Her eyes widened in amazement. In the blackness beyond the door, she saw the unmistakable glitter of gold! Expelling her breath noisily, she walked into the room, holding the torch aloft as she stared at the walls.

The entire room was made of black stone, and all four walls were covered with gleaming gold writing—strange symbols that were meaningless to her. She stood in the very center of the room and turned slowly, seeing each wall come to life as the torchlight struck it.

Then she walked over to one wall and held the torch close to it. What strange stone. It was smooth and black—so black that it seemed to swallow the light. She reached out to touch it and saw that the symbols had been carved into the walls, then the spaces filled with gold.

There was so much of the strange writing that she had stared at it for several minutes before she saw the finely drawn figures of dogs. She bent closer. No, not dogs. They didn't quite look like dogs. Their heads and chests were bigger, and some of them had huge fangs.

"Wolves!" she exclaimed, her voice reverberating in the empty room. Wolves! She shivered, frightened for the first time since she'd come down here.

She'd seen drawings of wolves in her storybooks. They were huge, vicious creatures that inhabited the mountains far from the city—the most fearsome of all animals.

But she reminded herself that these were only drawings—no more terrifying than the drawings in her books, even if they *did* seem to come to life as the torchlight passed over them.

What a wonderful discovery this was! Far better

than she'd hoped for. The strange black stone, the gold, that beautiful, graceful writing. . . .

She walked around the room several times, her fear now completely forgotten. But then the torch began to flicker a bit, and she saw that she had precious little time left. There were fresh torches in the storerooms above, but she had a long trail of yarn to follow before she would reach them.

With a sigh of regret, she turned slowly once more to watch the light reflect off the gold, then began to gather in her yarn until she had closed the door behind her.

Only when she was once more back in the main storeroom did she realize that she should simply have followed her yarn trail instead of gathering it in.

But she was sure she could find the room again—and she was determined that it would become her secret place. Let her brother babble on about his old dungeon; she had found something far more interesting.

Chapter One

Jocelyn could barely contain the tidal wave of emotions that cascaded through her. Anger, guilt, pain, fear—they tumbled about wildly inside her. But none of them showed on her face. Since her brother's death seven years ago, she had been well schooled. After all, she would be empress one day, and she could not afford the luxury of giving in to her emotions.

But not yet, she protested silently as she walked across the soft rugs to the big, high bed. *Please don't let it happen yet*.

She came to a stop beside her father's bed. It wasn't fair. She needed his wisdom, his quiet support. And she knew she could not hope to have it much longer.

There was a sound behind her and she turned to see Hammad entering the room, his expression losing its customary gravity for a moment as he smiled at her. Hammad—her father's most trusted friend and the commander of the Ertrian army. So many times lately, she'd found herself watching him closely for any signs that he too might be ill. He was her father's age, and although he appeared to be strong and healthy, so too had her father until less than a year ago.

She fought down the panic that seemed always to lurk within her these days, then turned to see her father's eyelids flutter and finally open. His gaunt face creased in a welcoming smile as he looked from one to the other of them. Then he pushed himself up in the bed, settling himself against the pillows. Jocelyn made a slight movement to offer assistance, then subsided. He didn't like to be cosseted, not even by his beloved daughter. There were so many things he could no longer do that it had become important to let him do what he could.

His gray-green gaze held pain, as it always did when he refused the potions that eased the pain but clouded his mind. His voice, however, remained firm and clear.

"Jocey," he said, using the old nickname that he alone now used, "There is something you must do."

"Of course," she assured him. "Anything you ask. You know that."

He smiled. "Never commit yourself so freely, my dear. You must learn that now."

"But when it is *you* who asks. . . ." She protested, then stopped as he waved a thin hand in dismissal.

"I forget that there is little left for me to teach

13

you. Sometimes, I still see you as a little girl—not as a woman who will rule."

Then he fixed her with a penetrating stare. "You must go to the Dark Mountains—to see the Kassid and speak to their leader, Daken."

Jocelyn was struck speechless. She stared at her father, thinking that his mind must be confused, after all. When his gaze continued to meet hers unwaveringly, she turned to Hammad. His expression was impassive, but he gave her a slight nod.

"The Kassid?" she echoed. "But . . . but I thought. . . ." Her voice trailed off in disbelief.

"You thought they were only the stuff of legends," her father finished for her. "And they are. But they are also *real*. I have met Daken, their leader. It was he who returned your brother's body to me."

"But you said that he had been killed by wolves in Balek—not in the Dark Mountains."

"He was killed in the foothills of the Dark Mountains, between Balek and the lands of the Kassid. And it was they who found him and his party."

So many questions were swirling through her mind. She grasped at one. "How can you be sure that the Kassid didn't kill him?"

"I am sure. Daken is an honorable man. He too once lost a son, and he understood my pain."

But that doesn't mean he didn't kill him, she thought with an inner chill. How could her father trust such a man? All the old stories ran through her head, frightening her even more. She forced herself to concentrate on the issue at hand.

"Why must I go to him?" she asked, certain that

there must be some way out of this and wondering why he would even ask such a thing of her.

"Because the Menoans and the Turveans intend to make war against us."

"Both of them? But how could they? They hate each other. They've fought each other off and on for years." More years than she had—more even than her father had.

"No longer," Hammad said. "Arrat has married the daughter of the Turvean prince. They've formed an alliance against us."

Jocelyn turned to stare at him, then turned back to her father. She knew what they must be thinking. If she'd agreed to marry Arrat. . . She couldn't quite prevent a small shudder of disgust.

"This is not your fault, Jocey. If you had wanted to marry him, I would have opposed it. He's not fit to rule Menoa, let alone the Ertrian Empire.

"But he now rules Menoa, and to all intents and purposes, Turvea as well. Old Nadik of Turvea has been half out of his mind for years and his sons are wastrels who will gladly allow Arrat to rule as long as he keeps them in gold and women."

"Are . . . are you certain they mean to attack us?" Jocelyn asked, still unable to assimilate all this.

"Our spies tell us that Arrat is even now gathering an army in both lands." Hammad paused. "They can't possibly be ready to attack before next spring, but I'm sure they'll make war then."

"And you think that the Kassid will help us?" she asked doubtfully.

"I have hopes that they will," her father replied.

15

"Daken even warned me of such a possibility all those years ago."

"How could he have known?" she asked, even as she thought about those old stories again.

Her father shrugged slightly. "I don't know how he knew. Perhaps it was only a guess on his part—or perhaps he saw the future."

"Are the old legends about them true?" she asked, not even trying to hide her nervousness now.

He shrugged again. "I don't know what is true and what is merely legend. But I believe what I saw. None of us who met them that day had any doubts about their abilities as warriors."

"But how could you know that? You didn't fight against them."

"No, but we *felt* it. It is difficult to explain. Jocey, you must go—and go quickly, before the Dark Mountains become impassable. Winter comes very early there."

"But surely someone else could go. Hammad?" She turned to him. Not only did she not want to go to the land of the Kassid, she also didn't want to leave her father.

But both men shook their heads, and her father said firmly, "Hammad must remain here, to try to turn an army of game-players into real warriors. And no one else would do in any event. You are my daughter and you will be empress. Daken would expect such a request to come from one of us."

"We must have their help, Jocelyn," Hammad stated. "Except for myself and a few other senior commanders, none of our troops has ever seen battle. As Maikel said, they are mere game-players with blunted swords and cushioned arrows."

"But who have the Kassid fought? Why do you think they're any better prepared?"

"They have fought no one for even longer than me—but they are warriors. And they are legendary."

"You mean that there's a chance that Arrat would call this off if he knew the Kassid were our allies?" Jocelyn asked, beginning now to see a possible way out of the horror of war.

"We have that hope," her father nodded.

"Then I will leave tomorrow," she responded, sounding far more sure than she felt.

The sun was lowering in the western sky, sliding imperceptibly closer to the broad plains beyond the city. Jocelyn drew her cloak more tightly about her. Summer was nearly gone. Already, the topmost leaves on the trees in the park beyond the palace walls were brushed with gold and crimson, and the vast fields of grain that surrounded the city were ripe for harvesting.

She was walking on the high, wide outer wall of the palace grounds—a small, slim figure silhouetted against the heavens, instantly recognizable to those in the palace courtyard to one side and the people in the park to the other. Her gleaming auburn hair streamed out behind her in the evening breeze. Through wide emerald eyes, she stared at the city below.

She was alone now, but she'd walked here all her

life. And before she could walk, she'd been carried by her father. He believed, as had his father before him, that it was important for the people to see their ruler.

"It reassures them," he'd said many times. "They need a person to embody the empire—not just a palace on a hill."

And now she walked alone—her mother gone fourteen years ago, her brother nearly eight, and her father no longer able to climb up here. She walked alone and thought alone, and was more conscious than ever of that aloneness.

It was true that she was virtually always surrounded by people as she tended more and more to affairs of state. But that only increased her sense of isolation. Once, she'd been the darling of the court, loved and pampered by all. But with her brother's death and the certainty that her father had no intention of remarrying, all that had begun to change. And now with his illness and her assumption of most of his duties, the transformation was nearly complete. She was empress in all but name.

This is what I wanted, she told herself. *I wanted them to stop treating me like a child. I wanted them to stop seeing me as a future bearer of royal children to a husband selected for political reasons. I wanted to be an empress. I wanted it—and now I have it.*

But did she, really? If war came . . . She shivered and again drew the cloak about her. With each passing month, she'd become more comfortable in her role—dispensing justice, disbursing funds, planning new projects, doing all the things a ruler must do. And she believed that the court—even those who'd been openly skeptical of her ability to rule—were coming around. But wouldn't that all change if war came? War was for men.

And war could destroy so much, put an end to so many plans. In war, she knew that even the victor suffered greatly. And the vanquished... She couldn't even imagine that.

She stared at the sprawling city below her. There was so much she wanted to do. Very slowly and carefully, she'd been gathering around her younger courtiers with new ideas and high ideals. It was a frustratingly slow process, since she couldn't very well get rid of those who'd served her father. But in a few years, she knew, she could make a difference.

When her father's illness had forced her into affairs of state, Jocelyn had been shocked at the extent of corruption in this land she would one day rule. She'd known that corruption existed; she assumed it was the same everywhere. But she hadn't expected it to have reached the point that some members of the court didn't even try to hide it from her.

How could her father have allowed this to happen—or to continue, since she assumed it had begun long before his rule?

It was the one question above all that she wanted to ask him—and the one question she could *not* ask. He was a good man, and that was what frightened her most. Had there been a time when he too had wanted to put an end to it? Surely, there must have been. But if so, why hadn't he succeeded?

Ertria—and even Balek, a land conquered long

ago by the Ertrians—were prosperous countries. Ertria had thriving seaports and fertile fields, and Balek had the great wealth of its mines that produced gold and silver and coal.

Only within the past year had she begun to understand how all that wealth was concentrated in the hands of a few families. And those families schemed and cheated to avoid paying their taxes— taxes that could have been used to help the unfortunates who lived in squalor along the city's edges and out in the countryside.

And now war—or the possibility of war.

As she paused at a corner of the wall, she saw a long line of Royal Guards riding two abreast, returning from what Hammad and her father had called their "game-playing." They looked splendid in their dazzling white uniforms with her family's sunburst crest emblazoned on their chests, and their perfectly groomed horses prancing in unison.

These were the elite troops, but even she, a mere woman, could see that this was not an army, and these men were not warriors.

She watched until they vanished from view as they entered the winding streets of the city, en route to the garrison behind her. Then she lifted her head again and stared into the glowing red sky to the west.

The Kassid. She'd been avoiding thinking about them, and her stomach began to churn with fear as she forced herself to do so now. She knew that she would have refused her father's command if it weren't for the fact that her fear of war outweighed her fear of the mythical Kassid—though not by much.

How many of those old stories were true and how much was mere legend? No one seemed to know— not even her father, who had actually met them.

The Kassid had once lived in this land, together with the Ertrians. They were said to be a very ancient race who believed themselves to be direct descendants of the Old Gods to whom the present-day Ertrians paid little more than lip service.

They had kept to themselves and never married outside their own kind, unlike the Ertrians and Baleks, who had intermarried for centuries. They'd had their own enclaves within the city and in the surrounding countryside as well. In the incessant wars of those long-ago times, the Kassid had supplied the fiercest warriors. It was from her brother Arman, who had been far more interested in those ancient wars than she had, that she'd heard the many tales of Kassid warriors.

"They weren't human, Jocey," he'd told her once. "They could fight with inhuman skill—and they used magic as well."

She'd merely listened, a little girl happy to be taken into her older brother's life on any terms. His stories of the Kassid had sounded no different from the fabulous tales spun by her old nurses. She'd accepted them just as she'd accepted the tales of little people who lived in hollow trees and mighty serpents that lived beneath the seas. They were endlessly fascinating and wonderfully scary.

But what had once sent delicious shivers along

her spine now filled her with a very adult dread. The Kassid were sorcerers who called upon the powers of their ancient gods any time they chose. And of all those powers, none was more terrifying to her then and now than their ability to turn themselves into wolves, the most fearsome of all creatures.

She remembered now a drawing from an old storybook—ancient and tattered even in her childhood—of a half-man, half-wolf creature baring its terrible fangs. Wolves! And it was wolves that had killed her brother and his friends.

And now she was to go to meet with these Kassid, in the Dark Mountains far to the west that were supposed to be their ancestral home. She'd never even seen those mountains, which lay beyond Balek, although she'd heard tales of them from her Balek nurse. They were supposed to be so high that they tore through the very fabric of the heavens, and the peaks were said to be forever covered with snow and often crowned with clouds.

No one knew why the Kassid had left Ertria, but long ago they'd simply vanished, leaving behind them the empire their warriors had helped to establish. And as the years had passed, they'd slowly retreated into the shadows of legend, becoming the stuff of stories told 'round the hearth on cold winter nights.

After her meeting with her father, Jocelyn had summoned one of the Balek representatives to the court and asked him about the Kassid, hoping rather foolishly that he'd say they didn't exist. But instead, he'd confirmed her father's story: they were indeed real.

He himself had never met them, but he told her that the few Baleks who lived in the foothills of the Dark Mountains occasionally encountered them.

She'd asked him about all the old stories. Were they truly sorcerers? Could they change themselves into wolves? The man had shrugged. No one really knew. They kept to themselves and no one ventured into their lands. There were stories, of course.

She told him that she was going to meet with them and he nodded gravely. He'd heard that the Menoans and the Turveans had joined forces to make war upon the empire. The efficiency of the palace grapevine never ceased to amaze her.

He told her that he knew of a man who would make an excellent guide for them as they journeyed into the Dark Mountains. The man had actually met Kassid several times. At her request, he gave the man's name to Hammad, who would see to it that the man was found and was waiting for them when they reached the garrison at Balek.

She asked if he thought the Kassid would join them against their enemies. He had shrugged again. Who knew? If they did, it would surely be because they felt themselves threatened by the possibility of having Menoans and Turveans on their borders.

Could they be bought? she inquired. Would offers of gold induce them to fight?

He had shaken his gray head. "I doubt that, milady. My people have always believed that they have even more gold and silver and precious jewels in

23

their mountains than there are in all of Balek and Ertria combined."

So it all depended upon her convincing them that it was in their best interest to keep the empire from being overrun.

Jocelyn had by now reached the end of the wall, where it joined the wall of the garrison. Below her in the fading light, she saw that the Royal Guard was entering the courtyard. Seeing her, their captain brought the column to a halt and drew his sword, then held it across his breast in a salute. She nodded in acknowledgment, then sighed softly. Game-players. Not a warrior among them. How very vulnerable they had become during this long peace.

She had just reversed her direction to return to the palace when she spotted a tall figure approaching along the wall. Even at this distance, she knew who it had to be. No one else would have dared to disturb her solitary walks up here.

Eryk believed himself to be courting her. She didn't disabuse him of that belief, since it suited her purposes to continue the sham. She'd often thought that it might be a dual conspiracy—that he too knew it was a sham, but chose to continue it for reasons of his own.

Jocelyn had no intention of marrying Eryk or any other man. When she was gone, the throne could pass to one of her cousins.

Eryk was a nobleman whose vast wealth came from his family's shipping business and fertile farmlands to the east of the city. He was handsome and bright and considered to be the best catch in all Ertria by the many women who pursued him. He had also been one of her brother's closest friends.

On the whole, she considered him to be far more acceptable than any of the other nobles. She knew that he too schemed and cheated on his taxes, but she suspected that it was to a far lesser extent than most of the others. And he treated those who worked for him far better than most.

Sooner or later, his need to produce an heir would force him to turn his attentions elsewhere, but she hoped and believed that she would be able to retain his friendship. Certainly, he could be a powerful ally when she ascended the throne and could make some changes.

"You leave tomorrow for the Dark Mountains," he said after greeting her.

"For someone who spends so little time at court, you don't lack for information, Eryk," she teased him, then nodded gravely.

"It seems I have no choice."

"It would be wise in any event for you to visit Balek," he pointed out. "It's been two years since your father was there."

"I know. I kept intending to go, but with him so sick . . ." She trailed off with a sigh, then frowned at him.

"Do you think they intend to make war upon us, Eryk?" She knew he had his own agents in both countries.

"Yes. My agents sent back the same news as Hammad's spies. I'm sure they'll attack in the

25

spring. Some of my best farmland lies close to the eastern border, and I'm already worried about the spring planting."

"And did you know that the Kassid actually exist?" she asked, wondering if she were the only one who'd believed them to be mere legends.

He nodded. "My brother was with your father when they brought back the bodies of Arman and the others. He told me about them."

"I thought they were nothing more than old stories," she admitted. "And now I wonder how much of those stories is true."

"Let us hope that the tales of their exploits in battle are true. We will need them."

"Or the threat of them," she said. "My father and Hammad think that such a threat could make Arrat change his mind about making war."

"Arrat wants the empire," Eryk stated succinctly. "When he couldn't get it through you, he decided to take it by force. For the likes of him, a mere threat may not be enough—especially if he too believes the Kassid are mere legend."

She hadn't thought about that, but she knew Eryk was right. She would have to persuade this man Daken to come back here—or send some troops.

They left the wall and walked down the steps into the great courtyard, then passed through the public rooms of the palace. She was lost in thought as she continued on toward her rooms and stopped only when he hesitated.

"Am I invited to join you for dinner?"

She nodded absently. Eryk could be trusted to behave himself. Only once had he ever attempted to force himself upon her, and he'd apologized profusely afterwards for that drunken mistake.

They dined in her private salon, where the wall sconces had been lit, casting what might have been a romantic glow over them both. But romance— never high on her list to begin with—was very far from her mind this night.

And probably from his as well, she thought as she noticed that he too seemed lost in his thoughts. War would wreak havoc upon his businesses. Shipping would be disrupted and it was quite likely that if war *did* come, the initial battles would be fought on his lands.

She thought about the consequences of war and lost her appetite. So very much depended upon her convincing the Kassid—or rather, their leader, Daken, to help them.

"You're afraid to go to the Dark Mountains," Eryk said after a long silence.

She nodded. Few people ever saw her fears, but Eryk was one of them. His lifelong friendship with her brother gave him a special place in her life as well. He'd missed that fatal hunting trip only because he'd injured his leg in a fall from his horse. They'd grieved together over the loss of brother and friend.

"I don't blame you," he said, surprising her. "I know your father believes that the Kassid had nothing to do with the deaths of Arman and the others, but I've never been completely convinced myself."

"Do you have any reason to think they might have killed him?" she asked as yet another reason to fear this trip emerged.

27

66

"No," he admitted. "I know nothing more than the old stories about them. I suppose it's just that I needed to be able to blame someone."

"But they lived among us once," she pointed out.

"I know, but that was long ago—and they kept to themselves even then. So who knows if they can really be trusted? It might have suited their purpose to fight on our side then."

"Still, we have no choice, Eryk. We need them."

He nodded. "We must use them—but not trust them."

"That sounds rather difficult, if we expect them to save the empire for us."

"That, my dear Jocelyn, is a problem for you and Hammad to deal with—and your father, of course. All I ask is that my ships can come and go in peace and that my fields and storehouses don't go up in flames."

"Eryk, if there *is* war, do you think that my being a woman will be a problem?"

He chuckled. "So you've thought about that? Well, if it is, you could always marry me." He paused, then went on more seriously.

"It would be better if your father could live to see this through, but the people love you, Jocelyn. And there's the history of four hundred years of your family's unbroken rule over Ertria. Anyway, I think that's the least of your problems. We haven't even got an army worthy of the name."

"But we have Hammad—and a few others."

"Yes, the gods be thanked for that. But not even Hammad can turn a bunch of wine-swilling dandies into officers, and peasants into soldiers in so little time. The Menoans and Turveans don't have that problem. They've been fighting each other for years."

They finished their dinner and strolled for a time in her private garden. Eryk took her hand, an intimacy she was willing to permit him.

"How many men will accompany you?"

"Only twenty. Hammad thinks that to send more could be viewed as a threat by the Kassid."

"That makes sense—but it's not much protection."

"If the old stories are true, our entire army could afford me no greater protection," she said bleakly.

He stopped, then took her other hand as well. "I won't rest easily until you're safely back in the palace again."

She looked up at him. At times like this, she wished that she could love him. She liked him and was comfortable with him—but something was missing.

Then she was glad that whatever it was *was* missing. Love was a luxury she could no longer afford. Love was for the ladies of the court who had nothing better to do with their lives than to please their husbands and raise their children. She had an empire to rule—and a war to prevent.

She thanked him for his concern, and he leaned forward slowly to brush his lips lightly against her cheek. It felt pleasant, comforting. She knew he truly did care for her, in his way.

When he had gone, Jocelyn stood there amidst the fragrant splendor of her garden, thinking about mountains she'd never seen and a race of sorcerers she hadn't known truly existed—and a mission that must succeed.

The party rode out the next morning shortly after dawn. Jocelyn had awakened in the pre-dawn darkness to a feeling of deep dread so powerful that she lay there for many minutes, paralyzed by her fears.

Her testing had begun. All the work she'd done so far, all the exercise of statecraft of which she was so proud, seemed to count for nothing. The only thing that mattered now was the success of this mission.

Strangely enough, though, she was able to set aside her fears for her own safety, thinking instead about the empire and her people. She had no doubts that those fears would return when they reached the Dark Mountains, but for now, she concentrated on finding a way to prevent war.

Her father had insisted upon being awakened to see her off, despite Jocelyn's attempts to persuade him that they should say their good-byes the evening before.

She'd gone to his bedchamber to find him awake but in obvious pain. The physicians hovered nearby, ready to give him the potions that would ease the pain, but send him into a dull slumber. He sent them from the chamber when she arrived.

"Trust Daken," he told her. "Perhaps the old stories are true and the Kassid *are* powerful sorcerers—but we need their magic. And I know that Daken is a good man."

But how can you know that? she'd asked silently—and was still asking it an hour later as they

left the city behind and rode through miles of farmland that fed its ever-growing population. For all
she knew, this Daken might well have cast some
sort of spell on her father.

Saying good-bye to her father had been the most
difficult thing Jocelyn had yet had to do. She knew
his condition was worsening, although the physicians had assured her he would live for many
months yet. She wanted to believe them, but could
not quite rid herself of the thought that her father
might well have ordered them to tell her that.

At least twelve days of hard riding lay ahead of
them before they would reach the Dark Mountains.
During the first part of the journey, they would be
able to rest comfortably at night, staying at inns
along the Western Road. But once they entered Balek, they would be leaving that well-traveled thoroughfare for narrow, winding roads through
sparsely populated country, where they would be
forced to spend their nights in the open.

They might have chosen a more circuitous route
that would have allowed her to stay at the estates of
the Balek nobility, but speed was essential. Winter
would soon arrive in the hills of Balek and in the
Dark Mountains.

Jocelyn was traveling without her ladies and even
without maids—a decision that had certainly
raised some eyebrows at court. But there wasn't one
among them who could ride comfortably astride a
horse as she could, and riding side-saddle would
have slowed them down.

Her brother Arman had taught her to ride like a
man years ago, though of course she never did so

in public. Had her mother been alive at the time, she would certainly have prohibited such unseemly behavior, but her father had found it amusing, and she herself loved the freedom and the daring of wearing men's trousers.

Fortunately, the morning was cool enough to justify her wearing a long cloak that disguised her very unladylike attire. What her Royal Guardsmen would think when they saw their future empress in pants she couldn't begin to guess—but neither did she care. This journey would also give her an opportunity to show them that she wasn't some delicate, perfumed lady of the court, but a woman capable of doing what must be done.

She drew the cloak more tightly about her as they rode directly into the chill wind blowing across the plains. It seemed colder than was usual for this time of year, and she remarked on that to the captain who rode beside her.

"Yes, milady, I was thinking the same thing. It does not bode well for a lingering summer." He paused. "And winter comes even earlier in the Dark Mountains."

"Have you ever been there, captain?"

"Yes, milady. I was stationed for two years at the garrison in Balek. But of course we never went beyond the foothills."

"And did you see any Kassid?"

"No, milady. We were strictly forbidden to encroach upon their territory—even in pursuit of game. Some of the Baleks go there, though."

"And has anything ever happened to them when they do?"

"No, not as far as I know. But they don't venture far into the mountains, and perhaps the Kassid are more tolerant of them than they would have been of us. After all, they have lived peaceably as neighbors for many centuries."

"Then you're saying that the Baleks aren't really afraid of the Kassid?"

"Oh, I think they fear them—or perhaps respect is a better word. But they don't seem to worry about being attacked."

"That's strange, don't you think—given the fierce reputation of the Kassid?"

"From all I have heard, the Baleks in that area regard them as being men of honor who would never attack unprovoked."

Interesting, she thought. But she still didn't trust them. How could anyone trust a race of sorcerers and warriors? One would have been bad enough, but they were *both*.

"What else do you know of the Kassid?" she asked.

"All the usual stories we were told as children—that they are powerful sorcerers who employ magic along with their great skills as warriors."

"And what about those stories that they can turn themselves into wolves?"

"Most of the Baleks seem to believe that those stories are mere myths. There *are* many wolves in those mountains, so it's easy to see how such stories could get started."

Jocelyn felt considerably better after hearing that, although the thought of traveling into wolf-infested mountains certainly did not please her.

After all, she'd lost a brother to wolves. But a wolf that was truly an animal, no matter how fierce— and a wolf that was actually a man in disguise were two very different matters.

"Do the Baleks have any information about how the Kassid live?" she asked. She envisioned them as being a very primitive race, although that was based on pure conjecture. And she knew that such people often had tribal councils—which could mean that she'd have more than this Daken to deal with.

"I was told a story, but I have no way of knowing if it was true," he replied. "I was told that the Kassid elect their leader and that he then appoints a council of advisors."

"They *elect* him?" she asked in surprise. "You mean *all* of them, or just certain nobles or tribal leaders?"

"All of them, if what I heard was true. Even the women, though I cannot bring myself to credit that." He stopped abruptly, then stammered slightly. "I . . . I meant no offense, milady."

"None was taken, captain," she replied quickly, certain that what he said was not true. Surely these were just more myths.

But she continued to think about such a society. How could the common people be trusted to make such a decision? Wouldn't they elect whoever gave them the biggest bribe?

It wasn't very comforting to think that she could be dealing with a man whose behavior might be more base than that of the worst of her own nobles.

* * *

The days and nights passed. Jocelyn ached all over, often tumbling into bed at night in total exhaustion, only to drag herself out again in the pre-dawn darkness. But at least the inns, having been alerted to her arrival, provided her with maids, however ill-trained.

Soon, she wouldn't even have that small luxury. They were already nearing the end of their journey on the Western Road and would soon be traveling the narrow, winding trails through the hills of Balek.

Those hills had been growing in the distance ever since the end of their first week on the road. In this far western corner of Ertria, plains had already given way to gently undulating hills that were higher than anything she'd ever seen—and the Balek hills in the distance were higher still.

Jocelyn found it very disconcerting to see the land wrinkled like bedcovers in the morning, and she wondered just how much higher the Dark Mountains could possibly be. When she had put this question to the captain, he had smiled and told her that the Dark Mountains were quite beyond imagining. So she stopped trying to imagine them, just as she'd stopped trying to imagine the sorcerers who called them home. She simply rode westward, determined to achieve her goal without yet bothering herself with the details.

The Western Road was heavily traveled, and what might otherwise have been a tedious journey was enlivened by the various people they encountered.

About a week out of the city, they came upon a

Saranne Dawson

group of Sherbas, a strange sect Jocelyn hadn't seen
since her childhood, though she knew they were in
the city regularly.

The Sherbas contrasted sharply with the other
travelers, dressed as they always were completely
in black, with black horses and black-painted cara-
vans. Although they'd been around for centuries
and were known to be Ertrian, no one had ever
seemed to know much about them. They kept completely to themselves as they journeyed about the
country, carrying all their belongings in their cara-
vans and selling precious herbs. Even the royal physicians sent servants out to purchase these items
from them.

She asked the captain what he knew about them,
and he shrugged.

"There aren't many of them, milady, and they
always keep to themselves. As far as anyone knows,
they have no real homes. They trade their herbs
and potions for their needs, and I've heard that they
have gold as well. We keep an eye on them, but they
never cause any trouble."

"But does anyone know what their beliefs are?"
Jocelyn asked curiously.

"No one I've ever talked to knows, but there've
been stories that they worship the Old Gods.

"Someone told me a story once about coming
upon a group of them who had been attacked by
bandits—back before we succeeded in clearing
those vermin from the Western Road—and one of
them had been stabbed. When they tried to help
the man, they saw a strange symbol carved on his

left breast, just over his heart. But the man refused their help, so they never learned anything about it."

When the captain had finished his tale, Jocelyn turned in the saddle to stare at the small, black-clad band, as they disappeared over a hill. She felt a sudden chill, although the day was quite warm. But she shrugged it off quickly. There was already quite enough strangeness ahead of her, without allowing a small, harmless sect to trouble her.

The party also regularly came upon the convoys of huge carts pulled by teams of horses that carried coal to the city. The royal party had the right-of-way, but when the captain explained to her the difficulty of maneuvering the heavily laden carts off the road, she insisted that they be given the right of passage.

Occasionally, they passed smaller carts carrying gold and silver from Balek's other mines. The owners frequently accompanied them, wearing more of the precious metal on their persons than even the gaudiest of her courtiers would dare. A few even had fine chains of gold and silver decorating their horses.

And then, from time to time, she also saw those who brought these riches up from the earth. They were thin, unhealthy-looking men who lived with their equally ragged families in small villages where it seemed to her that only the close proximity of other houses held up their tumbledown shacks.

These, she thought, are the people I want to help—if I can prevent this war. She knew that if even wealthy nobles like Eryk would suffer from the war, these least fortunate would suffer more.

Aloud to the captain, she said, "There is too much poverty here, for all the wealth this land produces."

"Yes, milady. But the mines belong to those dandies we passed earlier." His tone was clearly one of disgust.

Jocelyn eyed the captain with growing respect. He wasn't afraid to speak his mind. Hammad had told her that he foresaw a bright future for this man and planned to bring him soon onto his personal staff.

"Is that the solution, do you think—to give them ownership of some mines? I had thought about trying to improve their wages and their living conditions."

"Land would be better, milady—just as it would for the farm workers. But the other improvements may be more possible."

"You sound like a politician, captain," she smiled.

"The gods forbid," he chuckled. "I am happy with my life in the Guards."

"Are you married, captain?"

"Yes, milady. We have two daughters, and we hope to have a son."

"And what do you want for your children?"

"A better life—and a peaceful one." Then, as though he feared that he might have offended her, he hurried on.

"But their lives are already far better than mine was. My father was a farm worker. And at least I know that if anything should happen to me, my

38

family will be provided for. None of these people have that."

Jocelyn nodded. Pensions for families of men at arms had been started long ago, and with Hammad heading the army, she knew that the money was getting to them, too—which had not always been the case in the past. Only in the army did there seem to be no corruption. But it proved that with good men in charge, the same could happen elsewhere.

And it also proved, she thought, that there were those among the peasantry who, like the captain, could attain far more than their families had before. Hammad had long ago begun the practice of seeking out talented men among the peasantry and sending them at a young age to the army's schools.

She became accustomed to the stares of other travelers and of the people in the villages, and she also became less concerned about her appearance. Many women out here rode as she did and wore the same loose trousers. And it was doubtful in any event that they knew who she was, despite her accompanying guards. To the rural Ertrians and the Baleks, their ruler was a distant being, far removed from their lives. They lived and died as subjects of a power they never saw.

Still, Jocelyn was glad for the opportunity to see this land and these people, and she understood now why her father had always undertaken journeys to the distant parts of his realm on a regular basis.

From now on, she thought, *when I make my plans, I will have real people and real places to think about*. But those plans depended upon the success of her mission.

They passed over the border between Ertria and Balek, a border marked by ancient stone cairns. The land itself changed quickly. From rolling hills and wide valleys, they rode into a rapidly changing landscape of steep, tree-covered hillsides and deep, narrow valleys.

It was the morning after her first night spent in the open that Jocelyn first saw the Dark Mountains. A steady drizzle had fallen all the previous day from heavy, leaden skies—but the morning brought sunshine and bright blue heavens. They crested the highest hill she'd yet seen—and there they were, outlined starkly against the sky, stretching from horizon to horizon before her.

She felt a sharp jolt of deeply primitive fear as she stared at that dark line that separated land from sky. The hills through which they'd been riding had a smoky, gray-blue cast to them when seen from a distance, but the Dark Mountains were pure black. She'd never seen anything so forbidding.

"Why are they so black?" she asked the captain, taking care to keep her fear out of her voice.

"There are two reasons, milady. First of all, the forests are all a type of very dark fir of a variety I've seen nowhere else. And the stone itself is black—so black that it seems almost to swallow light. I've never seen its like either."

A stone so black that it swallowed light. His description stayed with her as they rode on toward the Dark Mountains. An old memory stirred, something she hadn't thought about in years. But she could see it now with surprising clarity—that secret room deep in the palace cellars that she'd seen only once and had never told anyone about. The stone in that room had been just such a black, covered with that strange gold writing.

She'd never been able to return to that room. When she'd emerged that day after her explorations, several servants had seen her and had, of course, passed along the word about her wanderings until it had quickly reached her mother. She'd been strictly forbidden to go back down there, but her mother must have known she would ignore the warning, because when she'd sneaked back down a week or so later, a new wall had been erected to seal off the unused portions of the cellars.

She thought about that strange room as she stared at those distant black peaks. Could the stone have come from there? But why? There were many quarries just to the east of the city, quarries that had existed for centuries and had provided the mellow golden stone from which the rest of the palace had been constructed.

Why would anyone have carried stone all the way from the Dark Mountains those many centuries ago? It made no sense.

And then she recalled the drawings of wolves intermingled with the strange writing on the walls. The Dark Mountains were said to be filled with wolves. But there were stories that wolves had once lived much closer to the city, before the land had been cleared for farming.

Still, it was a puzzle that mixed uneasily with the strangeness of those mountains, leaving her with an even greater feeling of dread as they rode steadily closer to the end of their journey.

She stared at the mountains all through that day, though by its end, the blue skies had faded to a leaden gray, and the Dark Mountains had become nothing more than a faint smudge along the distant horizon when they reached the top of a hill.

The next day was her worst yet on the road. Mornings had been cold for some days now, but on this day, the cold lingered, and a hard rain pelted them every step of the way, sometimes driven by strong gusts of chill wind. The captain had suggested they remain in camp until the weather improved, but Jocelyn knew the suggestion was being made solely for her benefit, and she insisted that they push on.

She huddled beneath a cloak made of heavily oiled skins that kept the rain itself from penetrating—but nothing could keep out the damp chill of the day. By late afternoon, when scouts had been sent ahead to seek out a suitable campsite, Jocelyn roused herself from her stupor to see small pellets of ice striking her cloak and her mare's wet flanks.

The next day was no better, except that more of what fell upon them was ice pellets. She put on the warmest garments she'd brought with her and so kept out the worst of the chill. Even the Guards had by now forsaken their sparkling white uniforms and fancy red capes for dark, heavy woolen uniforms and oiled skins.

The journey became a cacophony of coughing and sneezing and the splash of hooves as the horses trod through ever-deepening puddles. If the captain had suggested again that they remain in camp, Jocelyn might well have agreed. She had never been so miserable in her very sheltered life.

Trying to find a bright side to this, she told herself that at least she didn't have to spend the day staring at the Dark Mountains. Thanks to the weather, they could barely see to the next hilltop.

Still another day of the same cold rain followed—but at the end of this day lay a reprieve. They would reach the garrison at the edge of Balek's largest city, a place the captain told her was really no more than a medium-sized village by Ertrian standards.

The hills grew steeper yet, and the footing was treacherous because of the mud. Jocelyn was prevented from slipping wholly into her misery by the necessity of guiding her mare carefully along the trail. Finally, when they had climbed yet another hill, the captain pointed to the mountain barely visible ahead of them.

"The garrison, milady. We've made good time in spite of the weather."

Jocelyn blinked away the wetness and stared for some time before she could finally make out the old stone fortress perched atop the hill. And then, even as she stared at it she could see a column of men on horseback moving in their direction. The captain had sent a man ahead some time ago to alert the garrison to their arrival.

"No palace could look better," she said sincerely.

The men from the garrison reached them quickly, and their commander greeted her with grave formality, which Jocelyn found rather amusing considering her very much bedraggled appearance. Then they made their way down to the valley and up the opposite hill to the garrison.

The commander expressed his concern over the weather. "The Baleks say that we'll have an early winter this year, and they seem to know about such things. I wouldn't be surprised to see snow very soon."

"Snow?" she echoed with a smile. "I've only seen snow twice."

"We see far too much of it here, milady," the commander said. "But not usually this early. It's almost certain that you'll see snow up in the Dark Mountains, though. Some of the highest peaks have snow year 'round."

Jocelyn was intrigued by that thought—at least until she thought about how cold it must be there, and then about what else she would find in those forbidding mountains.

"There is a man named Tanner I am told can act as a guide for us. Do you know him?" she asked the commander.

"Aye, milady. He is waiting at the garrison. A good man. He knows the Dark Mountains as well as anyone but the Kassid. He hunts up there and earns his living selling wolfskins."

"And the Kassid let him hunt on their lands?"

"He's been doing it for more than twenty years, and his father hunted there before him. But I think he doesn't venture too far into their lands as a rule."

Jocelyn was soon luxuriating in the amenities provided for her, even though the commander apologized profusely for the roughness of the accommodations. After her days and nights on the road, a warm bath, hearty food, and a real bed were true luxuries, and all she required.

Twilight brought clearing skies, although the wind seemed even colder. The commander said that if it died down, there would likely be frost in the morning. Even though she'd been forewarned, Jocelyn was still astonished at the difference in the weather here—and not at all eager to experience the even colder weather that lay ahead.

She dined that evening in the commander's quarters with her host, several local Balek officials, the captain, and Tanner, their guide. The commander suggested a few days' rest before they proceeded into the mountains, but Jocelyn shook her head.

"If you are right about winter coming early, then we must go as soon as possible."

The guide agreed. "I returned only two days ago, and I know that snow has already fallen in some of the higher passes."

"How will we find this man Daken, Tanner—or any of the Kassid, for that matter? Do you know where they live?"

"No, milady. I don't know where they live. But they'll find us when it pleases them."

She didn't much care for the sound of that. She was beginning to envision them wandering about in those mountains for days or even weeks. "But what if it doesn't please them?"

"Then we won't find them," he replied bluntly. "But if we go far enough into the mountains, they're sure to make themselves known."

"So you've never actually seen any of their villages?" the captain asked Tanner. His concern mirrored Jocelyn's.

The guide shook his graying head. "No, but I figure we'll just follow the trail up 'til it gets us somewhere. Haven't much choice anyway. Far as I know, there's only one trail through the higher passes."

"That should make it easy for them to guard their villages," the captain remarked.

"Who'd they need to guard them from?" Tanner scoffed. "Nobody's fool enough to mess with *them*."

"Have you seen them often, Tanner?" Jocelyn inquired.

"Often enough, milady. Like ghosts they are— not there one minute, then sitting there on their ugly horses the next. That's how I know when it's time to turn around."

"But they've never harmed you?"

"No'm. If they'd wanted to do me harm, I wouldn't be here now."

"Have you ever spoken to them?"

"Only once. I got caught up there late in the season, y'see, and there was a lot of snow. I was tryin' to find my way back down when they suddenly showed up and led me back. Prob'ly saved my life."

"My father says that Daken speaks Ertrian. Do any of the others?"

"One of the ones who found me did," he nodded. "Spoke it about as well as I do, I reckon." He grinned.

"I wonder why," she asked, more of herself than of the others. Why would any of them speak the language of a people they'd left several centuries ago?

She raised the issue of their government, and Tanner said that he'd heard the same stories that the captain had told her earlier—but not directly from the Kassid.

"But where could such stories have come from?" she asked. "Is there anyone else who has had more contact with them?"

The guide shook his head. "They're just stories. Been around for years."

"Have you ever seen Daken, their leader?" the captain asked Tanner.

"No, sir. I always asked if he was with them. Just curious, you know. They're a strange lot, they are. Wouldn't want to get on the wrong side of them."

Jocelyn went off to bed with the uneasy feeling that the closer she came to the mysterious Kassid, the less she knew about them. It didn't bode well for her mission. She'd seen enough of diplomacy to know that understanding your opponent was more than half the battle.

But how could she hope to understand a people who might not even be fully human?

Chapter Two

Jocelyn got her first close look at the Dark Mountains the next morning as she stood in bright sunshine atop the garrison wall. It was a moment she would never forget.

The highest mountains she'd yet seen were the Balek Hills through which they'd just ridden—and those hills had dwarfed the hill at the edge of the city where the palace stood.

"The name for them in the Balek language means 'touch the skies'," the commander told her when he saw her expression. "When I first saw them, I thought even that was inadequate. They don't just touch the skies; they tear a hole in the heavens themselves."

And so they did. They were an unending series of successively higher peaks which, instead of being rounded like the hills of western Ertria and Balek, were raw and jagged. They looked so sharp that she fancied she would prick her finger if she could touch them.

And they were black—a much denser black than they'd appeared from a distance. The color of pure evil, she thought with an involuntary shiver she hoped the others would attribute to the frosty morning.

Atop the very highest peaks, there was white— the ever-present snow she'd been told about— standing out in sharp contrast to the black below and the blue above.

But what she felt most of all was the sense of an immense, brooding presence that dominated everything around it—even the huge stone garrison perched atop its hill. They felt like the very end of the world, a monstrous barricade that made an unequivocal statement: Go no further.

"I don't see how we can possibly go there," she said, following her thoughts.

Their guide wasn't present, so it was the captain who responded. "I spoke at some length with Tanner last night. He says that there is a narrow pass through the mountains—so narrow that we will be forced to travel single-file much of the way. And he's certain that some of them will be snow-covered already.

"I don't wish to alarm you, milady, but he told me there are places where the drop at the side of these trails can be many hundreds of feet—perhaps even thousands.

"I must speak bluntly, milady. I don't want to go in there myself—and I especially don't want to take you up there. I fear that I cannot provide adequate protection for you."

Protection? she asked silently. The gods themselves could afford no protection against that place. And then she remembered that, according to old legends, the Dark Mountains were the home of the Old Gods, from whom the Kassid claimed direct descent.

Strangely though, the captain's candor had the perverse effect of strengthening her resolve. "We have no choice, captain. I appreciate your candor and your concerns, but we *must* gain an alliance with the Kassid—and that means going to them, not asking them to come here."

"I agree," the commander stated. "Although I share the captain's concern for your safety. And Hammad was right to order only a small force to accompany you. The Kassid will know that you come in peace."

"Do you believe they are men of honor, commander?"

"That is a difficult question to answer, milady. I have seen them only once—and then very briefly. I can say only that they made a powerful impression upon me. I was struck by their pride of bearing. I believed then—and continue to believe—that there is nothing they could not do if they chose to do it. I've spent much time since thanking the gods that they aren't our enemies.

"As to honor, who is to say? If they *are* sorcerers, and not wholly human, perhaps their very minds are different from ours. It is certainly a fact that without them, the Ertrian Empire could not have come into existence—and yet they chose to walk away from it when they might well have chosen to have it for themselves, or at least to demand a great share of it.

"And in all these years, they have never made war against us, even though they surely know the riches to be gained."

He smiled at her. "The question I continue to ask myself is whether they have left us alone out of some sense of honor—or because they consider us so beneath them as to be not worth the trouble."

Although she'd been listening carefully to all the information she could gain about the Kassid, none of it had impressed her as much as the words of the commander, who clearly had spent much time thinking about them as he lived beneath their mighty shadow.

It was time to leave. If she lingered here any longer, she would surely convince herself that it was madness to go there and seek to awaken what she could only think of now as sleeping giants.

After one last, lingering look at the Dark Mountains, she turned and descended the stairs into the garrison yard, where their horses and men awaited. A short time later, their party rode out into the foothills, led by the guide, Tanner.

The land through which they rode that day was far hillier than any they had passed through earlier, with tall, steep hills and deep, narrow valleys where swift-flowing streams twisted through forests of dark fir, and the few broadleaf trees were already displaying the golds and reds of autumn.

This was still Balek, but a place where no one

lived. Here and there, they passed the huts that hunters and trappers used as temporary shelters, but there were no permanent homes. And despite the bright sun, the temperature remained low enough that the horses' breath steamed in the clear air.

And always ahead of them, looming ever larger, were the Dark Mountains. By late afternoon, the sun had dropped behind the peaks, and the land shifted abruptly into the shadows of coming twilight.

They made camp in one of the little valleys, where Jocelyn would have the use of a hunter's hut, while the men made camp around it. The food was good, since they'd been freshly provisioned by the garrison, and she slept that night beneath heavy quilts that were carried by day on fresh packhorses also provided for them.

Jocelyn was warm enough and felt safe inside the tiny hut. But Tanner had warned her that this was the only night she could hope to spend with four walls around her and a roof over her head. No one had ever dared to build huts on Kassid land.

Tanner had also been regaling them with tales of his wolf hunts. If Jocelyn had been secretly hoping that wolves couldn't be as big and vicious as those portrayed in her old storybooks, that hope had been laid to rest. And yet, as she lay beneath the quilts waiting for the welcome oblivion of sleep, she clung stubbornly to a new hope—that their talkative guide might be exaggerating.

And she clung to this hope even though she knew that her brother and his friends—all of them experienced hunters—had been killed by wolves in these very mountains.

When she finally did fall asleep, it was to nightmares of huge, red-eyed, fanged creatures like the ones pictured in her books. They were chasing her and howling ferociously as she tried desperately to climb a sheer cliff of black rock.

Then the dream shifted, and the creatures pursuing her were the half-human, half-wolf monstrosities from other stories. They alternately howled and cried out to her in a guttural version of her own language.

She awoke with a start, certain she'd heard something. Only when a guard called out to her from just outside the door of the hut did she realize that the sound must have been her own cry. She told him it was nothing more than a nightmare—but it took a long time for her to convince herself of that.

She lay there under the heavy covers, drenched in sweat and shivering at the same time. Her throat ached, and she began to worry about the consequences of those rain-drenched days on the road. But she'd always been extraordinarily healthy and so couldn't believe that her body would betray her now.

When she awoke again, it was to the comforting sounds of the camp coming to life—men calling out to each other, horses whinnying. She lay there for a moment, longing for the peace and quiet and comfort of the palace. How far away that all seemed now, both in distance and time. It felt as though she'd been on this journey all her life.

She thought too about her father and worried

again that the physicians might have lied to her under his orders.

What she did *not* think about were the Kassid. She refused to let herself dwell on them, lest she lose her nerve and insist that they turn back.

For two days, they rode over and through hills that grew ever higher and darker, while the Dark Mountains themselves loomed over them like great giants waiting to devour them. She felt dizzy and disoriented when she tried to look up to the peaks now, and there were times when her breathing seemed constricted, when it seemed that her lungs could not draw in enough of the cold air that pierced her like a knife.

She learned to keep her eyes fixed on the trail ahead, not looking up at the mountains or even to the sides, where the trail often dropped away into increasingly deep abysses.

And at night, she lay awake listening for the howl of wolves, until finally, on the third night, she heard a faint, distant sound. She lept from her pallet and grabbed a cloak, then hurried outside to find others awakening as well.

"Was that a wolf?" she asked the nearest Guard.

"Yes, milady, it must have been. But . . ."

He broke off abruptly as an unearthly howl split the silence of the night—far louder than the sound she'd heard before.

"Calling to each other, most likely," the man said. "The sounds came from different directions, I think—but it's hard to tell up here."

She hoped he was right. Tanner had told them

that the mountains could distort sound and even bring back echoes of one's own voice. She saw him come out of his tent briefly, then disappear into it again and she felt better. Obviously, he wasn't concerned, so they couldn't be close.

Late the next morning, they came to a high plateau, the closest thing she'd seen yet to the plains of home. It was largely devoid of vegetation except for tall grasses that had already turned to a golden brown. A cold, damp wind blew down from the black peaks and the skies were beginning to cloud over once more.

"We're in Kassid land now," Tanner said, tilting his head to stare up at the sheer black walls surrounding them.

"It feels like snow," the captain remarked, pulling his heavy, fur-lined cloak around him.

"Right you are, Cap'n. Before tomorrow, most likely." Tanner squinted up at the changing sky.

"How much snow could there be at this time of year?" Jocelyn asked, aware of the dangers but still thinking about the lovely, gentle snows that occasionally fell at home.

"In winter, it gets deep enough to bury a man and his horse," the guide replied. "But it's not likely to be more'n a few inches this early." He paused, frowning.

"What's worryin' me is a Big White."

"What's that?" the captain and Jocelyn asked simultaneously.

"Snow that's comin' down so fast and blowin' around so much that you can't see past your horse's nose. Doesn't take a lot of snow, either—not with the winds that can come up in these mountains. All you can do is wait for it to blow over."

"And how long can that take?" the captain inquired uneasily.

Tanner shrugged his thin shoulders beneath the wolfskin jacket. "Maybe hours—maybe a day or two."

But there was no Big White. Instead, the snow came that night, falling in big, soft flakes that left a coating of several inches over everything. Then the sky abruptly cleared again. For the first time, Jocelyn saw the beauty of this place. The snow clumped thickly in the dark firs, weighing down the branches. It lay in crevasses in the black rock of the surrounding mountains. The brightness nearly blinded her as the sun rose behind them, and the cold air had a wonderful smell. She thought that if she were here under different circumstances, she would truly love this wild, strange country.

By late afternoon, when the sun had once again disappeared behind the tallest peaks, they had reached the beginning of the narrow trail that wound around walls of black rock. She tried to keep her eyes averted from the increasingly precipitous drop beside her, but again and again she found herself drawn to that frightening vista where she could occasionally catch a glimpse of a section of trail they had traveled earlier.

Although they had actually been in the Dark Mountains for the past day, she felt it for the first time now, as she realized there was no longer any distant vista of jagged black peaks. She could see nothing but the black walls that had closed around them.

When they rested for a time at a wide spot in the trail, she walked over to examine the rock closely. It *was* the same stone that she'd seen in that secret room at the palace; she was sure of it. The rock she touched now had that same surprisingly smooth but dull surface, and looking at it produced that same sensation of staring into eternal, overwhelming darkness. But how did such stone get all the way to the palace—and for what reason?

Jocelyn considered telling the captain about it. But that room had been her secret for all these years, and somehow, to talk about it now with him seemed a sort of betrayal. She decided to wait and discuss it with her father when she returned home.

When they stopped to make camp on a wide ledge overlooking a ravine they'd traversed earlier in the day, Tanner announced that this was as far as he'd ever come into the mountains. This, he told them was the spot where a group of Kassid had suddenly appeared to let him know that their tolerance of intrusions had come to an end.

Jocelyn and the captain exchanged glances in mutual acknowledgement of the fact that they would really rather not have heard this. The others heard as well, and the captain took the opportunity to remind them that if they encountered any Kassid, they were to keep their weapons sheathed and take no action that could be deemed provocative. The warning was necessary, but it did little to ease the growing tension within the party. Despite the fact that guards were immediately posted, they all began to scan the trail and the dark forests regularly, mindful of what Tanner had said about the Kassid tendency to appear seemingly out of nowhere.

Jocelyn retired early to her tent, fully expecting to have her sleep disturbed again by howls or by nightmares—the two had become much the same to her at this point. But the night passed peacefully. She awoke only once, shortly before dawn, drenched in sweat again and shivering in the cold despite warm coverings.

Her chest ached as she lay there breathing in the chilled air. The others were all complaining about breathing difficulties as well. She'd asked Tanner about it, since he alone seemed unaffected.

"You get used to it after a time, milady. I figure maybe there's just less air up here."

Jocelyn thought that a very strange statement. How could there be less air? It was all around them. More than likely, it was a combination of the unaccustomed cold and that closed-in feeling they all had after lifetimes spent in wide, open spaces.

Or perhaps, she thought with yet another shiver, the Kassid have put a spell on this place, to make it difficult for strangers.

Now that she knew they were truly encroaching upon Kassid land, Jocelyn could no longer ignore what lay ahead. It would be bad enough, she thought, to meet such as them in familiar territory, but to meet them in this wild, forbidding place . . . She shivered again.

By early afternoon of the following day, they had reached a high valley—and Jocelyn saw her first waterfall. Tanner had described them to her, and now she stared in wonder at the cascade of sparkling water rushing down from a sheer wall of black where small firs clung to a precarious existence.

There was a little pool at its base, from which a thin mist rose into the clear air. She bent and dipped a hand into it cautiously, expecting to find it icy cold, as the streams had been. But she gasped in amazement when she touched warmth. What she'd believed to be mist was in fact steam; the water was close to bath temperature.

Tanner nodded when she exclaimed over it. "I've run across them from time to time, but a lot of them smell bad—like eggs that have gone rotten." He gave her an impertinent grin.

"Perhaps milady would like a bath."

He'd read her mind. She glanced at the captain, who nodded.

"I'll keep the men away, but we'll be close enough to hear you if you call."

After they had withdrawn, Jocelyn hesitated, scanning the area nervously. She did indeed want a bath, but undressing out here in the open made her uncomfortable. Fastidiousness vied with modesty, and the former finally won as she hurriedly stripped off her layers of clothing and slipped into the shallow pool.

With the men's voices carrying clearly to her from just beyond a tree-covered rise, she relaxed and let the water's warmth soothe and cleanse her. The air was cold, but as long as she stayed submerged she was quite comfortable.

She lingered as long as she dared, then left the

pleasurable warmth and dried herself quickly. She dressed before the lingering heat could dissipate and had just pulled on a thick woolen top when she glanced up—and saw the wolf!

It stood there on a ledge off to one side of the waterfall, some twenty feet above her. It stood seemingly at ease, but its pale blue eyes were fixed unwaveringly upon her.

Jocelyn was paralyzed by a mixture of fear and fascination. It crossed her mind briefly that the creature was somehow less ferocious-looking than the drawings in her old books. *It's those eyes*, she thought as she returned its stare—those uncannily human-looking eyes. The color drawings had always shown wolves with burning red eyes.

It was also larger than she'd expected, with a broad, powerful chest. And its dark gray fur, tipped with white, was thicker and softer in appearance than the furs she'd seen.

Neither of them moved as they stood there staring at each other for what seemed to her to be an eternity. The sound of laughter floated over the rise, and the wolf shifted its gaze briefly in that direction.

Jocelyn was roused from her stupor by those sounds and began to back away slowly, hoping to put enough distance between them so that it couldn't leap on her.

The wolf shifted its gaze back to her but didn't move otherwise, except to bring its pointed, white-tipped ears erect. She backed still farther, trying to gauge when it would be safe to turn and run. And then she could stand it no longer and whirled about to flee, crying out at the same time.

Tanner was the first to appear, followed quickly by the captain and several other men. Jocelyn pointed and managed to gasp the single word, "Wolf!"

Later, when the captain brought her her cloak and boots, he said that Tanner had been the only one to catch a glimpse of it. Then the guide himself appeared, saying he'd seen it just as it climbed out of sight around the cliff's face.

Jocelyn shivered beneath the heavy cloak, only now realizing how close she had come to certain death. "I thought they would have red eyes," she told the guide. "The drawings in my books always showed them with red eyes. But its eyes were pale blue. And it was much bigger than I'd expected."

"Blue eyes, you say?" Tanner asked with a frown.

She nodded. "Why? Is that unusual?"

He shrugged. "I've never seen one with blue eyes. Mostly they have dark eyes. And it *was* a big one, from what I could see."

"Its eyes were definitely blue," she stated. "They seemed almost *human*."

As they set out once more, Jocelyn noticed that the usually talkative guide had become very quiet. The Captain had to ask him twice why he thought the wolf hadn't attacked.

Rousted from his thoughts, Tanner merely shrugged again. "Prob'ly wasn't hungry, that's all."

The captain cast her an anxious look, as though apologizing for the guide's rather abrupt answer. But she barely noticed because she was thinking about how she'd known somehow that it wouldn't attack her. Or was that merely the bravado of a survivor?

Tanner's continued silence convinced her that he had something on his mind and that it was connected to that wolf, so she waited until they had made camp for the night, then approached him as he sat alone in front of his tent, smoking a foul-smelling pipe.

"Tanner, something about that wolf troubles you—and you certainly know a lot about them. What was it?"

He shifted about uneasily, not quite meeting her gaze. By the time he finally spoke, her blood was turning to ice. She knew what he was going to say. Hadn't that same thought been lurking deep in her own mind from the moment she'd first met that pale gaze?

"Well, milady, it's them old stories. Mind you, I don't credit them, but . . ."

"You mean the stories about the Kassid being able to turn themselves into wolves," she stated flatly, doing her best to ignore a chill that was now bone-deep.

"Yes'm, them's the ones. Like I said, I never seen one with blue eyes myself—but my daddy did once. He was making a fire one night and he just looked up and there it was, just staring at him the way you said. It coulda got him easy enough—but it just turned and walked away.

"When he told us about it, he said that the old folks believed that the blue-eyed ones was really Kassid—that there was other stories like his, and the blue-eyed ones never attacked."

"Do *you* believe the Kassid can turn themselves into wolves?" she asked.

"The solemn truth, milady? I just don't know. Wolves are fierce creatures, the only ones in these mountains that will come after a man. So it's hard to credit one just turning away, even if it ain't hungry at that moment.

"And somethin' else, too. Wolves travel in packs. But all the stories about the blue-eyed ones, they were alone—like the one you saw.

"But I've met the Kassid. They prob'ly saved my life. And I know they ain't exactly like the rest of us, but that don't mean they can turn themselves into wolves. That's a sight more than I can believe."

I wish it were more than I could believe, Jocelyn thought as that icy fear wrenched about in her gut. How in the name of the gods could she possibly negotiate with a man when she feared that at any moment he might turn himself into a creature like that?

Later, as she lay awaiting sleep, she wondered why it was so much easier for her to accept the possibility of the Kassid's other talents. After all, wasn't she here because she believed they had magic—magic that could prevent war or bring them victory?

But changing one's very shape seemed so much *more* than other forms of magic—not just awe-inspiring, but deeply primitive and beyond fear.

Anyway, she told herself firmly as she finally drifted off to sleep, it isn't really that I believe in their sorcery; it's the fact that our enemies may believe in it.

* * *

Jocelyn awoke slowly from a deep sleep. She could hear the men's voices, although it seemed too dark for them to be up. She burrowed deeper into her quilts to escape the frosty air.

And then the screams began!

She jerked herself upright, both galvanized and paralyzed by terror. Outside her tent, the shouts and screams grew louder.

Wolves! They were being attacked! Her worst nightmare had come true! With her heart pounding noisily in her chest, she crept over to the tent flap, dragging a quilt with her as though it might afford protection from the creatures.

The scene before her *was* a nightmare—but there were no wolves in sight. In the flickering light of the big campfire, she saw the grotesque silhouettes of men fighting, many of them only half-clothed. The firelight gleamed off drawn swords, some of them already darkened with blood. Bodies were strewn about, and even as she watched in horror, still more screamed in agony and fell on those already lying inert. One man stumbled back into the fire as he fought off another, then cried out piteously as his clothing was set ablaze, sending sparks into the black night.

Paralyzed by shock, Jocelyn clutched the edge of the tent flap, trying to understand what she was seeing, knowing she must do something—and realizing, finally, that she herself was in danger.

Then she saw the captain, his sword drawn, fighting off several men as he tried to make his way to her tent. Suddenly, he cried out and his body arched, then fell forward. She saw the shaft of an arrow protruding from his back, surrounded by a rapidly spreading pool of dark blood.

Involuntarily, she cried out, then thrust her fist into her mouth to stifle the sound. The death of the brave and good captain roused her as perhaps nothing else could have. She scuttled backward, looking about wildly for her cloak. She had to get away. There was nothing she could do here, and she owed it to the captain to save her own life, as he had been trying to do.

She pushed the heavy cloak out the back of the tent, then crawled out herself, paying no attention to the hard ground that scraped her flesh beneath its light woolen shift.

The thick forest rose just behind her tent. She started to scramble up the hill, then stopped when she heard the anxious whinnying of the horses and realized they were tethered only a short distance away.

She peered back at the tent fearfully. There was no sign of anyone in it and the sounds of the battle continued unabated beyond the row of tents. So she moved sideways along the hillside until she reached the horses, then untied the first one with shaking hands and led it quickly up the hillside.

The trail lay at the top. They had descended into the ravine to make camp in what the captain had thought would be a safe place. The captain! She let out that cry of anguish now as she struggled up the hillside.

When she reached the trail, she lept onto the horse's back, sparing a moment to be grateful to her brother for having taught her to ride bareback. She gathered up the reins with trembling fingers, then kicked the animal into a run and flew along the trail. Several minutes passed before she realized that she was going the wrong way—heading deeper into Kassid territory instead of fleeing back toward Balek.

She was about to rein in the horse when she realized that if they came after her, they would be expecting her to head back toward Balek. So perhaps her unconscious choice had been correct, after all.

She shivered beneath the cloak as the horse galloped along the dark trail. The sounds of the battle faded away quickly. And then the moon came out from behind some clouds, bright and glowing in the black heavens. Finally, she pulled the horse over to the side of the trail and listened for sounds of pursuit. But the silence was broken only by the horse's heavy breathing.

She tried to think about her situation. Anger began to burn away inside her, temporarily driving out the terror. How dare they do such a thing? How could her father—and all the others—have been so wrong? Men of honor, they'd called them. What honor was there in attacking a sleeping camp? What honor lay in killing people who had clearly come in peace?

But then she reined in her anger, knowing it wouldn't serve her well now. She would find a way to avenge this crime—but first, she had to survive.

She stared around her at the moon-drenched landscape. She was sure they would come after her sooner or later. Did she dare leave the trail? Where could she go in this wild land?

Then she remembered the little stream at their campsite. It had to be down there somewhere in the darkness. If she found it and then stayed near it, she could make her way back to the camp. Surely not all of her Guards had been killed. Perhaps by now, they'd even managed to subdue the enemy.

It was only a hope, and she knew that. But for the moment, she could not face the possibility that they were all dead and she was alone in the mountains with those evil sorcerers.

So she wrapped herself in that hope as she urged the horse down the steep slope, then finally dismounted and led it as the way became too steep. Sharp stones gouged her bare feet, but the numbing cold kept the pain at bay. The heavy cloak impeded her progress, so she took it off and flung it over the horse's back. She was shivering, but her exertions made her less aware of the cold.

Finally, she found the stream by literally stumbling into it in total darkness as clouds hid the moon once more. She gasped at the icy cold and withdrew her foot quickly, then slid on a moss-covered rock and fell headlong into the stream. Shivering violently now in her wet shift, she threw the cloak around her and climbed back onto the horse.

The next hours would forever remain a blur to Jocelyn. She huddled on the horse's back, her wet shift clinging to a body that she knew dimly felt too warm. Each indrawn breath of the icy air pierced her like a knife. Her head throbbed painfully.

The horse walked slowly along the edge of the stream, now and then splashing into it as the bank became too steep. Snow began to fall at some point, drifting down soundlessly through the firs to settle on her and on the horse.

Her thoughts were thick and muddled. She was sure that she was going to die and thought she'd welcome that release. Then she thought of the captain who'd been so kind, and of the other good men under his command—and of her father. And she knew she didn't want to die here in this terrible place, so far from the warm, sun-drenched plains of Ertria.

For long moments, she *was* back there, riding with a warm breeze beneath sunlit skies, calling to her brother to wait for her.

Then the scene shifted and she was walking along the palace wall with her father, in the days before his illness. He was talking about the responsibilities that would be hers one day, and she was caught between a desire to rule and a plea that that day should not come too quickly.

Lost in these vivid hallucinations, Jocelyn was very slow to realize that the night was giving way to the soft gray of early dawn. A tentative light began to steal through the forest. The snow trailed off into a few fat flakes, although clumps of it fell on her as she brushed against heavily laden branches. Some birds began to call in the tall trees.

She was still only vaguely aware of all this when her horse suddenly lifted its head and gave a soft, questioning snuffle that jolted her back to cold reality. She reined it in quickly and listened. Voices! She must be close to the camp!

Relief began to flood through her. Perhaps the slaughter she'd imagined hadn't happened. All those bodies could have been Kassid. As she began to edge forward cautiously, she even allowed herself the hope that the captain's wound hadn't been as serious as she'd thought.

But she was still wary enough to strain her ears for confirmation that what she heard was her Guards. Then she stopped as the voices became a bit clearer. Just ahead of her, the stream made a wide curve around a hill.

She listened to the voices—and her hopes died. She still couldn't hear what they were saying, but the rhythms of their speech were alien. They weren't her Guards, and the fact that they seemed to be talking in normal tones told her that the worst had happened—either her men were all dead or those who remained had been taken prisoner.

Tears rolled down her cheeks and she made no attempt to wipe them away as they stiffened against her cold skin. They were gone—all of them. Hammad chose only the best for the Royal Guard, and from that elite group had chosen the very finest to accompany her. And she'd led them to their deaths at the hands of the very people they'd hoped would help them save the empire.

Her thoughts spiraled once again into the black abyss of despair. She felt herself once more beginning to lose her grip on reality. But even as she stared into that abyss, a part of her began to pull back, to remind her that so much depended upon her—a sick father, an empire, all her people.

There was within Jocelyn's fragile body a very powerful will, the kind of strength that had made her a rebellious child and then a woman determined to do what no woman was believed capable of doing—ruling an empire.

So she sat there quietly for a moment, stroking the horse's withers to keep it quiet, gathering in that strength and ignoring the shivers and pains of a body driven past its endurance. Then she slid off the horse's back, ignoring the tremors in her legs as she tied it loosely to a tree.

She began to drag herself up the hill, certain that the camp must lie just beyond the bend in the stream. Halfway up, she gave up her attempts to keep the heavy cloak wrapped around her and dropped it, then climbed the rest of the way in her still-damp shift. She no longer seemed to mind the cold, but each breath continued to stab at her lungs.

The crest of the hill was covered thickly with firs, and she paused to lean against one of them, listening once again to the voices below her. She could hear their words now, but the language was unknown to her.

As she crept carefully across the top of the hill, every tale she'd ever heard about the Kassid flashed through her mind. And then, at last, she saw them.

Some of them were busy tying the bodies of her Guards onto their horses, while others were taking down the tents or gathering up weapons. Off to one side stood a group of shaggy, thick-chested horses with surprisingly long and powerful-looking legs.

She remembered their guide's comment about their "ugly horses."

But she took in all of this with no more than a quick glance. What drew her attention were the men themselves. They were so big—bigger than all but the largest of Ertrians and far larger than the Baleks. They weren't wearing uniforms, but all were dressed similarly, in loose dark trousers of a rich-looking wool and high, fur-lined boots. Instead of cloaks, they wore strange sweaters in a mottled black and brown and gray that glistened in the sun and had a supple look she'd never before seen in a knitted garment.

These, then, were the Kassid, warriors, sorcerers—and murderers. Killers not only of her Guards, but also undoubtedly of her brother and his friends as well.

She continued to watch them, feeling strangely unafraid—almost as though she were invisible. She half-expected some sign of their sorcery or to see one of them suddenly transform himself into a wolf before her eyes.

The wolf image came to mind easily as she watched them move about with a grace that belied their size. And she thought about that wolf she'd seen. She was sure now that it had been one of them—a scout for this group, perhaps even one of the men down there now.

She wondered if their leader, Daken, could be among them. There was none who was dressed differently, none who appeared to be giving orders. For one brief moment, she allowed herself the hope that this could be a renegade group.

Then one of the men broke away from the rest and started off toward the spot where the little stream began to curve around the hill. Her gaze automatically followed him and came to rest on a man she hadn't noticed before.

She barely managed to suppress a gasp when she saw what he held in his hands. It was the long, brightly patterned scarf her mother had knitted her years ago—the scarf she'd been wearing wrapped about her head and neck.

She moved carefully through the trees to another vantage point where she could see the man clearly. The other man spoke with him briefly, then returned to the rest of the group.

She couldn't see his face at all, since his head was lowered as he stared at the scarf. But he seemed even bigger than the others, with impossibly wide shoulders and a broad chest beneath that strange sweater. His hair was gray and long by Ertrian standards, falling thickly to below his ears.

Totally oblivious to her presence, he continued to stare at the scarf, his big hands running along its length in what seemed—absurdly—to be almost a caress.

Then one of the horses in the camp whinnied—and Jocelyn froze as she heard a faint, answering whinny she knew must be coming from her own horse.

She ran headlong across the hilltop and scrambled down the other side to her horse, not even pausing to pick up her discarded cloak.

* * *

Daken stood there, absently running his hands over the scarf as he thought about the woman to whom it belonged. She must be Maikel's daughter. But where was she?

One of his men came up to tell him that all the bodies had been loaded onto the horses and their equipment and supplies loaded onto the pack animals. There were no extra horses. He issued final instructions, then turned his attention back to the missing woman. He was still debating what to do when one of the horses whinnied and he thought he heard a faint, answering whinny from somewhere downstream, around the bend.

He hesitated as he listened, but he heard nothing more. Sounds could be very deceiving, particularly in a narrow ravine like this, and he hadn't been paying close attention.

Then he decided to check it out anyway and went for his horse, calling out to two of his men to join him.

"Daken—look!"

He'd been peering up the stream, where low-hanging branches limited visibility, but at his companion's cry, Daken turned quickly in the direction the man had indicated. A moment later, the man brought back to him a deep red, fur-trimmed cloak.

Daken examined it. A woman's cloak—no doubt about it. Small, like the other items they'd found.

He stared up at the hillside where it had lain. "She must have managed to escape last night, then

73

came back this morning and went up there to check out the camp. She can't have gotten far."

He urged his horse forward, and within moments they found several hoofprints in the mud beside the stream. After that, they rode quickly.

No more than five minutes had passed when they spotted her, still following the stream bed. He could see that she appeared to be wearing nothing more than a light shift of the type women usually wore to bed. She was bent low over the horse's neck. At first, he assumed it was because of the low branches, but she remained in that position even when the bank widened into a clearing.

He knew she should have heard them by now, but he was within twenty feet of her before she raised her head very slowly and turned around, lifting an arm at the same time to sweep away her long red hair. Jocelyn. For some reason, her name came to him then.

When she saw him, she began to kick the horse with her bare feet, but it was too late. He closed the distance quickly.

Jocelyn knew there was no way she could hope to outrun them. They knew this land, and she didn't. But she could not just stop and let them take her. She kicked her horse, then cried out as fresh pains shot through her cut and bruised feet.

When she turned again, they were nearly upon her. The man in the lead was the gray-haired giant, and he was saying something. But she didn't hear it, because at that moment she lost her grip on the horse and slid to the ground.

74

She tried to get to her feet, but her legs wouldn't hold her and the world was tilting crazily around her. She heard her pursuers' horses snort in protest as they were reined in sharply. She struggled again to gain her feet, then sank back dizzily. The strange calmness of utter despair overtook her as large, booted feet suddenly appeared in her limited range of vision.

Jocelyn lifted her head defiantly, fully expecting to see a sword in his hand. She might not be empress yet—and now would *never* be—but she was determined to die like one. The pride of centuries of her family's history flowed through her in that moment.

But there was no sword in his hand; instead, there was her cloak. He knelt down beside her and wrapped her in it carefully. Then he lifted her into his arms as easily as she might have lifted a baby. Through a fog that was robbing her of her reason, she heard a deep voice speak in strangely accented Ertrian.

"You're safe, Jocelyn. No one will harm you."

Then, as he carried her to his horse, he asked, "That *is* your name, isn't it? You're Maikel's daughter?"

She said nothing. She wondered if she could deny it—and what the consequences of that would be.

He set her on the horse, then swung up behind her. "You're safe now," he repeated as he wrapped one long, heavy arm around her waist and urged the horse back toward the camp. Then he exchanged some words in his own language with the other men, and they rode on ahead.

Jocelyn was just barely clinging to consciousness. Her throat and chest ached, her feet throbbed, and she was burning with fever and shivering at the same time beneath the heavy cloak.

She knew she must have slipped into unconsciousness for a time because suddenly they were back in the camp and he was lifting her down from the horse, then once again cradling her in his arms. Even in her present state, she was still aware of his great gentleness, so very strange for such a big, hard man.

He carried her over to the campfire that was being hastily rebuilt by one of the men. After setting her down, he lowered himself down behind her, then surrounded and supported her with himself as he reached for a mug one of the men handed him.

"Drink this," he ordered. "It will help the fever."

He held the mug to her lips, and she opened her mouth, startled by the sound of her teeth chattering against the rim of the mug. It smelled wonderful, but when she managed to take a few sips, she found that it tasted bitter and immediately thought of poison. But there was something familiar about it, something that touched an old memory. A childhood fever perhaps?

She managed to swallow it in small sips. Her throat was badly swollen, but almost immediately began to feel better. The warmth of the liquid flowed through her with a soothing, tingling sensation.

Then a tall young man approached her with a

smile, carrying the boots she'd left behind in the camp. The giant who held her reached around and drew up the hem of her cloak to reveal her feet, then said something to the other man, who left quickly and returned a moment later with a small pot of salve and a wet cloth.

When she had finished drinking the contents of the mug, he set it aside and shifted her in his arms, then picked up one of her feet. His touch was gentle, but she still cried out in pain.

"I know it hurts," he said in that soft, deep voice, "But they must be cleaned or there will be infection."

"Can you sit alone?" he asked, and when she nodded, he moved around to kneel before her and wipe her feet with the wet, heated cloth.

She stared at him, now truly seeing him for the first time as the potion he'd given her began to clear her mind. He was not a handsome man—at least not by Ertrian standards. His features were too strong—prominent cheekbones, firm jaw with a deep cleft in the chin, and a rather aquiline nose above a wide mouth, all of it framed by that thick, gray hair. It was a harsh face, she thought, despite his present gentleness with her.

Then he looked up at her and smiled—and she found herself staring into pale blue eyes that immediately brought back the memory of that wolf. She shuddered, but he apparently thought it was from the pain he was inflicting on her as he cleaned her feet and then applied the salve.

"They will heal now," he said as he picked up her

boots and slid them onto her feet. "It would be better to leave them bare, but that could be dangerous in this cold, since you are unaccustomed to it."

He sat back on his heels and regarded her solemnly. "I am Daken—as you may have guessed. I met your father some years ago, after your brother's death.

"Your men are all dead, Jocelyn. They killed them all. I am sorry."

"Sorry?" she echoed in disbelief, meeting those strange eyes for only a moment, then looking around the camp to realize that the horses and bodies were gone. She turned back to him, anger flashing in her green eyes.

"You're *sorry*?"

He searched her face, then nodded sadly. "So I am right. You believe *we* killed them. They were dead when we arrived this morning, and there were three dead Menoans as well. They didn't even bother to take away their own dead," he said disgustedly.

"They must have followed you here, hoping to make it appear as though we killed you."

"Then why would they have left their own dead?" she demanded.

He smiled briefly, with, she thought, a hint of admiration.

"My guess is that they thought about where they were and decided to leave quickly. Or perhaps they heard wolves that were drawn by the sounds of battle."

They stared at each other for a long moment, during which she saw not him, but that wolf on the ledge. She looked away quickly, before he could see the fear in her eyes.

"Where are the bodies now?"

"We buried the Menoans, and several of my men are on the way back to the garrison with the bodies of your Guards. They should be buried in their own land. I dislike the thought of the Menoans lying in our lands, but there was no help for it."

Was he telling the truth? She wanted desperately to believe him—too desperately, she thought. Despite the lessening of her fever and her other pains, Jocelyn knew she was scarcely able to think about this rationally now.

No, she decided, I will not *believe him—at least not yet*. When this is over, when she was well again. . . .

"Will you take me back to the garrison?" she asked. She could recuperate there and then return to meet with him—or perhaps persuade him to come there. She hoped for the latter; she never wanted to set foot in this dark place of death again.

Daken shook his head. "You are not well, and our home is much closer." He looked up at the sky.

"We must leave now. It will begin to snow before we reach home."

Her hopes plummeted into an abyss of fear. So he was going to hold her captive. That meant that, despite his gentleness and kindness, this man was a cold-blooded murderer who had ordered an attack on a peaceful, sleeping camp.

"Snow?" she asked contemptuously, wanting to force him to admit the truth. "How could it snow?" She gestured to the blue sky above them.

A trace of a smile crossed his rugged face, and he

pointed behind her, where tall, snow-capped peaks thrust toward the heavens.

"There," he said. "The weather changes swiftly up here."

She looked where he pointed and saw nothing more than a few puffy clouds with dark undersides. But she could hardly dispute his statement. The weather *did* change rapidly here; she'd seen that even in her short time in these accursed mountains. In fact, she and the captain had joked about it.

The captain. She felt a resurgence of pain—pain for his loss and the loss of all the others as well. Her expression must have mirrored her thoughts, because Daken gave her a questioning look.

"They were good men." she stated stiffly. "They did not deserve to die in such a manner."

"No one deserves to die in such a manner," he replied, ignoring her tone. "But there are always those willing to kill in such a manner. Cowardice is a far more common trait among men than is valor."

He started toward the horses and the other men, who were already mounted, and she stared after him.

Make all the pretty speeches you wish, Daken. It does not change who and what you are.

Then she saw that her mount was being led by one of the Kassid. They had bundled up her belongings and tied them to its back. Daken led his horse over to her. "You will ride with me. Your horse will not be able to travel as fast as ours."

Before she could protest, he had lifted her once again into the saddle, then mounted behind her.

His long arm was once more wrapped securely about her waist.

She sat rigidly, keeping herself as far as possible from him. But she was tired after her sleepless night, and before long, she relaxed against his broad chest without even realizing that she was doing so.

Just as he'd predicted, it soon began to snow. As the trail became narrow and wound ever higher, she saw how easily the ungainly looking Kassid horses moved, picking their way with an amazing agility. Even Daken's horse, with its extra burden, had no difficulty with the increasingly treacherous footing. At one point, she turned to see how her horse was faring, but it was no longer in sight.

Daken apparently guessed her concern. "Our horses are not as beautiful as yours, but they've been specially bred for these mountains. Don't worry. We will get it to safety."

Then, after a brief silence, he asked her what she remembered of the attack. She was sure that he was going to use what she told him to proclaim his innocence, so she struggled to recall everything she could, while at the same time protesting that she could remember very little.

"But think about the men you saw, Jocelyn," he urged her. "Or did you see nothing at all of the battle?"

"I saw a little," she admitted, still struggling for those memories and trying to ignore the pain and horror they brought.

"How many of them were there? How were they dressed?"

81

She remained silent as she considered his questions. Most of her Guards had been only half-dressed, making them more easily identifiable. But the others?

"The Menoans we found were dressed like Balek hunters—and they are much smaller than we are," he prompted when she continued her silence.

"We had a Balek guide with us," she said, ignoring his implied question. "Did you find . . . his body?"

"Yes. We know him. He has hunted here for many years. His body is being returned to his people."

She felt a twinge of pain for the talkative guide, but her mind was focused on his questions. She was nearly certain that none of the men she'd seen were any bigger than her Guards, most of whom were very tall by Ertrian standards—though not so tall as the Kassid. And she was quite sure they hadn't been dressed like Daken and his men. But what did that prove? It could have been a separate group of Kassid, dressed differently to disguise their identity. And just because the men with her now were big didn't mean that *all* Kassid were so large.

"Perhaps you'll remember more when you are well again," he said. "But think about this, Jocelyn. The Kassid have lived in peace with your people for centuries. Your father and Hammad have no reason to distrust us. If they did, they would certainly keep a larger force at the garrison."

She knew he was right. There was no reason for the Kassid to attack—and all the reason in the world for the Menoans, who could have found out about her mission and tried to stop it. Unless, of course, the Kassid had made a secret alliance with the Menoans and Turveans.

"What could your enemies possibly offer us that would make us change?" he asked, as though he had read her mind. "There is nothing of theirs—or yours—that we want."

Jocelyn sat stiffly as all those old stories came pouring back. If they were true, this man was a sorcerer—perhaps the most powerful of them all, since he was their leader. Could he read her mind? The rational side of her denied all of it, dismissed it as children's tales. But far beneath that, a primitive fear was lurking.

They rode higher and higher into the mountains. The snow came thicker and faster. She could barely see beyond the horse's nose, but Daken and his men clearly knew the way, and their mounts remained sure-footed.

"How is your father's health?" he asked after a time. "We have heard rumors that he is ill."

"Yes, he is," she said. How could he have "heard rumors," when his people supposedly had no contact with the outside world? Was it sorcery—or had the rumors reached him through the Menoans?

"So that is why he sent you—his heir?"

"Yes."

"And he sent you to persuade us to join forces against the Menoans and Turveans, who plan to make war against you."

Where was he getting his information? It was

83

possible that the Kassid had spies like everyone else—but if they all looked like these men, how could they possibly disguise themselves?

Then she realized he was expecting a response. "I would prefer to discuss my mission later."

He chuckled. "So the future empress has already learned something of statecraft. Very well. We will wait."

Her fever was returning. She began to shiver again, and her head throbbed. She rubbed her temples absently. He reached for a flask tied to the saddle, opened it and handed it to her.

"Drink some more of this. It won't be warm now, but it will still help."

She took it and drank more of the bitter brew. Once again, it helped almost immediately—but not as much as before. And she began to feel dizzy again, just as they rounded a sharp bend in the trail and were struck full force by a howling wind.

Daken tightened his grip on her and leaned close to her ear. "You're in no danger. We'll be out of the wind soon. Try to sleep, Jocelyn."

The trail now had become a constant spiral upwards, with walls of black rock to one side and a swirling nothingness to the other. She had to gasp for breath, causing her chest to hurt still more. Whether she actually did fall asleep, or simply passed out, she didn't know. Neither did she know how much time had elapsed. But she came to suddenly with a painful snap of her head as he brought the horse to a halt. She could see nothing—not even the other men. Only swirling snow and blackness.

"Why have we stopped?" she asked, trying to keep the fear from her voice.

"I had hoped to show you our home from here," he said. "But it's difficult to see through the snow." He pointed up ahead.

"Can you see the lights?"

She blinked and peered through the snow and finally *did* see some lights. Two lights shone with particular brightness; she thought they must be bonfires. But how could they keep bonfires going in this weather?

"The brightest lights mark the entrance," he told her as he urged the horse onward again.

"How can you have bonfires in this snow?" She asked incredulously.

"They're not bonfires," he replied. "You will see soon enough. We will be there within the hour."

But she didn't see them again. By the time the party reached the huge, flaming cauldrons at the end of the bridge, Jocelyn had slipped once more into oblivion.

Chapter Three

Jocelyn returned to consciousness suddenly—or so it seemed to her. From a place of total nothingness, she opened her eyes to bright sunlight pouring in through sparkling glass windows whose edges glowed with jewel-toned panes.

Vague memories flitted through her mind: gentle hands, voices speaking soothingly in an alien tongue, cool cloths bathing her heated skin. Then another, more disturbing memory: a large, shadowy presence and a much deeper voice, also speaking softly in that strange language.

She blinked a few times in the sunlight, then forced the memories away as she confronted the reality—she was a prisoner here, a prisoner of the Kassid and their leader, Daken. Her last clear memory of him was sitting astride his horse, leaning against that solid wall of his chest as he pointed out the bonfires. Or had he told her they *weren't* bonfires?

With all this running through her mind, Jocelyn was very slow to notice her surroundings—then slower still to assimilate what she saw. She had believed that the Kassid were a primitive people, despite the tales of their sorcery, but what she now saw was luxury beyond even the palace.

Glass windows, such as existed in only the wealthiest of Ertrian homes were decorated with colored panes along the edges. Richly decorated draperies covered the windows. Ornately carved wood in a mellow, golden shade she'd never seen before. Thick rugs on the floor. Unlit crystal wall sconces whose bases had the gleam of pure gold.

The bed in which she lay was large and comfortable, if a bit hard, and the cover was made of that same strange, knitted wool Daken and his men had worn. She withdrew a hand from beneath the covers and touched it. What wonderful wool—if indeed it *was* wool. She'd never seen its like before.

She stared at all of this for a long time, first in disbelief and finally with a sense of wonder. Not even the palace—surely the grandest place in the world—was so splendid.

She recalled the story she'd been told that the Kassid possessed great wealth, and remembered as well Daken's comment that there was nothing the Kassid could possibly want from Ertria or its enemies.

Then she belatedly recalled her pains and the

fever. She took a deep breath and felt no pain knife through her chest. She wiggled her damaged feet, then pushed back the covers to examine them. The cuts and bruises were mostly gone. Only a few faint marks were left to remind her of her ordeal.

She was just beginning to wonder how long she had been here when yet another thought struck her. The room was comfortably warm, even though the fire had burned down to a few glowing embers. For a moment, she thought she might still have a fever. Perhaps all of this was a hallucination. But no, she was fine; that warmth was coming from the room itself, not from a fevered body.

Surely it should be cold! It had been snowing when they arrived. But in this room there was nothing of the dampness she associated with colder weather.

Moving slowly and carefully, she got out of bed. Her body was somewhat stiff, but there was no real pain. She stood there uncertainly for a moment, curling her toes into the soft rug, wondering again where they got that luxurious wool. Then she realized that she could feel a draft of warm air against one side of her face.

She turned in that direction and saw only a wooden grate covering an opening in the wall. The warmth was coming from there, and she soon saw similar grates in the other walls.

From a sense of wonder, Jocelyn moved quickly to uneasiness. How could such a thing be? How could all of this exist up here in these dark, wild mountains?

Sorcery! Despite the warmth, she shivered. How

could she possibly have forgotten what the Kassid truly were?

She started toward the windows, her mind already considering how she could escape from this luxurious prison. But then she stopped and whirled about as she heard the door open behind her.

A very tall, dark-haired woman stood there, dressed simply but richly in a long dress with wide, intricately embroidered sleeves. She wasn't beautiful, but Jocelyn thought her very striking. The woman smiled at her.

"You are well," she said with obvious pleasure. "That is good. Forgive my poor speaking. I have only a little Ertrian. I am Tassa."

Jocelyn wondered if she were Daken's wife. They appeared to be about the same age, and the woman clearly wasn't a servant. She returned the smile.

"Yes, I am well. Was it you who nursed me back to health?"

"I and others as well. We have healers. You are hungry?"

"Yes—very hungry."

"Then I will bring food," Tassa said with another smile and left the room, closing the door softly behind her.

When she had gone, Jocelyn noticed a dark green robe lying across a chair. It wasn't hers, but she assumed it had been left for her and put it on, once again admiring the fineness of the wool. The robe was both too large and too long, but she sashed it as best she could, then picked up the hem and started once again toward the windows.

She peered out, then shrank away with a gasp as

a wave of dizziness overtook her. Then she stepped back to the window again, this time better prepared for the sight before her.

Far, far below was a huge courtyard, at least several times as large as the main courtyard at the palace. It looked as though a market was in progress; hundreds of people were milling about in the bright sunshine.

Beyond the courtyard was a wall, perhaps about the height of the outer wall of the palace, but dwarfed here by the height of the building in which she stood. And beyond that were the ever-present mountains—except that now she was at eye level with some of the peaks, though a few snowcapped ones were taller.

The size of the courtyard and the height from which she was seeing it suggested a building of truly gigantic proportions, although she could see nothing of it from the window. And all of it—the wall, the courtyard, and the outer portions of the deepset windows—was made of that strange black stone.

I have touched the sky, she thought, recalling the Balek name for the Dark Mountains. And for a moment, she lost her fear in the sense of awe over this wondrous place that swept over her.

Then she heard the door open and turned, expecting to see the woman, Tassa. But it was Daken who entered the room, balancing a large silver tray easily on one big hand.

He smiled at her—that smile that brought such gentleness to his harsh features and even softened the impact of those ice-blue eyes. She stayed where she was, resisting the urge to clutch the robe more tightly around her.

She wouldn't have believed it possible, but he seemed even bigger in the confines of the room. He was wearing loose gray trousers and a matching shirt with flowing sleeves, and over it a vest in that strange, supple, knitted wool. The effect was elegant, despite the solemn colors and lack of decoration—far more elegant, she thought, than the overdone clothes worn by men at court.

He gestured to the food, still smiling. "Come and eat. You will need to regain your strength if you are to practice statecraft."

His tone was light and teasing, making it difficult for her to take offense. She lifted the hem of the robe and crossed the room, conscious the entire time only of him, although she kept her eyes on the tray of food.

When she had seated herself at the small table, he poured them both a dark brew from an ornate silver pot.

"This may be too strong for you. I can add some water."

She tasted it and immediately began to cough. He chuckled softly. "I thought as much." He added some water from a matching silver pitcher.

"Wh .. what is it?" she gasped.

"We call it taru. It's brewed from certain roots, then aged in vats."

"It's wine?" she asked doubtfully. It hadn't really tasted like wine.

"No—and it will not make you drunk. We have some very good wines, but you should not drink them yet."

Watered down, taru tasted quite good—and so did the food. The spices were strange, and she didn't recognize half of what she ate, but she devoured it while he contented himself with a cup of the taru.

She was about to compliment his cook when it occurred to her that she hadn't yet seen any evidence of servants. Perhaps Tassa had prepared it herself.

"Tassa is your wife?" she inquired politely.

He shook his head. "She is my sister. My wife died many years ago."

Jocelyn then recalled her father's having mentioned that Daken had lost a son. "Do you have any children?"

"A daughter," he replied. "She wants very much to meet you, and I doubt that I'll be able to keep her away much longer."

"How old is she?" Jocelyn couldn't begin to guess his age, although she was certain that he must be younger than her father. Despite the gray hair, he looked like a man in the prime of his life.

"Sixteen," he replied with a smile. "And already insisting that she's a woman."

Jocelyn nodded with a smile of her own. "Yes, I recall saying much the same thing to my father at that age. It seems to me that fathers never want their daughters to grow up, although they're forever urging their sons to do so."

He chuckled—a low, pleasant sound. "I think you're right, although in your case, your father must have been forced to accept your growing up, since you are his heir."

"But your daughter . . ." She stopped, remembering those stories about their form of government.

"My daughter will inherit nothing—except what I have to give her, of course. Our leaders are elected."

So it was true—in part, at least. "Who elects them?"

"Everyone who has reached the age of maturity. Then the leader appoints a council of advisors."

"Does 'everyone' include *women*?"

He nodded, his eyes glittering with amusement. "Of course."

"Then a woman could be elected leader?" she challenged.

"That hasn't happened yet, but I think it will one day. I have two women among my advisors."

"And how long have you been leader?"

"For fifteen years—since I was twenty-six."

"Twenty-six?" She stared at him. "But how is it that you were elected at such a young age?" She wouldn't dare choose even an advisor so young.

"Durka, who was leader before me, had nominated me. That is the custom. I myself have already nominated a successor. But Durka died young, in an accident."

"I find it hard to believe that your people would accept such a young leader."

"But you are very young—surely younger than I was then. And you may well become empress at a very young age."

"Yes, but no one elects me." Nor would they, she thought. Ertrians would never elect a woman to

93

rule them. She was intrigued by his suggestion that such a thing could happen here.

"Nevertheless, they will accept you," he replied.

"Because they have no choice," she stated bitterly before she could stop herself.

Their eyes met, and she thought she saw understanding there. But how *could* he understand? That momentary warmth she felt for him drained away. She could not afford such feelings for this man.

"Am I a prisoner here?" she asked him, forcing herself to hold his gaze steadily.

"No, Jocelyn—you are a guest. We did not kill your Guards and I did nothing more than to bring you to your destination."

She believed him. She knew that she might change her mind later, but at this moment, looking into those pale eyes, she believed he spoke the truth.

"Thank you for saving my life," she said simply.

He nodded. "I regret that we didn't arrive quickly enough to save the others as well."

She finished her meal in silence as he drank another cup of the taru. His honesty was encouraging her to ask the other questions most on her mind: Were they truly sorcerers? Could they transform themselves into wolves? But she remained silent out of fear of what the answers might be.

By the time she had finished the meal, she felt herself growing tired and frowned at the cup she had just drained. Could it have been drugged? But he'd drunk two cups with no obvious effects.

He stood up. "You should rest now. You were very ill, Jocelyn—perhaps more than you realize. It will be some time before you regain your strength."

"How long have I been here?" she asked, realizing that she should have asked that question before.

"For five days. For the first two days, the healers were not certain they could save you. I think you must have been ill even before the attack on the camp."

"Five days?" She stared up at him, aghast, then nodded in response to his implied question.

"Yes, I hadn't been feeling well. We rode for several days in the rain, and the air in these mountains seemed to disagree with us."

He nodded. "When our people returned here many years ago from Ertria, they also found it difficult to breathe for a time. That is another reason you are tired now."

"But why is that? Tanner, our guide, told me that he thinks there's less air up here—but that can't be true."

He shrugged. "Perhaps it *is* true. We don't really know."

He reached down to assist her to her feet, then held her hand for a moment. It felt rough and warm against her soft skin. Their eyes met and held for a moment before she pulled her hand free and backed away, confused by the heat generated within her by that brief contact.

Then she felt warmth of a different sort as she moved closer to that grate in the wall. She gestured to it, grateful for something to distract her.

"Where does that warm air come from?"

He glanced at it briefly, then smiled at her—a knowing smile, she thought.

"Magic," he pronounced, then turned to the door.

"We will talk more later, Jocelyn. Rest now—and know that you are safe here."

He left, closing the door behind him. She stared from the door to the grate and back to the door again, shivering despite the warmth and his words. Safe? How could she be safe in the home of sorcerers?

But the days passed and Jocelyn and Daken didn't talk. She usually saw him at some time during each day, but on those occasions he confined himself to small talk, always in the presence of his sister and daughter.

Jocelyn, however, didn't force the issue. First of all, even though she was much better, she still tended to tire easily. And whether by accident or design, Daken tended to appear at the times when she was feeling her worst.

And secondly, she was slowly gaining information about the Kassid from the two women—especially Daken's daughter, Rina. Sometimes, though, it seemed that she was learning more through what was *not* being said.

Rina had become her almost constant companion. She was sixteen and already taller than the petite Jocelyn, who quickly discovered that the Kassid were indeed a very tall race. Rina had big brown eyes flecked with gold, deep-set like her father's, and a mass of chestnut curls that Jocelyn assumed must have come from her mother. She was pretty, bright, and very inquisitive—and she spoke excellent, if heavily accented, Ertrian.

Rina asked many questions about Jocelyn's life

and the Ertrian court, and Jocelyn answered them all candidly, hoping that this would be reciprocated when she asked Rina questions about the Kassid.

She explained that she would become empress only because of her only brother's death and that the usual role of royal daughters was to make important marriages and bear more royal children. She didn't bother to hide her disgust with this state of affairs.

Rina was aghast, unable to believe that people could be forced into marriage for reasons other than love. She asked how Jocelyn had managed to escape such a horrible fate.

"I might not have," Jocelyn admitted, "except that by the time I was of marriageable age, my brother had died and I had become the heir." She added that her father was disinclined to force her into marriage, having himself been fortunate enough to have married for love.

"He told me once that being emperor was difficult enough without also having to live in a loveless marriage."

"So now you can marry for love?" Rina asked. "You *will* marry, won't you, since you'll have to have an heir yourself?"

Jocelyn shook her head. "No, I have no intention of marrying, because I refuse to let a man rule in my place. And that is exactly what would happen. He wouldn't truly be the emperor, of course, but it would be to him that everyone would turn, not to me.

"As for having an heir, I have cousins who are busy having babies. When I see how they turn out,

I will simply adopt one of them as my heir. It happened once before many years ago, when an emperor had no sons of his own."

"So your father could have done that, too?"

Jocelyn nodded. "He could have—but he didn't. He said that I am more fit to rule than any of my cousins—and he's right."

When Jocelyn began to ply Rina with questions as well, the girl at first seemed to speak freely. She confirmed that Daken had said earlier about their manner of choosing a leader.

"It seems very strange to me," Jocelyn said, shaking her head. "How can people be trusted to elect the best leader? Surely there must be unscrupulous people who would bribe others to vote for them?"

Rina looked shocked. "Oh no! That would never happen. We are all taught in school the traditions of our people and the importance of electing a good leader."

"Do all children go to school, then, not just the children of the wealthy?" Jocelyn asked.

"Of course," Rina responded, apparently surprised that she should think otherwise. "We don't really have wealthy people here, Jocelyn. Some have more than others, but no one is rich the way your nobles are rich. And no one is as poor as your peasants."

How could that be? Jocelyn wondered, then began to understand as Rina told her that no one owned land. The Kassid believed that all of the Dark Mountains belonged to *all* of them, not to any one individual, and that the only way anyone acquired more wealth than his neighbors was by possessing some talent in abundance or by working very hard at something deemed to be difficult by the tribe as a whole, such as mining.

Jocelyn decided that she needed some time to think about this strangeness, and turned instead to the role of women in their society, a subject she'd found fascinating ever since she'd learned from Daken that women too voted for the leader and even served as his advisors.

"Do you think a woman could be elected leader of your people?" She asked Rina.

Rina shook her head—a bit angrily, Jocelyn thought. "Not unless certain things change. There are . . . requirements, you see, and women can't meet them now. But Father thinks that should change."

"What are the requirements?" Jocelyn asked. Daken hadn't mentioned any.

Rina hesitated and Jocelyn had the impression that she was struggling with a desire to divulge something she'd been told not to talk about. She was wondering how she could encourage the girl when Tassa joined them. Something in the girl's expression suggested that the matter should be dropped. But when Jocelyn attempted to pursue it later, after Tassa had gone, Rina changed the subject with all the adroitness of the born diplomat.

Not wishing to antagonize the girl or to get her into trouble, Jocelyn did not press for a response. But she wondered if the answer could lie in their sorcery. Was it possible that only men possessed the means to make magic?

Certainly it seemed to her that Rina and Tassa

and the few other women she'd met thus far possessed no magic. Daken, on the other hand, she could not so easily dismiss. There was something about him, something that defied description—something she felt at a deep, unknowable level. And to a lesser extent, she felt it also with Jakka, the young man Daken had designated as his successor and the only other Kassid male she'd truly met, though she saw others from time to time.

She feared Daken, although he had never given her cause to do so—and she was certain that fear came from a deep, instinctive knowledge that he did indeed possess magic, even if he chose not to use it in her presence.

One day when all three women were gathered, Tassa was struggling with her limited Ertrian and voiced her regret that she had not kept up her skill in Jocelyn's tongue. That prompted Jocelyn to inquire why they studied Ertrian in the first place.

"We all learn it in school," Rina answered. "But unless we use it after that, like Father does, it's hard to remember it."

"But when does your father use it?" Jocelyn asked.

The two women exchanged glances, and Tassa immediately turned back to explaining about the knitting of the beautiful wool Jocelyn had admired. She'd already explained that the wool came from animals that resembled goats more than they did sheep.

Once again, Jocelyn did not press for answers, certain that if she became too insistent, she would learn even less—and perhaps provoke Daken's wrath.

But the questions were piling up in her mind. To whom would Daken speak Ertrian? She already suspected that the Kassid were sending out their own spies, but if that were so, *they* were the ones who would have to speak fluent Ertrian, not Daken.

And if the Kassid were content in their mountains, why would they bother sending out spies in the first place? Surely they couldn't believe anyone would dare to attack them here.

Furthermore, why was Daken continuing to avoid any serious discussions with her? She'd now been here for nearly two weeks, and other than an occasional spell of tiredness, she was fully recovered.

Her status in this strange place seemed so tenuous, so very fragile. She was treated with utmost respect and kindness by everyone she encountered—including, of course, Daken himself. But she continued to feel as though she were walking a very fine line in this place and that one misstep could plunge her into a very different world, one she couldn't imagine and didn't *want* to imagine.

For this reason, she temporized, making no demands upon Daken. It seemed important to stay with the rules of diplomacy, which stated that the host should be the one to raise the business at hand. But she had no reason to believe that an isolated people like the Kassid would recognize those protocols.

Although she saw little of him, Daken occupied

a very large role in her thoughts—which she told herself was only natural, given the fact that it was he whom she would have to persuade to form an alliance with Ertria.

But she was uneasily aware of the fact that he would have been in her thoughts regardless of his position.

He didn't behave like any ruler she'd ever met or even imagined. He displayed none of the usual trappings of power. He dressed like everyone else, and she'd discovered that his suite in the fortress, while apparently somewhat larger than others, was no more luxurious. There were no servants or courtiers hanging about, and she'd even found him in the kitchen once, preparing his own breakfast.

She'd even had a few occasions to observe him with his men, and she'd been shocked at his behavior. Anytime she was present, he insisted that everyone speak Ertrian, which she assumed was intended to reassure her that no one was plotting against her. On these occasions, she'd heard him use phrases like "Perhaps you should . . ." or "Well, we might want to . . ." instead of simply issuing orders as her father—or she herself—would have done.

If he weren't who he is, she thought, he would certainly be thought weak when he talks like that. And yet the others clearly respected him, even though that respect wasn't accompanied by the usual bowing and scraping to which she'd long since become accustomed.

Daken, quite simply, fascinated her in a way no man had ever done. When they were together, she felt his presence so keenly that she often forgot there was anyone else there. And even when he was absent, which was most of the time, something of him lingered in the suite. Jocelyn had once been awed by the aura of power that had hovered about her father before his illness, but she knew now that she was truly seeing power for the first time.

He's a sorcerer, she thought with an inward shudder. And perhaps she'd misunderstood sorcery. Perhaps it wasn't flashes of light and puffs of smoke and illusions. Perhaps his magic was more subtle.

And she never looked into those pale blue eyes without being reminded of that wolf—and of the wolf that might be contained within this man as well.

When Jocelyn's fever had not returned for three days in a row, Tassa and the old woman healer who had attended her declared that she could venture outside if the weather permitted.

The days had in fact been quite sunny and everyone was remarking about the unusual warmth, but when Jocelyn at last ventured out into the great courtyard, she quickly realized that what the Kassid described as "warmth" was in fact about as cold as it ever got at home.

Rina accompanied her as they walked out into the courtyard to attend the thrice-weekly market she had seen from her windows—and it was then that she began to grasp the true dimensions of the Kassid fortress.

She'd seen enough of the interior to know that it was huge, but as they walked out into the center of the courtyard and Jocelyn turned to stare back at it, she was astounded. Even from this vantage point, she couldn't see all of it.

The great fortress was built entirely of that strange black stone and was quite literally carved out of the mountain itself. And there were windows everywhere. She stared at it in silent astonishment. How could such a thing have been built? Its very existence was the strongest evidence she'd yet seen for the Kassid's possession of magic.

"When was this built?" she asked Rina when she could tear her eyes away from it for a moment.

"We believe that it was a gift from the Old Gods," Rina told her, "A gift they gave the Kassid when they left this world."

"And the glass windows?" Jocelyn asked. "Have they always been there as well?"

"Yes, although some have been replaced over the years. The making of them is a precious skill, passed down in one family."

Then Rina pointed to one protruding corner of the fortress, where sunlight glared on a huge expanse of glass that had just caught Jocelyn's attention.

"See all those windows up there? That is our winter garden. We grow herbs and vegetables and some flowers in there."

Jocelyn marveled anew at the idea of an indoor garden. At the palace there was a small protected courtyard where some flowers and herbs could be grown through much of the winter, but even in Ertria's much milder climate, they often died.

They continued to walk about the courtyard and

presently came to a section Jocelyn hadn't seen from inside. She stopped and stared. Before her was the entrance to the fortress. A wooden bridge, wide enough for two horses to walk abreast comfortably, stretched across a ravine. Huge ropes, thicker than her waist, angled down from somewhere high in the fortress itself to the far side of the bridge. And on the near end of the bridge were two giant stone urns. Flames leapt up many feet from both of them and she realized that they must be the lights she had seen through the snowstorm the night Daken had brought her here.

"The bridge can be pulled up if necessary," Rina explained, "by using those ropes. It makes a terrible noise. Father says no one could ever attack us here with the bridge drawn up, but of course the only time they pull it up is to test it."

Jocelyn, who had always thought the palace to be very safe on the hill behind its walls, suddenly felt her home to be very vulnerable by comparison to this place.

"Do those fires burn all the time?" she asked.

Rina nodded. "There are pipes running into the bottoms of the urns."

"I don't understand," Jocelyn frowned. "What is in the pipes?"

Rina hesitated and Jocelyn wondered if she'd asked another indelicate question. But the girl held out her hands in a gesture of helplessness.

"I don't think there's a word for it in your language. We call it bol. It's a smelly black liquid that comes out of the mountain, and it burns."

Jocelyn stared at the flames, thinking about the

heat that poured from the grates in the walls. Could this bol be the source of that, too? She turned to Rina as she began to ask the question—and found herself staring instead into Daken's pale blue eyes.

"Bol is the magic that heats our rooms," he confirmed with a smile and a wry emphasis on the word 'magic.' "There are furnaces throughout the fortress and it is piped into them as it is into the urns."

"And this has always been there, too?" she asked, having just about exhausted her capacity for amazement.

"Yes. As Rina has probably told you, our home was a gift from the gods when they departed this world. A very generous gift."

"I am . . . astounded," she admitted. "This place is not at all what I expected it to be."

He laughed. "And you have yet to see all of it."

"I'm not sure I could stand any more surprises," she admitted with a rueful smile.

"Then we will wait."

"Rina said that not all of your people live here. Do the others live in similar fortresses?"

"Similar—but much smaller. And some live in separate houses during the summer months, to tend their crops and livestock."

Rina took Jocelyn's arm impatiently. "Come, Jocelyn. We must hurry if we are to get to market while the selections are good."

Rather reluctantly, Jocelyn allowed Rina to lead her away. She had very much wanted to go to the market—until Daken happened along.

But to her surprise—and apparently to Rina's as

well—he followed them. Rina threw him an astonished look.

"*You're* coming to market?"

He nodded and his wide mouth quirked with amusement. "And that means you won't be able to flirt with all the boys."

Rina rolled her eyes and her fair skin flushed brightly. She spoke in rapid, obviously exasperated Kassid. Daken reminded her to speak Ertrian before their guest, and Jocelyn laughed.

"It isn't necessary. Some things don't require translation."

Jocelyn found the relationship between father and daughter intriguing. Like Rina, she had also lost her mother at a young age and consequently had been very close to her father. But as she watched the two of them, it struck her that her father's attitude toward her had been one of affection and indulgence, while Daken had often displayed a great interest in every aspect of his daughter's life and showed great patience in listening to her complaints and dreams and plans.

As they moved among the many stalls, Jocelyn quickly saw that she herself had become a major attraction at the market. People stared at her with unconcealed curiosity, but nowhere did she encounter any hostility.

There were a surprising number of men at the market, something she'd noticed before as she'd watched from her window. Many of them, she observed, had been relegated to a baby-minding function as their wives selected merchandise, and seeing these big men display such an open, honest affection toward their children fascinated her. Apparently, Rina's motherless status wasn't the only reason her father took such an interest in her.

She felt, as she always did in the presence of the men, that vague uneasiness, that deep certainty that these were not ordinary men. But even among the women she saw a difference as well. They had a calm self-confidence and displayed none of the behavior Jocelyn was accustomed to seeing in women when men were present.

As always, she was aware of Daken's presence. People spoke to him familiarly, greeting him as a friend and neighbor, not as a ruler, and no one stepped aside to make way for him.

She lost her awareness of him only when they came to a stall where the sparkle of gold and silver and precious gems caught her eye. Jocelyn had two weaknesses—unusual jewelry and perfumes. And the jewelry she saw displayed here was exquisite. Some stones she recognized, but others were unfamiliar to her, and the workmanship was superior to anything she'd ever seen.

The man and woman behind the stall were clearly pleased with her interest, although she had to communicate with them through Rina.

"Would you like something?" Rina asked her.

"Oh yes—but I have no way to pay for them."

"Then Father can just—"

"No, please, Rina, that would be—"

But Rina was already off to find Daken, who stood only a short distance away. Jocelyn stood there uncomfortably as Rina pointed out the two bracelets Jocelyn had admired most. Daken picked them up, then took her gloved hand and slid them onto her wrist.

"A gift," he said with a smile.

"Thank you," she murmured, feeling both pleased and embarrassed. She was increasingly uncomfortable with such gestures of familiarity from him, though she tried to tell herself that it was only because she was accustomed to the far more formal life of the court.

Then it seemed that Rina had to give her a present as well. She knew that Jocelyn liked perfumes and dragged her off to another stall, where pots of herbs and salves and oils covered a large table. Daken followed along after them.

Rina spoke in Kassid to the woman at the stall, then turned to Jocelyn. "She will create a scent that is just right for you."

The woman scrutinized Jocelyn for a moment with bright black eyes, then began to mix various things together in a tiny pot. Jocelyn was excited. She'd tried creating scents herself a few times, but had never been satisfied with the results.

"Give her your hand," Rina instructed.

Jocelyn did so and the woman rubbed a small amount of the concoction onto the inside of her wrist. Jocelyn inhaled it and exclaimed with delight. It was perfect. Then Rina took her hand and sniffed.

"Oh, that's lovely—and it's just right for you. Don't you think so, Father?"

Jocelyn, who had for once quite forgotten his presence, was caught by surprise as Rina lifted her hand to Daken, who obligingly bent over it.

"Yes, it is," he agreed.

Their eyes met—and something shifted irrevocably in Jocelyn's world. For one brief moment, she forgot who he was, who she was—and everything else. Liquid warmth surged through her, leaving in its wake a strange sort of languor, a ripe heaviness that she'd never felt before. She looked away, embarrassed over that reaction and fearful that he might somehow have guessed it.

Then Rina's youthful enthusiasm came to her rescue. She tugged Jocelyn along to the food stalls, where they bought sweets and some soft cheese made from the milk of the strange creatures that produced the supple wool.

Jocelyn quickly set aside that disorienting moment with Daken as she enjoyed being carried along by Rina's high spirits. Not since her own childhood had she been to a market. After that, things had been brought to the palace for her inspection, and the pure joy of exploration had been lost.

Then, as they began to walk back to the fortress, Rina paused to speak to some friends and Daken turned to her.

"Would you like to go for a ride, Jocelyn? I thought you might like to see the view you missed when you came here—if you're feeling well enough, that is."

Surprised by the invitation, she still nodded quickly. But she found herself hoping that Rina would join them even though she was fully aware of the irony of such a wish. For days now, she'd

been waiting for a time to speak with him alone—
and now that it seemed she would have that opportunity, she feared it.

She sat down on a nearby bench while Daken
went to fetch the horses and began to eat some of
the marvelous sweets Rina had bought while the
girl finished her discussion with her friends. When
Rina came over to her, she told the girl that they
were going riding, then invited her to join them.

"I don't think Father would appreciate that just
now," Rina replied. "I think he wants you to himself
for a while."

Rina's choice of words was undoubtedly the result of speaking a foreign tongue, but Jocelyn's reaction was a warm flush that made her look away
quickly as she pretended to be busy unwrapping
another sweet.

Does she know—or has she guessed? Jocelyn's
fear of Kassid magic was never far from her mind,
and now she wondered if they might *all* be able to
read her mind. She couldn't quite believe that, but
decided that she must guard her thoughts and feelings even more than she usually did.

Then she saw Daken coming back across the
courtyard, leading two of the ugly Kassid horses,
and for just a moment, she saw him as she knew her
people would see him—a huge man who radiated a
carefully controlled power that surpassed anything
she'd ever seen before.

Even if he refuses to ally his people with us, she
thought, I must persuade him to accompany me
back to the palace. She knew there had to be spies

111

at court, and any who saw him would surely carry such reports back to Arrat that he would be dissuaded from attacking.

This thought calmed her by forcing her mind back to the purpose of her visit here and made her determined that, even if Daken had intended this to be no more than a sightseeing ride, she would raise that purpose with him.

It was time to conclude her business here and go home. At no time since her arrival had she felt such a powerful urge to return to the familiar routine of the palace.

Daken stopped before her. "Are you certain that you feel well enough to ride?"

She nodded. "And as you can see, I'm dressed for it as well." Beneath her cloak, she was wearing trousers.

He chuckled. "Much more practical than your previous riding clothes, although I doubt that you wear either in Ertria."

She thought about the thin shift she'd been wearing when he'd found her and very belatedly became embarrassed about it. A treacherous flush began to creep through her skin and she quickly averted her face, reminding herself that it was far too late to be concerned about that now.

Daken lifted her into the big, comfortable Kassid saddle much as he might have done with a child. The brief contact between them left her dizzy, and she fought it by telling herself that he probably did think of her as a child. After all, she was closer in age to his daughter than she was to him.

That realization was very comforting.

They walked the horses across the courtyard and onto the bridge, where Jocelyn made the mistake of looking down into the ravine. She gasped as the dizziness returned—for a very different reason.

"That's why I didn't bring you your own horse," he said, moving closer to her and laying a steadying hand over hers as she grasped the reins. "Our horses are accustomed to this, but the men had to blindfold your horse to get it across."

She kept her eyes straight ahead until they had reached the far side of the long bridge and tried not to think about the return trip. The rock-strewn bottom of the ravine had to be a thousand feet below them. And she'd once believed the outer walls of the palace to be as high above the surrounding land as it was possible to be!

They set out on the narrow trail, and both bridge and fortress were quickly lost from view. Despite her growing anxiety over the talk they must have, and despite her present uneasiness with him, Jocelyn was glad to be riding again. During those long weeks on the road, she'd thought she might never want to ride again in her life.

Daken remained silent as they trotted along the trail, where a thick fringe of firs rose along one side and a sheer wall of black stone thrust up on the other. She stared at that light-swallowing blackness.

"Does this stone exist anywhere else?" she asked him.

He appeared to be rather distracted, but presently shook his head. "I don't think so. The word for it in our language means 'stone of the gods', and our traditions say that it exists only here, in the place that was once their home."

Then how and why did it get from here to Ertria? she wondered silently. But perhaps he had provided the answer. She knew that her own people had once worshipped the Old Gods. Maybe that part of the palace was older than anyone thought and the stone had been brought there to create a place to worship them. But that still didn't explain that strange writing, although it *could* explain the drawings of wolves, which had probably always roamed this place.

She was just beginning to think about wolves when he spoke again.

"It will snow tonight," he said, peering up at the sky that was already beginning to fade from bright blue to a milky white.

"Tassa and Rina say that winter will come soon," she said, then after a moment's hesitation, added:

"And I must get back to Ertria before the trails become impassable."

She had hoped her words would provide a subtle reminder of her business here, but if they did, he chose to ignore it as he lapsed into silence once more.

The trail was narrow and he was riding ahead of her at the moment. She stared at his broad back and tried to fight down the fear that, despite all evidence to the contrary and in spite of his words, he *was* holding her prisoner here. She wanted very badly to trust this man—perhaps *too* badly, she thought now.

His continued silence as they rode along was unnerving. Daken wasn't overly talkative, but neither was he usually so taciturn—or so distracted. Rather belatedly, she began to worry that he might already have made a decision not to help her and was finding it difficult to tell her that.

No sooner had that thought entered her mind than she began to consider how she could make him change his decision. But he interrupted her bleak thoughts by reining in his horse.

"Look, Jocelyn. This is what I tried to show you the night I brought you here."

She reined in her horse quickly. She'd been staring at the black wall to one side of the trail and had failed to notice the opening in the screen of firs to the other side.

"Ohh!" She gasped as she stared in the direction he indicated. The fortress loomed above them now—and she was seeing it for the first time in its entirety.

Except for the great fires in the urns and the bridge and the fading sunlight that still reflected off some of the windows, it would have been nearly invisible as it wrapped itself about the contours of the black mountain. She gazed upon it in speechless wonder and knew that no matter what sights she saw over the rest of her life, she could never hope to see anything that would equal this. She told him that, then added:

"Only the gods could have built it. I can truly see that now." And she knew that she was silently acknowledging that the Kassid were all that legend had made of them—and all they believed themselves to be. No one looking upon this sight could believe otherwise.

He turned to her with a slight smile. "But I think you came here not believing in us—or in our magic."

She was startled by his words. "I . . . didn't know what to believe. My father didn't tell me that he'd met you until he ordered me to come here. Until then, I thought the Kassid were mere legend."

He turned away to stare at his home. "Like most legends, some is truth and some is exaggeration."

All the questions she wanted to ask remained caught in her throat. His tone and his abrupt lapse into silence again told her that she would gain no further information now.

Then he turned back to her again—and his expression made her blood run cold.

"There is no easy way to tell you this, Jocelyn. The Menoans have invaded Balek. They now control the Western Road."

"No!" She cried, unable to believe it. "My father and Hammad said they couldn't invade before spring."

"Which is undoubtedly why they chose to attack now," he replied. "Surprise is a great advantage."

"But the garrison?" Surely they hadn't taken it!

"They are some distance east of the garrison, but I have no doubt that they could take it as well. The number of men at the garrison has been allowed to dwindle over the years."

He paused and stared hard at her. "I think you

do not yet understand their purpose in taking the Western Road."

It meant that she could not return to Ertria. But then she realized the larger implication.

"Coal! they have cut off the coal supply for Ertria—and winter is coming!"

Ertria had a few coal mines, but most of its fuel came from Balek. And the open plains of Ertria could provide very little firewood.

"Yes—and gold and silver as well. Without them, Hammad will have some difficulty in raising an army."

He paused briefly, then went on in a softer tone. "I think they also want to keep you from returning to Ertria. Their spies at court would have reported that you are here with us."

"But I'm not that important," she protested, "Not while . . ." She stopped as she saw the look on his face. And then she knew. She gripped the reins tightly as her blood ran cold.

"My father," she said in a choked voice.

He reached out to her, then stopped and instead swung quickly out of his saddle. He lifted her from her horse and swung her to the ground, then folded her into his arms.

"He's gone, Jocelyn. He died a week after you left."

For long moments, she let him hold her. A huge emptiness gaped within her. He'd known; she was sure of that now. He'd known he wouldn't live to see her again. Perhaps he'd even sent her away in part to spare her those final days.

She'd believed that she'd been preparing herself for this, that when it happened, she would be ready to accept it. But she'd been wrong.

In the midst of her pain, she found both anger and denial. Abruptly, she pushed out of Daken's arms.

"How do you know this, Daken? Where do you get your information?" This could be some sort of ruse on his part.

"Word had already reached the garrison when my men returned the bodies of your Guards."

"Then you've known for more than two weeks—and you didn't tell me!" She shouted the accusation at him, trembling with anger.

"You weren't well, Jocelyn," he replied evenly.

"And how do you know about the Menoans?" She demanded, still unable to control her anger.

"We have our sources. I merely waited for confirmation before telling you."

"Who are your sources? I demand that you tell me who's been spying for you."

He smiled at her, the indulgent smile of a parent confronting a temperamental child. "You *demand*? For one who has been behaving as though you believe I might be some sort of demon, you've become very bold, little one."

His gently chiding tone had the effect of calming her anger. Instead, she drew herself up haughtily.

"I came here to ask for your help, Daken. My father said you were an honorable man and he thought you might help us. But that doesn't mean that I have to trust you as he did."

"You're wrong about that," he said quietly. "You

must trust me more—because you're *here*, in my land and under my protection."

Jocelyn felt tears stinging her eyes, tears for her father and for herself. Tears of anger and frustration and pain. Her father was gone. Her lands had been invaded. Her people would freeze this winter. And she was the prisoner of a man who might well be plotting against her even as he pretended to console her.

But she would not let herself shed those tears now. She held them back with an act of sheer will and walked back to her horse, swinging herself into the saddle without waiting for his assistance. Then she set off back to his fortress.

Daken watched her struggle to control herself and her agile leap onto the horse, and he thought— certainly not for the first time—that there was far more to this woman than jewelry and perfumes and the fine clothes he'd seen among her belongings.

As he mounted his horse to follow her, he recalled that moment when he'd first seen her, fleeing into a strange land in her nightclothes, surely knowing that she would be caught. And he recalled too her vain attempts to struggle to her feet when they'd caught up with her. She must surely have believed she was facing death—but she hadn't faced it with a bowed head or with pleas.

There was great pride and courage within her, as her father had said—and intelligence as well. But he found himself seeking more, wanting to see the woman beneath that cool reserve, even though he knew it was a dangerous quest.

During the long winter, there would be important

decisions to be made. His people would depend upon his judgment, even though the decision would ultimately be theirs. And he could not afford to let his own judgment be clouded by desire for a woman who could never be his.

Still, as he thought again about that long-ago conversation with her father, he wondered if Maikel might not have had just such a hope.

Chapter Four

Jocelyn remained in her room for two days. Trays of food were left outside her door, and she took care to eat most of it, certain that if she didn't, Daken would force his way into the room.

She grieved for her father, but that grief was all mixed up with Daken's other news of the enemy invasion. Her mind would drift from memories of her father to her fears for her empire's uncertain future—and that would give way at some point to an irrational belief that her father had betrayed her by leaving her now. Then she'd promptly feel ashamed of those thoughts and return to the good memories, only to start the cycle all over again.

After a time, she reminded herself that her father had entrusted an awesome responsibility to her— a responsibility he might well have chosen to give to one of her male cousins. She knew that his advisors had counseled him to do just that—with the possible exception of Hammad, who had more than once expressed his belief that she was capable of ruling.

How certain she'd been that she was indeed ready to rule—and how naive that now seemed. During the past year, she'd increasingly made decisions without first consulting her father, but she saw now that she'd been able to make those decisions only because he'd been there.

She, who had always before prided herself on her strength—disdaining the traditional female role—now began to think of herself as being no stronger than the silly, simpering women of the court.

And invariably, when she thought of her own weakness, her mind would turn to the one man who personified strength—Daken. Then she would give in to brief bursts of hatred for him, condemning him for being who he was and thereby making her seem ineffectual by comparison.

But regardless of these feelings, she knew she could not ignore him. Not only was she his guest—or prisoner, for she couldn't quite rid herself of that uncertainty about his intentions—but so much now depended upon him. War, which had heretofore been only a threat, was now a reality, and Jocelyn left off her pain and grief to face that reality.

The Menoans had to be confident indeed to have invaded Balek now. She wished that she knew more about the coal shipments, but she'd never paid the matter much attention. She *did* know that there were great storehouses on the edge of the city where the shipments arrived for sale. Would those storehouses already be full—and if so, would that be enough to see her people through the winter?

The fact that she was ignorant in this matter only served to reinforce her feelings of inadequacy.

She wondered if Hammad would attempt to regain control of the Western Road. Or was it possible that the Menoans had taken it as a ruse, hoping to draw Ertria's woefully inadequate forces there while they attacked the city itself?

Again, her inadequacies made themselves felt, but this time, she thrust them aside. That was Hammad's business, and she had complete faith in his judgment. Hadn't her father told her once that she could never hope to gain for herself all the expertise of her advisors and must learn to trust them?

Thoughts of the city facing the twin dangers of an inadequate coal supply and a possible invasion shifted her attention to the court. It seemed so very distant to her now—another world, far away in both space and time.

In her absence, her uncle, her father's younger brother, would have been set up as regent. He was a pleasant, self-effacing man who wrote poetry and patronized the arts and had no interest whatever in ruling. But Hammad could be counted on to see that he was treated as ruler until her return.

The worst that could happen, she thought with disgust, was that her greedy, unscrupulous nobles would steal even more. Her uncle was incapable of preventing that, and Hammad would be too busy preparing for war.

Still, for all their thievery, Jocelyn was certain that none of them would attempt to usurp her throne. As long as they could continue as they were, they would remain loyal to her family. Her problems there lay in the future, when she tried to curb their greed. And it was even possible that their concern for the future of the empire would force them to rise above their thievery for now.

The reality of war hung over her bedchamber like a dark, thick miasma. She paced the room endlessly, pausing now and again to stare out at the jagged black mountains. The snow Daken had predicted had come and now covered the scene with a blanket of white that stood out starkly against the black stone.

How could she persuade Daken that it was in his interest to support her? What arguments did she have to use? What incentives? No rulers of Ertria had faced such a problem for centuries. The empire had been so powerful that any negotiations with other people proceeded from that great strength. But that strength now seemed a sham to her.

The empire was built with Kassid power, she thought—and now it can survive only with that power. Yet why should the Kassid help? What was there for them to gain?

She wondered what there had been for them to gain by helping all those centuries ago. The history texts were vague about that, and it was a question she'd never considered before.

Who were these people? How did they think? She had been living among them for several weeks now, but they were still strangers to her.

She shuddered, despite the warmth of the chamber. She had walked among them, talked with them, shared their lives—but she was certain now that they showed her only what they wished her to see.

She recalled Daken's evasiveness on the subject of their magic. Did it really exist—or were they merely trading on the legends, much as the Ertrian Empire had traded all these years on its legendary power, a power she saw now was made possible only by the divisions between its enemies.

Part of her wanted to believe that the Kassid possessed no magic at all, that they were only ordinary people living in an extraordinary place. But deep down, in that place where rationality is shut out, she was certain they did indeed possess magic. She hadn't seen it—but she felt it in that deepest part of herself.

Furthermore, unless the legends were true, her empire was lost. Together, the Menoans and Turveans could field an army far superior in numbers to the Ertrians—and they were seasoned warriors who had been fighting each other for years. Not even the addition of Kassid troops could tip the balance—unless they brought magic with them.

When she awoke on the third morning of her self-imposed isolation, Jocelyn knew it was time to demand some answers from Daken. But she dreaded facing him. His mocking response to her demands before, however gently spoken, still rankled. His attitude toward her seemed to be one of indulgence, not one of respect.

And she had certainly not forgotten that moment at the market when their eyes had met and she had all but melted like a foolish, lovesick girl. She was appalled at her behavior—and determined that it would not be repeated.

She decided to dress the part of an empress, thereby signaling her intentions. So she put on her finest gown and the best jewels she'd brought along, did her best to arrange her hair in one of the elaborate styles she wore at court, then dabbed on the perfume Rina had given her, ignoring the memory of Daken that rose once more with its fragrance. Then she left her chamber to seek him out.

Daken's suite was large and contained a great room he used for affairs of state, even though there was no throne and no courtiers lurking about.

When she walked into it, she found him gathered with a group of men and women she knew to be his advisors, since she'd met them before. She hesitated in the doorway, not wanting to intrude upon their discussion, even though she suspected it had to do with her.

Daken's back was to her, but someone must have informed him of her presence because he turned and then stood quickly, starting toward her with a welcoming smile.

Despite her stern warning to herself, Jocelyn felt again that warm, melting sensation, that total awareness of the two of them that blocked out all else. And when he stopped before her and reached out to take both her hands in his, his simple greeting became a caress.

She withdrew her hands. "I'm sorry to interrupt you," she said formally, "but I must speak with you as soon as possible."

He gestured for her to join them. "The discussion has been about you in any event."

She allowed him to lead her to a chair in the midst of the group, feeling decidedly ridiculous in her formal attire. All of those present, including Daken, were dressed in the loose, casual clothing they always wore. They acknowledged her with smiles, but did not rise or offer formal greetings. Accustomed to the prescribed rituals of the court, Jocelyn felt her determination begin to wane.

One of the women, who was seated next to her, took Jocelyn's hand in hers. "We are all very sorry about your loss, Jocelyn. Words are not very much help at such a time, but you should know that our thoughts have been with you."

"Thank you," she murmured as the others nodded in response to the woman's speech. "But my father would have expected me to think first of my people—and so I must."

Then she turned to Daken. "I must return to the palace. Since the Menoans haven't attacked the garrison, I can find an escort there and return to the city by another route. I am hoping that you can provide me with an escort to the garrison."

"We have been discussing that, Jocelyn, because we knew you would wish to return. But we believe that it would be unwise for you to leave here.

"The winter storms have already begun here in the mountains and in Balek, and the trails could become impassable at any time. Also, the garrison could scarcely spare any men to accompany you.

"We also can't be certain that there aren't still

127

more Menoans lying in wait along those trails, guessing that you would attempt to return to the city. They would be unlikely to kill you, but capturing you would be a great advantage to Arrat."

Jocelyn remained silent. She could not refute his arguments, since she had already made them to herself. But she had hoped there might be a way.

"You would be safest here," an older man said. "The Menoans would never attempt to capture you here."

She nodded her acquiescence, then looked straight at Daken. "And what will happen in the spring? I must speak the truth. If you don't help us, Arrat will overrun the empire. As both my father and Hammad have said, the Ertrian army is no more than a group of game-players. They know nothing of war."

The words had very nearly stuck in her throat, but she saw no other course of action than to throw herself on the mercy of these people.

"We have made no decision about that," Daken told her. "Our people have not known war for even more years."

"But there are the legends," she persisted, knowing she was now treading on very dangerous ground. "Just knowing that you are going to join us may prevent Arrat from attacking."

"Perhaps," Daken said with a shrug. "But he has already sent men close to our borders. I think he will simply dismiss those legends—as you yourself did."

She wanted to ask if the legends were true, but the words would not come. She met Daken's eyes and knew that she truly didn't want to know if he were more than a man.

"We have some time yet to reach a decision," one of the others pointed out. "And we must seek the advice of the people on such a grave matter."

Jocelyn didn't bother to conceal her shock. "Seek their advice? But you are the leaders. Surely you can make such a decision."

Daken shook his head. "No, Jocelyn. We must ask the people. After all, it is they who will suffer if we go to war—both the men who must fight and the women who will be forced to take over their work here."

He paused for a moment, gazing at her steadily with those pale eyes. "I will tell you this. I believe that we should aid you. Arrat is a vicious, greedy man who will not stop even if he conquers the Ertrian empire. Sooner or later, he will decide to attack us as well.

"But even though I believe this, I am not happy about sending men into battle to save your empire. I told your father that the Ertrian empire is so corrupt that it doesn't deserve to survive. People starve while your nobility wrap themselves in riches. Men die every day in the mines that provide that wealth—and when they die, their families starve."

His voice was low, but harsh—harsher than she'd heard before. She sat there stiffly, terribly aware of her own fine gown and jewels.

"I am aware of the corruption," she replied. "But I cannot change that if Arrat takes away my throne. And he would certainly be no better."

"But probably no worse, either," Daken persisted.

"The stink of corruption is much the same in all those lands."

Jocelyn was shocked by his disgust, delivered with an arrogance she wouldn't have believed possible in him. She felt hurt, personally betrayed by this man who had been so kind to her. Still, she covered her feelings and told him of her plans to change all that he despised.

"Your father once had the same hopes, Jocelyn," Daken said in a gentler tone. "He was essentially a good man, but he lacked the will to make those changes happen."

She opened her mouth to defend her father, then closed it again. Hadn't she thought the same thing in that deepest, most secret part of her mind?

"And you think that I lack that will also," she stated flatly.

"That remains to be seen. You are young—and you're a woman. You could be easily taken advantage of."

She bristled. "You don't know me well enough to make such an assumption, Daken. And you were scarcely older than me when you became the leader of your people. Furthermore, you have women advisors yourself, so how can you fault me for being a woman?"

She saw the other women present smile at that. Perhaps she might have some strong allies there; it was worth remembering.

"I'm not faulting you for being a woman, Jocelyn," Daken said with the smallest trace of a smile. "I was merely pointing out that it is a disadvantage

130

in your land. Your nobles may well tolerate your rule as long as you don't interfere in their various businesses. But to make the changes you say you want to make, you *must* interfere."

"I am aware of that," she replied frostily. "And I also know that I cannot expect such changes to happen quickly."

Daken leaned back in his chair, stretching his long legs before him as he continued to regard her thoughtfully. "Have you considered that if you do one day succeed with all your plans, your people might decide that they want power for themselves?"

She hadn't—and it showed in her expression.

"That, I think, is why your father lacked the will to make such changes. Power is like strong wine. When you have drunk too much of it for too long a time, you cannot give it up. Your family has had such power for many years. It is in your blood as much as wine is in the blood of a drunkard."

Never before had anyone dared to criticize her family this way. Jocelyn went quickly from shock to anger.

"How dare you say such things about my family? We have ruled an empire for centuries—while you are nothing more than an *elected* leader. I came here to ask for your help, but I will not be treated like a—a common peasant."

By the time she had reached the end of her diatribe, she knew that she had just thrown aside every lesson she had been taught—and probably her chances of gaining his aid as well. She was horrified at her loss of control and unable to face the consequences. So she stood up and walked out of the room as quickly as the remaining shreds of her dignity would permit.

"Daken," said one of the women gently, "I think you were a bit harsh with her. She is young, and she has just lost her father."

"But she is also empress now," Daken said, staring at the doorway through which Jocelyn had just disappeared. "And she needs to hear the truth."

And, he thought with satisfaction, now I know that there is passion indeed beneath that cool exterior. And such passion could certainly be channeled in other directions.

Then he brought himself up short. He'd satisfied his curiosity, but he could afford no other satisfaction. There was an old proverb among his people about the foolishness of starting something that could never see a happy ending.

Jocelyn returned to her bedchamber in a red haze of anger. No one had ever dared to speak that way to her before. How dare he compare her family— the most powerful family in the world—to drunkards?

While she was still fuming, Rina appeared to offer her sympathy over the loss of her father and to ask if she would like to visit the winter garden, something Jocelyn had already expressed an interest in seeing. Jocelyn accepted her sympathy as graciously as possible, then sent her away rather curtly.

No sooner had Rina departed than she regretted

her behavior. After all, she had no quarrel with the girl. Still, she didn't go after her to apologize; she was feeling disinclined to make any apologies at this point.

But Rina's appearance had the effect of taking the sharp edge off her anger, and that very quickly led to recriminations. But recriminations served no purpose; what was done was done. She could not take back her words, and in any event, had no desire to do so.

Instead, she looked on the bright side. For all his cruel words, Daken had still said that he believed his people should come to her aid—and even here in this strange place, that must count for something. He'd made it clear that he favored the alliance only out of self-interest, but she couldn't fault him for that.

Still, there was a small, deep pain within her, the shriveled remains of a hope that he might help because it was *she* who asked, and not just because it was in his interest to do so.

Could she really have been so foolish as to think of him in such terms—she, who had never had a foolish, romantic notion in her entire life? He was far too old for her, he certainly wasn't handsome— and he was no longer even kind. Furthermore, she could never trust someone she didn't understand, and she knew she would never understand these strange people, whether or not they were truly sorcerers.

She set aside her thoughts about Daken, which didn't bear too close a scrutiny at this point anyway, and thought instead about his people. How would

they reach such a decision? Wouldn't they think
only about the hardships of going to war and refuse? How could Daken and his advisors trust them
with such an important decision?

There was a knock at her door and she hurried
to it, thinking that it must be Rina again and wanting to apologize to the girl. But when she opened
it, it was Daken who stood there. She said nothing,
but stepped back to let him enter. Apologizing to
Rina was one thing; apologizing to this man was
quite another.

"Would you like to go for a ride?" he asked. "The
day is pleasant and the snow is not yet too deep on
the trails. I know you're not accustomed as we are
to being confined during the winter."

Was this invitation a subtle form of apology? She
decided to treat it as such and nodded. He left and
she changed quickly into riding clothes, then hurried out to meet him in the courtyard. The air was
cold but still, and the sun shone brightly. She accepted his help to mount, and they rode out across
the bridge.

Jocelyn was determined not to repeat her earlier
outburst. It appeared that she was being given a
second chance. Possibly he had attributed her in-
temperance to the death of her father—and it was
even possible he was right. Certainly it had been
uncharacteristic of her.

Snow lay thickly on the dark firs and clung to the
black rock along ledges and crevices, but the trail
posed no problem to the sure-footed Kassid horses.
She recalled what the guide Tanner had said about

the depth of the snow up here in the winter and told Daken.

He nodded. "That's why a day like today should not be spent indoors. Before long, it will be impossible to leave the fortress."

He paused briefly. "Speaking of your guide, have you considered what his death must mean for his family? I know that you have pensions for the families of your Guards, but not for such as him. And yet he too died in your service."

Jocelyn stiffened. Had he brought her out here to continue his tongue-lashing? She stifled her anger and admitted that she had not considered it.

"If you would change the way your nobles behave, you must first change yourself, Jocelyn," he said, but not harshly this time.

"But there is nothing I can do for them now," she replied defensively.

"No, not now—but in the spring."

"But it might be now that they will need it," she said, now horrified that Tanner's family might suffer because of his service to her.

"They will be all right. It has long been our custom to provide for the families of those who die on our lands. Gold was sent back with his body."

She stared at him in amazement. "But you had nothing to do with his death. And surely you don't take responsibility for those killed by wolves or in some sort of accident?"

"It's not a question of responsibility. It is a matter of knowing that people will go hungry, and knowing too that we have more wealth than we need."

She lapsed into silence. Although there'd been no accusation in his voice, she felt its sting anyway. She thought about the sickly-looking miners she'd seen on her journey here and how she'd condemned the greedy mine owners for their failure to provide for those men and their families—and yet she'd given no thought to Tanner's family.

"You are right, Daken," she said after a lengthy silence. "I have learned a valuable lesson."

He smiled at her. "I think there is much you could learn this winter, Jocelyn. If you wish, you may attend our council meetings. Perhaps we can even help you with your plans."

"Thank you," she said sincerely. She could already see the value in talking her plans over with people who had no stake in the outcome.

"How will you inform your people so that they can make their decision about whether or not to aid me?"

"The Council members and I will meet with them in small groups to discuss the matter. Documents explaining the situation have already been sent to the other fortresses, and they will send their answers back here."

"And how do your advisors feel?" she asked.

"Most of them support my position, but a few are as yet undecided. None is opposed. But they will all be objective in their discussions with the people."

Jocelyn felt greatly relieved. Despite what he said about the people making up their own minds, she thought it highly unlikely that they would go against their leader and the majority of his council.

"It might be good for you to attend some of Rina's

classes while you are here," Daken went on. "You will learn that our children are taught to take their responsibilities very seriously and to set aside their own desires and comforts when those conflict with what is best for the future of all of us."

Jocelyn doubted him, but was disinclined to argue the point. She considered herself to be a rather astute observer of human nature, and she knew that people always acted in their self-interest. She politely accepted the invitation.

By this time, they had left the main trail for one that was both steeper and narrower, and she heard a distant roaring sound that she couldn't identify.

"What is that sound?" she asked uneasily.

"You will see," he replied cryptically, guiding them down a hillside through the forest.

The roar was deafening by the time they had descended to the bottom of the steep ravine. The horses were moving slowly now, picking their way carefully, but displaying no nervousness at the noise.

And then she saw it—at first through the trees, then in its incredible entirety as they rode out into the open. She reined in her horse and stared, transfixed by the sight before her.

The waterfall was many times the height of the one under which she'd bathed, and the volume of water much greater. It cascaded in a great, noisy river down over the black rock. Great shards of ice covered the sides of its path and at its base was a churning pool much larger than the one she'd bathed in.

"There are many waterfalls here," he shouted

over the din. "But this is the highest. Most young men feel the need to climb to its top at some point."

She stared up at the distant top, unable to imagine how anyone could climb those jagged rocks. "Did *you* climb up there?" she asked.

"I'm afraid so," he said with a smile. "But when I look at it now, I'm rather glad that I don't have a son. Fortunately, girls have more sense than boys."

They turned the horses around and started back up the hillside. When they had reached a point where she could speak without shouting, she told him about the waterfall she'd seen on her journey here—and then told him about the wolf.

"Tanner said it probably wasn't hungry," she finished, trying on a smile she hoped didn't look false. "He also said that wolves with blue eyes are very rare, and that his father had once had a similar experience with one."

She could not bring herself to look at him—to see those same pale blue eyes. She was sorry she'd told him about it. She did not want her worst fears confirmed.

"They *are* rare," Daken agreed. "And Tanner was probably right; the wolf wasn't hungry."

Jocelyn listened for a false note in his voice, but could find none. Feeling better now, she asked if he'd ever seen such a wolf.

"Several times. All of us have. After all, this is our home."

"The truly strange thing was that I wasn't really afraid—at least not while we stood there staring at each other. Later, of course, I was terrified."

"People react differently to dangerous situations. Your escape from the attack on your camp shows that you handle danger well. That is a good quality for a leader, Jocelyn."

His compliment pleased her—perhaps too much, she thought as she wondered if it might not have been merely an adroit way of moving the conversation away from dangerous grounds.

When they reached the trail again, he paused to stare up at a large bird circling overhead—a hawk, she thought, though a much bigger one than she'd ever seen. After watching it herself for a moment, she lowered her head and stared instead at his strong profile.

They rode mostly in silence back to the fortress, stopping once more at the spot where it was visible across the ravine. Once again, she marveled at their "gift" from the gods. But what else had those gods given them?

"You have yet to ask the question that must be uppermost in your mind, Jocelyn," he said in that low, deep voice. "Does it frighten you to think that we might have magic?"

She nodded before she could stop herself as she stared into his eyes and saw not Daken, but that wolf. She averted her gaze quickly.

"That magic could save your empire," he said softly.

"Yes, I know." She still couldn't look at him and hated herself for her weakness.

"The magic too was a gift from the gods, given to us when they departed this world so that we could always protect ourselves."

139

"Then it is true. You *are* sorcerers." She tried to keep her tone neutral, but she still could barely speak the word 'sorcerer'.

"No, not sorcerers. We cannot conjure up visions at will. Our magic exists only for the defense of this land—and even then, it is nothing we do ourselves, but rather that which is done *for* us."

"I don't understand," she frowned.

"It's difficult to explain—especially since I have only the stories passed down over the generations. But it is said that for every Kassid warrior who rides into battle, there are ten more riding with him unseen."

"Ghosts?" she gasped, her green eyes widening in disbelief.

He smiled. "So we believe. But their weapons are *real*."

"But if it is nothing that you yourselves do, how can you be sure these—these ghost warriors will appear?"

"We must trust to the rightness of our cause," he replied. Then he heaved a sigh. "But I must tell you that I will be a very reluctant warrior—as will the others. War is an unnatural thing."

Jocelyn thought about all the times she'd listened to her brother and his friends extolling the glories of battle and expressing the hope that they might one day go to war. She'd always thought that it was what all men wanted. Even the nobles often talked of the glory of war—though of course they meant those wars to be fought by someone else.

Yet here was the leader of the most famous warriors in their world admitting that he had no taste for it. It made no sense.

"Is that why your people left Ertria all those years ago—because they had tired of war?"

"In part, yes," he replied. "The gods called us home to this land, so that we could live in peace."

At that moment, they came upon a hunting party returning with fresh meat for the fortress. Jocelyn rode in the midst of the group, feeling again that differentness, that otherness, that she'd felt before with Kassid men. But why should she feel that? If what Daken said was true, they had no real magic of their own, merely the faith that their gods would provide for them in battle.

There is more, she thought. *He has not told me all the truth.*

True to all predictions, winter came with a vengeance to the Dark Mountains. Snow fell intermittently for three days, sometimes coming down so fast that Jocelyn saw nothing but a wall of white beyond the windows and sometimes drifting down slowly through the gray light.

She was delighted, though a bit awed too by this inundation. Snow fell rarely in Ertria, and on those occasions it vanished almost as it touched ground. But here, it fell and fell—and stayed, changing the shape of everything, rearranging the world beyond the fortress.

She spent part of her day with Daken and his advisors, listening as they discussed their own problems and also explaining the workings of her court and the problems she encountered.

She was fascinated by the outspokenness of Daken's advisors, who disagreed vociferously among themselves on some occasions and with Daken on others. She began by thinking they were being disrespectful toward him—then ended up wishing aloud that her own advisors would speak their minds more freely.

The snow finally stopped during the morning of the fourth day, and the sky cleared to a brilliant blue. Rina appeared early in the afternoon, stating that school had been let out for the day so that they could enjoy the break in the weather.

"But how can you possibly go outside?" Jocelyn asked. It looked to her as though the snow was far too deep.

Then, even as they stood at the windows, she got her answer. Teams of two horses each began to move slowly through the snow in the courtyard, dragging between them a wide, curved wooden device that pushed the snow before it. When the horses began to have difficulty moving it any farther, it was lifted up by the riders, then dropped again after depositing what looked like a miniature mountain of snow.

The areas in between had been swept nearly clean and men came along on foot to open gaps in the rows of piled snow. They were followed in short order by boisterous groups of children who began to play in the great mounds.

Jocelyn laughed in delight as she watched the children build miniature fortresses and pelt each other with snowballs. She told Rina that she'd made snowballs once, but it hadn't worked very well, because there was little snow to begin with and it had melted quickly.

"Come join us," Rina urged her. "I will lend you some clothes and boots."

Jocelyn was still watching the children and opened her mouth to protest that she was too old for such activities. But Rina had already run off to get her some clothes and by the time she returned, it seemed too late to refuse.

The moment she stepped out into the courtyard, she felt like a child again, remembering all the times she'd wished for snow like this. She picked up some snow, telling herself that she would just see if it made better snowballs than the soft, melting variety she'd seen so long ago.

And before long, the empress had begun a mock battle with Rina and her friends, who showed no respect at all for her exalted rank.

Daken came out into the courtyard and immediately saw Rina and her friends, weaving in and out between the high mounds of snow as they pelted each other with snowballs.

Then he looked around for Jocelyn. Since she hadn't been in the suite, he'd assumed that she'd come outside with Rina. He was about to risk being caught in the crossfire to ask Rina where she was, when he spotted her.

His wide mouth curved into a smile and then he laughed outright as she scrambled over the top of one of the mounds and aimed a snowball at a group of girls who were attacking from the other side. She was wearing clothes borrowed from Rina and he would never have noticed her if her cap hadn't fallen off, spilling that beautiful red hair down over her shoulders.

He withdrew quickly into the shadows of the covered walkway, certain that she wouldn't want him to see her. Then he stood and watched as she gamboled with the girls, virtually indistinguishable from them when she had once again tucked her hair beneath the cap.

Seeing this unexpected side of her was a bittersweet experience for Daken. The pleasure came from knowing that she could set aside that formidable reserve, but watching her with his daughter and her friends brought home to him that age difference between them—a gap not obvious when she met with him and his council.

Jocelyn remained coolly impersonal with him, but it was obvious that she and Rina had become close, and it was through his talkative daughter that Daken had learned most about her. He'd already known that she'd refused Arrat's proposal of marriage, but Rina had told him that Jocelyn had no intention of marrying anyone. He'd assumed that now that she'd become empress, she'd marry that Ertrian nobleman who'd been pursuing her for so long.

He thought wryly that he could have done without that particular piece of knowledge. It would be far easier to control his own feelings if he knew that there was someone else in her life.

Daken was increasingly uncomfortable with his

feelings for Jocelyn. In the years since his beloved Erina's death, Daken had carried on discreet affairs with several widows, but he'd never been able to convince himself that he wanted to marry any of them and they'd finally given up and found other husbands. He'd been without a woman for a long time now, and he knew that that fact alone made his situation dangerous.

Still, if it were only a question of wanting a warm, soft body in his bed, there were others who were willing.

She is not for you, he told himself. *The gods would not look kindly upon such a union.* He was too old for her. His life was here, while hers lay far beyond the Dark Mountains in the warm plains of Ertria. It would be foolish—and Daken was not a foolish man.

"On a day such as this, I really do wish I were young again."

Daken turned, startled out of his thoughts, to find Sheela, one of his advisors, standing next to him. She smiled.

"Are you too re-living your youth, Daken?"

He managed to return the smile, though he suspected it might be a bit guilty, given the direction of his thoughts.

But before he could respond, he saw Sheela staring at the group of girls with a frown.

"Is that Jocelyn out there?" she asked in a tone of disbelief.

"Yes—and I don't think she'd care to have either of us see her."

Sheela laughed. "What a remarkable young

woman! It is easy to forget how young she is—or it was until now."

"My thoughts exactly," Daken replied drily.

She turned to him, one dark brow raised in enquiry. "Somehow, I think we might mean different things. Daken, she is truly lovely and possessed of great courage—but she is not for you."

He nodded, not at all offended by her candor. They were both cousins and life-long friends. "Once again, you have spoken my thoughts."

Sheela gave him an arch look. "I've spoken your mind perhaps—but not your heart, I think."

As they talked, neither of them had noticed that the snowball battle had moved closer to them as a group of girls came around the end of one of the snow hills. They both heard the shouts and laughter and looked up just as a snowball hurtled past Daken's head, missing it by inches as it thudded against a pillar.

The group moved on, laughing, but the one who had thrown the snowball stopped and stared at him as her face flushed bright red, contrasting sharply with a pair of emerald-green eyes. He smiled at her, and Sheela called out a greeting. Jocelyn returned the smile and Sheela's greeting, hesitated, then hurried off to rejoin the girls.

That evening, they were all gathered around the big fireplace in the great room of Daken's suite—Jocelyn, Rina, Tassa, Daken himself, and Jakka, Daken's aide and nominated successor, who was unmarried and seemed to divide his time between Daken's family and his own.

Jocelyn had come to anticipate these quiet evenings when they gathered here while the winter winds howled beyond the windows. Some days ago, she'd told Daken how much she enjoyed such times.

"Winter is a time for drawing together," he'd told her. "During the rest of the year, we're all busy with our separate lives, so this is a time for being together—for sharing."

She thought about those words now as she watched him sitting on the rug before the hearth with Rina, discussing her schoolwork. She'd been touched by the simple honesty of his words and his willingness—so rare among the men she knew—to talk about his feelings.

Rina's gray kitten crawled up onto his leg and he picked up a ball of yarn, then unwound some and dangled it before the kitten, who immediately began to leap at it.

Jocelyn thought about her behavior this afternoon. What must he think of her? How could he take her seriously when she'd behaved like a child? She'd been mortified to find him there.

He tossed the yarn ball in her direction, letting it unwind as it rolled. The kitten quickly became entangled in the yarn as it scrambled after it, and before she could reach down to help it, Daken got up and came over to pick it up, holding it in one big hand as he freed it from its temporary prison. Jocelyn watched him, thinking how gentle he was. Then, just as her thoughts began to veer off into disturbing fantasies, he set the kitten down and looked up at her.

"You enjoyed yourself this afternoon—but now you're regretting it."

She was once again shocked and a bit fearful at his uncanny ability to read her thoughts. Whenever it happened, she told herself that her thoughts merely happened to be transparent—but that deep fear of sorcery lingered.

"Yes, I did enjoy it—but I fear that I behaved like a child."

"You did," he acknowledged with a smile. "But what was the harm in that?"

"The harm" she stated candidly, "is that such behavior could make it difficult for you and your people to take me seriously."

"Ahh," he said as he once again lifted the kitten to disentangle it from the yarn, "and you struggle always to be taken very seriously."

"Well, of course I do. When I was a child, I was the pampered pet of my father's court. No one ever took me seriously. But since my brother's death, I've worked hard to change that. And now that I'm empress, it's even more important."

"Do you take *yourself* seriously?" he asked, his pale eyes boring into her.

"Yes, of course, but . . ."

"Then that is all that is necessary. The rest will follow in time."

"Do *you* take me seriously, Daken?" She asked, meeting his level gaze with one of her own.

"I take you *very* seriously—although I enjoy the other side of you as well, when you permit it to be seen."

"Sometimes I fear that you think of me as a

148

child," she persisted, though she knew she was treading close to dangerous territory

He nodded slowly, his gaze shifting to the kitten again, creating the momentary impression for her that he was embarrassed.

"Yes, I think I do—and I shouldn't. But those feelings play no part in my decision to ally my people with yours—and that is what's important to you, isn't it?"

With his final words, spoken after the briefest of hesitations, he turned back to her again—and she was sure she saw a subtle challenge in his eyes.

Once again, as during those moments at the market, Jocelyn felt something shift within their relationship. That quiet challenge, his slightly lowered voice, even the way they seemed to lean closer to each other without actually moving—Jocelyn felt and saw and heard it all as that liquid heat stole through her. The conversations of the others in the room faded to an indistinct murmur as they stared at each other for what could not have been more than a second but seemed forever.

The kitten had lost interest in the ball of yarn and began to dig its tiny claws into the hem of her gown. Just as she bent to pick it up, he leaned forward to reach for it, too. His hand covered hers, and his head brushed lightly against her arm. They both stopped—and their eyes met again.

Carefully erected guards fell away. In his clear, pale eyes, she saw a desire so powerful that she could only respond with the truth—a confused truth of inchoate longings and fears.

The moment passed, and they joined in the conversation of the others. Daken avoided her glance, but she wasn't aware of it because she was carefully avoiding his as well. They both knew that an invisible barrier had been breached, however briefly, and that it would happen again.

Chapter Five

Days and then weeks passed. The snows grew ever deeper and the weather colder still. Jocelyn fitted herself into the winter life of the Kassid as best she could, and they were unfailingly kind and gracious to her, although she continued to find their informality disconcerting.

As she stared out from the warmth of the fortress into the bitter cold of the mountains, Jocelyn worried about her people. Was there enough coal in the storehouses to see them through the winter? Certainly, Ertrian winters were mild by comparison with what she saw here, but they were still cold and damp enough to cause great suffering.

And despite the Kassid's kindness, she felt out of place here, without any purpose. There seemed to be nothing more she could do to affect the decision the Kassid would make regarding an alliance, and this powerlessness frustrated her, making her long for her life at the palace, where she could indeed influence events.

She attended some of Rina's classes, where she saw first-hand how Kassid children were educated to their responsibilities in this strange society. She was surprised to see Daken appear in one of the classes she attended. He was there for more than an hour, patiently answering questions the children put to him and encouraging them to give their opinions regarding matters before his council.

A few times, when she could no longer stand being confined inside the fortress, Jocelyn dressed in the warmest clothes Rina could provide, then went out to walk along the covered walkway that ran most of the length of the courtyard. The cold truly astonished her. Within moments, her face felt numb, and not even Rina's warm mittens could prevent her fingers from turning icy. When she hastily returned to the warmth of the fortress, Tassa saw her reddened face and brought her an ointment, telling her that she must begin to use it regularly to protect her fair skin.

Tassa also began to instruct her in the complicated craft of knitting the beautiful sweaters Jocelyn so much admired. She'd never been much interested in knitting, although her mother had tried to teach her many years ago. Furthermore, this yarn was far more difficult to work with because of its slippery texture. Nevertheless, Jocelyn saw it as a task to help her wile away her time until the arrival of spring.

She both longed for spring and dreaded its arrival. She would be able to return to Ertria—but she would be returning to war.

Despite her attempts to keep herself busy, Jocelyn grew increasingly frustrated by her lack of a place in the scheme of things here. It was definitely a new experience for her. Even before her brother's death had elevated her into the position of heir to the throne, she had been important, if only as the darling of the court. And since that time, she'd always been at the very center of everything in that bustling court.

Added to this frustration was her relationship with Daken. She saw him constantly, but they were never alone, and she suspected that he was going to some pains to keep it that way.

She knew she should be grateful for what must surely be his attempt to maintain a proper distance between them—but she wasn't. Daken had aroused something within her—a curiosity? a need?—and now he was leaving it unsatisfied. Besides, *she* was the one accustomed to drawing such lines, and it rankled that that decision had been taken from her.

Jocelyn refused to examine too closely her feelings toward Daken. When they were together, she would find herself concentrating on some detail about him—his big, but surprisingly graceful long-fingered hands, his wide mouth, the sheer size of the man. And then she would begin to drift off into vague fantasies that often ended only when their eyes met.

She could not look into those pale eyes without remembering that wolf and shuddering inwardly over those old stories about the Kassid. Surely they

Saranne Dawson

could not be true. She'd seen not a single scrap of
evidence that they had magic of any sort—except,
of course, for the fortress itself. And even Daken
claimed not to have seen their magic, but only
heard tales of it—tales he believed implicitly.

Daken, she'd noticed, wasn't the only one to have
those eerie pale blue, nearly colorless eyes, although they didn't appear to be common among
the Kassid, who for the most part were dark-haired
and dark-eyed. Still, some time had passed before
it occurred to her that she saw those strange eyes
only among some of the men. There were a few
blue-eyed women, but theirs were a much deeper
blue.

She considered mentioning this observation to
Rina, but decided against it. After all, even though
she had gotten to see and meet many residents of
the vast fortress, her observations were still limited
to no more than a fraction of its population. Besides, she could think of no acceptable explanation
for her interest.

And yet, she could not forget that wolf—or the
guide Tanner's tale. In her dreams, she would see
it standing there on the ledge, staring at her with
that uncannily human gaze—and then it would be
transformed into Daken's figure, watching her
through those same eyes.

If anyone had asked her whether or not she believed in Kassid magic, Jocelyn would certainly
have said no, despite her dreams and despite that
lingering sense of their differentness. But a discussion one evening with Daken left her once again

154

with the certainty that there were secrets she had not yet learned—and perhaps would never learn.

It began out of her frustration over the lengthy process of reaching a decision regarding her request for an alliance. Jocelyn asked him how he could tolerate such a situation, how he could rule without power.

"But I *do* have power, Jocelyn," he insisted with a smile. "The best form of power is that which is rarely and lightly used."

"Are you saying that you could overrule your council, or your people?"

He nodded. "I could. And I have done so a few times. But I choose those times carefully and examine my reasons closely."

"Then even if your people decide not to ally themselves with Ertria, you could overrule them?"

"No, I would not overrule them on that."

"You wouldn't—or you couldn't?" she persisted, becoming ever more frustrated at their confusing system of government.

He shrugged. "It is much the same."

"I will never understand you, Daken. I've never met a man who seems so powerful and yet behaves like the weakest of peasants."

She had spoken without forethought and immediately regretted it. But he merely smiled.

"Perhaps that is because I am both. That is the difference you cannot understand, Jocelyn. I do have great power, but only because it was freely given to me by my equals."

She turned away, having heard his unspoken

condemnation. She had gained her power only because she was descended from generations of unlimited power.

"I was not suggesting that you have power only because of your family's history. Your way is different, that's all. And there is great power in you, Jocelyn—more, perhaps, than you think."

She made a dismissive sound. "You're wrong, Daken. I have power only as a result of birth. Without that, I would be nothing—because I'm a woman."

"Do you dislike being a woman?" he asked quietly.

"What point would there be in that?" she asked with a frown. "I can't very well change it."

"But I think you would do so if you could, and that must make you very unhappy with yourself." He paused briefly, then went on. "I think you probably feel the need to wield power too often and too strongly, to compensate for what you believe to be your female weakness."

She stared at him, coming dangerously close to hating him in that moment. But she managed to keep her voice level.

"You couldn't possibly understand, Daken. You don't know what it is to be a woman—and you don't understand the world I live in."

"I think I do understand what it is to be a woman," he said in that same low tone. "At least to the extent any man can understand. My wife and I were very close, and I came to value her often very different way of seeing things. That is why I've chosen to have female advisors.

"And I was present at the birth of both my children—Rina and our son who died. So I have some understanding of that part of being a woman as well."

"You were present at birthings?" she asked, too shocked to even think of hiding it.

He nodded, his amusement over her consternation very plain. "It is our custom. A father cannot give birth to his children, but he can at least provide comfort and support to the mother."

"But ... but that's *horrible!*" She herself had never seen a birthing, but she'd certainly heard the women talking about it. For a man to actually *see* such a thing. . . . She was quite simply beyond imagining that.

"I thought it was beautiful," he said in that simple, honest way that still surprised her.

Beautiful? From what she'd overheard, it was anything but that! The women of her court spent hours complaining in great detail about their travails.

"Well, perhaps it is—but it doesn't matter to me, since I will never have children."

She thought it politic to change the subject, so when he made no further comment, she asked him why he hadn't remarried—a matter of some considerable curiosity to her, but one she'd never felt comfortable about raising with Rina.

He shrugged. "I've found no one I want to marry."

"But don't you want a son?"

"I have a daughter. If Erina had lived, we would certainly have had more children."

"All men want sons," she stated.

"Only in a world where women are valued less."

She was convinced he was being dishonest with her and it made her angry. "Don't try to tell me that women aren't valued less here, Daken," she scoffed. "You suggested once that a woman could become leader of your people—and yet none ever has, and Rina told me they can't."

"It's true that none has yet, and it's also true that there are at present certain requirements that women cannot meet. But I think that will change."

"What are those requirements?" she demanded, recalling how Rina had deftly sidestepped that question.

He stared at her in silence for a very long time, then slowly shook his head.

"There are things about us that you could not understand, Jocelyn—and I think you would not *want* to understand them."

He got up then to tend the fire, and she knew he would say no more. Had it been her imagination, or had he actually sounded regretful? She wasn't sure.

She shivered, even though the room was comfortably warm. It was clear to her that he was referring to sorcery, that he hadn't told her all the truth about himself and his people.

Perhaps, she thought, only the men are sorcerers, since they use their power in war—and perhaps one must be a sorcerer to become leader.

The Kassid had once again become a dark mystery to her—unknown and unknowable.

* * *

More days and nights of snow and bitter cold passed. The Dark Mountains were now deep in winter. Jocelyn began to doubt that spring would ever come, and her dreams turned into nightmares of being locked away in the black fortress forever.

She began to lead two very separate lives. Outwardly, she remained the same, but inwardly, she lived in a hidden world of fears where seemingly normal, pleasant people transformed themselves into wolves or called down lightning or cast spells upon her.

But not even those dark imaginings could quell her fascination with Daken. She would lie in bed at night reliving some incident during the day—a certain look he'd given her, a tone of voice, a casual gesture.

Daken wore his affections openly, unlike any other man she'd ever known. From a kiss on Tassa's cheek to thank her for some special favor to hugs for Rina to an arm draped across the shoulder of his young aide who was worried about his father's health—Daken showed affection to everyone.

And she too was included in this. He was extraordinarily sensitive to her moods, knowing when to suggest a walk outside or how to draw her out of the bleakness that would come over her as she thought about her home or the loss of her father.

Was there anything different in the way he treated her? This was a question she asked herself endlessly.

It seemed to her that there *was* a difference, that he was at the same time both more restrained and more intense with her. Or was she merely confused by her own feelings?

She became more and more frustrated over the failure of the Kassid to reach a decision regarding an alliance. It occurred to her at this point that since the other fortresses were now unreachable until spring, she would have to wait until then for a decision.

She asked Daken about this, not even bothering to hide her impatience. She'd long since given up on the art of diplomacy.

"There will be an answer before spring," he told her. "The matter is being debated among them now."

"But how can those in the other fortresses let you know their decisions when the trails are closed?"

"We have magic for that," he replied with a smile, letting her know by his intonation that it wasn't really magic.

"What magic?" she inquired, unable to think of any way such a thing could be accomplished.

"I will show you," he said, turning away from the window where he'd been gazing at the snow that appeared to be letting up after two full days. "That is, if you're willing to walk a long distance."

She walked to the window and peered out at the courtyard that was buried beneath several feet of snow. "How could we walk through that?"

"We won't. The walk is inside the fortress, although part of it might feel like the outside."

Despite the many hours she had spent roaming about the huge fortress, Jocelyn knew that she had yet to see all of it. The hallways were endless and there were many levels.

So they set out, after she had gathered up a cloak to wear over her gown. She'd recently gone back to wearing the gowns she'd brought with her, after realizing that she was becoming entirely too comfortable in trousers. Most of the younger women here wore them regularly, but she knew she could not dress in such an outrageous manner when she returned to court. There were some things not even an empress would dare to do.

Daken offered to carry the heavy cloak for her until it was needed, and their hands brushed lightly as she gave it to him. Her breath caught in her throat and she looked quickly away, knowing that this was yet another moment she would be reliving tonight in her bed.

It seemed that they walked for miles, up and down sets of stairs, through twisting corridors where children played and people stood gossiping.

Finally, they reached the winter garden, which Jocelyn had visited with Rina, and Daken suggested that they stop there for a few moments. He was trying hard to slow his stride to match hers, but given the difference in their heights, she was still forced to walk fast to keep up with him.

They stepped through the doorway into the moist warmth of the garden, and Jocelyn marveled anew at the lush plants growing in this glassed-in space. Just as they entered, the first tentative rays of sun poured in through the windows, and Jocelyn felt an unexpectedly sharp longing for her home. Daken, attentive as always to her moods, raised an enquiring brow.

"It feels like a summer day in here," she explained. "The only thing missing is the smell of the sea."

Instead, the huge space was filled with rich, earthy smells overlaid with the fragrances of the various herbs that were grown in long, dirt-filled rows.

"I have always wanted to visit the sea," he said. "It is difficult to imagine anything that vast."

"You could return with me in the spring," she said impulsively, then added quickly, "if your people agree to an alliance, that is."

"If that happens, I will accept your invitation," he responded with rather more formality than was usual for him.

They walked slowly along the rows of herbs. There were so many different varieties. She'd asked Rina about them, but the girl hadn't known the names of many of the ones that were unfamiliar to Jocelyn. Nearly half the space was devoted to herbs.

Daken came to a stop before some straggly-looking bushes—the first thing she'd seen in here that wasn't doing well.

"It appears that our hope of growing berries in here is doomed to failure," he commented. "This is the third winter we have tried."

"What kind of berries are they?"

"We call them mis berries. The word 'mis' means ledge or rocky outcropping, which is where they grow. They are difficult to gather for that reason, but well worth it. It seems that they prefer to live only in difficult places."

"Like the Kassid," she said with a smile.

He laughed. "We don't think of this as a difficult place. It's simply our home."

She walked over to the windows and rubbed away the mist that had formed on them. "It *is* a beautiful place, Daken. I fear that when I return to Ertria, it will seem very dull by comparison."

She turned to him as she spoke and for one brief moment saw pain in his eyes. He turned quickly and started back along the rows, and after a moment, she followed. But the pain in him had lodged in her as well. In a few months, she would leave this place forever—and even if he returned with her, it would be to go to war.

It would be better if I had never met him, she thought, *because now I will never be able to forget him—or this place.*

They left the winter garden and soon after that began to ascend into the upper reaches of the fortress. Jocelyn was lost in a private misery that forced her for the first time to face up to the fact that Daken had come to occupy a place in her life that no other man had ever held.

Have I fallen in love with him? she asked herself. The question, coming so suddenly and seemingly out of nowhere, devastated her.

No, she couldn't have, she told herself firmly. Such a thing couldn't happen to her. Love was for those silly women who had nothing else of importance in their lives. She had an empire to rule, and once she was able to rule it, she would surely be able to look back at this time as nothing more than a strange interlude—a time out of time.

Lost in her thoughts, she was failing to keep up with him and also failing to notice that the hallways had grown quite cold. She climbed the next set of stairs and saw him waiting for her at the top, holding out her cloak for her.

"There are more steps to climb," he said when she reached him. "Are you feeling well enough to continue?"

She turned around so that he could drape the cloak over her shoulders. Then, before she could reach around to free her loose hair, he slid his hands beneath it and lifted it. His fingers grazed lightly against the sensitive skin of her bare neck. The sensation sent shock waves through her, and she moved away from him quickly.

"I'm fine," she said quickly, if a bit breathlessly, then attempted to make light of the moment.

"This magic of yours had better be worth the trip."

"You will have to judge that for yourself," he said as he led her down yet another deserted hallway.

"Does no one live up here?" she asked, realizing now that they hadn't seen anyone since leaving the winter garden.

"No. This part of the fortress has never been occupied. As you can see, the heat doesn't reach here." He smiled at her. "Apparently, even the gods had their limitations."

She smiled, but the smile held a trace of nervousness. They were alone—truly alone for the first time since he'd brought her here. Excitement vied with fear, alternately sending curls of heat and shards of ice through her.

He, however, seemed totally unaffected by their isolation and she began to wonder if what she had been feeling was completely one-sided. Daken was a complex man, easy and open with his affections, yet closed off from her as well. Unknown and unknowable. That phrase echoed through her mind, bringing back once more the image of that wolf.

Why don't I just ask him outright? she thought. Perhaps he was even inviting that question when he said that there were things she didn't want to know.

But she couldn't do it. It was far easier to live with the question than to face the answer.

Finally, they reached the end of a long, empty corridor where a heavy, carved door stood closed. Jocelyn stared at it as he reached out to grasp the big brass handle. For one brief moment, she was back in the palace cellars again—a little girl on a forbidden journey of discovery.

It was no different from the other doors here, she told herself as he pulled it open. Indeed, she was sure that the carving was much the same. But the doors in the occupied portions of the fortress were kept polished and radiated a mellow golden warmth. Rina had told her that the wood came from a special kind of fir that lent itself handily to such intricate carving.

This door, however, was darkened with the dust of centuries—just as that door to the secret room in the palace cellars had been. And she realized now that she would never have the opportunity to discuss that room with her father.

A carved door led to a room of black stone, where figures of wolves danced in the torchlight amidst strange writing. A Kassid room, she whispered to herself; surely a Kassid room. Only that ancient writing remained unexplained; she hadn't seen its like here, though she'd seen their writing many times.

A Kassid room deep inside the palace of Ertria. What did it mean? Who could explain it to her—except perhaps this man? She was suddenly sure that he knew about it, that it was part of the secrets he withheld from her.

But there was no time now to think about it further. The door opened into a narrow, winding staircase, dimly lit by slits in the black stone walls where both light and cold poured in. They must be in the tall tower she'd glimpsed from the courtyard at what she thought was the far end of the fortress.

Round and round they went. The steps were made for bigger strides than hers, forcing her to take ungainly skipping steps to ascend ever higher.

Then another door, identical to the one below—and to the one in the palace cellar. The air was very cold, and when they passed the slits in the walls, an icy wind blew down on them, whistling slightly as it forced its way through the openings. She pulled up the hood of her cloak as her ears began to burn from the cold, and she was drinking in the cold air in icy gasps by the time they reached the top—and yet another door.

She'd expected to find herself outside on a wide

ledge that was partly visible from the courtyard. But instead, she followed Daken into a circular room about twenty feet in diameter. There were two windows high up in the black stone walls—too high for her to see out of them. A thick, jewel-toned rug of the type she saw everywhere in the fortress covered most of the floor, and a stone fireplace was fitted into one curved wall, with a fire laid but unlit. There was no furniture of any kind—only piles of big embroidered cushions scattered about the hearth. On the hearth itself sat a gold tray with a wine carafe and gold cups, more simply wrought than the ornate, jeweled vessels used by all the Kassid.

Daken went over to the fireplace and set the wood ablaze with the torch he'd picked up before they began their long climb. Then he gestured to yet another door in the curved wall.

"This way to the magic," he said, opening the door.

"Does someone live here?" she asked curiously, trying not very successfully to fight off the effects of this intimate scene.

He shook his head as he pushed open the outer door. "No, this is a place I come to when I wish to be alone to think. Our leaders have always used it for this purpose. And the watchers use it to warm themselves."

"Watchers?" she echoed as she stepped into the icy blast of wind pouring through the door. She hadn't seen any guards anywhere since she'd come here. Why would they possibly need them?

He drew her through the door and closed it behind him. "Not guards—signal watchers and senders. This is our means of communication."

They had emerged onto a wide stone balcony at the very top of the tower. Jocelyn failed to notice the object he indicated as she stared in wonder.

Surely, she thought, *this* is where one can truly touch the heavens. It was, she was sure, the highest point in the fortress. Below her were the tile roofs of the residential areas, jumbled unevenly as they rose out of the black stone.

Still ignoring the object he'd pointed out, she walked over to the low wall, then shrank back with a gasp. For one heart-stopping moment she could actually feel herself falling through endless space into a ravine so deep and dark she couldn't even see its bottom. She staggered back as she felt its terrifying pull. Then two arms reached out to grasp her, pulling her back against a reassuringly solid body.

"You're safe," he said, his mouth close to her ear as he bent to her. "You're not really falling."

She stood there breathing hard as she began to regain her sense of balance. He was right, of course; she'd never truly been in danger. But that awful feeling . . . She shivered and his arms tightened about her.

"Why did it feel as though I were falling?" she asked in a voice that trembled slightly.

"I don't know, but many people feel that up here. For you, it must be worse, since you are unaccustomed to what we consider to be ordinary heights."

His head was still bent to her and his low voice was soft against her ear. Her fear subsided—to be replaced by an overwhelming sense of him, of his closeness. She stifled a protest when he finally dropped his arms and moved away.

"I brought Rina up here when she was little, and she had nightmares about falling for many nights after. But now she likes to come up here. There is no other place in the fortress where one can see so much of the mountains."

It was true. She'd been so preoccupied with that terrifying abyss that she'd paid scant attention to the rest of the scene.

The Dark Mountains marched off in an endless, disorderly parade. A few distant peaks seemed as high as the tower—but none was taller. The stark contrast of snowy patches against the black rock was dazzling. Even though the sky was now clearing, clouds clung to the higher peaks as though they'd been caught there and prevented from moving on.

It was, she knew, another scene she would never forget—the very essence of this strange, wild land.

Then, as she turned slowly to see it all, Jocelyn finally noticed the strange device he'd tried to show her earlier. It was a huge mirror, many times larger than anything she'd ever seen—and it was mounted atop a wooden structure. Ropes dangled from the edges of the frame that held the mirror, tied loosely around the supporting legs. Daken walked over to it and she followed.

"This is how we communicate with the other fortresses. We have a schedule for all the fortresses. Two of them can send and receive signals directly, but the third must communicate through one of the other two."

"I don't understand." She frowned.

He pointed to the ropes. "These raise and lower the mirror and change the angle so that it reflects the sunlight, then turns away from it. Watchers at the other fortresses can see the light."

"But what can that tell them?"

"Long ago, a code was worked out, based on tilting the mirrors at various speeds. What the watcher sees is either quick bursts of light or a longer, steady light. When the weather permits, each fortress sends an 'all's well' signal each midday, followed by other messages if there are any."

He stared up at the sky. "It is time now, but there may not be a signal today, since the sky is just now clearing." He pointed off to their left.

"Watch in that direction, and to the right as well. If they come, the signals will be from there."

The sun dipped behind a cloud, then emerged a moment later—and when it did, she saw a flash of light, then another from some distance away. The light remained steady for a long moment. Daken began to loosen the ropes, then tilted the big mirror, and Jocelyn quickly shielded her eyes as it caught the sun.

"It's not a perfect system, since it depends on sunlight," he said as he held the mirror in place. "But it works well enough."

After a few moments, both distant lights winked out, and then Daken lowered the mirror and retied the ropes.

"So there were no messages," she said, hiding

her disappointment. She'd let herself hope that a message might come regarding the alliance, though she knew it was foolish to expect it to come just because she was up here this day.

"No, they wouldn't be likely to have any, since the weather was uncertain."

Jocelyn stared at the device, oblivious for the moment to the cold wind whipping about her. She was fascinated by it and began to imagine how such a thing could be put to use in Ertria.

"It could work for you as well," Daken said, "although you would have to build tall towers to hold the mirrors, since you have no mountains."

She nodded, envisioning a line of such towers stretching across the plains and even connecting the islands that were also part of her empire. She was eager to discuss it with Hammad, whose men could surely build the towers.

But not if they must go to war instead, she reminded herself suddenly and began to shiver.

"Come inside," he said, taking her arm. "The fire will have warmed the room by now."

After the howling wind and bitter cold, the room was cozily warm and intimate with its richly colored rug and the big, embroidered pillows. Even the simple act of shedding their heavy outer garments seemed laden with sensuality. Jocelyn forgot all about her plans to build mirror-towers as the warmth of the room combined with the voluptuous heat spreading through her. A small inner voice warned her that they should leave this place quickly, but she ignored it. Here was where she wanted to be—alone with him.

He poured them both some wine and they both seated themselves on the cushions, a careful distance between them. It seemed essential to talk of something now, so her mind went back to the mirror-tower, which did indeed intrigue her.

"We could build mirror-towers," she told him. "And we have sunshine most of the time—more than you have here."

But she couldn't quite hold onto that dream, and bleakness overtook her. "But we can't build them if there is war," she finished sadly.

"There *will* be war," he stated as he stared into the fire. "I told your father that long ago. Ertria has let itself become too weak. All that was lacking then was a strong and greedy man like Arrat."

"But how could you have known it would come to this?" she asked fiercely. His nearness was overwhelming her, and she lashed out at him in a perverse attempt to deny that.

"You have lived here apart from the rest of the world for centuries now. I didn't even know the Kassid were *real*—I thought you were only a legend. And our Balek guide told me that only a few of his people had ever seen you, let alone talked to you. Do you have spies, Daken?"

He met her gaze levelly and shook his head slowly. "I cannot tell you how we get our information, Jocelyn. There are people who must be protected. And in any event, we are doing no more than you yourself do."

"But we have no spies *here*," she pointed out acerbically.

172

"That is true enough—but you would if you could."

She said nothing because she knew he was right. How very safe they were, here in their mountains. Even if the Menoans and Turveans overran all of Ertria and Balek, the Kassid had no real cause for alarm. No one—not even Arrat—would be foolish enough to attack them. She said as much to Daken in a bitter tone.

"I think he might be foolish enough to try, but he would never defeat us. It is the fact that he may *try* that made me decide we should ally ourselves with you, and it is that fact that will decide the others as well.

"These mountains are sacred to us. No war has ever been fought here, and it would be an insult to have an army in our land, even if we know we could destroy it with ease."

Her anger with him was spent. She knew she had manufactured it in any event. "I do not understand you, Daken. Just now, you spoke like a warrior— and yet you claim not to be a warrior at all."

"Perhaps that is because only the very strongest can afford to let themselves appear to be weak," he suggested. "I do not think of myself or my men as warriors, and we feel no need to prove ourselves. We are who we are—who we have always been. And we have great faith in our heritage—our gifts from the gods.

"If my people agree to this alliance as I believe they will, we will destroy Arrat and his army. We could do that even without Hammad's army."

For just a moment, Jocelyn could actually *feel* his pride, his certainty. "Yes," she said after a brief silence, "I believe you could do that. My father believed it, too."

He picked up the carafe to pour them some more wine and she held out her cup, watching the firelight reflect off the gold and remembering again the golden drawings on the walls of that secret room.

I want to tell him about it, she thought. *I must trust him. How can I not, when he will save my empire?*

She raised her eyes from the wine cup, then drew in her breath sharply as her eyes met his. He had leaned close to her to pour the wine—and now did not move away. What she saw in those pale eyes stopped all words and all thoughts.

With great slowness, he set down the carafe, then raised his hand to touch her cheek, his fingertips barely grazing it as he stared at her.

"I want you, Jocelyn," he said in a slow, quiet voice. "I can think of many reasons why this shouldn't happen, but reason plays no part in it."

She couldn't speak. It felt as though her heart had suddenly leapt into her throat. When he withdrew his hand after a moment, she finally found her voice—to make a sound of protest. He did not move away from her, but merely turned his face to stare into the fire.

"You are my guest, and I would never take advantage of that. You have no cause to fear me."

She realized then that he must have seen fear in her eyes and made another sound of protest, stronger this time. He turned back to her.

"I don't fear you, Daken. I ..." She faltered, knowing too late that it would have been better to let him think that.

"Maybe you don't fear *me*, but you fear what might happen between us. That decision must be yours."

"It would be wrong—foolish," she amended quickly. There couldn't be anything wrong about what she felt now.

"Foolish," he repeated musingly, staring down at his wine cup. "Yes, it would be that."

She was confused. He wasn't playing by the rules as she understood them. She'd been taught that men always sought to take advantage of a woman's innocence, that they were insatiable creatures who lusted after every woman.

"There is always some foolishness in love, I think," he went on after a long pause. "Though perhaps one should grow less foolish about it as one grows older."

"L—love?" she stammered.

He smiled at her and reached out to take her hand, enfolding it between both of his. "Yes, Jocelyn—love. There is one thing that I know age does bring—and that is the ability to distinguish between mere lust and love. It is, I think, a distinction women seem to learn at a much younger age."

"Are—are you saying that you *love* me, Daken?" she asked in an incredulous tone that still had a tiny quaver in it.

"Love does not happen so quickly, Jocelyn. Only lust comes so fast. But I know that something more

175

than lust exists between us even now." He raised a dark brow.

"Do you find it so difficult to believe that a man could fall in love with you—or is it only that you have heard those words too many times before? Or perhaps you think I'm too old for such things?"

"No," she protested. "I mean, I don't think of you as being old. I . . . I've just never been sure how you felt about me."

"And you are also not sure how *you* feel about *me*," he stated.

Then, before she could begin to formulate a reply to that, he stood up and drew her to her feet as well.

"Come. We should go back now—back where it is safer for both of us."

When he released her hand, she let it rest against his chest and tilted her head to stare up at him. She wanted only to hold onto this moment, to feel forever what she felt now. And then, as they stared at each other, she knew she wanted him to kiss her. Her lips parted slightly, although she had no words to say to him.

His gaze lowered, resting on her parted lips and the pulse point that beat erratically in her throat. She felt the touch of his eyes as she might have felt his lips.

He moved slightly, taking a half-step away from her and beginning to turn toward the door. But then he halted, turned back, and drew her almost roughly into his arms with a deep groan.

Jocelyn's world exploded in a white-hot blaze as his lips traced hungry, greedy kisses across her brow, her cheeks, her nose, and the eyes she closed because the world was spinning wildly.

And then at last, he claimed her mouth, covering it with aching tenderness as his hand caressed her hair. She was totally surrounded by him, cradled within his broad shoulders as his hands slid slowly down to draw her more fully against him.

She stiffened involuntarily as his tongue began to probe at hers in a gentle invasion that sent new shock waves through her. He withdrew quickly, but she reached up to grasp his head and pull him back again.

He made a low sound of satisfaction as he resumed his slow exploration of her mouth. She arched to him as his hands slid still lower, pressing her to him. When she felt that hardness thrust against her, the world exploded anew—but she could not prevent the small cry that poured from her mouth into his.

Immediately, she could feel him gathering together the unraveling threads of his self-control, and she wanted to protest, to tell him to ignore the fear she couldn't seem to control, to take her quickly beyond that fear.

But even as the words were struggling up to her throat, he was slowly moving away from her.

Daken heard his ragged breathing as he slowly, unwillingly, released her. He was caught between a wanting so powerful that it rocked him to his very core and the increasingly loud clamor of his shame that he was taking advantage of her innocence.

He hadn't intended this when he'd brought her

up here. He'd wanted only to show her the signaling device—and, admittedly, to enjoy the pleasure of her company for a time, away from the others.

But as shame beat back the flames of desire, he admitted that even if he hadn't intended it, he'd surely *wanted* it to happen. It was a very small distinction, but a necessary salve to his conscience.

How could this woman—not of his own people, far too young for him, and as wrong for him as any woman could possibly be—have sent him spiraling back to the heated passion of adolescence?

No, he thought, she has not sent me back to my youth, because even then I did not feel this. Then I merely lusted after a woman's body. Now I want *this* woman—*all* of her.

He sent a silent cry of anguish to the gods. Why had they sent this woman to him, when they knew he must let her go? Why were they allowing him to glimpse something he could never have?

He loped easily through the deep snowdrifts, then began the long ascent to the peak where a silvered moon hung suspended in the black night.

His thick coat kept out most of the chill, and he ignored the rest as he reveled in that incomparable sense of freedom. How long had it been? Years now.

When he finally reached the peak, the moon slipped behind a thin cloth of clouds. He stared out across the lower peaks and the deep ravines. The lights of the fortress gleamed in the blackness—distant now, as he'd wanted it.

The other mind slipped over his, never quite covering it, but rather blending with it, making him neither wholly himself nor completely other. The pain ebbed. The anguish waned. This is what he had sought and he welcomed it, knowing with the mind that was still his that it was only temporary.

Chapter Six

"The word for it in our language means a turning, a move toward spring," Daken told her, casting a wry glance toward the window. Snow was falling thickly.

"Often at this time, there is a period of warmer weather. But the festival goes on regardless of the weather."

They were alone in the great room of Daken's suite, following a council meeting. Nearly two weeks had passed since that trip to the tower, and this was the first time she'd been alone with him since that fateful day.

Daken had disappeared the day after their trip to the tower, and two days had passed before Jocelyn asked after him. At first, she'd thought he was merely avoiding her, but then, when he failed to appear for dinner and wasn't present among the group that gathered for the evening, she began to suspect that it was more than that.

Still, she had waited before inquiring because she feared that she might sound too eager, too interested. Tassa and Rina both knew that they had gone to the tower, and Jocelyn didn't want to arouse suspicions.

When she'd finally asked Tassa on the morning of the third day, Tassa had said only that he was "away," and Jocelyn had been unwilling to push the matter any further. Surely she couldn't have meant away from the fortress—not in the midst of yet another snowstorm. Then she'd recalled his statement about using that room in the tower as a place to get away, to think. So she assumed he must have gone there—and she knew what must have been on his mind.

He'd apparently returned sometime during the night of the fifth day. When she'd gone to bed that night, the door to his bedroom had been ajar, as it had been earlier. But when she'd gotten up the next morning, it was closed. He'd appeared late in the morning as she and Tassa were returning from the market that was held during the winter months in the Great Hall of the fortress.

Jocelyn had been shocked at his appearance. He seemed thinner, almost haggard-looking, and she'd even noticed a slight tremor to his hands. But Tassa had said nothing, so Jocelyn too had remained silent.

There was something else that had been different

about him in those first few days after his return—something Jocelyn could feel, but could not explain, even to herself.

Daken quickly reverted to normal, however, and although the incident remained in her mind as a worrisome mystery, she allowed it to diminish in importance as Daken once more seemed to go to considerable lengths to avoid being alone with her.

As she drifted with her thoughts, he had been busy explaining the history and activities of the upcoming festival that was clearly an important event in the life of the Kassid.

He fell silent, and she'd been so preoccupied that she didn't know if he had finished or had simply guessed that she was less than attentive. Their eyes met, and she was about to apologize for her inattention when he spoke.

"A message was received yesterday from the other fortresses. There, too, the debate over going to war continues. But I have sent word to them that a decision must be reached within a week."

"Within a week?" she echoed, feeling both apprehensive and eager. "But why?"

"There are preparations to make if we are to go to war—and now that the Turning approaches, we have little time left."

Then he turned away from her and rested an arm against the mantel as he stared into the fireplace.

"Are you having second thoughts?" she asked nervously. "Or do you think that the fact that they're taking so long means that the decision will be against an alliance?"

He shook his head without turning. "No, my belief is still the same, and I think the people will agree with me. But I am not looking forward to going to war."

"It may not come to war," she suggested hopefully. "If Arrat learns that you have allied yourself with us—"

"We cannot depend on that," he said, cutting her off. Then he turned toward her again, crossing his arms over his broad chest as he gave her a level look.

"Jocelyn, if my people *do* decide against an alliance, you must stay here until it is over."

"I can't," she protested, certain now that he must believe his people were going to decide against it. "If there is to be war, I must . . ."

"You must what?" he asked harshly as she faltered. "You must go back to be killed or captured? There is nothing you can do. War is a man's affair. And Hammad will need every man he can find to fight it. If you are there, he will be forced to withhold a large force to defend the palace and protect you."

"No!" she cried, even though she knew what he said was true. "I am empress and I must be there with my people."

He shook his head. "As empress, your first duty should be to keep yourself alive—and out of Arrat's hands. He probably wouldn't kill you, but you may wish that he had."

She wrapped her arms about herself and shuddered as she conjured up an image of that odious little man.

"I cannot stay here," she said succinctly, "Regardless of the outcome."

"And I will not permit you to return to certain death or capture," he stated with equal firmness.

She lifted her chin and looked coldly at him. "You have just admitted to holding me prisoner here, Daken."

He shook his head. "Only winter holds you prisoner now."

"But if your people agree to an alliance, then you will permit me to return—even though there could still be war?"

"I would prefer that you remain here in either event, but I am willing to take you back to the palace if we fight alongside your army."

"That makes no sense. I would still be in danger."

"No. Your own guards and some of my men could protect you adequately. Besides, it would not then be a lengthy war, and the enemy will never reach the city."

"Daken, you will forgive me if I say that I don't quite understand your certainty that you will win—that you can summon the magic you've spoken about. Hammad told me once that the worst mistake a commander can make is to underestimate the strength and talents of his enemies."

"Under ordinary circumstances, Hammad would be right. But when the Kassid fight, the circumstances aren't ordinary."

She regarded him with something close to amusement. Those words were the closest she'd ever heard him come to boasting.

"That is no idle boast, Jocelyn," he said softly.

"Perhaps not—but neither is it necessarily the truth. How can you be certain that the spirits of your ancestors will agree with the decision of your people? You told me that your magic lies in their presence in battle. But what if *they* don't think this is a necessary war?"

"Their spirits live on in us. If we choose war, they will be with us. Perhaps you will come to believe that soon."

Jocelyn was about to ask him what he meant by that, but Jakka, his aide, walked into the room at that moment and she took the opportunity instead to excuse herself.

She admired his unquestioning faith in a magic he'd never seen, but she couldn't bring herself to share it. She continued to believe that the benefit of an alliance with the Kassid lay in the legends of their prowess—not in the reality of their presence.

When Jocelyn awoke on the day before the beginning of the festival, she was nearly willing to cast aside her doubts about Kassid magic. After days of leaden skies and regular snowfalls, the weather had abruptly begun to change late the previous day. And now, as she stood at her windows, she saw brilliant blue skies. Then there was an impatient rapping at her door, and she quickly put on her robe and opened it to admit a very happy and excited Rina.

"Do you see, Jocelyn?" The girl grinned, gesturing to the windows. "The weather has changed. Hurry now. There is much to be done."

And so the Empress of Ertria, Balek, and sundry

scattered islands spent the day in the kitchen—a place she'd seen only once or twice at home, and then only as a child.

During the festival, she learned, people drifted from one home to another throughout the fortress, partaking of whatever food and drink was being offered.

She was amazed at the quantity and variety of foods the Kassid had, even in the midst of winter. The winter garden was only one part of their ingenuity. Until the snows became too deep, the men went on numerous hunting and fishing trips, and much of what they brought back was stored frozen in deep snow, to be thawed and eaten during the long winter. The rest of it was preserved by ancient methods that left it tender and spicy—much more tasty than the preserved meats and fish sometimes served at the palace.

Daken appeared regularly during the day to deliver the frozen meats and fish and to bring Tassa a cask of wine for her special cakes. Jocelyn smiled at what was obviously a long-standing game between him and Rina to see if she could prevent his sneaking off with various delicacies.

On his first trip, though, he apparently felt it his duty to remind her that she needn't take part in the work.

"And what else would I do?" she asked him with a smile. "I'm not an empress here, Daken, and there is much to be done."

Their eyes met—and neither of them looked away. Another, silent, conversation began then, an acknowledgement that neither of them had forgotten that day in the tower—no matter how much they'd tried to pretend otherwise.

How much longer can we go on like this? she asked silently. *When will this hunger consume us both?*

And from him, only those same words as before—the decision is yours.

What more might have been said—or rather, *not* said—they would never know, because a noisy group of Rina's friends came into the kitchen at that moment, breaking the silent conversation.

Late in the day, Rina took Jocelyn out to the cleared courtyard, where a space had been set aside for ice sculptures. Rina and her partner had to prepare their ice, which they would begin carving the next day. The judging was on the final day of the three-day festival.

There were more than two dozen teams entered in the contest to see who could create the most beautiful sculpture. Each team began with a huge pile of snow that had to be molded into a desired shape. Then, when they had created the outlines of their various sculptures, they poured water over the snow. By morning, it would be a solid block of ice, which they would then carve with picks and knives.

The designs were kept secret, but Rina had shown hers to Jocelyn. Her sculpture was to be a great bird, lifting its wings to soar into the heavens. Jocelyn could not imagine how such a thing could be created from ice, but Rina was confident of her abilities and those of her partner, a youth in whom she had clearly more than a passing interest.

While she was helping Rina and her friend pile

the snow into a mound, Jocelyn saw other young people practicing for another event of the festival—the "snow-walker" race.

Snow-walkers were devices made of wood and leather that were then strapped over boots. The fronts curved upward slightly, but otherwise, they resembled over-sized soles for shoes. She hadn't tried them herself, but she'd already seen how easy they made it to walk in the snow. The race began at the bridge, then continued onto the trail on the far side before returning once more to the bridge. Since no one was allowed on the actual trail until the race began, the contestants were practicing in the courtyard.

Rina paused to watch some of her friends who were contestants. "Several of the men have been working on a new type of snow-walker," she said. "They're calling them 'snow-runners' because you can go very fast on them. I haven't seen them, but Father says they're long and thin—as long as the person is tall."

"But how can they possibly walk in something like that?" Jocelyn asked.

"They're really intended to carry you downhill," she explained. "Then you have to take them off and carry them up again. Father thinks they could be very dangerous, although he's already tried them himself, of course." She said the last with a grin.

"When he was younger, he always won the snow-walker races—and the summer races as well. In fact, he won just about everything. Now, of course, he says he's too old."

Jocelyn immediately thought about the hard

body that had been pressed against hers—certainly not the body of an old man. Then she spotted him as he emerged from the fortress and lifted a hand to wave at them before turning in the other direction.

If all I am to ever have of him is memories, she thought, *then I want more than I have now*. She must find a way to tell him that. Why did she find it so difficult? Was it because, deep down inside, she still feared that he was more than a man?

The busy day was finally over, and darkness brought the eve of the Turning. They gathered in the great room of Daken's suite before a blazing fire and drank the sweet, spicy wine that Tassa served warm.

Jocelyn noticed a small pile of logs to one side of the hearth. They were much smaller than the big logs for the fire. She stared at them quizzically, seeing that someone had stripped away all the bark, leaving only a smooth, pale surface. There were four of them, all cut to the same length.

Just as she was about to ask what they were for, Daken picked them up and gave one to Rina and another to Tassa, then brought one to her. When he saw her puzzled expression, he turned back to his daughter.

"Have you explained this tradition to Jocelyn?"

Rina shook her head. "No, I forgot about it—I mean, I forgot to explain. There was so much else to do."

"It doesn't matter," Daken said gently when he saw his daughter's embarrassment. "Jocelyn can decide now whether or not she wants to take part."

He turned back to Jocelyn, still holding the last

189

log. "It is traditional at the time of the Turning to carve into a log a word or words to describe that which you have liked least about yourself during the past year. Then all the logs are piled into a great bonfire that will be lit tomorrow night, the first night of the festival.

"The belief," he said with a slight smile, "is that the fire will cleanse you of that particular behavior. Whether that is true or not, it does provide a time to reflect on what you've done and who you are— and who you wish to be."

Jocelyn took the log from him. Somehow, she wasn't surprised by this tradition. It seemed all of a piece with what she knew about the Kassid. She'd spent enough time with them to know that they seemed constantly to be trying to improve themselves in one way or another.

Rina and Tassa had already begun to carve their logs with small knives, and Daken now produced one for her. She took it, then frowned at the log. "I must give this some thought."

"How fortunate you are to have to think about your failings," he said drily. "For most of us, the only thought required is to decide which of our many failings is the worst."

Jocelyn laughed. "That is exactly what I meant."

She found the exercise intriguing. She frequently berated herself for her many flaws, but she'd never tried to consider them all at once—and then decide which was worst.

She knew she was often impatient. That particular flaw came to mind in light of Daken's very great patience. And yes, she was sometimes insensitive to others whose lives she affected. Daken had pointed out that unpleasant trait in regard to Tanner, the dead guide, and he also provided a contrast by his constant concern for the welfare of those around him.

Her frown deepened. It suddenly seemed to her that, despite these admittedly serious flaws, her biggest problem was a lack of a sense of completeness, the understanding of self that confers self-assuredness. And once again, she knew that she had thought of this because she saw that quality existing in abundance in Daken.

She made an involuntary sound of disgust. All she seemed to be doing was measuring herself against Daken—to her very great disadvantage. He had taken a seat near her, and she realized she'd made a sound only when he spoke in a low, amused voice.

"Searching oneself can be a difficult undertaking."

"Especially if one does it by comparing oneself to another," she replied without thinking.

He laughed softly. "I have had many more years to work on myself, Jocelyn—and I still have very far to go." Then he laughed again.

"Of course, if you *weren't* referring to me, then I will have to reconsider what I put on my log—change it to arrogance."

"No, Daken, arrogance is not one of your faults," she replied. "Do you tell each other what you put on your logs?"

He shrugged. "Sometimes. And sometimes not."

She stared at the log he hadn't yet begun to carve. "Will you tell me what you will put on yours?"

"I have been thinking about it, of course; we all do that. But this year, I have thought more about it that in the past. The word I will carve is 'tchupizh'. It's difficult to translate. The Kassid language has far fewer words than Ertrian because we often express a whole idea in one word." He paused, frowning.

"It is too much pride—but more than that. Too much certainty that nothing can change me. That is an inadequate explanation, but I can do no better with it."

He lapsed into silence and began to carve his log. Jocelyn wondered what had prompted his decision. If any man seemed unlikely to change, it was Daken. But then her thoughts were interrupted as Rina spoke up.

"I am going to cleanse myself of inattention— carelessness. I spend too much time in my head and not enough paying attention to others."

"I think that is a problem of your age, Rina," Jocelyn said with a smile. "You are at an age for dreaming. But you're also very wise to know that. I certainly wouldn't have at your age."

Rina smiled at her and Jocelyn thought for the first time that Daken wasn't the only one she would miss when she left here. She'd grown very fond of the girl, and thought that her affection was returned.

Tassa was busy carving her log, but said nothing. She was a very private woman, though always kind and generous. Jocelyn had learned from Rina that Tassa had long ago planned to marry a young man who died in a climbing accident, a sport practiced by many Kassid men. According to Rina, there'd never been anyone else in her life.

Jocelyn glanced over at her as she bent over the log and suddenly thought she might be seeing herself in years to come. I too am going to lose the only man I could love, she thought with a deep, deep pain that seemed to wrack her very soul.

She didn't want to look at Daken in that moment, but her eyes slid in that direction anyway. His gray head was bent to his task, his long fingers holding the delicate knife with great dexterity. She had already seen how he wiled away the long winter evenings by carving wonderful likenesses of forest creatures.

She knew so much about him—and so little, she thought sadly. There were things he would never tell her and she would never ask about. How could she possibly love such a man—and yet she knew she did.

She began to carve her own log. When she had finished, she wasn't satisfied with the results, but it didn't really matter. She knew what she meant. She wanted to rid herself of her foolish dreams, of that deep-down belief that if she wanted something badly enough, it would happen.

Jocelyn awoke the next morning to another day of brilliant sunshine—and once again, to impatient rapping at her door. She hurried into a robe and opened it to find a positively glowing Rina standing there, actually dancing in place in her eagerness to get on with the festivities.

Rina's enthusiasm was infectious. Jocelyn could remember her own eagerness for such events when she was Rina's age—the carefree joys of childhood she hadn't thought about since the burdens of her present position had begun to weigh so heavily on her.

Within the hour, they were out in the courtyard, where Rina's partner in ice sculpturing was already hard at work amidst the other teams. Slivers of ice flew in the clear, cold air, accompanied by the dull thunks of picks, hammers and chisels.

Jocelyn watched them for some time. The rules didn't permit her offering her own assistance. Then, when standing in one place became uncomfortably cold, she began to wander about the busy court-yard. She hadn't seen this many people out here since the snows had begun and the market had moved indoors. Everyone she encountered was in high spirits, adults as well as children.

She saw people beginning to bring their carved logs out to the large space set aside for the bonfire and paused to inspect them. She couldn't read the written Kassid language as yet, since she was hav-ing more than enough difficulty with the tongue-twisting spoken language.

As she stared at the logs, some of which were nearly covered with writing, she thought again about that secret room at the palace. Unless her memory was inaccurate—and she didn't believe it was—there was no resemblance at all between the golden writings on those walls and the writing she saw here.

But the rest of it was so very clearly Kassid, she though—the black stone, the drawings of wolves, even the door to the room. Every time she thought about that mysterious room, her thoughts were accompanied by a nameless fear. Deep down, at a level she could feel but not explain, she knew that the room held some very great significance. How could it not? It was an alien presence within the very walls of her palace, the palace built by her own ancestors.

Why don't I ask Daken about it? she wondered. Was it because she feared the answer—or because she knew he was already withholding things from her and she wanted to keep that room as her own secret?

She pushed away these thoughts as several more people came up to place their logs on the growing pile. Then she thought about her court and wondered if she could start such a tradition there. It could certainly prove useful, but she smiled wryly as she thought about her arrogant courtiers pondering their weaknesses.

"Did Rina wake you at first light?" a familiar deep voice asked, drawing her quickly out of her reveries.

She turned and smiled at Daken as he tossed his log onto the heap. "No, not quite. But I'm afraid I've caught her enthusiasm. Are you entering the races?" She saw that he was carrying a pair of snow-walkers.

"Rina said that you thought you were too old for such things," she teased. "But she said you always won."

He laughed. "Size has its advantages, and so does the fierceness of youth. No, I'm not racing. I'm part of the team that will check the trail before the races begin. There is always the danger of a zhakash." Seeing her frown of incomprehension, he hastened to explain.

"Sometimes, the snow on the mountain above the trails can break loose. If it's bad enough, pieces of the mountain can fall as well. It rarely happens up on this trail, but we need to check it to be sure."

"But what do you do when it *does* happen?" she asked, imagining the trails obliterated by snow and rock.

"Most of the time, it's simply an inconvenience. We just take another trail. But there are a few places where that isn't possible. Then there's nothing to do but dig our way out. That hasn't happened in many years, thank the gods."

At that moment, several other men called out to him from across the courtyard, and he excused himself to join them. Jocelyn watched him walk away, balancing the snow-walkers easily on one wide shoulder. She felt such an indescribable sense of loss when he left her—even now, when she knew she would see him again. How would she survive the permanent loss to come?

For one brief moment, a moment she knew she could never allow herself to repeat, Jocelyn wished that she weren't the Empress of Ertria—that she could be an ordinary woman and stay here forever with this man.

But the moment passed quickly as that longing gave way to anger with herself. Such weakness was unacceptable. She wasn't a woman; she was an empress. It was understandable that she would indulge in such foolishness here, but this was no more than an interlude in a life that had been ordained years ago, when her brother Arman had lost his life at the edges of these very mountains.

She began to walk through the bustling courtyard until she reached the far end, where children's excited voices could be heard. Small mountains of snow had been piled up there and dozens of children were swarming over them, either careening wildly down the slopes on their big wooden discs or dragging them back up again.

Jocelyn had seen these discs before. They were curved slightly like saucers and polished to a perfect smoothness to make them glide through the snow more easily. Along each side were raised portions with handles that allowed the child to more or less guide them. She found them fascinating, and every time she saw them, she had to fight down an urge to try it herself.

A few adults stood about, keeping an eye on the children. Jocelyn saw that Sheela, one of the women members of Daken's council, was among them and went to join her as they watched the children's antics.

"It scarcely seems possible that winter is half gone," Sheela said, shaking her mostly gray head as she tossed back her hood. "But for you, I guess that the time has passed very slowly."

Jocelyn murmured assent, although she too believed time had passed quickly.

"You must miss your friends and family," Sheela continued, "but what you face when spring comes cannot be pleasant."

Once again, Jocelyn retorted to banalities. She did in fact miss a few people—Hammad, several cousins, the new people she had begun to gather as advisors. Even Eryk. But the sad truth was that there was really no one at the palace, now that her father was gone, to whom she felt really close. It was the price of being who she was.

"I am heartened by the response from the other fortresses," Sheela went on. "Since they are even farther from the borders with your lands, I had expected them to feel less urgency. It speaks well of them that they think not only of themselves, but rather of our people as a whole."

Then she frowned at Jocelyn's confusion. "Has Daken not told you?"

"Told me what?"

"The word came yesterday from the other fortresses. They have voted in favor of the alliance."

She hesitated, then shrugged. "Daken is very protective of you—too protective, perhaps. He probably decided to wait until the decision is made here. The other fortresses are quite small, so even though their decision is important, it is here that the matter will truly be decided."

"Perhaps he doesn't yet know," Jocelyn suggested, fighting a rising anger with Daken.

"Oh, he knows. We spoke of it yesterday. Do not be angry with him, Jocelyn. His intentions were good—and it is his support for your cause that gives it hope.

"I know he's told you that each of us makes up our own mind, and that is true. But in a matter as grave as this, we all look to our leader for guidance. Our leaders are always respected—but none more than Daken. We would have to look far back in our history to find a leader like him. Durka, the leader before Daken, once remarked that greatness sat easily on Daken's shoulders, and I think he was right."

"Sometimes it seems to me that his greatness is a burden those around him are left to bear," Jocelyn remarked without thinking.

Sheela laughed. "I could not have put it better myself. In fact, Erina, Daken's wife, once said much the same thing."

"She did?" Jocelyn was very curious. No one ever seemed to speak of her.

"We were very close," Sheela told her. Then her eyes seemed to have shifted to the past. Jocelyn remained silent, not wanting to force her to relive an old sadness, but hoping she would continue. After a time, she did.

"Erina loved Daken and he loved her—but she was always very fragile, in body and spirit. It always seemed to me that she needed a little less greatness in a husband, and Daken needed someone stronger. Do you understand?"

"Yes, I think so," Jocelyn replied. "But why hasn't he remarried?"

Sheela shrugged and turned again to watch the children. "Sometimes I think he realized his mistake—realized that he needed someone stronger. There've been women, of course, although not for a long time after Erina's death. But then it seemed that he just became content with his life as it is, although . . ."

Her voice trailed off and Jocelyn prompted her. "Do you think that has changed?" She was thinking about what Daken had explained to her as he'd carved his log the night before.

"I think he may be finding it difficult now to remain content," Sheela said, casting her a look that seemed both sad and amused.

Suddenly, the volume of noise from the slopes increased, and both women saw that two children had collided part-way down the steep hill. Their discs slid off to the sides, creating still more havoc, and the two who had collided were now tumbling down the slope, arms and legs floundering.

By the time it was all sorted out, and the anxious adults had determined that no one had been injured, Sheela said she had to hurry off to the crafts fair, where she had volunteered to help. Jocelyn wanted very much to pursue their conversation, but was forced to let it go.

The rest of the day passed in a blur of activities. Jocelyn returned several more times to check on the progress of Rina's ice sculpture, at the same time bringing food and warm drinks for both her and her partner. With each visit, she could see more of the giant bird taking shape under their skilled hands.

She also went over to the bridge to watch the snow-walker races and marveled at the speed and agility of the contestants as they seemed to skim along on the awkward-looking devices. She'd expected to find Daken there, but he was nowhere to be seen.

The inside of the fortress was a beehive of activity as well. There was a market and the crafts fair and more games for children. At one end of the Great Hall, a group of mostly older men were playing a complicated-looking game that involved rolling wooden balls through a maze of tall wooden cylinders. From the sounds of the crowd gathered there, she guessed that the object was to strike the cylinders and knock them down.

The wide hallways of the fortress were crowded with merrymakers, and since most of them were much taller than she was, Jocelyn began to feel as though she were back to her own childhood, scampering about amongst the crowds at the palace.

The doors to all the living quarters were flung open, and people drifted from one home to another, laughing, talking, drinking, and eating. Delicious aromas wafted out from every doorway, and Jocelyn received many invitations to partake of this or that delicacy or the host's special wine.

By the time she finally reached Daken's quarters, she was over-filled with food and a bit dizzy from having sampled too much wine. But she was also very optimistic about the outcome of the vote because so many people had told her they agreed with Daken.

One elderly gentleman, who had perhaps had a bit too much wine, said that the Kassid had an "historic interest in the welfare of the Ertrian empire," by which Jocelyn assumed he meant that long-ago time when Kassid warriors had fought to help create the empire. She knew that the Kassid had a strong sense of history and thought it likely that many others would feel that way as well.

The door to Daken's suite stood open as well, and she walked into the great room to discover a substantial crowd present and Daken himself pouring the wine. Tassa was nowhere to be seen, and Jocelyn belatedly realized that with Rina busy with her sculpture, she should have offered to help with the guests. Tassa had probably been confined to the kitchen all day.

As soon as he saw her, Daken poured another goblet of wine and brought it to her. She knew this was the special wine he made himself, but she put up a hand to refuse it.

"I'm afraid I've had too much already," she stated ruefully. "Is Tassa in the kitchen? I must go help her so she can get out for a while to see everything."

"She's already doing that," he replied, peering at her closely. "Perhaps you should rest for a while. Otherwise, you might miss the evening's activities."

"I think you're right," she said, horrified to realize that she was swaying slightly and her eyes weren't quite focussing properly. As long as she had kept moving in the crowds, she hadn't noticed it.

Daken circled her waist with one long arm and led her off to her bedchamber. Very embarrassed now, she protested that she was fine.

"You will be if you get some rest. Some people make much stronger wine than I do, and you're not used to it. I should have warned you."

He opened the door to her bedchamber, then dropped his arm. She started to sway against him, then caught herself and instead protested that she might miss the judging of the ice sculptures.

"I'll come get you," he promised, then backed away and closed the door behind him.

Jocelyn walked rather unsteadily to the bed, then fell onto it without undressing. Despite the hum of activity all around her, she fell asleep very quickly.

Something was brushing lightly against her cheek. Still struggling up from sleep, Jocelyn put out a hand—and touched warm, calloused flesh. Her eyes snapped open to meet the eyes that haunted her dreams—the eyes of the wolf. Daken's eyes. She gasped—whether because she thought it was a dream or knew it wasn't, she couldn't have said. He quickly withdrew the hand that had smoothed her tangled hair away from her face, then straightened up and backed away from her bed.

"I knocked, but you must have been sleeping deeply. Wine will do that. I've brought you some tea to help you wake up."

She sat up in the bed, struggling away from the dream and away from the havoc wrought by his touch. It was still daylight, but the shadows were lengthening.

"Have I missed the ice sculptures?" she asked in a husky voice that owed as much to his presence as to sleepiness.

"No, that's why I woke you now. There is time yet." He handed her a cup of the strong brew the Kassid drank in the morning. His movement seemed oddly stiff and formal.

"Thank you," she murmured, taking the cup. Their fingers touched lightly, then withdrew quickly—as though each had touched something hot.

"Have you seen the sculptures? Is Rina finished?" Despite her fondness for the girl, the ice creations were the last thing on her mind at the moment. But it was essential now, as that voluptuous warmth spread through her, to preserve a sense of normality.

"She must be finished by now," Daken replied. He stood there awkwardly for a moment, then took a seat on a nearby chair. "I went out earlier, but she sent me away, telling me I couldn't see it until it was finished. For some reason, Rina seems to think I demand perfection in everything. She's much like her mother was in that regard."

Jocelyn smiled at his words, recalling the conversation with Sheela about the burdens of living with someone like Daken. "Well, perhaps you could show an imperfection or two yourself from time to time. It might help."

She'd spoken lightly, a smile on her lips and in her voice—but rather to her surprise, he took her words very seriously.

"I'm not perfect, Jocelyn. In fact, I've never been more aware of that than I am at the moment."

Their eyes met—and held this time. She wanted to look away, to prevent the heat and chills that seemed to be chasing each other endlessly through her. She could feel the tension in him—his self-control was held by a taut leash in danger of snapping at any moment.

The cup shook in her hand. He saw it and stood up slowly, coming to stand once more beside the bed. His movements seemed slow and deliberate as he took it from her and set it on a nearby table. Then he turned back to her, and a question was asked and answered in a heavy, heated silence.

He sat down on the edge of the bed, and his weight sent her tumbling into an awkward position against him. She moved—not away from him, but just to make herself more comfortable. And this time when their eyes met, she raised her hand carefully, letting it come to rest against his cheek in an unconscious imitation of his earlier gesture. It was the most she dared, but far less than she wanted—and she knew that she had told him that when he turned his face into her hand and his lips brushed against her sensitive palm.

A low, strangled sound rose within her. She tried to catch it in her throat, but failed. It felt as though a storm were gathering inside her—dark, mysterious, threatening.

She leaned toward him and felt him hesitate for a moment before gathering her into his arms with a deep groan that echoed through her as he buried his face in her neck.

But she was hungry for the taste of him and drew his mouth up to meet hers as she threaded her fingers through his thick gray hair.

The sensations were almost too much to be

borne. For a moment, she was afraid she might fall away into some unimaginable chasm as a powerful need pulled at her.

Their bodies were twisted and awkward, arms and legs bumping into each other. And then the clumsiness was gone as they lay back on the bed and his hands began to roam greedily over her. Tremors that began in one ended in the other— fine, strong threads of passion that bound them to each other.

No one had ever touched her so intimately—but she wanted more. Her clothing chafed against her heated flesh, begging to be released from its confinement. What should have been frightening was an impediment to be dispensed with.

She arched her body to his, and this time did not shrink away when she felt that hardness. Through her mind ran all those stories she'd heard about the pain, the humiliation, a woman's duty, not her pleasure. All of it passed through her mind and was gone; she knew it could not be that way with him.

His mouth moved warmly over hers and his tongue probed lightly at her own. Moments, hours, could have passed this way as they lay there, lost in a world of their own creation.

Then he slowly lifted his mouth from hers and propped himself up on one elbow as he stared down at her. Long strands of hair had fallen across his face and she reached up to smooth them away, wanting more but pleased just to be able to touch him.

Once more, he turned his face into her hand and kissed it—bringing them back to where it had begun. She understood the gesture. What had started could not be finished now. She was aware of the fact that she should be relieved, but felt instead only a frustration.

"Rina will be expecting us," he said hoarsely.

She nodded, not yet trusting her own voice. In the unspoken conversation beneath those words, he was saying that this was the only reason they had stopped, and she was agreeing. But it seemed that he required the words to be spoken after all, because he sat up, moved slightly away from her, then spoke in a more normal voice.

"Do you want us to become lovers, Jocelyn?"

"Yes," she said succinctly, not wanting there to be any doubt about it. She guessed that he might try to find doubt in her because she knew he had his own.

Their gazes locked, and after a moment he smiled. "You are determined not to leave me a way out, aren't you?"

She nodded, a smile hovering about her own lips.

He stood up then, putting still more distance between them before he spoke again. "I have never wanted a woman so much before. I fear what will happen to us, Jocelyn—but I fear more the pain of *not* having you."

"Yes," she said. There was no need to say anything more. They had no promises to make, no future to talk about. They both knew that all they had was this time together—to create memories.

Chapter Seven

A large crowd had already gathered around the ice sculptures, and Jocelyn felt a pang of guilt as she saw Rina scanning it anxiously, obviously wondering where they were.

She felt disoriented as Daken took her arm and led them through the throngs. She barely heard the remarks made to him, mostly in the Kassid tongue, but occasionally in Ertrian for her benefit. Even through her thick cloak, she could feel the heat of his touch, and the conversations around them were drowned out by the memory of their words—or rather, *his* words and her agreement.

Then they reached Rina, and Jocelyn understood what people had been saying—the sculpture was magnificent. The last rays of the lowering sun touched the tips of huge wings arched to take flight. And the details were truly astonishing. Somehow,

Rina and her partner had managed to create feathers out of ice, giving the impression that a real bird was poised just beneath the translucent, glittering ice, ready to cast off its covering and fly away.

"Rina, this is wonderful! What talent you have!" Jocelyn hugged the girl impulsively.

Rina grinned tiredly. "It took us longer than we'd thought. We just finished. Have you seen the others?"

Jocelyn admitted that she hadn't, but said she was sure none could be the equal of this.

"Everyone is saying that," Rina nodded proudly. "But there's a very good bear, the best I've ever seen."

Jocelyn and Daken made their rounds, viewing all the ice creations. The bear was indeed very good, but Jocelyn thought it lacked the spirit, the animation, of Rina's great bird. One team had even carved a larger-than-life likeness of a Kassid warrior, complete with the short sword she learned from Daken was their weapon of choice in battle.

Jocelyn stared up at the expertly carved face. There was no doubt in her mind that the sculptors had intended it to be Daken, although he professed not to see that.

That ice-warrior remained in her mind as they made their way back to Rina. She wished that the two youths who had carved it had chosen something else. This was not a night when she wanted to be reminded of what lay ahead for them. In this safe place, war seemed such a very distant thing, and she wanted only to keep it that way for as long as possible.

When they reached Rina, the trio of judges was moving slowly around the bird, the crowd having fallen back to make way for them. Jocelyn watched their faces and thought they seemed impressed, although they might well have schooled themselves into that expression to hide their decision until the last moment.

But when the announcement was made, the great bird was pronounced the winner with much praise. Daken was the first to congratulate his daughter, lifting her high into his arms with a shout of joy.

Then, together with the glowing Rina, Daken and Jocelyn made the rounds of the fortress as the activity moved back indoors again. Tassa, who had been forced to miss the judging for other duties, joined them as they moved from one home to the next, where Rina's skills were praised by all.

Jocelyn took great care this time not to accept too many glasses of wine, although she had more trouble turning down all the delicacies being offered.

From time to time throughout their leisurely journey, pale blue eyes would meet emerald green in silent promise, and Jocelyn would feel her world spinning dizzily.

But once, when she looked away from Daken to find Rina watching them with a curious expression, Jocelyn allowed reality to intrude. What would Rina think—and Tassa as well? Would they understand that this time was all they had, that what was happening between her and Daken already had an ending even before it had begun?

Abruptly, she recalled her father saying to her

once that one should never begin that which cannot be finished.

The great courtyard of the fortress was overflowing with people when they walked out into the cold, clear night. Rina had told her that no one ever missed the bonfire unless they were too ill to be exposed to the cold.

By contrast with the gaiety of the day, the mood of the Kassid was now more solemn than she'd yet seen. People spoke in low, hushed tones or simply stood together in silence as the last of the carved logs were tossed onto the huge pile. She had brought her own log out earlier, and stood now with Rina and Tassa. Daken had disappeared some time ago. She scanned the crowds, seeking him, then found him standing with his advisors at the front of the crowd before the pile of logs.

At that moment, he spotted her, too, and beckoned her forward. Rina took her arm.

"Come, Jocelyn. Father wants you to join him."

Jocelyn made her way through the crowd with Rina holding her arm. She detected a certain tension in Rina and immediately wondered if the girl had guessed what was happening and disapproved. It would be natural, she thought, but she hoped that she was wrong.

When they reached Daken, he took her hand. "As our guest, you should be here where you can see the ceremony."

She thanked him, but gently withdrew her hand, mindful of Rina's presence. Daken glanced at her in silent question, but said nothing. Then a group

211

of men began to circle the small mountain of logs, pouring something over them.

"Bol," Rina told her. "To start the fire. Sometimes the smoke is terrible, but there's no wind tonight, so it shouldn't bother us."

Jocelyn thought that Rina still seemed tense, but then she realized that the feeling of tension was in the very air. Apparently, the Kassid regarded this moment as being very important.

Then a part of the crowd gave way to permit the passage of a boy and a girl who were carrying torches. As Daken took both torches from them, Rina whispered that they were the winners in the snow-walker races and had lit the torches from the urns at the bridge.

Considering the solemnity and the tension in the crowd, Jocelyn was expecting some sort of speech or ceremony, but Daken merely flung the torches into the middle of the huge mound of logs. Within seconds, flames lept into the darkness as the logs caught with a great roar. The crowd moved back a bit, and Daken now came to stand beside her.

At first, Jocelyn could barely hear the singing over the roar of the flames, but when Rina and Daken quickly joined in, she listened carefully, trying to pick out words she knew. Her knowledge of their tongue was still quite limited, however, and after a moment she gave up and simply enjoyed Rina's clear soprano and Daken's surprisingly good bass.

The singing continued until the flames began to die down. Thousands of voices joined in the bitter cold night that seemed to lend an extra clarity to their tones. And then the huge crowd fell silent.

Suddenly, the silence was broken by strange sounds that seemed to be coming from various directions. They were obviously musical instruments of some sort, but the sound was unlike anything she'd ever heard—mournful but strangely stirring as well. Daken leaned close to her, his arm around her waist as he spoke into her ear.

"They're called bezhras—a very ancient instrument played only at the Turning."

By now, Jocelyn was able to make out the figures standing on the outer wall of the fortress, spaced along its entire length. And she was sure there must be more somewhere in the fortress itself, perhaps atop the many towers.

The strange music went on and on, the rhythms occasionally repeating themselves. The crowd remained absolutely still, and that strange tension seemed to be increasing. She could feel it even in Daken's arm as he kept it about her waist.

Finally, when the fire had at last died down to mere embers, the music stopped. But the crowd didn't move, and Daken drew her more closely to him. She looked up at him uncertainly, but his head was lifted as he seemed to be staring off beyond the wall.

And then she heard it, accompanied by soft exhalations from the crowd. Far, far away, beyond the walls of the fortress, the rhythms were being repeated. The music was faint but startlingly clear in the cold, dark night.

It didn't last long, dying away even as she strained to catch it. It was impossible to guess how far away it was, let alone in which direction, but she thought it seemed to be coming from several different places. Lovely as it was, she couldn't help thinking that the musicians were putting themselves at great risk to be out there. Daken had said that the trails were truly treacherous.

The end of the distant music brought an end to the strange tension that had gripped the crowd, and they once again broke out in laughter and conversation. She thought they sounded very relieved and wondered if everyone worried about those poor musicians. But if so, why did they send people out there?

She wanted to ask Daken about it without seeming to criticize their traditions, but before she could do so, he dropped his arm from her waist and siezed her hand instead.

"Come. I will show you what the bezhras look like."

He led her over to the steps that had been carved into the thick outer wall. The musicians were just then descending. They seemed pleased by her compliments and her interest in the bezhras and showed her how they were played.

Jocelyn found them as strange as the music they created. They consisted of large leather sacks in which very faint designs could be seen, and from which a series of dark wood pipes decorated with gold protruded. Daken told her that their origins were lost in antiquity. The Kassid had always played them, it seemed, and the haunting music was passed down through the generations to a select few who mastered the difficult art of squeezing the sack and blowing into the pipes.

"It must be dangerous for the musicians who went out there to play," she said as they walked back across the nearly deserted courtyard.

He was silent for so long that she feared that despite her carefully neutral tone, she had insulted one of their traditions. She was about to apologize when he finally spoke.

"No one goes out there, Jocelyn. That was music from our ancestors."

"Wh—what?" she stammered, totally forgetting now about respect for tradition. "Are you saying that was *ghost* music?"

"Yes."

Surely he wasn't serious, she thought. This was just another joke, like the time he told her that the heat in the fortress was magic.

But then she thought about their belief that the ghosts of their ancestors rode with them into battle. Even though they had by now entered the fortress, she drew her cloak more tightly around her and shivered.

"The spirits of our ancestors remain in these hills, and on this night, they remind us of their presence," he said solemnly. "We call to them with the music— and they answer. The only other time we would call would be to summon them to battle.

"There were some who feared that they might not answer this time—that they might remain silent as

Saranne Dawson

a way of telling us that we should not go forth into battle again. But they have answered—and now I think the decision to go to war will be made."

Jocelyn didn't know what to say. She was glad that he seemed so certain now of the alliance, but she simply could not accept that the music she had heard had come from Kassid spirits.

Echoes, she thought suddenly. Surely it must have been echoes she'd heard. She remembered the guide Tanner showing them how voices could echo here in the mountains.

But hadn't that ghostly music seemed different? The rhythms had been the same, but the sequence had been different. Surely no echo could do that.

As soon as they reached Daken's suite, she excused herself and went to her room. She was badly shaken by his insistence that what she'd heard was ghost music—Kassid magic. Time and again, she'd denied to herself that such magic existed, because until this night, she'd seen no evidence of it other than the fortress itself, and it was sufficiently ancient to permit her to disregard its origins.

But now, if Daken were to be believed, she had her proof.

Still, she resisted accepting that proof. People could deceive themselves; she already knew that. She didn't doubt that Daken and his people *believed* that music to have been created by their ancestors—but that didn't necessarily make it so.

And yet, no other explanation presented itself to her as she stood at the window, staring out into the darkness beyond the fortress walls.

Suddenly, she was overcome with longing for her

home—for a place where she understood what was happening around her. The pain was sharp and all-encompassing—far worse than anything she'd felt since coming here. And never had her home seemed farther away.

Then she knew that she didn't want to be alone with her thoughts. So she took off the trousers she'd worn all day with a heavy Kassid sweater and put on one of the gowns she'd brought with her. It was a simple woolen dress in a deep emerald shade that matched her eyes. Over it, she wore a matching vest with fine gold embroidery.

The gown had a deep vee neckline and she decided to wear one of her favorite necklaces with it, a fine gold chain strung with emeralds and pearls. As a final touch, she took out the large, heavy gold ring with the carved insignia of her family. She wanted desperately to recapture her real life beyond these mountains and to remind herself that she was Ertrian and not like these strange people who believed their ancestors returned to speak with them through music.

When Jocelyn entered the great room, Daken and Rina and Tassa were all there, gathered before the fire. Rina immediately exclaimed over Jocelyn's necklace. She'd never seen pearls and was astonished when Jocelyn explained that they came from sea creatures who grew them inside their bodies.

She resolutely kept her eyes away from Daken, who remained seated on the thick rug before the hearth, but she could feel his gaze upon her nonetheless.

Both Rina and Tassa were clearly enthralled with

the idea of such lovely things coming from the sea they'd never seen, and Jocelyn decided she would have necklaces made for both of them when she returned to Ertria. It would make a splendid repayment for all the many kindnesses they'd shown her.

Rina and Tassa began to talk about the day's events and then about the remaining days of the festival. There would be more games, and dancing as well. Rina ran off to her room and returned with a beautifully embroidered dress. She held it up to Jocelyn with a grin of triumph.

"It will fit, I think. This is a dress for dancing. There wasn't time to make one for you, so I borrowed this from my cousin, who has outgrown it."

Jocelyn admired the dress, but then shook her head ruefully. "Unfortunately, the dress will not make me a dancer. Can I learn the steps before tomorrow evening?"

"Oh I'm sure you can. They aren't difficult," Rina assured her.

She then began to talk about the performance of her dance group, who would entertain before the general dancing began. "It's very noisy," she laughed. "We wear special shoes that tap out the rhythms."

"Rina is the best of the group," Tassa said proudly, "even though she had to be forced to take lessons at first. Her mother was a wonderful dancer."

Rina leaned close to Jocelyn, then said in a loud whisper, "Father can't dance—or at least that's what he tells me."

Daken had been silent, but now he turned from

his contemplation of the fire and smiled at his daughter. "Then perhaps tomorrow night, I will *prove* to you that I can't dance."

After that, though, he lapsed into an uncharacteristic silence as the women talked. Soon, both Rina and Tassa proclaimed themselves to be tired and said their good-nights. Jocelyn got up, too, but Daken suddenly looked up at her.

"Please stay for a while, Jocelyn—unless you are tired, too."

She hesitated, then walked back to her chair. She wasn't tired, but she was feeling very confused and still badly shaken over the ghost music.

He stood up and turned his back to the fire, making himself a large, dark silhouette. The flames flickered behind him, and the word "sorcerer" once again came to her mind. She trusted nothing at this point—not that music and not the scene before that in her bedchamber. What was real and what was illusion?

"The music of our ancestors troubles you," he said, making it a statement, not a question. "You still distrust our magic."

"Yes," she replied. "Daken, in my world, ghosts are for children's stories."

"And so were the Kassid until you came here," he said. "But now the Kassid and their ghosts will save your empire."

For a moment, she didn't grasp the significance of what he'd said. In her mind, she was seeing that gulf between them grow ever wider. *I have accepted that we don't have a future*, she thought bitterly, *but now we don't even have this time.*

219

Then his words got through to her and she stared at him. "Do you mean that a decision has been reached—that your people have decided to aid us?"

He nodded. "Word was received from the other fortresses a few days ago. I didn't tell you because no decision had been reached here. There was a group that would not decide until they had assured themselves that the ancestors hadn't turned their backs on us. But now that they have heard the music, they too are willing to fight."

Jocelyn had been perched rigidly on the edge of her chair, and now she sank back with a happy sigh. "If only there were some way of getting word to the palace."

"It may be possible," he stated. "Several men have volunteered to try to get through to the garrison. If they succeed, then word can be passed from there. We can also learn if any attempt has been made by the Menoans to capture the garrison."

"Could I go with them?" she asked eagerly, then subsided when she saw the sudden pain come to his eyes. She wanted to leave, but she didn't want to leave *him*.

He shook his head. "You cannot travel the way they will take, Jocelyn. And even if you could, it would be too dangerous."

There was something in his phrasing and his tone that troubled her, but she didn't pursue it. The truth was that she was glad he had refused her request. She was frightened by the evidence she now had of Kassid magic—but she knew she loved him anyway and wanted to stay here with him for the time allotted to them. Whether she went home now or in another two months would make little difference to the empire—but it would make a very great difference to the empress.

She stood up and extended both her hands to Daken in a formal gesture of gratitude. "Thank you, Daken. Even though the decision was made by all your people, I know that they would not have agreed if you hadn't declared yourself to be in favor of the alliance."

He took her hands with a slight smile. "So tonight you are once again the empress. When I saw you dressed like that, I thought you might have somehow found out already."

She withdrew her hands reluctantly and shook her head. "No. I was merely feeling very homesick and decided to become my real self again."

"Oh? And who have you been until now?"

"I'm . . . not sure. So much has happened."

He nodded, then turned to pour them both some wine. "I think we might celebrate our alliance—if not the war to come."

They drank the wine in silence, both of them thinking about the war they didn't want. Then Daken set down his glass and gave her a level look.

"Jocelyn, you must come to accept us for who and what we are. There will be doubts enough among your people. We *do* have magic, and those who fight alongside us will see that. I think that you have never quite given up the belief that the Kassid are mere legend, despite having spent time with us. Your people will be frightened—both of war and of us, and while you cannot allay their fears about war, you can help them to understand that they have nothing to fear from us."

When she said nothing, he reached out to take her hand. His voice dropped lower.

"And you also must accept *me* for what I am. I want you as much as ever, but I will not come into your bed as anything other than my true self."

"There is more, isn't there—more to being Kassid, I mean? It isn't just the presence of your ancestors?"

The silence that followed that was very great. For a moment, he seemed ready to drop her hand and walk away. Then, instead, he looked straight at her and nodded.

"Yes, there is more."

She saw the fear in his eyes and felt that fear tremble through her as well. A deep, dark abyss opened between them as they stood there with their hands clasped.

"I don't care about the rest of it," she said fiercely. "I love you, Daken—and we have so little time."

She felt him relax—but not completely. Then, finally, he drew her hand up to his lips.

"Perhaps the rest of it doesn't matter. But I want you to be very sure of that, and you cannot be sure unless you know all of it. Think about this, Jocelyn. We will talk tomorrow."

Jocelyn did indeed think about it—far into the long winter night. Was it cowardly not to want your worst fears confirmed? Bravery was not a quality spoken of in connection with women; courage was male. And of course, for that very reason, Jocelyn had determined that she would always be brave. A ruler must always display great strength and courage.

But it wasn't the ruler who faced this situation; it was the woman. Only because of Daken was she able to see the difference between the two.

She tried to rationalize away her fears. He could be referring to *anything*. It could simply be more about their ancestors.

But she knew it wasn't just the ancestors. And as if to confirm that, when she finally fell asleep, her dreams were haunted by wolves—and men who became wolves.

Daken was absent all the next day, and Jocelyn wondered if he might be planning to stay away for days as he had done before. But she recalled his teasing remark that he would show Rina at the festivities that evening how he couldn't dance.

She spent the day enjoying the games and practicing the dance steps. As Rina had said, it wasn't complicated. The formal dances at court required far more skill and attention.

When she had changed into the dress Rina had borrowed for her, Jocelyn found Daken and Tassa awaiting her in the great room of the suite. Rina had already left to join her dance troupe.

Jocelyn could not contain her surprise at Daken's attire. She had never seen him in anything but dark clothing—yet here he was dressed in flowing white trousers and a loose white shirt partially covered by a brightly embroidered vest. Tassa wore white as well, and she would learn that the Kassid always wore that color for their dances.

Daken lifted his arms in a gesture of surrender. "Well, here I am, as promised. You said that I should let Rina see that I am not as perfect as she believes, and she will certainly see that tonight."

Jocelyn laughed, glad for his light mood, though she knew he would not have forgotten his promise that they would talk.

"Have you never danced at the festival?" she asked curiously, recalling that Tassa had said his wife was an excellent dancer.

"Long ago, when I was young and foolish and trying to impress Erina. She was very good and made me feel as clumsy as a hobbled horse. I hope that you haven't become too good in the course of one day."

"Not really," she lied, wondering if she could fake clumsiness.

They entered the Great Hall to find it well filled. Those who didn't intend to dance themselves had gathered on the wide balcony that surrounded the high-ceilinged hall. But on the floor, all was white, with vari-colored accents. It was an impressive sight.

Daken's presence on the floor was greeted with amazement and much good-natured teasing that didn't require translation. She, to her delight and gratitude, was the recipient of many expressions of solidarity and promises that Arrat would never again trouble her empire. The Kassid might have taken their time deciding, but now that the decision was made, they seemed almost eager to go to war.

As they found a place from which they could watch Rina and the others perform, she commented to Daken on her observations.

"It seems that the warrior blood in the Kassid has been awakened. I confess that I am rather surprised at that myself."

"But you don't share it?" she asked.

He shook his head. "I am still a reluctant warrior. But I will do what must be done."

As the musicians and Rina's troupe arranged themselves, Jocelyn thought about a conversation she'd had with Hammad prior to her departure. He had expressed those same sentiments. When she'd questioned how it was that the commander of the army could be so reluctant to go to war, he had told her in his blunt manner that that was as it should be. "A commander who wants to go to war is a very dangerous man," Hammad had said.

He and Daken will like each other, she thought. If only they could be meeting under better circumstances.

Then the music began, and Jocelyn put all thoughts of war from her mind. After the solemn music of the previous night, she hadn't quite known what to expect. But the Great Hall was filled with the sounds of pure joy. Some of the instruments were familiar to her, but others were strange and intriguing. It was the music of a people who loved life, and perhaps for the first time, Jocelyn did not feel that differentness that had so often troubled her.

When Rina and her fellow dancers began their performance, the music died down to mere background accompaniment, and the sounds that filled the hall were the rhythmic tappings of many feet. Jocelyn had already seen the strange shoes with their thick soles and pieces of iron nailed on. She'd thought they couldn't possibly dance in such clumsy looking shoes—but they did.

After the performance, Jocelyn and Daken sought out Rina, and Jocelyn saw that all of the performers were perspiring quite heavily. There was indeed a price to be paid for dancing so lightly in those shoes.

Rina admired her father's costume and made him promise that he would dance with her after she'd had some refreshments and recovered from her efforts. Then she left with the others, and at the same time, the general dancing began.

People danced in groups as they did at the palace, but with the much simpler steps, conversations were possible and there was much laughing and teasing of Daken and encouragement for her own efforts. When Daken circled her waist to whirl her about at one point, he bent close to her ear.

"You did not tell the truth, Jocelyn. You dance as well as anyone here."

So much, she thought, for trying to appear clumsy. She'd never been very good at dissembling.

"And I have yet to see you trip over your feet," she replied just as they parted.

Later, when she watched Daken partner Rina, she decided that his only problem was his size. He stood out even among the very tall Kassid both in height and breadth, and in the confines of the dance groups, he had very little room to maneuver.

Next Daken partnered Tassa, who had dressed for dancing but had to be persuaded out onto the floor. Jakka, Daken's young aide, asked Jocelyn to join him, and she was once again caught up in the merriment.

"I am looking forward to visiting Ertria," Jakka told her, hastening to add that he wished it could be in peace. "What I want most is to see for myself what the sea looks like."

"If there is war," she said, "it will be fought on the plains. The Menoans would never challenge us at sea and the Turveans are land-locked."

Then, seeing his disappointment, she told him that the city was on the sea and he would see it in any event. "Perhaps," she added, "I could arrange for you to go out on a ship, though."

"After we have sent Arrat back into his hole," Jakka stated confidently. "I would like that."

She stared into his handsome young face with those same pale blue eyes and prayed silently that he would survive to take advantage of her offer.

They were so confident, she thought. But weren't all men like that when they ventured into battle? Even with death all around them, did they not believe that they would emerge whole? How else could they fight?

When the dance was over and Jakka had escorted her back to where Daken and Tassa stood talking with some other people, Jocelyn stared at Daken and for the first time thought of the possibility that *he* could be killed.

Jakka was Daken's nominated successor, and he was about the age now that Daken had been when

227

he'd become leader. That thought was chilling, and her expression must have shown it, because Daken quickly asked her what was wrong.

She shook her head. "Nothing—only a stray thought. I am enjoying myself." Then she went on quickly to talk about the differences between the dancing here and the highly stylized form practiced at the palace.

But once that fear had arisen, it refused to be put from her mind. She could not bear to think that Daken could die protecting her empire. Somehow, war had to be prevented.

The festivities were still under way when Daken caught her eye later, after she had danced a round with one of his advisors and listened to yet another statement about the certainty of victory.

She knew even before he spoke that he was going to suggest they have their talk. Music and laughter surrounded her, and she resented the intrusion. But she met his intense gaze and nodded.

They slipped through the crowd and walked back to the suite. The halls were empty and more silent than she'd ever seen. Jocelyn let herself hope one last time that she was wrong—then steeled herself to learn that she was right.

He poured them both some wine, added a few logs to the fire, then turned to face her. She wished that he'd take her into his arms, but he remained apart—and there was no mistaking his nervousness.

"For the first time in my life," he began in a low, musing voice, "I have found myself questioning the need for honesty. And I think too that I now see what it is to be . . . different. That, I suppose, is the price we Kassid have paid for our isolation. If we had continued to live among your people, this conversation would not be necessary and we could instead be doing what we both want to do."

He paused, and their eyes met and heat coursed through her chilled body. She started to rise from her chair, to go to him, but he put out a hand to stay her even as his eyes reflected his hunger.

"From the beginning of time, Jocelyn, there have been those among us who are considered to be especially blessed. It is our belief that these blessed ones enjoy a special closeness to the old gods.

"There are never more than fifty in each generation—and sometimes less. And they are always male. Why, we don't know. It does not follow families; it just happens.

"It has always been our tradition that the leader must be chosen from among the blessed ones, but I think that should change. The qualities that make for a good leader are not always found among us, and there are many not blessed who have those qualities.

"Nevertheless, following that tradition, I have nominated another of the blessed as my successor."

"The eyes," she said in a near-whisper, thinking of Jakka.

"Yes. All Kassid babies are born with eyes that color, but most of them change within the first few weeks of life. That is the first sign."

He paused, then went on in a more hurried manner. "Wolves have always lived here in the Dark Mountains. We believe that they were here even

Saranne Dawson

before the arrival of the old gods and then formed a special bond with them. The gods were so taken by their grace and beauty that they wanted it for themselves as well. And so they used their magic to transform themselves into wolves whenever they chose. That gift was then passed on to the blessed ones among us."

He stopped, his gaze intent as it held hers in supplication. "I know you have cause to fear and hate wolves because they killed your brother. But we cannot control them; they are wild creatures. They will not attack any Kassid, perhaps because of that bond."

She swallowed hard, trying to dislodge the painful lump in her throat. Her hands had turned to ice and she unconsciously twisted them in her lap, trying to warm them. But a strange sort of calmness was stealing slowly over her.

"The wolf I saw at the waterfall—with blue eyes. That wasn't really a wolf."

"No, it was one of us. We didn't know you were coming, and it was pure chance that he came upon your party. When he returned to tell us, we debated what to do—and so lost precious time that cost the lives of your guards."

"But how . . . ?" The question poured out before she could stop it. She knew what she had to know now. Why was she tormenting herself further?

"It happens the first time at around the age of twenty. There is no way I can explain the feeling, Jocelyn. It is simply a knowledge that comes to us—and a need, a need that is even greater than

230

the need a young man has at that age for a woman, and in some ways not so very different from that.

"When we are young, most of us make the change often—just as we want a woman as often as possible. But as we grow older, the need lessens, although it can still be powerful.

"I had not made the change in years—not since Erina's death sent me into the mountains for nearly a month. It was a selfish thing to do because Rina needed me then, but as I said, sometimes the need can be very powerful."

Belatedly, she realized what he was saying. "And you . . . made the change after we went to the tower that time? That's where you were?" She remembered how haggard he had looked upon his return.

"Yes. I was greatly troubled." He paused, then went on softly. "It's the freedom, Jocelyn—the freedom from pain. We are still ourselves, but *different*. It is as though two minds exist at the same time, and the other, the wolf-mind, numbs the pain. Wine can seem to do the same thing—but it is different."

"Then you have to *want* to change?" she asked fearfully. "It can't just *happen*?"

"No, we must want it—and I could never change in your presence, or in the presence of anyone else unless a life were in danger. That usually happens only in battle, which is how the stories you heard came to be."

He came over to her and knelt before her, taking her cold hands between his warm ones. "Jocelyn, you have nothing to fear. With you, I am only a man."

"There were drawings in some of my storybooks," she said in a thin, unnaturally high voice. "They showed a creature that was part-man and part-wolf."

"No," he said, bending over her hands and brushing them with his mouth. "It isn't like that. "The change happens in the blink of an eye."

"B—but how does it *feel*?" she asked, wondering if she could ever forget those drawings.

His warm breath fanned against her hands as he laughed softly. "It feels, my love, the way it feels when a man and woman are joined. But I think you cannot yet understand that."

"No, I can't," she whispered.

"Then I will show you."

He rose to his feet, then reached down to draw her up and into his arms. For a long moment, they simply stared at each other. Then he smiled gently.

"I was so afraid you couldn't accept me," he admitted.

"I have no choice. I love you—all that is you."

He kissed her then, a slow, lingering kiss that poured the heat of desire through them both. Then he lifted her into his arms and carried her from the room, down the hallway to his bedchamber.

Chapter Eight

Daken set her onto her feet and she stood there, swaying slightly on trembling legs as he lit the fire, then dragged the heavy quilt and some pillows from the bed to the hearth before turning back to her.

She was suddenly unsure. Oh, she was certain that she wanted him—the heat that was spreading through her and causing her to tremble all over was proof enough of that. But she was unsure about whether she should give in to that strange feeling.

All the times when, as a child, she had hidden behind draperies or around corners, listening in on conversations among her mother's ladies, tumbled through her mind. She saw the distasteful expression on her aunt's face as she'd delivered her lecture to her orphaned niece on the subject of intimacies between men and women. And she saw too her cousin, weeping piteously on the morning after her wedding night.

Daken came to her, and she involuntarily shrank away from him. He simply stood there silently until she knew that he was waiting for her to explain herself—or accept him.

"I'm afraid," she said when her confused mind could produce no other words.

He reached out then to take her hand, and led her over to the quilt, then gently pushed her down onto it and sat down beside her, close, but not touching.

"I too was afraid the first time," he said quietly, then smiled at her look of astonishment. "Perhaps there are differences, but fear is fear. I thought I might hurt her; I've always worried about that because of my size. And I thought too that I would be . . . inadequate. I've never understood why men seem to have such a need to prove their manhood, while women simply accept their female selves— or so it's always seemed to me.

"I don't know what you've been told, but I think it may be very different with your people. If fear is introduced at an early age, it must be difficult to ignore it when the time comes."

"I used to hide and listen to the women talk when I was little," she admitted. And then she told him about her aunt's lecture, and about her cousin.

"But what about your mother and father?" he asked. "You said that your mother died when you were ten. You must remember something of them—of how they were together."

She nodded slowly, wondering why she hadn't

thought about that. "They were happy. They loved each other very much."

"But you forgot that—and remembered the fear," he stated.

"Yes."

Once again, he took her hand, holding it carefully in his much larger one. "Let me show you how good it can be—for both of us."

She nodded, although some of that fear and uncertainty remained.

He piled the pillows behind him and drew her onto his lap. Through the soft, light fabric of his trousers and her dress, she could feel the rock hardness of his thighs—and then that other hardness.

For a long time, they stayed like that, kissing and touching cautiously, his desire on a taut leash and hers building slowly. Daken feared that at any moment, some unconscious movement on her part, some involuntary sound, would snap that leash. Jocelyn struggled to understand the hunger that was surging through her—and then stopped trying to understand it.

Their clothing fell away gradually, almost unnoticed by either of them until new sensations were revealed in their absence. When her dress had been cast aside, leaving her in the light shift beneath, and when his shirt had joined it, she pressed herself against his hard, bare chest and felt her nipples grow taut beneath their nearly nonexistent covering.

He felt it too and drew her back, then lifted his mouth from hers and covered the aching tips instead, rubbing a tongue against that light veil. Jocelyn cried out in pleasure, and when he mistook that for pain and withdrew, she clutched his head and drew him back again. He laughed softly, and his warm breath fanned against her sensitive skin.

He lingered over every moment, savored every reaction, no matter how small. Never before in his life had he been so immersed in a woman, so attuned to her slightest nuance of movement and sound.

Jocelyn's total awareness of him told her that he too felt every tiny shudder of her awakening body—felt it and played upon it as an accomplished musician plays upon his beloved instrument. In his hands, she had become the instrument from which the very best was drawn for the pleasure of them both.

Their remaining clothes became an unwanted barrier and joined the heap on the floor. Jocelyn stared at him as he stretched out on his side; she'd never seen a naked man before, and despite the evidence she'd felt beneath his clothing, she was unprepared for the reality. Those old whispers of pain came back to hiss through her mind.

He saw her fear and took her hand, guided it to him, then felt her touch—soft and tentative at first, then increasingly bold and exploring. A groan of need driven almost beyond endurance escaped from him, and she drew back immediately.

She thought that she had inadvertently hurt him, then understood that it was pleasure and not pain when he drew her back again. How very strange he felt—hard and smooth.

Then with another groan, he slid his hands beneath her and lay her down onto the quilt. Propped up on one arm, he stared at her in the light of the fire. His gaze traveled slowly over the length of her, then returned to her face.

"You are beautiful," he said simply.

She knew she was; she'd been told that all her life. But for the first time, she *felt* beautiful and knew that it had nothing to do with the beauty that others saw in her.

He began to kiss her, moving after a moment from her mouth to her neck and then to the dark, hard nipples. He drew them into his mouth, each in turn, suckling them gently, and when he left them at last to trail kisses down over her rib cage, she protested and tried to draw him back again.

But he resisted this time and moved lower, pausing to dip his tongue into her navel before moving still lower when she gasped with pleasure.

His mouth had reached the thatch of springy hair before she quite realized that he was invading that most secret of places. She stiffened involuntarily. He raised his head and smiled at her, then moved on to caress her thighs, her knees and down all the way to her toes.

The ache inside her was growing, but it had centered now in that secret part of her, as though everything she'd felt from the first moment he'd touched her had now come together in that place.

He returned to her mouth, covering it hungrily as his hand traced a light path up her leg, along the inside of her thighs—and stopped at the gate to that throbbing need.

She moved slightly, the motion unplanned—and

then his fingers were touching that moist warmth, exploring carefully as he lifted his mouth from hers and stared at her. She knew what he saw—and made no attempt to hide it. The need had become uncontrollable, a wild thing inside her, struggling to be free.

It seemed to her that all the times their eyes had met over these months had now merged into this moment, when no question need be asked because the answer was there.

He was slow and careful even when she wanted him to be fast and reckless, to match her own wild abandon. The pain was brief—gone and forgotten as her body accepted him and made him welcome.

The rhythm built within them, ancient and timeless and all-encompassing. His hardness drove against her softness again and again as a new urgency began to assert itself, a reaching beyond themselves for something unique and powerful.

And then they found it. From one moment to the next, that pounding rhythm became a long, shuddering crescendo that filled their world and then ebbed away slowly, leaving small aftershocks that trembled through them both.

Sated, still enveloped in the soft afterglow, they lay curved about each other, arms and legs entwined haphazardly, as though neither one was quite sure yet which limb belonged to whom. They didn't speak for a long time, since both of them found words to be superfluous.

Jocelyn reached for thoughts, grasped at them, and found them to be elusive. How could so many women have been so wrong? Was it he—this man

238

she'd believed she already loved, although she knew now that she hadn't understood what the word meant?

Or was it magic—Kassid magic? Could there be more that he hadn't told her? A small ripple of uneasiness ran through her, disconnecting her from him for a moment and making her aware of his very different body.

It *was* magic, she decided, but not Kassid magic. It was the unique magic of love, of becoming one with someone after struggling toward that oneness in words and thought.

She thought she should be saying all this to him, but instead remained silent, listening to his quiet breathing. Was he asleep? The question had barely been asked in her mind before she too fell away into oblivion.

Daken resisted awakening, fought it because the dream was too pleasant. He drifted as long as possible in that strange place between sleep and consciousness, feeling her beside him, an arm resting lightly on his chest, long hair spilling feather-light against his shoulder, a slim leg resting atop his.

But no matter how hard he tried, it was a place he could not remain—and so he awoke and opened his eyes.

For one brief moment, he felt a surge of icy fear. Dreams, no matter how pleasant, had no place in the waking world—yet she was still there.

He moved slowly, carefully shifting onto his side to stare at her. She made a sleepy, contented sound and accommodated herself to his movement.

The memories began to flood through him. He smiled as he let them surge forth. He felt them with a sense of wonder. Not ever—not even in the beginning—had it been this good with Erina. And yet he'd loved her. But if that had been love—and he was sure it must have been—then what was this, this sense of wholeness?

He continued to stare at her, seeing the woman but thinking now of the empress. What had the gods done to him, giving him this woman he could not keep? And why, as he lay here with her, did he believe that he could?

There were those among them who claimed from time to time to hear the whispers of the gods, but Daken had never been one of them. In fact, he believed that the gods paid them little attention, apart from a distant sort of benevolence. But now it seemed he *did* hear something—words he strained to hear but couldn't quite understand.

The whispers of the gods, said those who believed in them, always spoke of good things.

Her dark lashes began to flutter against her fair skin, and then, before he was prepared for it, her emerald eyes were staring at him in shock.

He leaned over to kiss her, then kept his mouth close to hers. "We are real, Jocelyn. This is no dream."

She nodded, unable yet to speak. In that brief, waking moment, she had been certain it was only a dream. Then the memories that had inundated him flowed through her as well. He seemed to understand that, because he remained silent and unmoving.

Then, after a time, he kissed her again and his hand began to trail lightly over her body, raising a pleasant, tingling awareness. She turned on her side and pressed herself against him and felt his arousal with a quickening of her pulse.

This time, it seemed that they moved in slow motion, capturing and holding each sensation. He was more careful still, certain that she must be bruised and sore. She was bolder, both letting him know what she wanted and exploring the still strange terrain of his body with curiosity.

But if the prelude was different, the mind-shattering conclusion was the same—that increasingly rapid and desperate climb to the peak and then the dazzling fall into ecstasy.

They slept again and awoke to sunlight stealing around the edges of the draperies. This awakening was different. Already, they had grown comfortable in each other's arms. It seemed to them both that they had known no other way—that there could *be* no other way.

As they shifted arms, legs and bodies, seeking still greater closeness, they heard muted sounds beyond the door—Tassa and Rina. Jocelyn raised her head in sudden alarm, but he drew it down again, claiming her mouth with a lingering kiss.

"They know," he said in a low, husky voice. "We left the dance early, and the door to your bedchamber is open. Our feelings have not been hidden, beloved. If they are surprised, it is only that we've waited so long."

"But what will Rina think?" Jocelyn was putting herself in the girl's place, wondering how she would have felt if she'd discovered that her father had put another woman in her mother's place. Perhaps he had from time to time, but Rina would have had no knowledge of it.

"Rina is very fond of you," he said without concern, then proceeded to drive all thought from her mind.

It was mid-morning before they left his chamber, and both Rina and Tassa were gone. Daken left, too—and Jocelyn was alone with her thoughts.

For a time, she thought of nothing but that glorious awareness of herself, an awareness given to her by Daken, who had shown her again and again during the night the pleasures her body could provide. Small pieces of that night would fill her mind, leaving her with a voluptuous certainty that this body she lived in had undergone a dramatic transformation.

Still, as that feeling began to subside, all the thoughts she had suppressed rushed in to fill the void. Her worst fears about the Kassid—about Daken himself—had been confirmed. A wolf lived inside the man she loved.

Daken began to emerge in her mind as two men—the gentle lover and the dark Kassid sorcerer. She loved him and knew that the price of that love was acceptance of his differentness. It seemed to her to be not too high a price, and when she was being totally honest with herself, she would admit that his differentness was a part of his attraction—the thrill of the unknown and unknowable.

Tassa returned to the suite as Jocelyn was about

to leave, and she discovered to her very great relief that the older woman treated her no differently. She let herself hope now that Rina too would accept what had happened.

But when she returned to the suite late in the day, she found Rina and Daken there, talking quietly. His arm was draped around her shoulder, and the girl had obviously been crying. That rush of heat Jocelyn felt at the sight of Daken cooled quickly as Rina looked up and saw her.

Rina, however, leapt up and ran to Jocelyn, then hugged her tightly. "Don't leave us, Jocelyn. I want you to stay. Father loves you and needs you—and so do I."

Jocelyn held Rina and stared beyond her to Daken, her own pain now growing to meet the girl's. All through the day, she'd thought only of the time when they could return to his bed. Not once had she thought about the future they didn't have.

"I have explained to her that we love each other, but cannot stay together," Daken said, the pain reflected in his eyes as well. "She will understand in time."

Struggling to keep the anguish from her voice, Jocelyn kissed Rina's smooth brow. "I love you too, Rina, and I'm glad you want me to stay. But I cannot. Remember that I am the leader of my people as your father is the leader here. You would not want him to give that up—and neither can I."

Rina nodded finally and hugged Jocelyn again, then left them alone. And as the days passed, she seemed to understand—or at least she said nothing more.

Saranne Dawson

Daken's bedchamber became a place of enchantment, a refuge from the dark future. There, they brought pleasure to each other and to themselves—and lived from one passionate moment to the next.

But there were times—though both tried to hide it—when they stared at each other with haunted expressions. A single word, a sentence left incomplete, a casual reference to the future—any and all these things tormented them by pulling them, however briefly, out of their passion for each other.

The days and weeks passed. After a brief hiatus during the festival, the snows came again. Soon, the hills of snow piled up in the courtyard became so high that men began to shovel it into carts and carry it to the bridge, where they then dumped it into the ravine. But even when the courtyard had been cleared, the bitter cold kept nearly everyone indoors. Even the Kassid had limits to their tolerance for frigid weather.

Jocelyn had assumed that the men who had volunteered to go to the garrison were being delayed by the resumption of bad weather, and so she was surprised when two young men appeared one day in Daken's suite to say that they had news of the garrison.

As Jocelyn looked into their pale blue eyes, she suddenly realized how it was that they'd survived the trip—and why Daken had said that she could not "travel the way they would take." Only as wolves could they have made such a journey.

The garrison remained secure, they reported, and Balek spies had discovered that the Menoan force that had captured the Western Road had either been decimated by the winter weather or had retreated. Only a single squadron remained.

They told her that the garrison commander had received the news of the alliance with great pleasure and had quickly dispatched some Balek volunteers to the city to report the news to Hammad.

Word had also come from the city by a circuitous route that the Ertrians were faring well enough. The storehouses had been well-filled with coal before the Menoans cut off the Western Road, and the winter in Ertria had thus far been milder than usual.

The garrison commander had given them a letter for her from Hammad, but when she asked for it, they hesitated, shooting beseeching glances at Daken.

Then she understood even as Daken explained to her that as wolves, they could not carry letters. Hiding her discomfort at being forced to face this dark aspect of the Kassid, she merely nodded as Daken hurried on to explain that they had approached and left the garrison as men.

She wondered silently what the men at the garrison thought when they saw two men walk out of the mountains in the midst of winter—and then return again. Undoubtedly, new legends would be added to the old.

One of the men had read the letter and now repeated it to Jocelyn. Her uncle had assumed the title of regent in her absence. The nobles were behaving no worse than usual—and in a few cases, better, since they feared the war to come.

The court was still in mourning for her father,

who Hammad said had died peacefully with family members and himself in attendance. Near the end, Hammad had written, he had awakened briefly to say that the Kassid would be returning to Ertria.

Jocelyn was glad that he'd died secure in his belief that her mission would be successful, but she wondered if it had been merely a dying man's hope—or some strange foreknowledge.

The confinement forced upon her by the weather gave Jocelyn far too much time to worry about the future. Daken was increasingly busy, and the council meetings she'd attended were far fewer as he spent more time with his newly appointed military commanders.

So one day, when the snow had given way to brilliant sunshine and deep blue skies, if not to warmer weather, she asked Daken if they could visit the mirror-tower again. He too seemed to want to escape, so they set off late one morning, with Daken carrying a basket containing bread, wine and cheese for their lunch.

Unlike their previous trip, this time Jocelyn found others walking the hallways of the unused portion of the fortress. Daken commented that one could always tell how late in the winter it was by the number of people taking their exercise up here in these remote reaches of the vast fortress.

At one point, Jocelyn heard thundering footsteps approaching from an intersecting hallway and looked at Daken questioningly. But he simply stopped and drew her back against the wall as a large group of young men came running past.

When they had gone, he explained that it was

part of their military training, and what had been a pleasant outing became, for Jocelyn at least, considerably less so. She knew that the men were practicing their swordsmanship and archery in the Great Hall or in the courtyard, but she had avoided watching them just as she avoided anything connected to the future.

Still, it took only something like the sudden appearance of the future warriors to remind her that she could not deny that future completely.

They climbed the final staircase in silence, then entered the circular room. Daken lit the fire and they went out onto the balcony to find two men working on the tower. One of them explained that it had sustained some damage from the winds that had howled around the fortress the previous night, although the great mirror was intact.

Their work was finished by midday, and they all stood in the windy cold peering off at the distant mountains for the daily signals. Before long, they all saw the one long flash of light from the closer fortress: the "all's well" signal. Then, a few minutes later, the distant mirror at the other fortress began to blink on and off irregularly. This went on for many minutes as the men watched intently. Jocelyn peered at Daken to see if the news were bad, but his expression was impassive. One of the other men grunted unhappily at one point, however.

When the light blinked out for the last time, Daken told her that there'd been a zhakazh—a snowslide—near their fortress. It was bad enough to delay the arrival of the warriors from that fortress by a week or so in the spring.

"The rest of it was a personal message," he told her. "Normally, we do not permit those, since there would be too many. But an exception was made in this case. The grandmother of a woman at that fortress is close to death here, and her granddaughter wanted her to know that she has given birth to her first child. That happy news will ease her final days, though I know that she had hoped to live to see her first great-grandchild."

"How does she fare, Sattar?" Daken asked, turning to one of the men.

"Very poorly, Daken. I think this good news will arrive barely in time."

Jocelyn watched as the other man began to pull on the ropes to tilt the mirror and send a signal to the other fortresses. She was thinking again about the wonder of such a device. A sketch of it had already been drawn for her, showing in detail how it was constructed.

Someday, she vowed silently, when we have peace again, I will see that these towers stretch all the way across Ertria—and then even to Balek. Perhaps even into the Dark Mountains themselves.

But then that pain that was never far away these days seized her once again. What good would it do to be able to communicate in such a manner with Daken? It might only make the pain worse.

She had a sharp, sad vision of herself standing on the outer wall of the palace, alone, watching for such a signal to be relayed by the towers that marked the great distance between them.

But she'd become good at hiding this pain from

Daken, as she assumed he was hiding it from her. They talked often about the war to come—but never about its aftermath.

Still, she wasn't quite as adept as usual about hiding it this day, and when the two men had left, Daken drew her into his arms, parting both their heavy cloaks so that the warmth of their bodies could intermingle. No words were exchanged between them. There was no need.

Then she broke away from him, but held onto his hand as she walked over to the edge where she'd had that frightening episode before. When she stopped at the low wall, Daken circled her waist tightly.

"You were right," she exclaimed. "I don't have that feeling of falling this time."

They stood there for a time, staring off at the magnificent vista of mountains and deep ravines. Then, as the icy wind picked up, they went back into the circular room where the fire had heated it to a cozy warmth.

They ate their lunch in silence. Jocelyn knew what *she* was thinking about, but after a time, she began to wonder at his silence. He was better than she was at concealing his pain, though she saw it occasionally in his eyes.

Finally, he raised those eyes to meet hers. When he spoke, his voice was low and uncertain—very unusual for him. She felt herself stiffen involuntarily.

"I was not going to tell you about this, and I know that I may be raising false hopes. But the pain I see

249

in you cuts me to the bone, Jocelyn." He paused, then went on more quickly.

"There have always been those among us who claim to hear what we call the 'whispers of the gods'. I had never heard such things myself, and I admit that I doubted their existence. I've always thought that the gods pay no attention to us as individuals.

"But for weeks now, I think I *have* been hearing them. It's hard to explain—and harder still to determine if they're real or merely my own hopes." He paused, looked away, then turned back to her.

"I think that a way will be found for us to be together—to stay together."

She drew in her breath sharply as hope flared brightly within her. But just as quickly, it died again—not quite becoming cold, but no more than a faint, glowing ember.

"But how?"

He shook his head. "That I don't know. If the gods *are* whispering to me, they are not pointing the way. That is why I still doubt it."

There *is* no way, she wanted to shout. The only way that could happen would be if Arrat succeeds in conquering the empire and I am forced into exile here. But if that happens, even the Kassid will no longer be invulnerable and war will come sooner or later to the Dark Mountains as well.

"I spoke of this with one of the elders," he went on. "She has heard these whispers many times over her life, and they have always been accurate. She has no notion of what it might mean, but she reminded me that many of our people have always believed that there is magic that was lost over the years—more gifts from the gods that have fallen away, perhaps from lack of need."

Jocelyn said nothing. She did not dare let herself hope. She had come to accept that the Kassid had magic, but she could not believe that that magic could help the two of them. She considered it highly likely that Daken had been right when he'd said that the gods paid no attention to them as individuals.

They finished their lunch and sat for a time before the fire. Daken piled up the pillows and drew her onto his lap and what began as mere kisses and caresses quickly escalated. They had only to be in each other's presence to feel that hunger, and touching as they were now stoked those fires to dangerous levels.

When he began to peel away the thick Kassid sweater she had worn beneath her cloak, she put out a hand to stop him.

"Someone might come."

He pulled the sweater over her head, then smoothed down her hair and kissed her. "No one will come. This is my private place, and the midday message time has passed."

"But those men were here this morning," she pointed out as her voice grew husky with desire.

"And I knew they would be," he said, now beginning to pull off her heavy woolen trousers. "No one comes up here other than at midday without first asking my permission."

He stripped off her remaining clothes, then rid

251

himself of his own. Her fear of discovery merged into a fierce hunger as she stared at that big, hard body she'd come to know so well.

His eyes glowed in the firelight as he saw her watching him. They enjoyed this game—staying apart when their bodies clamored to be together. She was half-reclining on her heavy cloak, and now he did the same, keeping them tantalizingly close, yet apart. Almost always, it was she who could stand it no longer. When he teased her about it, she told him it was his age that made the difference, reminding him in her own teasing that he'd once thought himself too old for her.

Today was no exception. By the time she moved to him with a cry, her body had become so voluptuously heavy with wanting that she could barely move.

He lifted her quickly atop him and entered her with a deep groan, proving that his need did indeed match hers. Together, they rode the wild storm of passion as cries and groans echoed from the stone walls.

But if they lived for these wild joinings, they enjoyed too the quiet aftermath, lying together as their bodies slowly separated. He drew her down beside him and caressed her heated flesh that even now gave forth a muted response.

Then, after a time, he propped himself on one elbow and stared down at her intently. "Marry me, Jocelyn."

"M—marry you? But . . ."

He stilled her with a kiss, then began to toy with a few strands of her hair as he continued to stare at her. "There will never be anyone else for either of us; we both know that. It is all we have to give each other.

"There is another reason as well—a reason dictated by our positions. It is all well and good that Arrat will soon know we have formed an alliance, but alliances can be broken. An alliance formed through marriage, on the other hand, is a bond that cannot be broken. If Arrat knows we are married, he might well think twice about making war against you."

She felt a sudden anger at his calm, reasonable words, though she could not dispute them. "You sound like any other ruler, Daken—making a marriage for political reasons."

"That is *your* way, not ours," he pointed out gently. "I meant only that there is an advantage in the marriage that we should consider beyond the commitment we make to each other."

"You're right," she said after a moment. And he *was* right—about all of it. But would making that commitment mean less pain or more? In the end, she decided it would make little difference, except that they would be telling all what they already knew—that they belonged together even if they were to be forever kept apart.

"But when I am gone," she said, finding the words difficult to say, "not right away, but in time, won't you want other women?" She'd always understood men to be that way.

He didn't answer immediately, but she saw the hurt in his eyes and looked away. He reached out to draw her back again.

"Jocelyn, there will be no other women—and there wouldn't be even if we didn't marry. I've known that for a long time—even before I took you into my bed."

When she opened her mouth to speak, he put a finger to her lips. "I know what you're going to say—that I probably felt the same way when Erina died. You're wrong. I didn't think about other women for a long time, of course, but there was never that certainty that I feel now. What we have found comes only once in a lifetime to a very few, and it is enough for me that I have had it for a while. Living in the memory of what we've had will make me happier than sharing my bed with another woman."

She hadn't intended to cry. She was always careful not to let him see her pain, lest it make his worse. But the tears began to roll down her cheeks silently, and she buried her face in his chest. He'd put into words all that she too felt—except that it would never be enough for her to remember what they'd had for a while.

Jocelyn stood patiently as the two seamstresses fit the creamy white wool gown to her. The fabric was finer than anything she'd seen yet—even here, where the wool from those strange goat-like creatures was already superior to that in Ertria.

She had designed her wedding dress herself, having already decided to wear it for the ceremony at the palace as well. The neck was high and plain, which would allow her to display the most elaborate piece of jewelry she owned—a gift from her father when he had officially named her his heir. It was a magnificent creation of gold and silver woven into tiny chains and threaded with diamonds, emeralds, and pearls. She wished that she had brought it with her, although as she'd observed wryly to Daken, she hadn't exactly come here to be married.

The sleeves of the gown were snug to the elbows, then flared out to her wrists, a style she liked but one with which the Kassid seamstresses were unfamiliar. The bodice was closely fitted, and the long skirt was a full circle, allowing the beautiful fabric to move in sumptuous ripples when she walked.

Finally, the seamstresses had finished, and she was left alone in her bedchamber—or rather, that which had been her bedchamber. Now it had become a refuge—a place she hastened to when that terrible sadness overtook her.

Worst of all, she felt now that she was alone in her sadness. Daken truly seemed to believe in these "whispers of the gods." How she wished she could share his faith. Her people nominally worshipped the gods; the palace had more than its share of mumbling priests. But only the ignorant peasants truly believed in them anymore.

And yet, there were times when she remembered that ghostly music on the first night of the Turning, and she questioned her lack of belief. If the spirits of the ancestors truly existed, didn't that mean that the gods existed as well?

She walked over to the window and saw that the break in the bad weather had brought the men outside for arms practice. Usually, she tried to avoid seeing them, but today she forced herself to

Saranne Dawson

stand there watching. In another month, Daken had told her, the weather should permit them to leave the fortress to begin the long journey back to the palace—and to war.

Half of the men were practicing with the stubby-looking bows and arrows, aiming at targets set up against the outer wall. The targets were silhouetted warrior figures, and as she watched, she saw arrow after arrow pierce the spot where the heart would be. The Kassid were skilled bowmen; they shot for hunting and for pleasure as well.

The rest of the men were lined up in opposing rows, practicing with their strange short swords, which had been blunted with pieces of leather. She'd told Daken that Hammad was going to be surprised at these weapons, since the Ertrian army used swords twice that length.

"I doubt they'll continue to use them once they've seen the advantages of these," Daken had replied confidently.

Something was changing in him, she thought. More and more when she looked at him, she saw a warrior. He remained the same gentle, affectionate man she so loved—but there was a subtle difference now. She felt it, but couldn't explain it.

She hadn't really expected to find him out there, but when she did, she was surprised that she hadn't noticed him before. Perhaps it was because the men nearest him were almost as big as he was—a rare occurrence even here.

The man lined up opposite him was as tall as he was, though not as heavy. When the two lines began to advance cautiously across the twenty feet that separated them, Jocelyn looked away. She could not bear to think of Daken fighting, even in practice.

But even so, she might have looked back if there hadn't been a tap on her door just then. When she called out, Rina poked her curly head around the edge of the door and scanned the room with a disappointed look.

"I thought I might see you in your gown."

"They just left to make the final adjustments." Jocelyn smiled. To her very great relief and pleasure, Rina was happy about the marriage. She hadn't been sure that would be the case, since the girl had said nothing about their relationship after that one time.

"Shouldn't you be in school?" Jocelyn asked as Rina came into the room and flopped onto the bed.

"I was helping Tassa and the others. Father said I could."

Jocelyn sighed. "I should be helping them as well. I'm afraid that I'm just too accustomed to having servants to do such things."

"They can manage. Everyone loves to help for wedding feasts. Jocelyn, do you think you could persuade Father to let me come with you when you go home? I really want to see your palace and the wedding there, too. But he says it's too dangerous."

"He's right," Jocelyn said gently. "This would not be a good time. But as soon as it's safe for you to come, you will."

"But if it's not safe for me, then it's not safe for you, either."

"That's true enough—and your father tried to persuade me to remain here as well. But I *must* go.

257

I'm the empress, and I've been away for too long already."

Rina was silent for a moment, then looked at Jocelyn sadly. "How will you and Father stand it—being married and living so far apart?"

"We will stand it because we must," Jocelyn said, hoping she wasn't going to break down and cry again. "We've talked about it, and we plan to build a place for us somewhere that is halfway between the Dark Mountains and the city. That way, we can make annual trips to see each other."

"But that's awful!" Rina exclaimed. "I think that would be even worse than not seeing each other at all."

Jocelyn said nothing, but ever since Daken had ventured the suggestion, she'd thought the same thing. How could she face a lifetime of good-byes?

"Father told me about the whispers of the gods," Rina said. "He believes there is a way you will be together. I think it is only his hope that is whispering to him."

"I fear that you are right," Jocelyn admitted. "But he says that your people have always believed there is magic that has been lost over the years."

"Well, if it's lost, it's likely to remain lost," Rina replied unhappily.

She got up from the bed and walked over to the window. "Father loved you from the very beginning, you know. It was in his eyes when he sat here while you were so sick."

"But he didn't know me then," Jocelyn pointed out.

"I think he knew what you would be like. He said

you were brave and strong—and beautiful, too, of course." She turned and grinned.

Jocelyn thought about the first time she'd looked up into his eyes, and about his great gentleness with her. If she hadn't been so sure then that he was responsible for the deaths of her Guards, she knew she would have felt the same.

The golden rings lay in a golden box, side by side in a bed of deepest black. Jocelyn and Daken were alone in the suite. All the others awaited them down in the Great Hall, the only place in the fortress large enough to contain the crowd that wanted to celebrate their leader's marriage.

Her gown had been delivered only a short time ago, and it fit her perfectly, proving that the Kassid seamstresses were at least the equal of her women at the palace. She had decided against any other adornment after Daken had told her about their custom of exchanging rings.

Daken was dressed in what she assumed was his most formal attire—a loose-fitting black shirt and trousers in the same fine wool as her gown. The full trousers were tucked into high black boots polished to a mirror-shine. Over the shirt, he wore a black wool vest heavily embroidered with silver and gold threads.

Jocelyn smiled as she thought about the reaction of her court to such attire. The men at court very nearly outdid the women in their fondness for bright colors and jewelry of all kinds.

He'd already explained to her that it was their custom for the couple to exchange rings in private, to be followed by a lavish feast. It signified, he said, that marriage was both a very private and a very public affair.

She bent over the box containing the rings and saw that they had carved designs.

"The carvings are ancient symbols for good fortune, health, and happiness," he said when he saw her examining them. Then he picked up the smaller of the two rings and slid it onto her finger, then stood there staring down at it.

"I know that I was the one who wanted this marriage, but now I realize how unnecessary it is—except perhaps to prevent war. I think we have been married in spirit from the very beginning, Jocelyn. There is a line from an old love poem that I now understand, after all these years—*You are the missing part of my soul, the part I never knew to be missing until you made me whole.*"

He drew her hand to his lips, and when he released it, she lay it against his cheek.

"What a beautiful poem," she said in a husky voice. "I confess that I have little faith in the gods—or *had* little faith until I met you. Now I think perhaps they have proved their existence—and their mercy for my failure to believe. They have given me you, a man I would never have dared to dream could exist."

As she spoke, she picked up the other ring and slid it onto his finger, noticing almost absently that her hand was trembling—not from the fear that most women felt at such a time, but from the sheer force of the love she had for him.

In a very brief period of time, she had gone from

one who disbelieved in love to a woman truly over-whelmed by its power.

They held each other quietly for a long time, her head resting against his chest and his long arms encircling her gently. Lately, they'd found so often that they had no need to speak with words. What they felt seemed to pass from one to the other without words.

Finally, Daken dropped his arms, then picked up her hand. "If we don't go down there now, we may be the first couple in the history of my people to forgo the pleasures of the feast for the pleasures of the bed."

She laughed. "Does tradition dictate that we must remain there very long?"

"Long enough to eat, in any event," he smiled. "Unfortunately, I've noticed that you take quite a long time at that for one who eats so little."

"I'll be faster tonight," she promised, stretching up to give him a quick kiss. Then she shook her head ruefully.

"One would think that tonight will be the first time we've made love."

"Every night *is* a first time for us, zherisa," he replied, using the Kassid word for 'beloved'.

And so it was, she thought. No matter how many times they made love and no matter how well she had come to know her own body and his, the flames of passion engulfed them anew every time they touched.

Daken led her to the balcony overlooking the Great Hall, and as soon as they were spotted, the huge crowd grew silent for a moment and then erupted into shouts and whistles and clapping. The Kassid, she had learned during the festival, could be a joyfully raucous group—even those like Tassa who were normally restrained.

There was eating and drinking and music and dancing, all of it happening simultaneously. What a pleasant contrast it made to the false posturing and rigidly prescribed behavior of her court. The Kassid simply enjoyed themselves and each other.

And children were present as well, down to the tiniest babes in arms. No one ever brought children to court. She had advisors whose children she'd never even seen. Only she and her brother had ever been to court as children, and then they'd been coached strictly about their behavior, forced to play the role of small adults.

The Kassid, by contrast, were very indulgent with their children. Little ones scampered about among the adults playing games with abandon, and other than making certain they didn't get hurt or over turn the heavily laden tables, the adults ignored their antics.

"Daken," she said after watching all this, "I fear that you are going to hate my court very quickly."

"From all that you have told me about it, I wonder that *you* can tolerate it."

"I've never known anything else—until these past few months," she pointed out.

And she wondered if she *would* be able to tolerate it. She knew that she had changed greatly during her time here—and yet the court would have remained the same.

As soon as the traditional toasts had been made

and the songs sung, and after they had circulated through the crowd and complimented those who had worked so hard for this, Daken took her hand and leaned close to whisper that they could now make their escape.

"But we've been here only an hour or so," Jocelyn protested. They would never be able to get away with this at the palace.

"They will enjoy themselves without us," he said as he began to lead her away. "And they will forgive us for having other things on our minds."

As soon as Daken had opened the door into the suite, he swept her into his arms and strode down the hallway to his bedchamber. She gasped when she saw it.

"Oh Daken, this is wonderful! But the winter garden must be bare of flowers now."

Huge golden and silver vases had been filled with all the lovely flowers she'd seen in the winter garden. Their scent filled the large chamber. The fire had been lit, and on a low table near the hearth was a magnificent golden tray with jewelled edges, containing a gem-studded gold wine carafe and two tiny goblets.

He set her down and she walked over to the hearth. "I've never seen this before. It's . . . beautiful." It was in fact the most exquisite thing she'd ever seen. Words simply could not describe it.

"It belongs to us all," he explained. "It's very ancient. No one really knows its origins, so naturally there are those who say it too is a gift from the gods."

"They may be right," she said, picking up the

fragile goblet to peer at the tiny gems worked into intricate designs all over the cup and stem.

He picked up the carafe and poured a dark golden liquid into both goblets. "This is a special wine, made in very small quantities because the berries are quite rare."

He paused and smiled. "It is believed to have, ah, certain qualities that can prove beneficial on a wedding night."

Jocelyn had been sniffing at it, and when he finished, she very dramatically set it down, then took his from his hand as well.

"I think we had better forgo that tradition. There is such a thing as *too* much, Daken."

But they did eventually drink the wine as they sat naked before the fire. Perhaps it made a difference. In any event, Jocelyn was proved wrong—there could *never* be too much for them.

Chapter Nine

For the first time since her arrival in the Dark Mountains, Jocelyn felt warm. Not even Daken's warning that this was undoubtedly a false spring could dampen her pleasure at being outdoors again without so many layers of clothing. For two days now, they'd lived with the incessant sounds of melting snow dripping from the roofs and balconies of the fortress.

They rode across the bridge behind the first hunting party to go out in several months. Both men and horses were clearly in high spirits. Jocelyn had wanted to exercise her horse, but Daken had insisted that she ride a Kassid horse because the trails would still be icy in places. Having seen the incredible agility of the ungainly animals, she'd acquiesced.

The hunting party soon turned off onto another

trail, leaving Daken and Jocelyn alone on the main trail. Because this part of the trail lay in sunshine most of the day, it was nearly bare, although deep snow still covered the steep slopes and hung in great, dripping clumps from the tall firs.

They rode in a companionable silence, although they exchanged frequent glances. It seemed that they couldn't keep their eyes from each other for very long—as though each still doubted the other's existence.

Daken had become an extension of herself—the eternally mysterious, unknowable part. He was open and honest and willing to discuss his feelings, but the mystery remained. Most of the time, she simply ignored that mystery, but every so often, something would happen to threaten her peace of mind.

Jocelyn thought about a conversation the day before with Tassa, as they'd both watched the men-at-arms practice in the courtyard. She was forcing herself to watch this now, knowing she must accept what almost certainly lay ahead.

Tassa was normally a quiet woman, rarely exposing her feelings. But after a long silence, she had turned to Jocelyn with a proud gleam in her eyes.

"Now I begin to understand what it means to be Kassid," she said. "Always I have known who and what we are—but it seemed so much a part of the past. Now I can *feel* it. Do you feel the difference, Jocelyn?"

Jocelyn acknowledged that she had and Tassa had gone on.

"Something that has slept for centuries is now awakening. Perhaps it is the ancestors. Even though they've not yet been called to battle, their spirits know what is to come. I hate war—as we all do—but there is something good in this feeling."

As they rode along in the bright sunshine, Jocelyn cast a sidelong glance at Daken and continued to think about Tassa's remarks. She *did* feel the difference, though not in the way Tassa had. She'd felt that differentness in the Kassid from the beginning, but the feeling had grown steadily stronger these past few weeks.

She felt it most of all, of course, with Daken. From the beginning, she'd sensed his quiet pride, but now that pride seemed to come rather close to arrogance, as though it had been honed to a sharper edge. His behavior toward her and others hadn't changed—but *something* had changed.

She broke the silence between them by relating to him that conversation with Tassa.

He nodded. "She is right. Something *has* awakened in us. Our legends tell us that the old gods created the Kassid to defend their sacred mountains, and if that is true, then we were warriors from the very beginning. We've been at peace for a very long time now, so we have perhaps forgotten our purpose." He paused, then went on in a softer tone.

"And may the gods grant us a long period of peace again, when this is over."

Jocelyn, who tried to hold her tongue when he spoke of certain victory, didn't succeed this time.

267

"Hammad has fought and won many battles. In fact, he's never lost. And yet I know that he cannot be this certain of victory."

"Hammad is not Kassid," Daken said succinctly, with that trace of arrogance that she often heard in him now.

As they lapsed into silence again, Jocelyn began to think about the long journey back to Ertria—back to a life that had grown very distant indeed. How would her court react to this army of proud warriors who would be descending upon them? Might they not fear the Kassid as much as they feared Arrat's army? They wouldn't have the advantage she'd had of seeing these people in their normal lives. What they would see was an army of fierce, arrogant warriors, led by a man whose mere physical presence would be intimidating to them.

And a man who was married to their empress, thereby gaining even greater stature and power. They might well believe that Daken had gotten what Arrat had once sought, and that one evil had been exchanged for another. Furthermore, if Daken showed his dislike of the way the court operated, some of them could well decide that they would be better off with their empress married to Arrat.

She continued to think about that for a time, then reluctantly faced up to feelings that had been growing stealthily within her for some time. Didn't she too fear that Daken would usurp her authority—not deliberately, but simply by being who and what he was? By marrying him, hadn't she placed her right to rule in even greater danger?

She hated these thoughts, because she loved the man. But they were the thoughts of an empress, not a woman, and she would soon become empress.

While she lingered in her thoughts, Daken had led them off the main trail and onto another that was just barely discernible. Now those thoughts vanished beneath a rush of pleasure as they emerged from the thick woods.

Before them lay a great meadow, a long, south-facing slope where the dark firs had given way to open land. The sun had melted away all the snow, and the field was ablaze with brilliant scarlet and purple flowers with long, feathery leaves. They rippled in the light breeze, creating a scene of such astonishing beauty that Jocelyn was totally entranced.

"I had hoped they would be blooming," Daken said with satisfaction. "These flowers exist nowhere but in this meadow and a smaller one not far from here."

He dismounted and tied his horse to a tree at the meadow's edge, then lifted her from her saddle. She stood there, still staring at the scene, thinking of nothing at all except that there was no place else she wanted to be. After a long winter when the outdoors was always black, gray, or white, these brilliant flowers beneath a blue sky seemed truly a miracle.

Magic, she thought. Is it any wonder that the Kassid believe in it, living in such a place?

After he had tethered her horse, Daken came up to her and took her hand, then began to wade through the flowers that were knee—high to him but reached nearly to her waist.

She pulled them both to a halt. "Daken, we're trampling the flowers."

He laughed and waved his free hand around them. "There's a whole field full of them. The few we trample will be back next year."

She shrugged and gave in, although it still seemed wrong to her to mar the exquisite beauty of the place. They waded through the wonderfully sweet-smelling flowers until they had reached the very center of the meadow. Daken stopped and drew her into his arms.

"I want to make love to you here. I've been thinking about this for days." His voice was low and husky as he buried his face in her unbound, wind-ruffled hair.

"Here?" she gasped, already feeling the powerful pull of her never-ending need for him. "But . . ."

"We're alone. If anyone else should come along the trail, they'll see our horses and stay away."

Jocelyn felt both terribly exposed and strangely excited. Both emotions trembled through her as he pushed the cloak from her shoulders and began to undress her with fumbling fingers that betrayed his urgency.

Freedom! She'd never felt such a wonderful, wild freedom. The warm breeze played over her bare skin and surrounded her with the lush fragrance of the flowers. Their brilliant colors added a rich sensuality to a scene that needed no more.

Daken was much faster at casting off his own clothes. They embraced, her soft curves molding themselves easily to his hard angles. The flowers nodded their approval and a few feathery stems brushed against their naked skin.

Then they fell onto the cloak he had spread, surrounded by the heady scent of the flowers and the deeper, darker aroma of rich, damp earth.

There was a different, richer texture to their lovemaking this day—an urgency to match the perfection of the scene and a certainty that this was a moment to be captured in its uniqueness.

The miraculous meadow became part of their shattering climax—brilliant flowers exploding against the blue sky as they offered up their own version of perfection.

Afterward, they lay there with their bodies entangled and sated, simply staring up through the nodding scarlet and purple flowers to the heavens, saying nothing and, for the moment, wanting nothing. They lingered over long, slow kisses, intoxicated by the day, the place—and each other.

Finally, he got to his feet, then helped her up. Once more aware of their vulnerability here, she reached for her scattered clothing. But he seized her hand and began to wade once more through the flowers, this time down a gentle slope.

"Where are we going?" She asked, looking around them nervously.

"Down here," he replied. Ahead of them, the meadow ended abruptly where two steep slopes merged.

She opened her mouth to protest, then stopped as the sound of rushing water became clearer, separating from the softer sigh of the breeze.

It was a small waterfall—or rather, two waterfalls, since one diverged above them and two fell into the pool several yards apart. A mist hovered over the pool and the breeze carried to her that faint, mineral scent.

He sat down on the rocky ledge, then slid into the pool and lifted her down as well. The water reached nearly to her shoulders and was wonderfully warm.

"We have company," he said quietly, then began to turn slowly to face the rocky source of the waterfall.

Jocelyn saw the wolf even before his words could have an effect on her. Her body stiffened. He turned back to her and began to stroke her back soothingly.

"He won't hurt us."

She stared up at the creature. It was too far away for her to see the color of its eyes, but not even Daken's soothing hands and words could quell her fear.

"Is it one . . . one of *you*?"

"No, it's an ordinary wolf. But they never attack us—and you are safe because you're with me. It's just curious about us, that's all."

The animal apparently had satisfied its curiosity, because a moment later, it began to descend from the rocks and then disappeared around the edge of the hill. Only then did it occur to her to question how he knew of its presence, when his back had been to it.

He shrugged. "We can always tell when one is near—just as they know when we're around. I just felt its presence."

Jocelyn did not forget the beauty of the day, but that night as she lay in his arms, the wolf and the man once again merged into a nightmare. When she cried out and he woke her gently, she pretended she could not recall the dream—and wished that were true.

Will I ever see this place again? I have learned so much here, and I have known such happiness. Jocelyn's eyes misted over with tears and her throat constricted painfully as she stared across the ravine at the great black fortress. It seemed another lifetime ago that she had come here believing herself to be the captive of a people whose very existence she had doubted.

The long line of Kassid warriors in their dark garb stretched back to the bridge and beyond into the courtyard that wasn't visible from this spot. Daken had called a brief halt as they both stared back at the ancient home of the Kassid.

He reached over to cover her hand, and she tried to blink away the tears before turning to him. How could she explain them?

"Nothing in life is certain, Jocelyn. But I believe we will both return one day. Otherwise, I'm not sure I could allow either of us to leave."

She nodded and swallowed. "No matter what happens, my heart will always be here."

Paying no attention at all to the men behind them, Daken leaned over and kissed her on the mouth. "And mine will be with you."

Then they urged their horses onward, and the long line of warriors followed. All through the gray, overcast day, the column wound its way down from the highest peaks. At times, Jocelyn could look up and see the rear of the line on the trail high above them. It was an impressive sight—one she wished their enemy could see.

In the final weeks before their departure, that quiet certainty that the Kassid projected had become her certainty, too. She felt, as Tassa had put it, that awakening of ancient forces that had lain dormant in the Dark Mountains for centuries. She no longer doubted that victory would be theirs; she worried only about the cost of that victory for them all.

She slanted a glance at Daken as they rode side by side on a downward-spiraling trail. The sun had broken through the clouds and now reflected off the crest sewn onto his heavy knit tunic. All the men wore this crest, and when she'd first seen it, she'd thought it vaguely familiar. He'd told her that it was the ancient symbol for their people. She hadn't given it much thought then, but when he turned to her and she saw it again, a memory suddenly stirred.

She *had* seen it before—on the walls in that secret room at the palace. She was sure of it. Or was she? So many years had passed, and she'd seen it only that one time. How *could* she possibly remember one symbol among so many on those walls? But then, hadn't she already decided that the room had something to do with the Kassid?

There is an explanation, she thought. *When we get to the palace, I will have that wall torn down and*

274

then I will take Daken down there. But in the meantime, she continued to keep her secret.

They made camp that night in the place where Jocelyn had first met Daken—and where her Guards had met their deaths at the hands of the Menoans. Daken had told her that the size of their force required them to make several camps, but this was the safest and he preferred to have her here.

She nodded her agreement, but as the camp was set up, she wondered why he should be concerned about her safety here. It seemed more likely to her that he wanted her to come back here, to face up to both the past and the future.

How could she not face the future, she thought, when everywhere she looked, she saw warriors? And so she did. The men were different. They were more disciplined and more intense, and even without the uniforms and weaponry, she would have felt that difference.

The men slept in the open, in large sacks of oiled hide with the wool on the inside. They reminded Jocelyn of over-sized versions of the sacks babies were frequently put into for sleeping. By day, the sacks were rolled up and stored behind the men's saddles.

A tent had been brought along for her and Daken, and he had it set up slightly apart from the rest of the men to afford them some privacy. Night fell quickly, and after the evening meal, Jocelyn retired to the tent, while Daken remained for a time with his men.

She was lost in thought about the other time she'd been camped in this place, when the quiet of the night was suddenly shattered by the unearthly howling of wolves.

A chill swept through her as the eerie sounds rose and fell—so many of them that it seemed the entire camp was surrounded. She drew her cloak around her and reached for the tent flap—then stopped.

What if those howls weren't real wolves, but the Kassid? The chill deepened to freezing terror. Despite all that Daken had told her, she still feared she would find those creatures from her old story-books out there.

I love him and he loves me, she told herself as she reached again for the flap. *He would never frighten me this way*.

She stepped outside to find the men gathered about the campfire as before, paying no attention at all to the continuing howls. Their nonchalance in the face of the unearthly din was nearly enough to make her doubt her own ears.

As she stood there uncertainly, Daken got up and started toward her. Never had the sight of him been more welcome, and it calmed her enough to make her think about the very great difference between this time and the other time she had been here.

"How can you just ignore them?" she asked, raising her voice slightly to be heard above the howls.

"There's no danger. They're simply letting us know that they're aware of our presence. It will stop soon. Come sit with us if you like."

The men nearest the fire cleared a space for her, and several of those she knew repeated Daken's soothing words. But her heart still beat faster with each new wave of the rhythmic howling, until she would have sworn it was keeping time with them.

"Do they know what is happening?" she asked, thinking about that unique bond between the Kassid and the wolves.

"They may," he acknowledged. "Certainly they have never seen this many of us traveling together. They're intelligent creatures, so they may well suspect that something's afoot."

And then it stopped—not gradually, but all at once, as though some sort of signal had been given. The silence made her nearly as nervous as the howling had.

"Would they warn you if the camps were going to be attacked?" she asked.

"Yes. There have been many times over the years when they have warned hunting parties of the approach of bears or wild dogs."

"But this wasn't a warning?"

He shook his head. "They have a language of sorts, and this was simply a greeting."

They both went back to the tent shortly thereafter. Jocelyn was tired after the day's journey, and her nerves were still raw from the encounter with the wolves—but none of that could prevent her from wanting him. Their time was growing short.

Their lovemaking had both a fierceness and a special tenderness to it these days, and this night was no exception. She held his big, hard body to her tightly, not even letting go as she finally fell asleep.

* * *

Saranne Dawson

Jocelyn found herself swiveling her head about regularly, checking all around them—but for what? The land was empty. They were out of the Dark Mountains and into the much lower foothills where no trace of snow lingered, save for a few very sheltered spots. It was Daken who finally explained her uneasiness.

"It's the open land," he said with a sympathetic smile. "We are all feeling vulnerable."

He was right, of course. She could see the men around them doing the same thing. Her mind spun back to the first time she'd seen those mountains that were now behind them. How dark and forbidding they'd seemed then—and now she felt vulnerable without their protection. How would she feel when they reached the broad plains of Ertria? And what about Daken and the men? They'd never been in flat land before. Even the horses must find it strange, although they moved with their usual surefootedness over the ridges and through the valleys.

Now that they were no longer restricted to narrow trails, the Kassid army had spread itself widely across the land and looked even more forbidding—huge waves of black-clad men swarming over the sides of the hills. She wondered if the Menoans would have spies hiding in the thick woods, and what they must think. When she asked Daken about it, he nodded.

"I hope they do. The sooner they know we are coming, the better."

"Will we reach the garrison today?" she asked eagerly, wanting to hear news of home.

"We should be there by nightfall," Daken replied. "We will need to spend a few days there, I think. We must buy some provisions from the Baleks, unless the garrison can provide for us."

"The garrison is always well-stocked," she told him. "The commander told me that they always keep on hand enough provisions to last them a year."

Then she turned in the saddle to look back at the army behind her. "But you brought so much with you." She'd been astonished at the number of pack horses accompanying them.

"The men are used to eating well," he replied with a smile, "and I'd prefer not to have to ration food just yet."

But Jocelyn was still staring back at the huge army. "Daken, we must have some of the men from the garrison accompany us to the city. The people will be terrified when they see your men."

"They probably will be anyway. But I plan to ask the commander to send as many men as he can spare. He can replace them with Baleks. They would certainly fight hard to defend their home, if it should come to that."

"I doubt the commander would agree to that," she said, recalling the time some years ago when the Baleks had requested to man the garrison themselves. Hammad and her father had been in agreement that the garrison must remain in Ertrian hands, even though the Baleks had been peaceful for many years.

"The commander will agree if he is ordered to do

so by his empress," Daken stated pointedly. "Those men could be put to much better use defending Ertria. If war comes here, it will be much later."

Jocelyn said nothing. She was becoming aware for the first time of the possibility of clashes between her and Daken. And what about Hammad and Daken? She now realized that she'd been foolish to think that this alliance could be managed so easily. The man and the woman might love each other, but the empress and the leader of the Kassid were likely to have their differences.

"Empires are not lasting things, Jocelyn," he said in a quiet voice. "Inevitably, the strains of keeping together different peoples causes discord."

"But the Ertrians and the Baleks have lived together peaceably for generations," she protested angrily. "I have Balek advisors and there are always Balek nobles at court, where they're accepted fully."

"Those at your court have an interest in maintaining things as they are. They've probably become more Ertrian than Balek."

"Are you suggesting that I should give up the empire?" she challenged him.

"I am merely thinking ahead a bit—to a time when you could perhaps loosen its bonds a bit. There will be Baleks and Islanders fighting in this war, and they could be rewarded by being given more control over their lives."

Jocelyn retreated into an icy silence. She was thinking about the way the Kassid lived and the implications that could have for her own people. Was he really saying that the Kassid would demand a "reward" for their service—the dissolution of the empire?

And they'd be within their rights to make such demands, she thought nervously. The empire could not win without them.

The only comfort she had was the certainty that Daken loved her and was unlikely to force her to take any action she found unpleasant. But as she recalled that time he'd harangued her before his council, the doubts crept in.

They rode on for the rest of the day mostly in silence. Jocelyn was so preoccupied with her thoughts that she paid no attention to the group of men who now rode beside Daken, conversing with him in their own language. If she hadn't been lost in thought, she would have realized it was the first time he'd permitted that in her presence.

It was late afternoon, nearing twilight, when they crested a hill and saw the garrison for the first time, perched atop its hill some distance away.

"Jocelyn," Daken said, breaking his long silence, "If I tell you to turn around and ride to the rear, do it immediately and without question. Do you understand?"

She stared at him, stunned by the peremptory tone of his voice. He'd never spoken to her in such a way before, and coming as it did after his suggestion that she should dissolve the empire, it sent chills through her.

"Have you noticed that we've encountered no Baleks?" he asked in a more normal tone. "We should have come upon some hunting parties—especially at this time of year."

"But . . . what are you saying?"

"I think it is possible that an unpleasant surprise could be awaiting us at the garrison."

"You think the Menoans could have taken it?" she gasped. "But you said that their force was decimated."

"Perhaps they've had reinforcements. And they may be planning to have us ride right into a trap. They'd never attempt to attack us out here—but if they can get some of us inside the garrison before we know what's happening . . ." He shrugged his wide shoulders.

"I would send you to the rear now, but I'm sure they'd be watching us, and that would tip them off that we're suspicious."

"But if they've captured the garrison, how can you possibly take it from them? You have many more men, but that garrison is impregnable."

"I'm sure that's what the Menoans think if they're there," Daken replied evenly.

Once again, she heard that absolute certainty in his voice, but this time she was not reassured. Even if the Kassid could retake the garrison, it would only be after a long and bloody battle that could be intended to keep their army here while the Menoans and Turveans attacked Ertria.

"They intend to keep you here," she told him. "That way, they will be able to overrun Ertria."

"Yes," was his only reply as he turned once more to his men and began to speak rapidly in the Kassid tongue.

Daylight was failing now as the sun fell away behind the Dark Mountains. The Kassid army advanced at a measured pace toward the garrison, crossing the valley and climbing over a low hill, then descending once again into the narrow valley below the garrison.

"Daken, look!" Jocelyn pointed excitedly to the watchtowers at the corners of the garrison. Men in the dark green winter uniforms of the Ertrian army were patroling along the wall and could be seen in the towers themselves. She could almost make out the Ertrian crest emblazoned on their tunics.

"They're Menoans in Ertrian uniforms," Daken replied succinctly.

Then, even as he spoke, the great wooden doors of the garrison were opened and she could see more men in uniform just inside, awaiting them in formation.

"How can you be sure?" she asked in a whisper, even though they were still a considerable distance away from the doors.

"I trust my instincts—and those of my men."

His certainty convinced her, even though she wanted very much to believe he was wrong. She drew her cloak more tightly about her to conceal her tremors.

He put out a hand to touch hers briefly. "You'll be safe. Just do as I say. They won't attack now. They want to get as many of us inside as possible—and they'll also want to get you out of the way. I'm sure Arrat has made it clear that you are not to be harmed."

That scarcely reassured her, and she doubted that Daken had intended it to. They both knew what

283

Arrat wanted from her—that which she had already refused him.

When he saw that his troops had filled the small valley, with the rearmost spread about the crest of the hill behind them, Daken signaled a halt.

For many minutes, the only sounds were the restless shuffling of the horses and the creaking of saddle leather. Jocelyn attempted to match Daken's calm, although she felt as though her heart had lept into her throat.

Finally, three men rode out of the garrison, and Jocelyn could see that the one in the middle wore the uniform of the garrison commander. It wasn't the commander she had met, but she knew that Hammad had intended to recall him to the city.

She let her hopes rise. Daken could be wrong, for all his instincts. Surely these were Ertrians! Perhaps they had been momentarily disconcerted by the sight of the Kassid army. And the commander's lapse of protocol could be laid to the newness of his command.

The trio rode directly toward them. Daken sat motionless, awaiting them. She tensed, hope vying with fear. And then the men came to a halt, some twenty feet away. The commander drew his sword and she tensed, though she sensed no movement on Daken's part. But he simply raised it and crossed it over his chest in a salute to her.

"Welcome, milady! We have prepared a suite for you."

His Ertrian was excellent, and if she hadn't already been suspicious, she might well have missed the traces of a Menoan accent. After all, the only

Ertrian she'd heard for months now had been spoken with a heavy accent.

She nodded, not quite certain what to say, and glanced at Daken. But he was ignoring her as he addressed the man.

"She will remain outside with me. A wife's place is with her husband—empress or not."

Jocelyn had to exert considerable control over herself to prevent her shock from showing itself to the man. She'd never heard Daken speak like that, but she realized that it was the kind of voice she had expected to hear the day she collapsed at his feet.

The commander was clearly befuddled, and she rushed in to fill the silence. "This is Daken, Commander. He is the leader of the Kassid—and my husband. I thank you for your kindness, but I prefer to remain with him, and he wishes to remain with his men."

The man stared at her, then looked at the vast army arrayed about him. If his accent hadn't already given him away, the brief look of fear she now saw would surely have done so. Finally, he nodded curtly.

"As milady wishes."

"We will make camp here tonight," Daken stated. "And then we leave in the morning for Ertria. What news is there of the Western Road? If the Menoans still control it, we will take it back."

Once again, the commander's mask slipped briefly. "They have gone. The road is clear."

Daken nodded. "A wise move on their part, though it only prolongs the moment of their dying."

Once again, the man darted a glance beyond them. Jocelyn thought he looked positively pale beneath his plumed helmet. He gave her one last salute, then actually backed his horse a few paces before wheeling about and riding hastily back to the garrison. As soon as he was out of earshot, Daken began to chuckle quietly.

"A messenger will undoubtedly be leaving the garrison tonight to carry the news to Arrat. I think we will permit that."

"What will happen now?" she asked with a nervous glance at the retreating men.

"We will capture the garrison and then go on to Ertria. When I suggested that the garrison should be left under the control of the Baleks, I hadn't anticipated this—but now it will have to be that way. It's unlikely that any of your men are left alive."

"But how can you possibly capture the garrison? Won't you be playing right into their hands by staying here to fight them?"

Daken turned from her briefly to tell several of his men to begin setting up camp. Then he turned back to her.

"We will surprise them. There is a tunnel beneath the garrison, with an opening on the far side of that hill." He gestured briefly. "It's actually a natural cavern such as frequently occur in this area. The Menoans won't know about it."

"I've never heard of such a tunnel. How do you know about it?" And she was reminded of all the things he seemed to know.

"It's very ancient," he said, not really answering her question. "Like the garrison itself."

Then, perhaps to forestall any further questions on her part, he told her that he intended to have their tent set up in a prominent spot, but when it was dark enough, she would be taken to the rear of the lines for the night.

"I don't really expect them to try anything, but I want you out of the way, nevertheless. I'm afraid you'll have to make do with a sheppa."

"Sheppa" was their name for the sleeping sacks. But Jocelyn wondered how he could possibly think that she would sleep.

As darkness settled over the land, she sat at one of the campfires and tried to eat the food brought to her by a youth—one of many brought along to tend the horses and prepare the meals and run various errands.

She felt useless, even though Daken had warmly praised her behavior toward the fake commander. And she was also back to those gnawing doubts about him. How did he know so much? Who were his spies? They must be Baleks—and now he wanted her to hand over the garrison to them. What more would he want of her?

The empress has doubts, she thought sadly—but the woman loves him. Did that dichotomy exist in him as well?

The camp settled down for the night. Jocelyn went to her tent, but was there for only a short time when Jakka, Daken's aide, appeared with a group of a dozen youths.

"They will lead you to safety, Jocelyn," he told her, then turned to the boys. "You know your orders. Under no circumstances do you join in any fighting. If anything goes wrong, you take her and return to the mountains."

The boys all nodded solemnly, but she could see that they longed to be part of the battle.

Then several other men joined Jakka, leading horses. They all mounted quickly and rode off into the night. Jocelyn frowned.

"Where are they going?" she asked the boy who was put in charge.

"To see the Baleks in town. They will have to take over the garrison now."

As they led her through the sleeping bodies, Jocelyn turned to look back at the garrison. Things were already spinning out of her control. The Menoans had captured the garrison—and now the Kassid would take it back and give it to the Baleks.

She had a sudden, powerful longing to be back at the fortress. She was shocked to realize that it was the fortress she thought of, and not the palace. The palace was where she belonged, where she could regain that control she felt slipping away.

Staying within the shelter of a patch of woods, they crossed the low hill and descended into the next valley. There she found several other boys, with horses. They began to chatter away in Kassid until their leader reminded them that they were to speak Ertrian. He smiled apologetically at her.

"Please do not take offense, Jocelyn. It is just that we all wished to see the battle. But we would not have been permitted to be there even if it hadn't been for you. Promises were made to our parents."

"I understand," she said, "and I'm not offended. But there won't be much to see in any event, will there? Daken plans to sneak in through the tunnel."

"Yes, but then he will open the gates for the others." He shrugged unhappily. "We won't even see that."

Jocelyn stared into the darkness where she could just make out the intervening hillside. "We could if we went back up there."

The boy hesitated. "Jakka told us to stay down here until someone comes for us."

"But if I were to insist upon staying up there, you would have to join me, wouldn't you? I cannot bear not to know what is happening."

"Uh, well . . ."

What followed was rapid-fire Kassid as the other boys overheard the conversation. Finally, the leader gave her a grin and another shrug. "You are right. We would have to stay with you."

So they tethered the horses and went back up the hill, stealing through the woods until they reached the top, where they could see the garrison clearly. Lights gleamed in the tower, and the reflected glow of torches could be seen beyond the high walls.

They had brought their sheppas along, including one for her, and now they arrayed themselves at the crest of the hill, crawling into the sacks, then turning over onto their stomachs so they could watch the garrison. Jocelyn was surprised at how quickly she felt warm inside the bulky sack.

Nothing happened for a very long time. The Kassid camp was quiet, with only a few campfires burning brightly. As the moon rose high, the guards on the garrison wall and in the towers could be seen.

And then, just as she was losing the battle to stay awake, the howling began. She drew herself up quickly. It wasn't like the other night in the mountains; there were far fewer of them here. But the sounds were just as eerie.

Josek, the boys' leader, began to laugh softly. "That should give the Menoans something to think about."

"Have they followed you?" she asked.

"Probably. But they will go no farther than here. The mountains are their home."

The howling would reach a crescendo, then die away, only to begin again some time later. She thought that if the creatures were capable of thought, they couldn't have designed a better torment for the Menoans. Silence punctuated by renewed howling was sheer torment—even worse than the continued howling of the other night.

Then, in one of the silences, it occurred to her that these might not be ordinary wolves. She turned to Josek, but found she could not ask the question. Even in the darkness, she had seen his pale eyes. He was one of the "blessed," though he couldn't be old enough yet to make the change.

She began to drift into a doze, stirring only when the howling was renewed, so she wasn't sure how much time had passed when she was suddenly jolted awake by other sounds—distant shouts.

"They're in the garrison!" Josek exclaimed in a loud whisper.

They all strained their ears, listening to the rising sounds of men shouting. Jocelyn knew that the boys must be envisioning the battle even as she tried *not* to. Where would Daken be? Was he in danger? She could not let herself believe that he was.

Then the big doors of the garrison were suddenly flung open, visible because of the fires revealed in the courtyard beyond. Dark figures could be glimpsed moving about in the flames. And then darker figures could be seen advancing up the hill to the open doors. In the space of a few seconds, it seemed that the entire Kassid army had sprung to life.

The shouting died away gradually, and the flames were extinguished except for torches. The Kassid army began to retreat back down the hillside, but at a leisurely pace.

"It's over," Josek said happily. "We've got the garrison."

A short time later, several Kassid rode into their little camp just as they themselves were returning to the spot where they were supposed to be. They confirmed that the garrison had been taken, and with no loss of life for the Kassid, although there'd been a few injuries.

"Daken sent us to fetch you, Jocelyn," the one man told her. "He thought you might prefer to spend the remainder of the night in more comfortable surroundings."

"Is he all right? Was he hurt?"

Saranne Dawson

"He is well," the man assured her. "The Menoans were taken completely by surprise, thanks to the tunnel."

"And my men—are any of them left alive?"

"Only the garrison commander. He's been badly beaten, but he'll survive."

Chapter Ten

As soon as she rode into the garrison, Jocelyn asked to be taken to see Daken. She knew she should also visit the garrison commander, but at the moment, she badly needed to reassure herself that Daken was whole.

She was led through a maze of unfamiliar corridors and then shown into a small room. Daken had been seated on a chair at the bedside of the man she assumed must be the commander. Several Kassid physicians hovered about them.

He turned and rose when she entered the room, blocking her view of the commander, to whom she paid no attention in any event as a surge of relief carried her into Daken's arms.

"It's over, maiza," he murmured against her hair, using the Kassid word for wife that was also a term of endearment. "For now, at least."

She clung to him, totally oblivious of the man on the bed, who had struggled into a half-sitting position and was gaping at her unabashedly. The empress would surely have remembered her duty to a loyal follower; the woman did not.

Then, as Daken reluctantly released her, she caught sight of the injured man and gasped. "Revi! You are the new commander here?"

He managed to draw his badly swollen mouth into a sad sort of smile. "My first command—and my last, I'm sure. I'm sorry, Jocelyn."

Jocelyn turned to the curious Daken. "Revi is an old friend of my brother's, and he's married to my cousin."

It was obvious that he was in considerable pain, but Jocelyn was reassured when the physicians told her that he was in no real danger.

"Some broken bones and bruises—and a badly wounded pride," Revi told her. "They tricked me."

She would have asked more, but Daken intervened, saying that Revi had already given him an accounting and he would tell her later. Revi needed to rest. So she left him to the ministrations of the physicians and followed Daken from the room.

"It appears that the Menoans have a fondness for disguise. The garrison has always been open to Baleks. Merchants and others come and go all the time. The Menoans had left their camp near the Western Road, and garrison scouts saw them headed back toward Menoa. But it was only a ruse. Over a few weeks' time, they managed to sneak men into the garrison disguised as Baleks. They apparently hid in the unused portions of the garrison and then struck in the night, opening the gates to the rest of their men, who had returned by another route."

"Poor Revi," Jocelyn murmured. "To lose all his men on his first command. He's right. Hammad will never give him another command."

"He's young and inexperienced, and he simply followed the loose security of his predecessors. Hammad should take that into account."

"Yes, he should," Jocelyn agreed. "And I will speak to him about it. Unlike most of the nobles, Revi truly wanted a career with the army, and I think he is a good officer, despite this."

"And he will be a better one in the future," Daken stated.

Then he stopped outside a door that was guarded by two of his men. "We spared the lives of three Menoans so they can carry the news back to Arrat. They're in here."

One of the Kassid guards opened the door, and they walked in to find three young men dressed in the dun-colored uniforms of the Menoan Army. All three stared fearfully at Daken, then gaped at Jocelyn with a faint light of hope. They assumed they would not be killed with a woman present.

"Do you speak Ertrian?" Daken asked.

One of them nodded eagerly, and Daken addressed him in that language.

"Your lives will be spared so that you can carry a message back to Arrat. You will tell him that the garrison has fallen—and you will also tell him that the Kassid have allied themselves with Ertria. I am Daken, leader of the Kassid—and this, as you

295

surely know, is the Empress Jocelyn, who is also my wife."

He paused to wrap a long arm about Jocelyn's waist, then continued in an almost jocular manner. "You may also tell him that any army that can walk through the stone walls of a garrison can easily trample his army."

Then he released Jocelyn and took a few steps toward the three men, dwarfing them all. They all cringed and staggered backward, one of them knocking over a chair in his haste to get away from this giant.

"Tell Arrat to remember carefully all the legends of the Kassid—because they are all true. If he persists in this foolish war, he will learn far more than he wants to know about Kassid magic."

Then he called out to the guards at the door and told them to take the men to the gates and give them horses and weapons, after which they were to be escorted to the Menoan Road. The badly shaken men stumbled out of the room, and Jocelyn turned to Daken with a smile.

"So you walked through walls?" She laughed. "Will they really believe that?"

He returned her smile. "I have no doubt that they will. They know nothing of the tunnel, and they know we didn't come in through the gates." Then he quickly sobered again.

"But I also doubt that it will prevent war. By all accounts, Arrat is a stubborn man. However, those three will spread tales about our magic, and that should strike fear into the hearts of Arrat's army. Fear can make men careless."

"Daken," she said, drawing herself up as though anticipating an argument, "I want to know how you knew about the tunnel."

He took her arm and began to lead her from the room, but she resisted.

"Come along," he urged, "so that we can both get some sleep. We knew about the tunnel because this garrison was built by the Kassid centuries ago. We built it for the Baleks' protection, and for years, both Kassid and Baleks served here."

"But who were you protecting the Baleks from—and why did you abandon it?"

"We abandoned it because a decision was made by our people to stay within our mountains. The Baleks themselves used it for years after that, and then the Ertrians came."

"You didn't say who you were protecting them from," she reminded him as they entered the garrison commander's suite.

"From the Ertrians, of course," was his calm reply.

"I don't understand, Daken. The Kassid fought alongside my people, not against them."

"That's true—but that was long before the Ertrians decided to conquer Balek."

"But if the Baleks regarded you as their protector, how could your people have simply abandoned them?"

"For the same reason we left Ertria. A decision was made not to involve ourselves further in the wars of the time. We simply went back to our ancestral homelands."

There was more to this, she thought, but he was

already stripping off his clothes and she became aware of just how tired she was and how she wanted nothing more now than to fall asleep in his arms.

Beyond the walls of the garrison, the Menoans climbed on their horses and rode off into the waning night, turning back regularly to make sure that the Kassid weren't following them.

From time to time as they rode toward the border, they heard the howls of wolves that seemed to be keeping pace with them.

When they reached the border two nights later, the howling abruptly stopped. And by the time they carried their message to Arrat, they had also spread the word about the sorcery of the Kassid—and about their giant leader, who had taken the Empress of Ertria as his wife.

They remained at the garrison for several days while Daken and his men recruited Baleks to man the garrison, together with a small group of Kassid. Since it was clear that Revi, the garrison commander, would be unable to travel for some time, Jocelyn accepted the offer of a local Balek nobleman to accompany them to the city, together with some of his own men. All agreed that the presence of a well-known Balek, together with her own presence, would serve to allay the fears of the people they passed along their route.

Two young Baleks were dispatched to the city, carrying messages from Revi and Jocelyn for Hammad, informing him of the garrison's fall and recapture by the Kassid, and alerting him to their arrival as well.

Finally, they set out. They rode hard, covering the distance in far less time than Jocelyn had when she'd first come to the Dark Mountains. She was by now eager to return to the palace, but still she kept swiveling about in the saddle to catch her final glimpses of the mountains as they retreated from jagged peaks to a dark smudge on the horizon, and then vanished.

Both Daken and his men were clearly uneasy as they left behind the low hills of Balek and entered the vast plains of Ertria. Jocelyn felt some of that uneasiness herself, but quickly readjusted to the land she'd always known.

It was easy for them all to believe that war was no more than a vague possibility. Traffic had resumed in earnest on the Western Road, with the coming of spring and the absence of the Menoans, and everywhere the land was being readied for the spring planting.

The long line of Kassid warriors seemed incongruous here even to them, and despite her presence and that of the Balek nobleman and his entourage, the many people they encountered gaped at them in both awe and fear.

They stayed each night at an inn, the proprietors of which were given advance notice by the Baleks. The Kassid army spread themselves about in camps, hunting whenever possible to replenish their food supplies.

On these occasions, which afforded Ertrians their first close look at the Kassid, Jocelyn saw how they shied away from Daken, while attempting to appear natural and at ease.

When a maid was sent to their room just after their arrival at the first of their inn stopovers, the girl was so uncomfortable in Daken's presence, and he was so clearly unhappy about her that Jocelyn sent her away, then made sure that none were sent at future stops. But she worried about how he would adjust to the constant presence of numerous servants at the palace. She couldn't very well get rid of *them*.

"What is their purpose?" he asked when she tried to prepare him for life at the palace. "What do they do that you cannot do for yourself, apart from bringing bath water and tending your clothes?"

"Daken," she said, tired and exasperated after a long day on the road, "I lived as the Kassid live in the Dark Mountains—and you will have to learn to live as I do when we get to the palace."

He gave her a baleful look, then finally nodded. "Very well, but keep them away in the morning. When I awaken, I want to be with you—and you alone."

That, at least, she knew she could do, so she felt somewhat better. But having spoken those words, she now saw the full truth of them—she could and had adjusted to his way of life, but he could never live as she did.

And that, of course, thrust her once more into the darkness that lay ahead—because Daken would never *have* to adjust to her way of life. After the war—if there *was* a war—he would be gone.

Still, her eagerness to be home again and to

plunge herself into the affairs of state kept her from dwelling overmuch on the future as they rode across the sun-warmed plains. Deep inside, she knew that she would not be returning to things as they'd been before, but she ignored those warnings.

Then one day on the road, an incident occurred that was to trouble her greatly, though she took care to hide it at the time.

She was riding with Daken and the Balek entourage at the head of the Kassid army when they came upon a group of Sherbas, the strange sect she'd encountered on her trip to the Dark Mountains. They were traveling in the opposite direction and as the two groups drew near, the Sherbas pulled their horses and their black-painted wagons off the road.

Then, to Jocelyn's amazement, they all prostrated themselves on the ground in front of the party. Both Jocelyn and the Baleks stared at each other in surprise; no one had ever seen them do that before. And then it dawned upon Jocelyn that the object of their adoration was *Daken*! At first, she assumed they must be terrified, but before she could think of a way to deal with that, they had risen again and she saw no fear at all in their faces.

Daken merely inclined his head to them and thanked them for moving from the road. As soon as they were out of earshot of the Sherbas, she commented on their unusual behavior, keeping her voice as level as possible.

"Most likely they were just afraid of us," Daken replied with a shrug.

"Do you know anything about them?" she asked,

Saranne Dawson

still in a casual tone even though she was now deeply troubled.

"Not much," he replied. "They have been around for centuries and cause no harm to anyone as far as I know."

"But what about their beliefs?" she persisted.

"I know nothing of that. They live in your land. Surely you must know something of them."

Jocelyn admitted that she knew nothing of their beliefs, only that they seemed to have no home, but always traveled about, trading their herbs for their needs.

"They have fine herbs," Endrok, the Balek nobleman put in. "Although I've always wondered how they grow them when they seem to travel all the time."

How indeed? Jocelyn kept her expression calm, but her thoughts were churning. It was possible, of course, that the Sherbas had some secret place known only to them, which was what Daken suggested in response to Endrok's comment. But she was thinking about all the herbs grown in the Kassid winter garden, and presumably outside in the summer. At least some of the herbal potions used by the Kassid were the same as those traded by the Sherbas.

That alone proved nothing, she told herself. They might even be growing them on the edges of Kassid land, a wild, uninhabited region.

But when she put that together with their behavior toward Daken, her suspicions grew.

And still later, as she recalled her questions to Daken about where he was getting his information

302

about life beyond the Dark Mountains, she was nearly certain that she had her answer—the Sherbas traded information with the Kassid for the herbs.

They were the perfect spies, she thought. They traveled all over Ertria, Balek, and even Menoa and Turvea. No one paid them any attention or considered them to be anything more than a group of harmless eccentrics.

She understood why Daken would not be willing to admit this in the presence of the Baleks, but when she raised the matter again that night in the privacy of their bedchamber and he merely shrugged it off, those small doubts that had lain dormant in her came together in an icy knot that lay cold and heavy inside her.

Why did he find it necessary to keep such a thing from her? Surely it shouldn't matter now.

"My Guards!" Jocelyn pointed excitedly to the white-uniformed riders astride their equally white horses bearing down on them in a cloud of dust along the Western Road.

They were about a half-day's ride from the city, passing through fertile fields where peasants were busy tilling the soil. The closer they came to the city, the more intense became Jocelyn's longing to be home, to be back in a familiar place where the dark questions that continued to haunt her would seem less threatening.

But even as she spoke, she remembered that the men she referred to were well and truly *her* guards now, and that brought back the grief over the loss of her father that she hadn't felt in months. As long as she was in the Dark Mountains, a part of her had continued against all reason to believe she would find him here when she returned. These men would soon swear their fealty to her alone, as their ruler. Hammad controlled the army, but the Royal Guards were under the direct control of the emperor—and now, the empress, for the first time in the history of the empire.

Sadness and responsibility fell heavily over her as the gap between the groups closed. She sent a sidelong glance to Daken and felt yet another wrenching pain. He was her husband and she loved him—but she was no longer sure that she trusted him. That too contributed to her eagerness to be home.

As the Guards drew close, Daken called a halt to his army and they waited for the others to arrive. Then Jocelyn recognized Hammad riding with the commander of the Guards. Her heart swelled with love for this man who'd been like a second father to her.

Daken dismounted, then lifted her from the saddle. With his arm encircling her waist, they waited for the others to dismount. When Hammad lept from his horse with the agility of a much younger man, Jocelyn temporarily forgot her exalted rank and broke away from Daken to run into Hammad's arms.

"Ahh, Jocey. Little one, I have worried so much about you." If Hammad found her behavior less than seemly, he gave no hint as he kissed her brow, then held her away from him to look at her fondly.

"It appears that I worried in vain."

Jocelyn quickly led him to Daken and introduced the two men. They shook hands, and Jocelyn couldn't help smiling at the way they discreetly sized each other up. Then Hammad stared beyond them to the huge army that had halted just a short distance away, stretching far back along the road.

"You are more welcome than I can say, Daken. I thank you for rescuing the garrison, and I am eager to hear the details."

"The Menoans killed all but Revi, Hammad," Jocelyn said sadly. "He was badly beaten, but will recover. The garrison has been left in the hands of the Baleks, with a few Kassid troops as well."

Hammad exchanged a long look with Daken, then nodded. "For the time being, we will leave it that way."

"What is the word from Menoa?" Daken asked.

Hammad shook his gray head. "Mixed reports. Arrat's army continues to gather near the border, but our spies say there appears to be some dissension in the ranks." He paused and gave Daken another long, considering look.

"It seems that some of Arrat's commanders are not eager to face men who can walk through walls."

Daken merely nodded, and when Jocelyn was about to protest that the story wasn't true, he signaled her to be silent. Realizing that he might believe there to be enemy spies even here, she subsided. The Guards were certainly loyal, but they could tell Hammad the truth later.

Then she saw Hammad looking from Daken to her with a slightly puzzled look and realized only then that she hadn't yet told him of her marriage.

"Daken and I are married, Hammad. We will have another ceremony here, of course."

Hammad smiled and nodded. "You have just confirmed another strange tale brought to me by our spies."

Then he turned to Daken apologetically. "Forgive me, Daken. I meant no offense, but I have known her since birth and I quite frankly never thought to see her married."

He looked from one to the other of them again as Daken once more encircled her waist. "I take it that this is no mere marriage of convenience, to seal the alliance."

"No," Daken said, "Although we hoped it might impress Arrat."

"And so it might," Hammad nodded, "Though if he isn't impressed by the other tales, a marriage isn't likely to dissuade him."

He took Jocelyn's hands in his. "Your father would have been very pleased, Jocey. He thought very highly of Daken. In fact, although he never confided this to me, I think he hoped this might happen when he sent you to the Dark Mountains."

"I suspect he did indeed hope that," Daken put in with a chuckle. "When I met him that time, he spent considerable time talking about his daughter to me."

"You never told me that," Jocelyn said in astonishment.

"For a very good reason, given your well-known disdain for marriage," Daken replied evenly.

Seeing the rebellious look he knew all too well,

Hammad quickly suggested that they be on their way. He told Daken that his men were busy preparing a camp for the Kassid army just outside the city, while the officers could be quartered within the palace itself.

They mounted again and set off. Hammad rode with them, and he and Daken were soon engaged in a discussion of the battle at the garrison. Jocelyn remained silent, thinking about their revelation. She could not believe that her father had seen Daken as a possible husband for her. Not once had he ever hinted at such a thing; in fact, she hadn't known of Daken's existence until she was sent to meet with him.

Was that the reason he'd never urged her to marry someone else? If the Menoans and Turveans hadn't joined forces to make war on them, would he have found some other excuse to send her to the Dark Mountains?

There remained in her just enough of that rebellious child to resent her father's scheming. But there was also a deep pleasure in the certainty that he would have approved.

When Jocelyn got her first view of the palace atop its hill, she cried out in delight to Daken, who had already spotted it. But the moment their eyes met, she saw—almost as though she were seeing into his mind through those pale eyes—the great black fortress. And when she turned again to the palace, it seemed diminished—and frighteningly vulnerable.

But as they rode into the city, her spirits rose.

The wide main thoroughfare was lined many-deep with Ertrians waiting to welcome their empress home.

Jocelyn had always been popular with the people. As a child, she'd been permitted to go about the city with her nurses, and then, as she grew older, she was often seen riding through the streets and walking regularly on the outer wall of the palace grounds. Her beauty alone would have made her popular, but Ertrians also saw her as being far more accessible than her father had been.

Then, too, palace servants had long carried gossip about her into the city, and in the taverns and markets, her spirit and her many kindnesses to servants were the subject of many tales.

But on this day, the people's attention was quickly diverted from their empress to the big, gray-haired man who rode beside her on a strange, ugly horse, followed by others dressed in black like him. The Kassid army had taken another route to their camp.

People stared and whispered and the word "Kassid" seemed to be on all lips. Jocelyn saw the same mixture of fear and awe that she'd seen before and guessed that the spies' tales had already circulated in the city—tales of men who walked through walls, men with great magic.

Daken accepted all this scrutiny without any outward sign that he even noticed it, and when she turned to look at him, she found his gaze always on the palace ahead of them.

When they reached the inner courtyard, Jocelyn

found her uncle, the regent, awaiting her with her senior advisors. They embraced, and she saw that he didn't even try to hide his relief that his onerous burden was now taken from him.

Her advisors, unfortunately, wore the same ingratiating smiles as always—hiding, she was sure, their nervousness about her plans for their future.

Then they were in the Great Hall. Jocelyn paused as she saw the golden throne on its dais, and for a moment, wanted to go to her suite instead. But she knew she must show no hesitation, so she walked in a measured pace, greeting people as she went, then took her seat, with Daken to one side and Hammad to the other.

As she faced her court, they fell gradually silent. But she saw that most eyes were on Daken. These were people who carefully masked their true feelings most of the time, but she could still see glimpses of that same fear and awe behind their polite smiles.

"My father sent me to enlist the aid of the Kassid," she said into the silence. "The alliance has been made."

Then she reached up to take Daken's hand. "This is Daken, the leader of the Kassid—and my husband."

The dozens of indrawn breaths told her that although they must have heard the rumor, they hadn't believed it. She wondered what they were thinking now. Probably they were already scheming to ingratiate themselves with him, believing him to be emperor in fact, if not in name.

* * *

Jocelyn watched Daken prowl about her luxurious suite. "Prowl" seemed an appropriate description, she thought. He looked like a dark, caged animal, trapped in unfamiliar and incongruous surroundings—like a wolf, forced from its harsh mountain lair into a world of soft pastels.

Standing here in her own world, Jocelyn began to question her acceptance of his magic. And the doubts were even stronger here in this suite, the emperor's suite—redecorated in the shades the servants knew she preferred. After all, it was here that she'd first heard the legends of the Kassid, told as children's stories.

But it was also here that her father had explained that the Kassid were *real*.

Then he stopped his pacing and turned to her with a trace of a smile. "I find your courtiers . . . interesting."

He did not mean it as a compliment, and she knew that. Her first instinct was to defend them. However despicable they might be, they were still *her* court, and her father's before her. But she could scarcely do that, when she'd complained loud and long about them herself. Instead, she thought about *their* reaction to *him*.

"They find you very 'interesting' as well."

He nodded, then leveled his pale gaze on her. "This seems a good time to repeat my promise, Jocelyn. I have no designs on your empire. I cannot help the behavior of your courtiers, but I can assure you that it will have no effect upon me."

She nodded, but she felt a wrenching pain inside.

310

Had it come to this—that he should feel compelled to state his intentions and that she should need to hear them?

He held out a hand to her. "In the mountains, I made love to a woman. Now I would like to make love to the empress."

When she walked across the room to him, he lifted her hand to his lips. When her eyes met his again, she saw sadness there.

"I confess that I need to know that the empress also loves me."

Jocelyn had already reached the limits of her patience, even though she'd been holding court for less than two hours. She thought with longing of the sessions at the fortress with their free and open exchanges. She doubted that she'd heard one honest word from any of the two dozen people gathered about her. Even her new advisors, the ones for whom she'd had such high hopes, seemed less open, though perhaps it was only because of the presence of their elders.

I dealt with these people for a year, she thought. *They are no different. What is different is* me.

She had trouble maintaining the formality required of these occasions. Her elaborate gown and hairstyle felt uncomfortable. She found it difficult, sometimes impossible, to hold her tongue. She wanted to banish the lot of them.

Daken had gone to the camp, and since Hammad was not at court, she assumed that he too had gone there. But then Hammad appeared, and she seized upon his arrival to end this tedious session. As soon

311

as the current speaker had finished his long-winded recanting of unimportant events, she raised a bejeweled hand.

"I wish to speak with Hammad privately."

It gave her considerable pleasure to see them all troop out unhappily, but that pleasure was very short-lived. She did in fact need desperately to speak with Hammad. Long into the night, while Daken slept beside her, Jocelyn had thought about those doubts that continued to plague her. In fact, she'd been able to set them aside only when they'd made love. In the cries and whispers of passion, she loved him more than ever—but in the sated aftermath, she worried about who and what he really was.

When the others had finally departed, she left the throne and gestured to Hammad to join her in a small alcove, at a table and chairs used by the court scribes. As they walked across the Great Hall, Hammad paused and took her hands in his.

"Daken is a fine man, Jocelyn. If you were truly my daughter, instead of the daughter of my heart, I could not wish a better husband for you."

"Thank you, Hammad," she said sincerely, then impulsively stretched up to kiss him on the cheek. They sat down and she sighed.

"I love him, Hammad, but I fear that I may love a stranger—or at least a man who has kept secrets from me."

Hammad appeared unperturbed. "Men and women have always kept secrets from each other, Jocey."

"Not like this," she insisted. "Hammad, I know

that Daken told you the truth about how they got into the garrison, so you know that no magic was employed."

He nodded. "I was very surprised to learn of that tunnel—and that the Kassid built the garrison. I'd always assumed it was built by Ertrians."

Jocelyn reminded herself that she must speak to him about Revi, the unfortunate garrison commander, though she knew that Daken had already put in a good word for him. But the garrison's origins didn't concern her at the moment.

"And has he told you about their magic—the magic they employ in battle?"

Hammad nodded. "I've never doubted it. There were old stories passed down through the generations in my family, going all the way back to an ancestor who fought alongside the Kassid centuries ago."

"Then you know about their ancestors—the ghosts who fight alongside them—and also about the . . . wolves."

Hammad nodded again, but his dark eyes were solemn. "This is difficult for you, Jocey—to love a man who is so different."

"Yes, but that is not what troubles me at the moment."

She then went on to tell him about the Sherbas and their strange behavior toward Daken, and about her own thoughts on the matter.

"They're the perfect spies—nearly invisible, traveling all over, regarded as harmless eccentrics by everyone."

Rather to her surprise, Hammad chuckled. "So

they are. Would that *we* had such perfect spies. But it is not their spying that troubles you."

She shook her head. "It's the way they prostrated themselves to him. They behaved as though they thought he was one of the Old Gods, Hammad. Do you know that the Kassid claim to be the direct descendants of the Old Gods—a warrior race created by them to protect their sacred mountains?"

"Yes, I know that is the story, and perhaps the Kassid have good reason to believe that, since they have been gifted with magic that the rest of us lack."

He sat there drumming his thick fingers restlessly on the tabletop. "We've never really known anything about the beliefs of the Sherbas. It always seemed enough that they were peaceable. But this conversation has reminded me of a story I heard many years ago.

"Someone once claimed to have seen one of them wearing a very fine and heavy gold chain—the finest he'd seen. And suspended from that fine chain was something he described as being nothing more than a piece of black rock."

"Like the black stone of the Dark Mountains," she said. And like the black stone in the secret room. But she would get to that.

"Perhaps they worship the Kassid as the embodiment of the Old Gods," he suggested. "But even if they do, I see no real cause for alarm, Jocelyn."

"Then why didn't Daken admit it?" she challenged him.

"That is a question only he can answer, Jocey. I suggest that you ask him."

"I probably would have, if it weren't for the . . . other thing."

When Hammad gave her a sharp look, she went on to tell him about the secret room. "I hadn't thought about it in years—until I saw that black stone in the Dark Mountains. Then I remembered it all, including the drawings of wolves."

She went on to describe the similarities between the door she'd seen in the fortress mirror-tower and the door to that secret room.

"They have different woods in the Dark Mountains, and it ages differently as well. But the final proof that it must be a Kassid room came when I first saw that symbol on their tunics. I'd already seen their writing, and it wasn't at all like the symbols I remembered. But Daken told me that the symbol on their tunics is the ancient symbol for their people, written in the old way. He said that their spoken language hasn't changed, but that they had simplified their written language centuries ago."

Hammad leaned forward attentively. "A Kassid room—here?"

She nodded. "I trust my memory, but I must see that room again."

"I agree. I will find some trusted men to take down the wall immediately. But you have not spoken to Daken of this, either?"

She fidgeted uncomfortably. "No, I haven't. I can't really explain it, Hammad. Perhaps it is only that I've kept it secret all these years."

"But you have just told me," he pointed out gently, then reached over to cover her fluttering hand.

"I still believe there is no cause for alarm, Jocelyn. But we will go to this room together to test your memory—and then, if we know that it is Kassid, you must talk to Daken about it. Once again, he may be the only one who can explain it."

"I know you've always had a great interest in history, Hammad, and a much greater knowledge of it than I do. I was hoping that you might know something that could explain it—or that Father knew about it and had told you."

"I know of nothing to explain it, and your father never mentioned it, so he must not have known, either. He would certainly have told me about it, if for no other reason than the one you mentioned. He knew of my interest in our people's history."

Hammad paused for a moment, staring off into space. His tone became musing. "I have always thought that our history is incomplete, somehow. Despite all the old manuscripts in the palace library, it seems to me that much is missing."

But Jocelyn barely heard him as her thoughts remained on that room deep in the palace cellars. "That room is Kassid, Hammad—and it was built at great cost. It must be important."

"Yes—but not necessarily threatening."

No, she thought, it might not be threatening, but it *was* important. There was a reason for her having found it all those years ago.

Chapter Eleven

Jocelyn had deliberately decreed that the marriage ceremony take place immediately, to forestall any plans the court might have to turn the event into a major spectacle. Already, they were upset at her refusal to have the usual lavish ceremony that was traditionally held to commemorate the ascendancy of a new emperor.

"After all," she had told the few who dared to complain, "we are already married. This is merely an affirmation of that marriage."

She had also warned the priests that she did not want their usual hours-long ramblings—though not in language quite that forceful. But in this, she was less successful.

Although one of her many titles was "Defender of the Faith" and she was nominally the priests' superior, they knew they could disobey her with impunity. The nobility of Ertria and Balek paid no more than lip service to the old religion, but the arrogant priests still had considerable power over the common people.

So she stood beside Daken in the Great Hall, carefully maintaining an expression of piety while they mumbled on interminably. The huge room was filled to overflowing, with an even larger crowd gathered in the inner courtyard beyond the open doors. It was traditional to permit several hundred ordinary people to attend, with individuals chosen by lot. Through the growing haze created by the incense, she could see the common folk just outside, straining to get a better view.

I would rather have them in here than these arrogant, bejeweled peacocks, she thought disgustedly. Her stay among the Kassid had decreased her already limited tolerance for her courtiers.

Then, when she forced herself to pay attention to the priests, she saw how they avoided looking at Daken. Perhaps she should have sent him to talk with them; they certainly seemed to fear him.

Then she began to drift off once more into her thoughts. Hammad had gathered together a few of his most trusted men, and she had gone to the cellars with them to show them the wall that would have to be torn down. Fortunately, it was in a part of the cellars that was rarely visited by servants, so the work should be able to proceed in secret. Hammad thought it would take them no more than two days.

She cast a quick, sidelong glance at Daken, who stood stoically beside her, no doubt wishing himself back at the fortress. How easy it had been to love him then—even after his revelations about their magic. Perhaps there was something in the very air in the Dark Mountains that made magic more acceptable. Or perhaps it was only that there she could be a woman, while here she had to be empress.

But I do love him, she thought, even if I no longer completely trust him. Distrust was in the air of the court as surely as magic was in the air of the Dark Mountains.

Finally, it was over, and a great cheer rose up from the people outside. The courtiers, of course, were far too dignified for such behavior.

Taking Daken by the arm, she led him down from the dais, through the overdressed crowd that parted in surprise—and out to the inner courtyard, where the equally surprised common people stepped back quickly, then began to bow and curtsy clumsily.

In a loud, clear voice, she thanked them for their good wishes and promised them that when the war was over, they would see many changes—good changes. Then, half-appalled at her own daring, she hurried back inside to more cheers. When her eyes met Daken's, he smiled at her and nodded his approval.

Some time later, as Jocelyn was beginning to silently count the minutes until they could escape, she saw one of Hammad's aides come into the hall and move purposefully through the crowd toward his commander. After a brief conversation, Hammad found his way quickly to Daken.

She knew something had happened even before

the two men approached her and suggested they retire to a small anteroom off the hall. And she quickly learned that she was right.

The Menoan and Turvean forces had joined at their common border and were on the move toward Menoa's border with Ertria. She didn't need Hammad to tell her that war was now inevitable. Their last, faint hope of avoiding it had been the sending of an emissary to Arrat to inform him of what he already knew—that the Kassid had joined forces with Ertria. Hammad reported that the emissary, a cousin of Jocelyn's, was now safely back within the borders of Ertria, and he'd sent one of his aides on ahead to report that his announcement had been greeted with a stony silence from Arrat.

After Hammad's announcement, the three of them stood there in silence as the revelry continued in the nearby Hall. Then there was a knock at the door, and Hammad went over to admit Eryk. Jocelyn had not seen him alone since her return, and now she took his hand to introduce him to Daken. Hammad, however, was uninterested in social pleasantries at the moment.

He told Eryk the news, then explained to Daken that the most likely point of invasion would bring the enemy quickly into some of Eryk's lands.

Eryk nodded solemnly. "I have already moved all the farm workers' families to safety. The workers have remained to prepare for planting, but I ordered that no planting be done until we could determine if there would be war."

"I am sorry that your lands will be caught up in

this," Jocelyn said sincerely. "Of all the landholders, you are the one who least deserves it."

"Yes, but he is also the only one who would trouble to move his people to safety," Hammad stated. "The others would simply remove everything of value and leave the people to their own resources."

Both Jocelyn and Eryk nodded in agreement with this, while Daken eyed Eryk with interest. This, he knew, was the nobleman rumored to be the most likely candidate for Jocelyn's hand.

Perhaps he would have made her a good husband, Daken thought. At least he seemed different from the others if those statements were to be believed.

Knowing what was to be believed was a very difficult thing in this avaricious and dissembling court. After only a few days here, he felt a nearly overwhelming urge to do exactly what so many of them seemed to expect of him—seize power for himself. But he reminded himself once again of the decision made long ago by his ancestors, and he knew it had been a wise one.

His gaze traveled from Eryk to Jocelyn and he felt a deep, aching sense of loss. Day by day, perhaps even moment by moment, she was slipping away from him to be reclaimed by the band of beribboned and bejeweled thieves she called her court.

And now there would be war. He'd known it would happen but had held out to her the hope that it could be prevented—and then had perhaps come to half-believe it himself.

"My people tell me that we are in for a spell of rain," Eryk said, "And they are uncannily accurate in their predictions. So the attack may be postponed."

Hammad nodded, then glanced at Daken. "Nevertheless, we must move quickly now that we are certain of their point of attack."

"We are ready," Daken replied, but his gaze was locked on Jocelyn, whose fair skin had gone quite pale.

Jocelyn leaned back in her warm, scented bath. Save for her maids, she was alone on her wedding night. Daken had gone to the camp, and tomorrow the Kassid, together with the Ertrian army, would begin the long march to the border.

There was, she thought, a certain benefit to knowing that the worst had happened. She couldn't say that she felt tranquil, but at least the agony of waiting was over.

Daken had come back to their suite with her, but only for a few minutes, and his mind was clearly elsewhere for most of that time. That difference she'd begun to feel in him from the moment the Kassid had made their decision had only increased. The man who'd held her in his arms and had sworn that he would return to her was a stranger—a mythical warrior come to life to save her empire.

She had believed him when he'd said he would return to her, but what difference did it make? When he returned, it would only be to say goodbye. He belonged to the Dark Mountains, and she belonged here—and their allotted time together was drawing to an end.

The bath water was growing cool, but she felt unable to move. One of the maids suggested that more warm water should be brought, but she shook her head. It seemed to be the only effort she could make just now.

How very strange the mind was. In the Dark Mountains, her life here had begun to seem like a distant dream. But now that she was back, her time there felt the same way.

She leaned back still more and closed her eyes. Immediately, her inner vision was filled with Daken and the times she had known even then she would never forget and others that had seemed unimportant at the moment, but had somehow been preserved anyway.

Tears began to fall down her cheeks unnoticed. Even if she never again saw the Daken she had loved, she had these memories to cherish. It would be enough. It *had* to be enough.

She drew into herself, curling up in the cooling water, floating with those memories and trying to hold at bay the doubts that kept trying to intrude. She was drifting in that strange place between wakefulness and dreaming, clinging to one while reaching for the other, when a low, urgent and very familiar voice intruded.

She opened her eyes to find Daken standing there, glowering at the maids, who were clearly caught between their fear of him and their duties to her.

"Go! Leave us alone!" he repeated.

The frightened women stared from him to her and she nodded. Her heart was pounding and she half-rose from the bath, frightened herself now as she stared at him.

"Daken, what is it? What's happened?"

His fierce expression softened even as he turned back to her. He lifted her from the bath, then quickly wrapped her in the towelling cloth.

"What has happened," he said in a calm voice that belied the tension she could feel in him, "Is that I had to see you again."

He carried her into the bedchamber and laid her on the bed, then began to rub away the wetness, lingering over her soft curves.

"I went to the camp, but I could not sleep there. Forgive me, maiza, for thinking only of war and not of you. Perhaps I have finally talked myself into being a true warrior at last." He gave a rueful chuckle and continued his ministrations, but more slowly, lingering over her breasts and the sensitive flesh of her inner thighs.

"I could feel the presence of the ancestors there; we all could. They are transforming us from men of peace into the warriors created by the gods.

"But a part of me resists that. A part of me wants only to be in your arms."

He paused, and his hands on her grew still. "I think they know that, and approve. If I have to kill, I must at least know why I do it. And I must have your love to give me courage."

She wriggled free from the constraining towel

and wrapped her arms tightly around him. Her tears were starting again.

"I thought I'd lost you—lost the man I love. You've been so *different*, Daken."

"I know," he said, kissing away her tears. "It is the war and this place—and our history. But none of it has anything to do with *us*, with the man and woman who love each other."

The night became a long, waking dream. Every kiss, every touch, every soft word of love, became a moment separated from the rest, but also one long continuum of sensuality. They were fierce with each other, but gentle, too. They drifted along the edges of sleep together, only to be pulled back again by erotic demands.

Although neither spoke of it, they both knew that magic touched them—a magic far beyond either of their understanding. It was ancient, timeless—and all-powerful.

Their footsteps echoed sharply in the heavy silence, and the torchlight flickered over empty corridors, illuminating nothing but the dust of centuries.

She might have been that curious child again, Jocelyn thought. She was even carrying a large ball of red yarn again—the same color she'd carried all those years ago, though the choice had been random, dictated more by size than by color. It surprised her that she could recall even that small detail.

But she wasn't alone this time, and she was glad of that. By an ironic twist of fate, the child had been braver than the adult was. But then, the child hadn't known what she would find.

"You told no one in all these years?" Hammad asked, his voice booming in the silence.

She shook her head. "I guess I just thought of it as a wonderful secret. Arman was always bragging about secrets he kept from me, or talking about things he did that I couldn't do—so it became *my* secret, something I'd done that he hadn't."

And it seemed to her now that she was intended to keep it secret, she thought—just as she was intended to discover it in the first place.

"Then I simply forgot about it over the years," she went on. "Or maybe I didn't really forget, but rather put it away with everything else from childhood. It was only when I saw that black stone in the Dark Mountains that I began to think about it again, and I had intended to talk to Father about it when I came back."

They were both silent for a few moments after that, each of them lost in a resurgence of pain over his loss. Hammad had come to her suite quite early, just after she had awakened to find that Daken had gone. Even as he'd told her that the men had broken through the wall in the cellar, Jocelyn had been struggling to decide if the night just past had been real. Then, after Hammad had gone and her maids had come in to help her dress, she knew, finally, that it *had* been real. Her body told her. No dream lover could have left her with this powerful awareness of herself—or with the small aches and pains of a night spent exploring the outer limits of a body's capacity for pleasure.

She felt it still, as they walked through the ancient cellars, and a lingering trace of the night's magic seemed to be following her as well.

She paused at the bottom of a small set of stairs, then chose the corridor that led to the left at an angle. Nothing was straight down here; corridors seemed to branch off at odd angles everywhere. And yet she felt so confident of the way—too confident for someone relying on a single, sixteen-year old memory. But she was still wrapped in the magic of the previous night and didn't question it.

"We've been moving steadily downward," Hammad observed. "I had no idea the cellars were this deep."

"How old do you think this part of the palace is?" she asked, knowing this his interest in history made him one of the few people likely to be able to make an accurate guess.

"No one really knows. It was built in stages, of course—over centuries, actually. It's possible to see where construction left off and was begun again years later, and we can guess that it might even have been partially torn down and rebuilt at times. But this"—he waved an arm around them—"has to be the oldest part. See how the stones are cut differently? Cutting tools were less precise back then.

"If I had to make a guess, I would say that this portion of the palace must be at least four hundred years old, perhaps even older. The oldest account we have mentions construction atop an older structure, but says nothing about what it was."

"But Hammad, my family's rule goes back only

a little more than three hundred years. If this is older, who built it?"

Hammad shrugged. "It might still have been built by your family, before they conquered the other noble families. Or it might have been built by one of the other families, then taken over by your family after the conquest. If my memory serves me correctly, there is mention somewhere of a desire to get rid of the old structure, as though it were associated with bad memories."

Another set of stairs loomed ahead of them. Jocelyn stopped, then hurried on excitedly. "This is it, Hammad. See how it curves down out of sight? That's exactly the way I remember it. It made me nervous not to be able to see what lay at the bottom."

Hammad followed her down the narrow staircase, chuckling. "It seems that you were even more adventurous than I'd given you credit for, Jocey. By the gods, you could have been lost down here forever! No wonder Maikel had the place walled off."

And then they were standing at the bottom, before the ornately carved door she remembered. Hammad held his torch close to it, examining it carefully.

"Excellent workmanship," he pronounced. "But I do not recognize the wood."

"The wood in the fortress comes from trees that grow only in the Dark Mountains, and when it isn't kept cleaned and polished, it looks just like this."

He took hold of the tarnished brass handle and

gave it a sharp tug before she could warn him. She had just recalled how easily it had opened for her. He too very nearly lost his balance as the door swung outward without protest.

They entered the room together, holding their torches before them. Their gasps were simultaneous. Jocelyn was no less impressed for seeing it the second time, even though it seemed to her now that it had always been there, just this clearly, in her mind.

The torchlight was swallowed by the utter blackness of the room—except for where it reflected with dazzling brightness off the golden drawings. Hammad stood in the center of the room just as she had, turning slowly as he held the torch aloft. Then he walked over to one wall and began to examine it closely.

"There! And there as well. Jocey, you were right! The symbol is the same!"

She already knew that. If she'd had any doubts left, they'd disappeared the moment she'd re-entered this room. She knew that she couldn't describe it to Hammad, so she didn't even try. This was a Kassid place—it *felt* Kassid. It had that feel of past merging with present that she'd sensed so often at the fortress. It had a presence that was both Kassid and somehow even more ancient.

A place of the Old Gods, she thought with a shiver. Built by the Kassid, yes, but at the instruction of the Old Gods. Not like the fortress, which had been created by the gods themselves, but rather something built on their orders after they had departed this world.

"And the wolves!" Hammad exclaimed, breaking into her thoughts. "They're everywhere!"

But Jocelyn was wondering how such thoughts had come into her head, and why she was so certain that the magic of the gods lingered here, after all these centuries.

The little girl who had discovered this place had felt none of that—but the woman felt it now.

And Hammad feels none of this, she thought as she watched him walk slowly along the walls, pausing now and then. *It is I who feel it—because I have been touched by Kassid magic.*

"They carved the stone, then filled in the carvings with gold," Hammad said. "An enormous task."

Then he turned back to her. "The Kassid *must* have built this, Jocelyn. There is no other explanation. That means that this place was theirs before it became ours."

He paused, then went on more slowly. "And that must mean that our history lies. The Kassid were more than an army of mercenaries who fought for us."

She nodded, the movement barely perceptible. They had ruled it all. She knew that now, though she could not have said *how* she knew it.

And now they had returned.

Rumors were everywhere. One had only to breathe the air of the city to take them in. Wartime only lent the ever-present rumors more urgency—and gave them more speed.

It was said that Hammad's forces had been defeated. But it was also said that they were victorious, and that the enemy was on the run, back across its borders. Those who spread the latter rumor were divided—Hammad and his men had followed them into Menoa; Hammad had ordered his army back at the border.

And the Kassid? Rumors of them were spoken in hushed tones, with the reverence reserved for the Old Gods. Were they not the children of those Gods, the ones most blessed? It was said that they fought with unimaginable magic—lightning bolts out of clear skies, ghosts who fought with real weapons alongside them. And wolves; stories of wolves were rampant. In some, the wolves accompanied the Kassid; in other tales, the wolves *were* the Kassid.

In all the rumors of the Kassid, they were victorious. Would the gods have it otherwise for those whom they favored?

And there were other tales, even more disquieting. It was said that this land, too, belonged to the Kassid, as surely as did the Dark Mountains—and that they had come at last to claim it again. All the world belonged to the Kassid; the gods had given it to them when they departed. Even Menoa and Turvea were part of that ancient empire, given up centuries ago for reasons known only to the Kassid themselves. Given up voluntarily, it was said—for who could have defeated them?

Daken, the gray-haired giant, had led his people back here to claim what was rightfully theirs. He'd cast a spell on their beautiful empress. Servants said she was besotted with him—she, who had disdained marriage. She was said to be distracted and short-tempered when he wasn't around.

And there was more—stories of how the Kassid elected their leader and shared the land and their great wealth equally. No man worked for another; no women and children went hungry.

And they would bring all this to the peoples of Ertria and Balek, now that they were reclaiming their empire.

The small, green-robed figure who walked once more along the palace wall knew more than they did—and less. Jocelyn received regular reports from Hammad's young aides, who took turns riding hard from the distant battlefields to bring her the news first-hand.

The enemy, trusting in its superior numbers, had launched a two-pronged attack. A part of the force crossed the border at the expected place, into Eryk's lands. There they were met by the Ertrian army and part of the Kassid force, who were slowly forcing them back, despite being outnumbered nearly two to one.

The aides passed on to her the tales told to them by men fighting alongside the Kassid. Wherever the Kassid went, strange, dark shadows rode with them, forms that seemed to shift from men to wolves and back again. The enemy fell in far greater numbers than could be accounted for—and many had not a mark upon them. These, it was said, wore expressions frozen in death that bespoke great horror.

There were reports, too, of Ertrians who had witnessed Kassid changing themselves into wolves. In one tale brought to Jocelyn, two Ertrians, who had lost both horses and weapons, were being attacked by a Menoan on horseback. A Kassid suddenly appeared on a hilltop some distance away. He lept from his horse and started toward them—and then it was no longer a man running, but a wolf. The wolf sprang upon the nearest rider, tore out his throat, and then dispatched the other just as quickly. As the Ertrians picked themselves up, the wolf ran back the way he had come, and then was a Kassid again before he reached his horse.

"It happened just like that, milady," Hammad's aide told her, snapping his fingers. "Kassid to wolf and wolf to Kassid—in a mere blink!"

But of the main Kassid force that had taken off after the other enemy force, there was no news. Jocelyn had never visited that region, but she knew what it was like—hilly, rugged land, unlike the rest of Ertria. It was also the source of Ertria's great deposits of iron ore; hence the enemy's interest.

"Hammad says they've made a big mistake," one of the aides told her. "They aren't used to fighting in such terrain, and the Kassid are. But the Kassid are out-numbered by more than three to one, milady. I was present when Hammad and Daken discussed it, and Daken said at those odds, the Kassid would be quickly victorious."

And they will be, Jocelyn thought now as she paced the outer wall in the waning daylight. She no longer believed that *anything* was beyond the capabilities of the Kassid. All that Daken had told her had been confirmed.

When she returned to the palace, she found the captain of her Guards awaiting her, his expression grim. The Guards, of course, remained in the city.

But at Hammad's suggestion, she had given the captain orders to learn what he could about the Sherbas, who were said to be in the city in record numbers.

She took him to her suite, not wanting to risk their conversation being overheard by anyone. And it was there that he told her about the rumors circulating around the city.

"It's the Sherbas, milady. They're the ones spreading the tales about the Kassid. By our count, there are at least a hundred of them in the city itself, and more are reported in the farms beyond.

"One of my men saw a Sherba openly displaying that black rock on a gold chain that you spoke about. And from many sources, we now know that they worship the Kassid. There's no doubt in my mind that they have always spied for them."

"So they believe that the Kassid have come back to claim what is theirs?" Jocelyn said softly.

"Yes, milady. That is what they say. The people remain loyal to you, I believe, but these Sherbas stir up their hopes. It is a dangerous situation."

And it would be more dangerous when the war was over, she said silently. When the soldiers returned and everyone knew how the Kassid fought, the people would worship them as the children of the gods.

"With your permission, milady, I will round up all the Sherbas and imprison them."

Jocelyn considered that, then shook her head. "To do so would only give credence to their tales. We must ignore them for now."

The captain was clearly disappointed, but he accepted her decision and left her alone.

Jocelyn paced about her spacious reception room. The Sherbas were only confirming what she'd already known—what she'd guessed down there in that secret room. Her family's four-hundred-year rule of this land was nothing more than a straw in the wind, blowing away as the Kassid returned to claim what was theirs.

That, she thought, was what had been decided in the Dark Mountains—not an alliance with Ertria, but a resumption of their rule over this land.

She recalled Daken's harangue about her family's rule. What he'd really been telling her was that it was to come to an end—that they'd given her family time, and it had been used unwisely. Now they would take it back for themselves.

Could she truly blame him? When she thought about how the Kassid lived, and then remembered the poor, pathetic people she'd encountered on her journey, she could do nothing more than agree with him.

Was their love too a sham? Had he married her merely to effect an easy transfer of power? When he'd said that the gods had whispered to him that they didn't have to be parted, had he really been telling her that he would remain here to rule Ertria?

"No," she said aloud. "No!" Their love was no sham, no Kassid magic trick. Whatever Daken's plans were, he would never harm her.

She was siezed by a sudden and powerful urge to return to that secret room. Before she could even

consider the wisdom of going down there alone,
she had grabbed her cloak and left the suite, then
slipped at the first opportunity into one of the little-
used corridors she knew well from her childhood.
A short time later, she was in the cellars, picking
up a torch. She'd brought no yarn with her this
time and knew she didn't need it.

The gold symbols flared to life the moment she
stepped through the doorway, seeming even
brighter than before. She walked over to a wall and
put out her left hand, as she held the torch in her
right. The light caught the gold of her ring as well—
the ring Daken had given her.

She stared at it, remembering the tiny symbols
carved into it. Daken had told her they were ancient
symbols for happiness and other good things. She
held her hand up to the torchlight and peered at
them, but the light wasn't bright enough to make
them out. It didn't matter; she knew they would be
similar to the writing on these walls.

She retreated to the center of the room and stared
at the walls. Something stirred—not in the room,
but within *her*. Were they voices? It seemed they
could be. She stood perfectly still for a long time,
but the voices or whatever it was became no clearer.

Still, when she left the room at last, she felt a
glowing warmth inside, a sense of peace that for a
time drove out her fears.

The excitement in the court was palpable—though
of course restrained, as befitted people who spend
their lives hiding their true feelings. News of the
victory had come to the court by way of one of

Hammad's aides, and Hammad himself was due to arrive at any moment.

Daken would not be with him. The aide had reported that after soundly defeating the enemy force that had been intent upon seizing the iron mines, Daken and his men had rejoined Hammad to drive the other enemy force back across the border into Menoa.

There hadn't been many of them left to push back across the borders, the aide reported. Between their heavy losses and numerous desertions, what was left was no more than a small force still loyal to Arrat.

Daken, the aide said, had taken his army to pursue them, since both he and Hammad agreed that Arrat must die. To leave such a man alive was to invite future troubles. But the feeble-minded ruler of Turvea was already suing for peace, having lost his wastrel sons in battle.

Jocelyn, waiting impatiently with the others, heard the clatter of hooves in the inner courtyard and came down from her throne as the courtiers made way for Hammad and his senior officers.

He looked gray and tired—and old. When he made to get down on one knee before her, Jocelyn took his arm instead and led him back to the dais. Already, her elation over the victory was being supplanted by guilt over the news she would have to give him.

She'd had two days since the Guards commander's report to consider what to do, and her position had hardened. She would *not* surrender either her throne or her power to Daken. She'd already acknowledged to him the past injustices, but she was determined to redeem her family's name. She would face Daken down, certain that he would neither harm her nor set his men against her own army. But she badly needed Hammad's wise counsel. She'd spoken to no one of this.

Her advisors would support her; she had no doubt of that. But they would support her only because they too had heard the tales being told of the Kassid's return to claim their land—and the stories of their strange beliefs. They would support her because they believed she would continue as her predecessors had done—tacitly accepting their greed and corruption.

Hammad made his formal declaration of victory, adding to what she already knew only the fact that reports had reached him that Arrat and his remaining troops had reached an ancient fortress in the Menoan hills and the Kassid were laying siege.

Perhaps it was another of their own fortresses, Jocelyn thought, built by Kassid who might well have knowledge of its weaknesses. Daken had commented to her after the fall of the garrison in Balek that except for the mighty Kassid fortress in the Dark Mountains, all fortresses were vulnerable and should have a secret means of escape.

When Hammad had finished his abbreviated recounting of the victory, Jocelyn thanked him formally on behalf of the court and the people and declared three days of festivities to celebrate. The Keeper of the Royal Purse watched her stoically. He had ventured the opinion that one day would do. She felt rather bad about rejecting his advice, since he was one of the very few honest men at court. But she hoped that a longer festival would serve to keep people's thoughts away from the Kassid threat.

Then, after allowing the court as little time as possible to congratulate Hammad—whose disdain for them matched her own—she hurried him off to her private suite.

As soon as they were there, he sank gratefully into a chair. "I am too old for this, Jocey," he said tiredly. "It is time I retire and you appoint a successor."

She nodded her agreement. It was more important to her to have this good man alive and able to provide her with wise counsel than to have him heading the army. She told him this, then sighed.

"Hammad, I wish that I didn't have to burden you now with what I have learned, but there is no one else I can go to."

She then told him about the Sherbas and the stories they were spreading, and about her own belief that they were accurate.

"Daken will not harm me, and I honestly believe that he does not want to fight the Ertrian army. He is essentially a man of peace."

She paused, thinking about their last night together and his confession that the warrior spirit of the Kassid had stirred inside him. Could she be wrong about him? Now that he had seen battle, now that he had taken up the sword himself, could he put it down again? But before she could voice these thoughts to Hammad, he spoke them for her.

"Victory is a heady wine, Jocey. Men become addicted to it very quickly—even men of peace such as Daken. Furthermore," he said, heaving a heavy sigh, "As you yourself have pointed out, he would have right on his side if he did decide to defeat us.

"And he *would* defeat us. Who could defeat an army augmented by ghosts of warriors past?"

"Then you are saying that I should give up the throne?" she asked in a suddenly choked voice.

Hammad shook his head. "No, I think you should wait and see what his intentions are. The Sherbas speak of their hopes—not of Daken's plans.

"When your father told me of his plan to seek the aid of the Kassid, I felt that we would be awakening a sleeping giant that, once aroused, might well trample us. But we had no choice. Without them, we would have lost—and then we'd have Arrat in place of Daken."

He paused a moment to accept the wine she belatedly offered him, then went on. "If the Kassid intend to fight us, they would not have risked themselves so many times in battle to save Ertrians. But there were many reports of such things.

"I think that Daken intends for you to remain on the throne and for you to rule the empire. But I believe he intends to demand that you make good on your promises to him of reforms."

After another pause, Hammad went on in a musing tone. "I think we will be able to guess his intentions when we learn the truth about our own history. If the Sherbas are right that the Kassid once ruled all this land, then the reason they gave it up is of great importance. If there is one thing I have learned about Daken and the Kassid, it is that they are true to the history of their people. They walked away once—and we need to know why."

"The Sherbas claim not to know," Jocelyn said distractedly as she thought about Hammad's words.

"But we haven't talked to the Sherbas. We've only heard their tales from our own people."

"Then I will invite their leaders here, and we will ask them."

Jocelyn had expected that the Sherbas would refuse to meet with her and had ordered that no coercion be used, but to her surprise, their leaders agreed to come to the palace.

The meeting was set for late in the evening, allowing Hammad time to rest from his ordeal and also allowing for the greatest possible secrecy. In the city and at court, the festivities had commenced, and the Guards brought the Sherbas in through their garrison and a backstairs route used only by them in their mission to protect their empress.

Hammad arrived at her suite just before the Sherbas. Jocelyn felt greatly relieved to see him looking much better. They talked about Daken's pursuit of Arrat without concern for his safety or success, and Jocelyn finally smiled ruefully.

"We both believe the Kassid to be invincible, don't we?"

Hammad nodded. "As they have always been. That is why we must learn the reason they chose to walk away before."

Then the Guards arrived with three Sherbas—

two young men and one very old man who moved slowly, but stared at her with bright, curious eyes before accepting the seat she offered.

She assured them that they were her guests and under her protection and thanked them for coming. Then she explained that there were rumors about in the city regarding the Kassid, with whom, she said, they appeared to have "some bond." Would they be willing to tell her about their history—and about their knowledge of the Kassid?

To her surprise, they were quite willing to do so. The old man's voice was strong and his bearing, despite his great age, was proud. Neither did he ramble as he told his story.

And as Jocelyn and Hammad listened in rapt attention, the history of their people was re-written.

The Kassid had indeed ruled the world ever since the departure of the Old Gods. They were, after all, the children of those gods. Because their empire was vast and contained many different peoples, they had encouraged local autonomy, contenting themselves only with resolving disputes that arose between various tribes.

Fortresses were erected in various areas, and the Kassid kept some troops in each to put down unrest and act as courts to resolve disputes. But most Kassid lived in their ancestral home in the Dark Mountains.

The Kassid, he told them, were fair and just, but the men who gained power under their loose rule were not. The result, as time passed, was corruption, greed and ever-increasing wars. More garrisons had to be built and more Kassid had to leave their beloved mountains to battle first one tribal ruler and then another.

Always, the worst trouble was in Ertria, the largest and richest of all their lands. Because the other lands were more peaceful, the Kassid withdrew from them over a period of years, remaining only in Ertria—and in its neighbor Balek, sparsely populated then as now, but a land of considerable wealth that had long ago caught the eye of greedy Ertrians.

"The Kassid built a great fortress in Ertria," he went on, "and kept a large force there. But if there were no outright wars, there were many assassinations. As soon as one family would seem to be gaining ascendancy, members of another would kill their leader."

Finally, the Kassid had apparently had enough. It became clear to them that they would have to choose the best from a bad lot and set that man up as a strong ruler.

"The man they chose was your ancestor, milady," the old man said. "And once they had chosen him, they abandoned their fortress and went home to the Dark Mountains. It was said that they acted on the whispered advice of the Old Gods, who called them home after their long ordeal."

The man made a gesture and went on. "The rest you already know, milady. No sooner had the Kassid departed than war broke out again, as the new ruler of Ertria sought to add to his lands."

"But the Kassid did not return?" Hammad inquired.

The old man shook his head. "The gods had spoken—and I think too that they were weary. You, milady, have seen their home, so perhaps you can understand why they chose to remain there."

"Yes," she said. "I can understand that."

"But where do *you* fit into this?" Hammad asked. "How did the Sherbas come into being?"

"The name 'Sherba' is an old Kassid term for 'Faithful'—and that is what we were—and are. We are the descendants of those who continued to hope that the Kassid would one day return to bring peace and justice to this land again. We were hounded and often killed by the new rulers of Ertria, and when it became too bad for us, we sought refuge in the Dark Mountains. The Kassid allowed us to live there for a time, until we were largely forgotten by the Ertrian rulers. Then we ventured forth again and became the sellers of herbs you see now. The Kassid provide them to us and give us gold as well.

"We wear black because that is the color of the Kassid's sacred land, and many of us carry a piece of that stone with us. Many wear a mark as well—the old Kassid symbol for The Faithful. And we wander because we have vowed not to settle on this land until Kassid peace and justice once again prevail here."

"And when you get the herbs and gold from the Kassid, you give them news of the outside world?" Hammad asked. Jocelyn was glad he forbore using the term "spy."

The old man nodded. "Always we have hoped they would return—and they are ever curious about the world beyond the Dark Mountains."

"And you now believe that they have come back to claim their lands?"

He looked her straight in the eye and nodded gravely. "They *have* returned—and their leader has married you."

Chapter Twelve

Rains lashed the city and the surrounding plains for days on end, beginning just as the victory celebration was ended. Jocelyn's mood was as dark as the skies as she waited for Daken's return. Several times, she returned to the secret room, hoping that the strange feeling that came over her there would be clarified. But it remained as elusive as ever, though she always left the room more at peace with herself.

She never doubted that the Kassid would be victorious and that Daken would return to her, however. So when the news came, she felt no particular elation, but rather a tense awareness that the final act was about to be played out.

The news was carried by one of Hammad's men. A small contingent of them had gone with the Kassid to capture the garrison where Arrat and his few remaining troops had holed up. Hammad brought the bedraggled messenger directly to her, so that they might hear the news together.

"Arrat is dead," the man told them. "Only a few men remained with him, and they too were killed. The others came out of the garrison to surrender, and Daken spared their lives." He paused and looked rather nervously from Hammad to Jocelyn.

"Daken said he spared them because the Menoans had suffered such heavy losses and they needed to maintain an army for defense."

Jocelyn shot a quick look at Hammad, but his expression told her nothing. The messenger went on.

"Not one Kassid life was lost—not one! There was a secret entrance to the garrison through an underground stream that provided water. The Kassid knew about it because they built the garrison. It was just like the garrison at Balek," the man said with more than a touch of awe in his voice.

"Daken himself killed Arrat, then ordered the men he spared to take his body back so that the people would know he was dead. He told them you would be sending an envoy, milady, to dictate the terms."

I may be sending the envoy, she thought—*but who will be dictating the terms?* When the messenger had gone, Hammad and Jocelyn were both silent for some time before Jocelyn finally asked what Hammad thought of Daken's insistence that the Menoans should have an army for defense.

"There's no doubt who he thinks they must de-

347

fend themselves *from*," she finished bitterly. "The Turveans have only the remnants of an army left themselves."

"He is remaining true to his history—and ours," Hammad said mildly. "If he were to leave them totally defenseless, he would be giving us an excuse to spread Ertrian rule over them as well."

"You approve of this?" Jocelyn asked in disbelief.

"I am merely seeing it from Daken's perspective," he responded neutrally, "and from the perspective of history as well."

"But he doesn't trust us. He doesn't trust *me*!"

"I believe he trusts your intentions—but good intentions are often not sufficient."

Then, after a brief pause, Hammad went on. "I think also that this proves that he does not intend to take control of the empire for himself. If he intended that, he would not be so worried about the Menoans and Turveans defending themselves."

Jocelyn hadn't thought about that, and now she felt a faint rise of hope. But no sooner did that hope stir than she realized that if those were Daken's intentions, he would not remain here, but would return to the Dark Mountains.

How tangled her thoughts were! If Daken remained, she would be empress in name, but not in fact. If he left, she would never know the joy of his love again.

After Hammad had left, she wondered for a time which she would choose, if the choice were hers to make. Would she willingly trade her throne for his love?

No, of course not, she told herself quickly, angrily. That is the kind of sentimental groveling other women engage in—but I am an empress.

But she thought after a time that her protest rang falsely.

Jocelyn had always been a light sleeper, so the faint noise from beyond the door to her bedchamber woke her, though not completely. She lingered for a moment in that in-between state, then sat up quickly when the door opened, admitting a faint light from the antechamber beyond which her maids slept.

A huge, dark form, made even larger by a cloak of dark, oiled skins, stood there—uncertainly, she thought. Behind him, she could see her maids, moving about nervously.

"Daken," she whispered, and knew only when she heard the agonized longing in her own voice how very much she had missed him. In the naked, raw emotion of her arousal from sleep, when she hadn't yet remembered all her doubts and fears, love and desire poured through her.

He turned briefly to glance at the hovering maids, then closed the door behind him. In the blackness of the room, she could see him only as a slightly different texture to the darkness. Then she heard the heavy cloak thud softly to the floor, the oiled skins crackling slightly.

She got out of bed, intending to ask the maids to bring a lamp, but collided almost immediately with a solid wall of flesh.

"Maiza," he groaned. "Oh gods, how I've missed you!"

The warrior is gone, she thought as he crushed her to him. *The man has come back to me!*

She struggled to free a hand, then reached up to touch his face, making a slight sound of surprise when she encountered his beard.

"I need to bathe and shave," he said thickly, "but I need you more."

The lamp was forgotten as they fumbled blindly to get out of their clothing, to reach beneath it for the heated flesh they both craved. When the clothing had fallen to the floor, they tumbled onto the bed already locked in an embrace.

There was no softness, no gentle exploring, no slow stoking of the fires of passion. His hardness slid into her melting softness immediately, driving them both over the edge and into that other plane, where nothing existed except an all-encompassing need. In the darkness of deep night, they broke through to a realm of brilliance, then clung to it until the darkness once again enveloped them.

They slept and awoke to remembered love, then renewed that love and slept again. And when Jocelyn opened her eyes to the morning light, she wanted to close them again and recapture the magic of the night.

One of her maids had crept into the room and was standing there uncertainly. Jocelyn raised a hand and sent her away, then lifted herself to stare down at Daken as he slept on.

At first, it was the face of a stranger she saw— one that sent a quick chill through her. His heavy beard was more black than gray, giving his rugged features a darkly menacing cast. But then, even as she stared at him, his lashes fluttered—and she was staring into those pale eyes.

He smiled and reached for her sleepily, drawing her back to him with a murmured endearment. The warrior vanished again. When he didn't move, she thought he had fallen asleep again. Her head rested against his chest, the bristly hairs tickling her skin that was already raw from his beard.

Then he began to caress her slowly. "Did I hurt you?" he asked in a fearful tone that was at odds with his menacing appearance.

She laughed against his chest. "Not permanently."

"The guards gave me no trouble, but those accursed maids of yours tried to stop me," he growled.

Jocelyn doubted that, but remained silent. Her maids were terrified of him, and she knew he resented their presence here.

"Hammad's messenger arrived with the news?" he asked as he continued to run his big, calloused hands over her.

"Yes." She didn't want to talk about this now. She didn't want to talk about anything.

"I do not want this again, maiza. I may be Kassid, descended from a long line of warriors—but I do not want to fight again."

"There is no reason you should," she said, hoping that was true.

"Is there no place we can go to escape from your court and those damned maids for a time?"

She should have thought of that, she realized. "There is a small summer palace on one of the islands, but it is early to go there."

351

"Let's go anyway—without the servants."

"But . . ." Jocelyn thought about the usual contingent of servants that went along, less than half the number required here, but too many, she knew, for him. She laughed.

"Daken, I cannot cook for us. I don't think I've ever even *seen* the kitchens at the summer palace."

"We'll manage. Tell them to pack food, then get us a boat. I want to go today."

And so they did. Jocelyn was quickly caught up in his need for them to be alone. She issued orders to her shocked majordomo and sent orders to the captain of the imperial boat, an arrogant man from whom she half-expected to hear a refusal.

Daken went to have a bath and a shave, and Hammad joined him to hear the details of the siege of the garrison. With the low murmur of their voices in the background, Jocelyn supervised the packing. She felt like an excited child again. She hadn't been to the summer palace for two years, since her father's health hadn't permitted the boat trip. But she'd always loved the place, with its airy rooms and the soft sand beach almost at its doorstep and the soothing sound of the sea to lull her to sleep.

When the packing was done, she summoned her senior advisors and informed them of her plans. They were predictably aghast, but she gave them no opportunity to protest, and in any event, the words they might have spoken died on their lips when Daken appeared.

The weather had cleared overnight and a stiff, warm breeze was blowing. As they rode to the harbor, Jocelyn recalled how the weather in the Dark

Mountains had changed so dramatically just before the Turning festival and wondered if Daken could have been wrong when he'd stated that the gods paid them little attention.

Jocelyn loved the sea, but her pleasure this time was even greater as she watched Daken. He made no attempt to hide his enjoyment and plied the captain with endless questions. That formerly unpleasant man underwent a dramatic transformation, answering Daken and even offering more information about wind and weather and the art of sailing.

Everyone, she thought as she watched them, has fallen under the spell of the Kassid. And when Daken then left the captain to walk across the deck to her, she forgot all about the threat that posed because she too was under the spell of this man. The only difference was that while others saw great warriors, she saw the passionate man who had said over and over again during the glorious night just past that he needed her.

Several hours later, as they sat in the comfortable chairs on the deck watching the sails billow with the stiff breeze and eating cheese and fruits, Jocelyn spotted the faint smudge on the distant horizon and pointed excitedly.

"There is Saba! Do you see it?"

He did, and they finished their meal as they saw the island grow larger, And then they were there, stepping from the boat onto the long pier as the crew unloaded their belongings and food supply. A short time later, the boat was gone and they were alone.

353

In fact, as Jocelyn explained to Daken, they were not completely alone on the island. There was a small fishing village on the far side, and the captain would call there to arrange for fresh fish to be delivered to them during their stay.

"Of course, we may be forced to eat it raw," she told him, teasing him gently about his refusal to bring servants.

"I can cook fish," he replied, looking about him with obvious pleasure.

Daken carried their things into the low, rambling structure, designed by a great-great uncle of Jocelyn's nearly a hundred years before. It was considerably less luxurious than the palace, but more than made up for that with its high, airy rooms and many windows open to the sea.

All the windows were shuttered, and Daken went around opening them, so that the musty smell of disuse was quickly replaced with the invigorating aroma of the sea. There was little dust, thanks to the shutters and the couple on the island who looked after the place during the winter. But Jocelyn still found it strange and rather intimidating to be here without any servants.

Before the day had ended, however, she was glad that he'd insisted on this trip. Never in her life had she been utterly alone with one person and it felt very daring and free.

They took off their shoes and walked on the soft, sandy beach, stopping regularly to examine the empty shells of sea creatures that had washed up and watching the birds that sought food along the water's edge.

Daken was fascinated by the sea. He said he hadn't known it was so restless, so constantly in motion, but had believed it would simply be a larger version of the lakes in the Dark Mountains. The captain had explained to him about tides, though, and he understood that now.

He wanted to swim, but Jocelyn, after dipping a hand into the water, declared that it was too cold. Daken, however, accustomed to the greater cold of the lakes in the Dark Mountains, stripped off his clothing and waded in, then began to swim in long, powerful strokes as Jocelyn sat on the beach and watched him.

When he emerged, naked and wet, her passion flared anew, and they made love on the beach, using his clothes as a bed, then reluctantly went inside when the sun dipped below the crest of the island behind them and the air began to grow cool.

They went to bed early and spent the night in a love that was no less passionate, but more tender as they now found it possible to control that passion. Jocelyn had told him about how she had often arisen before dawn to watch the sun come up over the sea, and Daken awoke her in the soft, gray light so that they could watch this wonder together.

Blissful days and nights followed. Daken proved that they could manage quite well without servants. Their meals weren't as elaborate as those prepared by the palace kitchens or by Tassa at the fortress, but they were good. When the fishermen brought them some of their catch, Daken got from them as well instructions on how to prepare them. Accustomed to the highly spiced or sauced versions

served by her staff, Jocelyn was pleasantly surprised to find the simple recipes Daken prepared
truly delicious.

Several small sailboats were kept on the island,
and Daken hauled one of them down to the dock,
then took it out, at first alone, so that he could be
certain he could handle it, and then with Jocelyn
aboard. The man of the mountains was rapidly becoming a man of the sea as well.

But there were times when she would find him
sitting on the beach staring at the sea with a
haunted expression. After seeing this several times,
she sat down beside him and asked if he were thinking of his home.

He nodded slowly, his gaze still directed at the
sea. "I had not thought to miss it so much. I like it
here, but inside, there is this need to go home. It
doesn't feel natural to me. I think perhaps the gods
have made us this way, so that we will never again
be tempted to try to set the world aright."

And so it began. Jocelyn, who had known that
they must talk, had carefully steered all conversation away from this subject, wanting to cling to
this beautiful time together. And Daken as well had
avoided it. It hadn't really been his intention to talk
now, but with that one remark, there seemed to be
no other conversational course they could take.

So she told him about the tales spread by the
Sherbas and about her meeting with their leader.
He sat quietly, but his gaze was now on her, not
the sea. And when she had exhausted her tale, he
confirmed that it was all true.

"It was the hope of my people to bring the life we

had to all, but we failed. We were so righteous, so sure that the rest of the world would accept what we believed to be the way people were intended to live.

"But in the end, the gods called us home to the Dark Mountains in much the same way that I now feel called to return. It is a pain, maiza, a need that grows ever stronger inside me."

He paused for a moment, staring intently at her, then went on in a bitter tone. "But I do not understand why the gods, who surely sent you to me, now demand that I leave you."

Jocelyn fought back her tears and thought again about that choice she'd once tormented herself with—her throne or him. She could give up neither, but she knew she must give up one.

They spoke no more of it then, as each tried to console the other, and soothing caresses and words turned slowly to lovemaking. But two days later, when the fisherman appeared, they asked him to have a boat sent to Ertria to summon the captain.

In the interim, they walked many miles on the strip of beach, bypassing the pain for a time by talking about Ertria's future. Daken urged her to be both bold and patient as she tried to make changes and suggested that she seek the counsel of the Sherbas, perhaps even making a few of them her advisors.

"They are a good people, dedicated to peace and justice, and they have no wealth or land of their own to sway their advice."

Jocelyn agreed with him, but knew it was going to be very difficult to bring into court such as they—

assuming, of course, that they would agree to come. Daken said they would, that he would speak to their leader.

He also asked her not to exact a tribute from their former enemies. Neither land was as wealthy as Ertria to begin with, he pointed out, and they had suffered great losses in the brief war.

"But that would make me seem weak," she protested, ever-conscious of being a woman who would presume to rule.

"No, it will make you generous," he insisted. "And even if they should think you weak, they cannot attack Ertria again. They have lost most of their army, and know, furthermore, that if they attack, they will again face the Kassid."

As for Balek, he wanted the garrison to remain in their hands and for Ertria to permit the Baleks to handle their own affairs.

"They can remain a part of the empire, but still rule themselves to as great an extent as possible. It is a rich land with few inhabitants, so they will always need protection. But their nobles are closer to their people than yours are, and I believe they would rule justly, save for the few who have remained too long at the Ertrian court and would most likely choose to remain there."

Then, when she despaired of her court, he told her that he would gather them together and let them know that her wishes were his as well, thereby letting them know that they risked the wrath of the Kassid if they attempted any insurrection.

"I know that that will make your authority seem less, maiza, but there is no other way. Just remember that it has less to do with your being a woman than it does with the fact that you will be forcing them to change."

In the end, she accepted that because, as he said, there was no other way.

They returned to the palace and she called her court together to hear Daken. He'd already met with Hammad and had that estimable man's full support.

Her courtiers were obviously nervous as they gathered in the Great Hall. Certainly they had heard the story circulated by the Sherbas, and Jocelyn thought that they probably expected her to announce that the Kassid would now rule the empire.

Instead, she introduced the beginnings of her plans—tax reform (and there was no doubt that they understood just what she meant by *that*; it was in their faces), free basic education for all citizens (they were too shocked at the first item for this one to register), and the inclusion of several Sherbas in her circle of advisors if they were willing.

"And that is just a beginning," she stated, looking from one stunned face to another. "When the people have been educated, there will be elections for a parliament to advise me."

Daken silenced the beginnings of protest that followed this announcement. "Your empress has convinced me that she should retain you as advisors, although I would have preferred to see you all put into the dungeons."

He paused, and although Jocelyn could not see his expression, since he stood beside her, she could certainly see the naked fear on their faces.

He went on to excoriate them for their corruption and greed and said that his men had not saved the empire to have this continue.

"The Kassid once ruled this land and then we withdrew, hoping you would make it a just place for all to live in peace. Instead, people starve while you parade yourselves at court wearing enough gold to fill all their stomachs for a lifetime.

"You will either work with the empress to achieve these reforms, or we will return and take *everything* from you. I will leave soon for the Dark Mountains, but we will come quickly if we are needed. Hammad's men will be constructing mirror towers across Ertria and Balek to signal us."

He paused, then went on in a quietly menacing tone that brought a chill even to Jocelyn. "Now I would have each of you swear to your empress that you will follow her dictates and take no actions to thwart them."

Jocelyn had known what he planned to say to them, but he hadn't told her that he intended to make them swear to obey her. It was, she thought, a brilliant move to force these arrogant men to make such a pledge on bended knee.

Hammad stepped forth first. Jocelyn thought this unnecessary, but she suspected that he and Daken had planned this, to show that he and the army supported her in what was to come.

The next man to step forth was Eryk. Jocelyn hadn't seen him and hadn't expected him to be at court, since he wasn't, strictly speaking, one of her advisors. She detected Hammad's hand in this; he was Eryk's uncle. And as one of the wealthiest and most powerful of the nobles, his support was essential.

The others followed. Most of them looked as though they'd just been forced to eat something exceedingly bitter, but one by one, they knelt before her and made their pledges.

When it was over, she dismissed all but Hammad and Eryk and extended a hand to each of them in gratitude.

"I have had it in mind for some time to educate the people who work for me," Eryk told her. "Both on my ships and on the farms—and even in the mines—new ideas are being tested. The time will come soon, I think, when it will be necessary for people to read and write and do simple sums just to do their jobs." He smiled at Jocelyn.

"Naturally, I am pleased that the court will do this at its expense, not mine."

"But it *will* be at your expense, to some extent, Eryk, now that you have promised to pay your fair share of taxes." Jocelyn returned his smile.

"I won't even mind that, since most of the others will be harder hit than I will. I've never cheated all that much—at least not by comparison with them."

Then he turned to Daken. "And I would like to know more about these signal towers. I may set up a system of my own for my lands."

Daken explained them, and Hammad told him of the plans to erect them, and Jocelyn sat there listening and thinking happily about the future.

She didn't doubt that, despite their promises, many would try to undermine her work. But as

Daken had said, with a combination of firmness and patience, she would prevail.

Only when they had returned to her suite did the future lose its brilliant promise and the bleakness of a life without Daken begin to set in again—a life that would begin tomorrow, since he planned to depart for the Dark Mountains with the dawn.

Most of his men had already returned, after resting a few days in their camp at the city's edge. Hammad was sending a few men with him as far as Balek, where they would train the Baleks to take over the garrison permanently. On the way, they planned to seek out an appropriate place to build another small fortress that would serve as a meeting place for Daken and her.

Once a year, they would meet there—and try to fit a year's worth of love into a few weeks. It was an imperfect solution, but the only one available to them.

They ate their dinner in her suite, then sat before the fire. Both were quiet and content for the moment to simply hold each other. Jocelyn realized for the first time that although she would certainly miss their lovemaking, what she would miss even more was simply his presence.

He filled her life and made it whole, though she hadn't known until she'd fallen in love with him that it was incomplete. He was always quick to sense her moods and draw her down from her angry flare-ups, or bring her up from the depths of despair. Now she would have to face that alone—and the despair would be even greater.

Then suddenly, she remembered the secret room, the Kassid place, that she had yet to tell him about. Whether she recalled it at that moment because she had recalled the peace she'd found there, or whether the gods themselves put the thought into her mind, she would never know—but later, she would be inclined to believe the gods had spoken to her.

If Jocelyn was beginning to find faith, Daken, at that moment, was in danger of losing it. The gods had continued to whisper to him that they would not have to be parted—and yet it was about to happen. As he sat there holding her on this last night, he wondered if they were playing a cruel joke on him for their own unknowable reasons.

His faith in the gods, at least insofar as their constant presence in his life was concerned, had never been as strong as that of many of his people. Never before had they whispered to him—and now they did so with lies. Perhaps he deserved it, for having so little faith.

Such were his thoughts when she suddenly moved out of his arms and spoke his name excitedly.

"Daken! There is something I forgot to tell you— a discovery I made many years ago."

Then she stopped abruptly. "No, I think I will show you instead. Come."

She led him from the suite, then through back corridors and down many steps until they reached a broken wall that looked to have been more recently built than its neighbors.

"My father had this built," she told him, "After he found out that I'd been down here exploring."

She led him over the rubble of the wall, then down long, empty corridors. At one point, after they'd made a turn, he began to worry that they'd become lost down here. But she seemed so intent and so purposeful that he decided to trust her.

And then, a few moments later, he felt something—a strong pull, a beckoning. This time, he turned into an intersecting corridor before she did.

"Do you feel something?" she asked in a hushed voice.

He merely nodded and began to walk faster, forgetting how difficult it was for her to keep up with him until he heard her rapid footsteps echoing in the silence. Then he forced himself to slow down.

"It's down there," she said when they reached a steep, narrow staircase that wound down out of sight.

He didn't have to be told. He had no idea what was down there, but he felt the presence of the gods very strongly.

At the bottom of the steps was a door. He reached out to touch it, instantly recognizing the wood and the workmanship.

"Kassid," he said, his voice loud in the small space.

"Yes—and so is what lies beyond it. I think the palace must have been built on the ruins of an old Kassid fortress."

But he didn't hear her. His hand was already on the tarnished brass handle. Unlike Jocelyn and Hammad, he didn't tug hard at it. He knew the workmanship of his people. No matter how old it might be, it would open easily.

He stopped just inside the room, watching as the torchlight picked up the golden drawings. A sayet—the sanctuary of the gods. Exactly like the one at the fortress. He heard her voice as a distant murmur as the peace of the place filled him. It was a long time before he realized that she had fallen silent, then turned to see that she had left the room. Forsaking that peace for the moment, he hurried after her.

She stood quietly at the bottom of the stairs. "It is a sacred place for you, isn't it? I could feel that, and I thought you would want to be alone."

He told her it was, and named it in his language. "There is such a room in the fortress—in all of the fortresses. We go there in times of trouble, to seek the peace of the gods. And we go there too to seek their blessings when we marry or when a child is born."

"But we didn't go there," she said, and he could hear the hurt in her voice.

"No. I chose not to take you there. I knew you didn't believe in the old gods, and it seemed wrong to take a non-believer there. When did you discover this room?"

She told him of her childish explorations and how she'd kept it secret, then told him how she'd realized in the Dark Mountains that it must be a Kassid place.

"I told Hammad about it when I returned, and he had the wall torn down so we could come down here to test my memory. Hammad didn't feel anything; his interest was only in the history. But I felt something, Daken—and I felt it again just now. A great sense of peace."

He nodded slowly. "That is what we feel. So even if you have not accepted the gods, they have accepted *you*."

"Such power frightens me, Daken, but I can no longer deny that it exists. To deny that would be to deny *you*."

He took her hand. "Come back into the room with me."

They went back into the blackness, this time leaving the torches outside. Jocelyn was terrified at the utter blackness, but with Daken's arms around her, that wondrous peace flowed through her again.

There they stood for a long time, wrapped in each other's arms, but not speaking. Jocelyn heard those indistinct murmurs and was sure that he must hear them better because he had become very still and attentive.

Then at last, he made a strange, choking sort of sound, and she put up a hand to seek his face. His cheeks were wet with tears.

"Daken, what is it? What's wrong?"

"Did you not hear them, maiza?" He asked in an unsteady voice.

"I . . . I heard or felt something, but not words."

He gathered her more tightly into his arms, then bent to find her mouth for a long, passion-filled kiss.

"We will not be parted," he said as he lifted his mouth from hers.

"The gods have decreed that we belong together."

"But how?" She felt herself beginning to soar

with hope and fought it. What the gods wanted wasn't necessarily what *she* wanted. She could not return with him, however much she loved him.

"This room," he said in a wondering tone. "This room and the room at the fortress. They are the gateways."

"Gateways? What do you mean?"

"I'm not sure about you—but I can pass from this room to the one at the fortress and back again. I do not know how it can be—but it is."

He took her hand and led her through the darkness to the door, and then out to where their torches had been left, in sconces at the base of the stairs. She was silent, wanting desperately to believe, but unable to accept that such a thing could happen.

Finally, she said, "Can you test it—try it now?"

He shook his head with a smile. "No, it is necessary for me to go back to the fortress for a time, maiza, and I will go as planned. But I will return."

Days merged into weeks and the weeks became a month, and then another month. And Daken did not return.

On the cool, gray morning when they'd walked together into the courtyard to meet his remaining warriors and Hammad's men, she had already begun to lose that faint hope that the magic of the gods would keep them together.

Perhaps he had too, because his final words to her, as he held her one last time, had been, "A part of me remains here with you, maiza. Cherish it and keep it safe until we are together again."

Her life was busy, and the demands upon her

were incessant and at times overwhelming. Her courtiers were balky, but stopped short of outright obstruction of her plans. Once or twice, she found it necessary to invoke Daken's name to remind them of their pledges, but for the most part, she relied on that combination of firmness and patience in which he had instructed her.

Hammad's men began the construction of the mirror towers, and plans were drawn up for the construction of a garrison near the Western Road at a point midway between the city and the Dark Mountains. The garrison would replace the one in Balek, now permanently handed over to the Baleks themselves. But it was designed to provide also a place where Jocelyn and Daken could meet.

The designers brought her the finished plans, which included a small structure entirely separate from the garrison, but still within its walls, that would be for their use. With walls of its own and a small garden, it was a miniature palace.

But Jocelyn's enthusiasm was muted. She viewed it as a place to which she would go with eager anticipation—only to leave in great anguish. Would it not be better to remain separate than to subject herself to such pain?

The nights were the hardest, of course—when she lay alone in her bed remembering their lovemaking and those quiet moments afterwards when they lay entwined in each other's arms, sometimes talking and other times simply luxuriating in the afterglow of passion.

Oftentimes, she would think how very ironic it

was that she, who had so disdained love, had found the greatest love of all. She paid close attention to those couples she saw at court on festive occasions, and she listened carefully to the talk among her ladies about their husbands. And she knew that none of them had what she and Daken had—yet they, at least, were together.

For Daken's sake, she wanted to have faith in the gods and even went from time to time to the small chapel in the palace—to the very great astonishment of the priests, who were accustomed to finding only palace servants or a rare pious court lady there.

But that faith eluded her, and had the priests been able to hear her thoughts on those occasions, they would have fallen to the floor to beg the gods' forgiveness for the blasphemy of their empress.

Strangely enough, the one place where she had in fact felt some supernatural presence—the secret room in the cellar—became a place she avoided. She often thought about it, and a few times actually started down there, but some inner voice warned her that she should stay away. And so she did, out of fear of offending the very gods she didn't believe in. Irrationally, she decided that they might take offense and then harm Daken if she intruded upon their place.

Some six weeks after Daken had gone, his parting words came back to haunt her—but with a very different meaning this time.

She'd been suffering from occasional bouts of great tiredness, but had ascribed them to her demanding schedule and ignored them. Then she awoke one morning and became violently ill only moments after getting out of bed.

It must be something I ate, she thought with annoyance. She'd developed a ravenous appetite recently and had only the day before devoured an entire box of sweets.

When she recovered quickly, she forgot all about it—until the next morning, when the sickness was repeated. Her maids suggested calling in the palace physicians, but Jocelyn, who never got sick, rejected their concern. She had an exceptionally busy day, and besides, whenever she saw the dark-clad physicians, it reminded her of their hovering presence at her father's bedside.

On the third morning, she rose and put on a dressing gown for a private breakfast with Hammad, who was about to depart to check on the progress of the tower construction, then go on to the Balek garrison, to see how things fared there.

The servants had barely set the food before them when the sickness struck again and she hastily excused herself. When she returned, it was clear that the maids had informed Hammad of the previous episodes.

"I'm fine now," she said, waving away his concern. "I think I've been eating too much, that's all. I seem to have developed an excessive fondness for sweets."

"Jocey," he said with a faint smile, "Have you considered another possibility? I've thought a few times lately that you've seemed tired, and that, together with the increased appetite and this sickness in the morning, brings to my mind those same symptoms in my wife years ago."

Jocelyn frowned at him as fear began to spread its ugly tentacles through her. Hammad's wife had died many years ago, after a lingering, wasting illness.

When he saw the look on her face, Hammad shook his head. "I was not referring to the illness that caused her death, but rather to the months preceding the birth of our daughter."

One fear died to be replaced by another as she continued to stare at him. "No!" she protested—but faintly. And then she wondered why she'd needed to have him, or anyone else, suggest that particular cause. She'd heard the symptoms often enough, and she knew that she'd long since passed the time for her monthly.

Very reluctantly, she called in the midwives, then tried to echo their pleasure when they confirmed that she was indeed pregnant. But she was not happy. What kind of life could she and Daken offer a child? Certainly not the warm security of two loving parents.

And yet, as she lay in bed that night with her hand pressed against her still-flat belly, she thought that she did truly have a part of Daken that would remain with her.

Could he have known? She rejected that notion. Surely he too would know how unfair it would be for them to bring a child into a world where its parents couldn't be together.

But he trusted in the gods to keep them together—or at least he had when he left. She doubted that he believed that now, and felt a pain at what she knew must be his very great anguish. She, at least, had never truly believed it in the first place.

For nearly a week, she sat at her writing table in the evenings, trying to formulate a message to him. But at the end of each evening, she tore it up, then burned the shreds of parchment in the fireplace. No words seemed adequate to express both her joy and her misgivings.

But she knew she would have to write soon, before her condition became obvious and the word reached him through the Sherbas, several of whom were now at court, while the others continued as they had always done—getting their precious herbs from the Kassid and then trading them for other goods.

One evening, after she had temporarily abandoned her attempts to write to Daken, Jocelyn was strolling alone in her garden. Spring was slowly giving way to summer, and on this evening, the day's warmth lingered in the night air. The garden was a profusion of scents beneath a pale full moon.

She had never felt Daken's absence as keenly as she did on this night that was so clearly made for lovers. Of course, before Daken, she had never thought of *any* night as being "made for lovers."

How many nights have I walked here in the past, she wondered, *without thinking of anything other than the beauty of the night?* Love had changed her. She saw so many things she had never seen before.

She pressed her hand to her belly and thought

about the baby. Would it be a boy or a girl? Which did she want? Daken, in all likelihood, would want a boy; he already had Rina. But wouldn't it be more difficult for him to have a son he saw only once a year?

She wondered if he would insist at some point that a son join him in the Dark Mountains. He might well do so, and how could she refuse? Then *she* would be the one to see her child only once a year.

She decided that she wanted a daughter. Daken would be less likely to insist that she go to live in the Dark Mountains. But then she thought about the closeness between Daken and Rina and knew that it would make no difference. The anguish they both felt would be made greater still.

She stood there in the soft night, balling her fists in helpless anger. How could he put his faith in gods that had brought them together only to pull them apart and then add this new pain?

But slowly, her hands relaxed and she began to stroll once more through the garden, stopping occasionally to inhale a particular fragrance. A calmness descended upon her, stealing through her so slowly that some time passed before she began to question it.

Then she recognized it as being the same feeling she'd had in that secret room—the room she had been avoiding without quite understanding why. And she knew, as surely as she had ever known anything in her life, that she must go there now.

She hurried from the garden through her suite

and down the corridors, then nearly ran along the back hallways and flew down the stairs to the cellars. With each step, the urgency to reach that room became stronger still, completely overwhelming rationality.

When at last she reached the carved door, she paused only long enough to set aside the torch before pulling it open. In the weak light from the torch that spilled over into the room, she saw the gold writings spring to life. Then she closed the door behind her and stood uncertainly in the utter blackness.

Her heart pounded loudly in the deep silence of the room. That sense of peace she'd felt earlier was gone. In its place was a sense of great powers, of unimaginable forces gathering in the darkness. But they seemed to be benevolent forces; she felt no threat from them.

Her breathing slowed, and she was no longer aware of her heart thudding noisily. Instead, she was tense with anticipation as those unseen forces gathered around her.

"Daken," she whispered, "come to me."

There was a sudden rush of something—a wind that stirred nothing, but seemed nonetheless to ripple over her skin, leaving it with a tingling awareness. She called his name again, more desperately.

And then she felt his presence—scant seconds before his arms came around her and swept her off her feet!

She still could see nothing in the darkness, so she grasped his shoulders, touched his face and threaded her fingers through his hair.

"Are you real?" she asked in a small, fearful voice.

"Yes, maiza, I am real." He lifted her face to his and kissed her hungrily.

And he *was* real—big and solid and hard as she pressed herself against him, still half-afraid that if she let go, he would vanish.

They held each other, saying nothing, for a long time. And then he came slowly into focus. She gasped as she realized that the golden drawings were glowing with a light of their own.

They both turned, still clinging to each other, and she could feel that his awe matched her own. As the gold gleamed still brighter, that wondrous feeling of peace and happiness spread through them both. Then slowly, the glow faded, until they were once again in total darkness.

As the light dimmed, Daken had moved them closer to the doorway, and now he opened it and they stepped out into the torchlit space at the bottom of the stairs. He closed the door behind them, then drew her into his arms once more.

"I tried to come before, maiza," he said against her mouth. "But the gateway would not open. I think the gods decided that you needed time—time to become empress."

She turned in his arms to stare back at the closed door. "But what if it will not open again?"

"It will," he assured her. "And it will open for you as well, when it comes time for our son to be born in the Dark Mountains."

"H—how did you know?"

"They told me. He is special to them. He will one day be both the leader of the Kassid and the

Saranne Dawson

Emperor of Ertria. It is the beginning of their plan for the world."

"The beginning?" she asked in confusion.

He nodded. "Beyond that, I know nothing."

Then he kissed her again and began to lead her up the stairs.

The magic enfolded them again as they reached her suite, but this time it was the magic of love—a magic they both understood very well.

Chapter One

"Strip him! Strip him naked! Let's have a look at what we're bidding on!"

The strident female voice rose on the sweltering air, stirring a ripple of movement in the sullen, sweating crowd. All glanced in the woman's direction. Then, with a collective sigh, the people turned back to the huge, raised platform in the city square.

"She's right," another female cried. "These males come too highly priced as it is. He's pretty enough but we're not buying his looks. We're buying his breeding abilities. Strip him, I say!"

The auctioneer, a huge, hairy bear of a fellow, grumbled and mumbled to himself as he strode over to the bare-chested blond man pinned between two guards. "Damn them," he growled. "I'm a busy man and haven't the time to display each slave that passes through here."

He halted before the prisoner. Hard, dark brown eyes slammed into his. The auctioneer paused, startled by the savage look of warning. Then he grinned, his aterroot-stained teeth gleaming in the midday sun.

"You've only yourself to blame, you high-and-mighty off-worlder," he said to the man. "Strutting out here as cocky as you please, flaunting yourself before these women. You're lucky they don't swarm up here and tear you to pieces." His smile widened. "We had that happen once, you know."

The auctioneer's hands moved toward the prisoner's breeches. "Now, be sensible and don't give me any—"

A booted foot snapped out and upward, catching the auctioneer squarely in the groin. "Be damned!" Gage Bardwin snarled. "I'll not add to anyone's entertainment!"

With a whoosh of exhaled air, the big man clutched himself and sank to his knees. His face twisted in agony. For long seconds he knelt before Gage, breathing heavily. A stream of aterroot juice trickled down his chin to drip onto his shabby tunic.

Behind him, female voices rose to a wild shriek, a cacophony of primal excitement mixed with a growing bloodlust. "Strip him! Strip him! Teach the arrogant male a lesson!"

A small, scrawny man hurried over, nervous and perspiring profusely. He mopped his brow with the back of his sleeve, then grabbed at the auctioneer's arm, tugging him to his feet. "Get up, you fool! You should know better than to stand too close to a breeder."

He pulled the auctioneer out of harm's way, then motioned over four more guards. "Do whatever is necessary." He indicated the prisoner. "Just give the women what they ask. I want this one sold and out of here before he starts further trouble!"

They advanced on Gage, all eyes riveted warily on his legs. He fought against the two men who held him, struggling to break free.

Helpless frustration welled in Gage. Gods, what else could go wrong? Beryllium shackles bound his wrists and arms, he faced four other men and he was trapped on an unfriendly planet with no weapons or money.

Curse the lapse of vigilance in that tavern on Locare, the final transport station before Tenua! If he hadn't been so exhausted from a particularly long and difficult transport process, if he hadn't imbibed one mug of Moracan ale too many or been so overly attentive to that seductive little barmaid, he'd have seen those off-world bounty hunters coming. But none of that mattered now. He'd been careless. He must extricate himself as best he could.

There was only one consolation. He *had* arrived at his destination, the capital of Eremita on the planet Tenua. He just wasn't in any position to do anything about it right—

With a shout, the extra guards rushed Gage en masse. Two leaped simultaneously for a leg. Another slipped behind to snake an arm about his neck and throttle him.

Gage fought wildly. He threw the full weight of his heavily muscled body first into one guard, then another. He managed to fling one man free of his right leg, then lashed out, kicking him full in the chest. The guard snapped backward, the wind knocked out of him.

Pivoting on his still encumbered leg, Gage kicked at the other man. Something flashed in his peripheral vision. A fist slammed into his jaw, then his gut.

The fourth guard.

Gage staggered backward, his knees buckling. Bright light exploded in his skull. Pain engulfed him. He battled past the agony, shaking his head to scatter the stars dancing before his eyes.

It was too late. The six men wrestled Gage to the platform, encasing him in a body lock he could only jerk against in impotent fury. His upper torso pinned, his legs held down in a spread-eagle position, Gage fought with all the strength left in him. Finally, as oxygen-starved limbs weakened, his powerful body could give no more. He lay there, panting in exhaustion, his face and chest sheened with sweat.

The sun beat down, its radiance blinding him. Gods, but it was hot on this hellish planet. So very hot. So draining . . . desolate.

A huge form moved to stand over him. "Proud, stupid off-worlder," the auctioneer snarled. "You'll pay dearly for your defiance before I'm done and satisfied, but first we'll give the women what they want."

He knelt between his prisoner's outspread legs.

With a smirking grin, the man grasped the front of Gage's breeches and ripped them apart.

"No, damn you!" Gage roared. With a superhuman effort he reared up, sinews taut, muscles straining.

The guards' grips tightened, strangling the life from him. A swirling gray mist swallowed Gage. He fell back. At the sudden lack of resistance the guards' holds loosened.

Gage dragged in great gulps of air, fighting past the loss of consciousness, sick to the very marrow of his bones. Sick with his sense of helplessness, of defeat.

It didn't matter that they'd bared his body. What mattered was the implied submission of the act— the utter *subservience*. And he'd never, ever, allowed another to use him without his express consent. Never, since that sol he'd confronted his mother . . . .

Rage swelled, white hot and searing. In a sudden, unexpected movement, Gage twisted to the side, dragging all six guards with him.

"Let . . . me . . . go!"

The endeavor took all he had. They quickly wrestled him back to the floor, slamming him down, crushing his head into the rough, splintered wood. Gage tasted his own blood, then his despair, bitter as gall.

"Damn you all! Let me go!" he cried again, choking the words past his sudden surge of nausea.

"Do as he says," a new voice, rich with authority, commanded. "Free him. Now."

The guards paused, looking up in surprise. The

auctioneer glanced over his shoulder. With a strangled sound he released Gage, then climbed to his feet.

"Domina Magna," the man murmured, bowing low to the woman who was Queen and ruler of the planet. "I-I am honored that the royal family chose to attend my humble sale."

"And why not?" the Queen's voice came again. "Haven't you some of the finest breeders in the Imperium? Now, get out of my way. Let us have a closer look at the male."

"As you wish, Domina Magna." The auctioneer stepped aside.

For a moment all Gage saw was color, a bright, vibrant swirl of crimsons, blues and greens. Then the hues solidified into folds of shimmering, ultralight fabric, and the fabric into gowns. Gage levered himself to one elbow and glared up at the two women.

One was young with glossy black hair tucked under a sheer veil and striking, deep violet eyes. She was dressed in a loose, bulky gown that completely disguised whatever figure she might have. At his direct scrutiny her lashes lowered. A becoming flush darkened her cheeks.

A maiden, Gage thought wryly, and as shy as they came.

He shifted to the other woman. She was equally striking—her ripe femininity blatantly accentuated by the voluptuous bosom thrusting from her low-cut, snugly molded dress. There was no doubt as to the quality of her figure.

She met his hard-eyed gaze and held it for a long moment before turning to her younger companion.

"Well, daughter? Are you certain he's the one for you?" Her bold glance lowered to Gage's groin. "Your maiden's flesh will be sorely tried by a man such as he. And he strikes me as none too gentle, if his antics a few seconds ago are any indication."

"Mother, please." The girl bit her lip, turning nearly as crimson as her gown. Her hesitant gaze lifted, meeting Gage's for an instant before skittering away to slide down the tautly sculpted, hair-roughened planes of his body.

The girl's eyes halted at the gaping vee of his breeches. A river of dark hair arrowed straight down from his flat belly to a much denser nest and hint of a large, thick organ before disappearing beneath the torn cloth. She swallowed hard, dragging her gaze back to her mother's.

"H-he couldn't help it. His pride was at stake. He had to fight them."

A slender brow arched in amusement. "Did he now? I think the sisters at our royal nunnery filled your head with too many tales of days long past. Days when men still possessed some shred of gentleness and integrity. And I think," the Queen said as she took her daughter's arm and began to lead her away, "that I called you back to your royal duties none too soon."

"Mother. Wait." The girl dug in her heels.

"Yes, child?"

"May I have him or not? You said it was my choice."

The Queen eyed her daughter, then sighed. "Yes, you may have him if your heart is set. The law dictates that you take a breeder before commencing a royal life mating. But heed my words. You'll regret it. He's not the male for you."

She glanced at the auctioneer. "We'll take him," she said, indicating Gage. "Have him sent to the palace immediately."

"Er, pardon, Domina Magna." The small, scrawny man stepped forward.

"Yes?"

"This is an especially high-quality breeder. He'll cost extra."

The Queen's lips tightened. "How much extra?"

"Five thousand imperials."

Her nostrils flared. "No breeder, not even one for a Royal Princess of Corba, is worth that much! I'll give you two thousand and not an imperial more!"

"But Domina Magna—"

"Enough!" The woman held up a silencing hand. "Another word and I'll forget I'm your queen and simply confiscate the male." She smiled thinly. "And everything else you possess as well."

"As you wish, Domina Magna," the little man croaked, bowing and backing away. "The breeder will be delivered immediately."

Triumph gleamed in the Queen's eyes. "Good. See that he is."

"You will mate with my daughter and impregnate her. An easy task, I'm sure, for a breeder of your quality," Queen Kadra proclaimed, leaning

386

back with an air of finality in her ornately gilded throne.

"Indeed?" Gage Bardwin drawled.

The woman glared down at the prisoner, her patience at an end. Though still bound and ensconced between two burly guards, the man was as defiant as he'd been on the auctioneer's platform. Obviously, more drastic measures were needed to ensure his cooperation.

She motioned to the guards. "Leave us."

At the order, Gage arched a dark brow. His lips twisted in cynical amusement.

Kadra waited until they were alone. "Have you had an opportunity to observe my palace?" She indicated the room with a regal sweep of her bejeweled hand.

Gage shrugged. "It appears adequate."

"*Adequate?*" Kadra nearly choked on the word. "It's *impregnable*, both from within and from without." Her smoldering gaze met his. "There is no hope of escape."

He eyed her, knowing there was more to come.

"You will service my daughter and impregnate her, or you will die. It's that simple."

"Is it now?"

Gage slowly surveyed the room. She was right. This chamber was just as heavily fortified as was the rest of the palace. The doors and windows were barricaded by a sturdy grillwork of what looked to be a beryllium-impregnated alloy. Not even a laser gun could cut through that metal. The exterior walls were of solid rock and several feet thick. Add to that the highly complex video monitoring system Gage had noticed in his journey through the palace, and escape seemed a near impossibility.

He clamped down on a surge of angry frustration and turned back to the queen. "And what's wrong with your own men that you must turn to an off-worlder for breeding purposes—especially for your own daughter?"

The Queen's grip on her chair tightened. "Tenuan men are not the issue here. I have given you a command. The consequences are clear. What is your decision?"

Gage's eyes narrowed. Damn her. She held the advantage—at least for now—and she knew it.

He was on a mission of vital importance. The issue of his pride, no matter how dearly cherished, paled in light of the threat of Volan infiltration. And there *were* potential benefits to stalling for time, for being in the Tenuan Royal Palace. Information could be gleaned, conversations overheard . . . .

"She's a pretty one, your daughter," Gage said, conceding the Queen a temporary victory. "What's her name?"

A smile glimmered on Kadra's lips. "Meriel. Do I take this to mean you accept my terms?"

"A mating with your lovely daughter in exchange for my freedom?" Gage nodded. "In reality, I win all the way around. How soon do you require my services?"

"My daughter's fertile time spans this very day. You will be bathed, dressed more appropriately, then taken to her. I expect several matings to assure your seed is properly planted. Do you understand me?"

Gods, there went his opportunity for leisure to explore the palace. Well, the girl herself might be the best source of information anyway. He nodded. "Yes. And on the morrow I am free to go?"

"But of course. There will be no further need for you."

"No, I'd imagine not." Gage paused. "Is there anything I need to know about your daughter? To ease the 'wooing', as it were?"

Kadra bristled at the barely veiled sarcasm. The insolent bastard! But why should she be surprised? Bellatorians were all alike—arrogant, unfeeling and endlessly belittling of Tenua and all things Tenuan. It was exactly that attitude that had finally prodded her to cut her planet off from the rest of the Imperium. She'd be damned if she'd grovel and beg for the few crumbs of support that the Bellatorian-led, exalted organization of planets deigned to toss her way.

Meanwhile, she'd deal with this particular Bellatorian as she saw fit, the only possible outcome his death. Kadra smiled grimly. She'd take great pleasure in seeing this breeder died as painfully as possible. She had enough problems without being forced to tolerate his arrogance.

"Meriel is gently reared, having just completed her girlhood training at the royal nunnery. She knows little of men. You will treat her with care and not subject her to any crudities. And you will be constantly monitored, so don't think I won't know what you do or say."

"Even to our mating?" Gage inquired dryly. "Will you be privy to that as well?"

The Queen's eyes narrowed. "I owe you no explanation of what I will or will not do. You're a breeder, not a compatriot. Use your body and use it well. That's what I bought you for."

LOVE SPELL

THE MAGIC OF ROMANCE
PAST, PRESENT, AND FUTURE....

Dorchester Publishing Co., Inc., the leader in romantic fiction, is pleased to unveil its newest line—Love Spell. Every month, beginning in August 1993, Love Spell will publish one book in each of four categories:

1) *Timeswept Romance*—Modern-day heroines travel to the past to find the men who fulfill their hearts' desires.

2) *Futuristic Romance*—Love on distant worlds where passion is the lifeblood of every man and woman.

3) *Historical Romance*—Full of desire, adventure and intrigue, these stories will thrill readers everywhere.

4) *Contemporary Romance*—With novels by Lori Copeland, Heather Graham, and Jayne Ann Krentz, Love Spell's line of contemporary romance is first-rate.

Exploding with soaring passion and fiery sensuality, Love Spell romances are destined to take you to dazzling new heights of ecstasy.

COMING IN SEPTEMBER 1993
HISTORICAL ROMANCE
TEMPTATION
Jane Harrison

He broke her heart once before, but Shadoe Sinclair is a temptation that Lilly McFall cannot deny. And when he saunters back into the frontier town he left years earlier, Lilly will do whatever it takes to make the handsome rogue her own.

_0-505-51906-2 $4.99 US/$5.99 CAN

CONTEMPORARY ROMANCE
WHIRLWIND COURTSHIP
Jayne Ann Krentz writing as Jayne Taylor
Bestselling Author of *Family Man*

When Phoebe Hampton arrives by accident on Harlan Garand's doorstep, he's convinced she's another marriage-minded female sent by his matchmaking aunt. But a sudden snowstorm traps them together for a few days and shows Harlan there's a lot more to Phoebe than meets the eye.

_0-505-51907-0 $3.99 US/$4.99 CAN

LEISURE BOOKS
ATTN: Order Department
276 5th Avenue, New York, NY 10001

Please add $1.50 for shipping and handling for the first book and $.35 for each book thereafter. PA., N.Y.S. and N.Y.C. residents, please add appropriate sales tax. No cash, stamps, or C.O.D.s. All orders shipped within 6 weeks via postal service book rate. Canadian orders require $2.00 extra postage and must be paid in U.S. dollars through a U.S. banking facility.

Name _____

Address _____

City _____ State _____ Zip _____

I have enclosed $_____ in payment for the checked book(s).

Payment <u>must</u> accompany all orders. ☐ Please send a free catalog.

COMING IN OCTOBER 1993
HISTORICAL ROMANCE
DANGEROUS DESIRES
Louise Clark

Miserable and homesick, Stephanie de la Riviere will sell her family jewels or pose as a highwayman—whatever it takes to see her beloved father again. And her harebrained schemes might succeed if not for her watchful custodian—the only man who can match her fiery spirit with his own burning desire.

_0-505-51910-0 $4.99 US/$5.99 CAN

CONTEMPORARY ROMANCE
ONLY THE BEST
Lori Copeland
Author of More Than 6 Million Books in Print!

Stranded in a tiny Wyoming town after her car fails, Rana Alcott doesn't think her life can get much worse. And though she'd rather die than accept help from arrogant Gunner Montay, she soon realizes she is fighting a losing battle against temptation.

_0-505-51911-9 $3.99 US/$4.99 CAN

LEISURE BOOKS
ATTN: Order Department
276 5th Avenue, New York, NY 10001

Please add $1.50 for shipping and handling for the first book and $.35 for each book thereafter. PA., N.Y.S. and N.Y.C. residents, please add appropriate sales tax. No cash, stamps, or C.O.D.s. All orders shipped within 6 weeks via postal service book rate. Canadian orders require $2.00 extra postage and must be paid in U.S. dollars through a U.S. banking facility.

Name _____

Address _____

City _____ State _____ Zip _____

I have enclosed $_____ in payment for the checked book(s).
Payment <u>must</u> accompany all orders.☐ Please send a free catalog.

BRIMMING WITH PASSION...
BURSTING WITH EXCITEMENT...
UNFORGETTABLE HISTORICAL
ROMANCES FROM LEISURE BOOKS!